Peter Schiffman

DIAMOND MEN

Doug Macdougall is a geoscientist and writer. He is a former Professor of Earth Sciences (now Emeritus) at the Scripps Institution of Oceanography, University of California San Diego. Born in Toronto, Canada, he currently lives in Edinburgh, Scotland.

www.dougmacdougall.com

BY THE SAME AUTHOR

Non-fiction
A Short History of Planet Earth
Frozen Earth
Nature's Clocks
Why Geology Matters

Diamond Men

Doug Macdougall

This novel is a work of fiction. Names, characters, places and incidents are either the product of the author's imagination or are used fictitiously. Any resemblance to actual persons, living or dead, events, or locales is entirely coincidental.

Copyright © 2016 by Doug Macdougall

ISBN: 1523422408
ISBN 13: 9781523422401

ACKNOWLEDGEMENTS

In writing this novel I have benefited from comments and advice from many people. I'd especially like to thank my readers: Andrew and Hilary Noyce, Brad Hill, and especially Sheila Macdougall, who probably now knows the book better than I do. Collectively, feedback from these readers has significantly improved the book.

Kit Foster produced the cover and I thank him for his excellent work and for his patience as we cycled through multiple iterations. Various members of the Macdougall clan – Sheila, Katherine and Christopher – provided input on those iterations. Special thanks also to Merav Israel, whose eye for artistic balance and subtlety of meaning helped steer the final version to the eye-catching cover it is.

The inspiration for this novel came many years ago from conversations I had with a dear friend, Al Levinson, who sadly is no longer with us. Al, Professor of Geochemistry at the University of Calgary in Canada, was an expert on diamonds and he took a keen interest in the Canadian diamond boom.

Finally, if memory doesn't fail me, a specific and important element of the plot – no spoiler here – came from an off-hand comment in the excellent book *Diamond* by Matthew Hart.

ACRONYMS USED IN THIS BOOK*

APB   All Points Bulletin

CBSA   Canada Border Services Agency, a government agency charged with managing the flow of people and goods across Canada's borders.

CFO   Chief Financial Officer.

CSIS   Canadian Security Intelligence Service, Canada's primary intelligence agency.

IRS   Internal Revenue Service, U.S. tax collection and tax law enforcement authority.

NDP   New Democratic Party, one of Canada's three major political parties.

NSA   National Security Agency, a U.S. government organization involved in communications monitoring.

RCMP   Royal Canadian Mounted Police, Canada's national police force.

| UBC | University of British Columbia, situated in Vancouver. |
| WWME | WorldWide Mineral Enterprises, a fictitious company that appears in this book. |

*Only acronyms that may be unfamiliar to some readers are listed here.

There are strange things done in the midnight sun …

ROBERT SERVICE

CHAPTER 1

Ensenada, Mexico, September 2012. The wind came down from the interior, hot and dry, blowing the coastal fog out to sea. Further north, in California, they called this wind a Santa Ana. It made you depressed and irritable, people said, and right now it was making Bill Thompson jumpy. Or maybe it was just his situation that was making him jumpy. He was sitting at the kitchen table of his Mexican beach house, sipping tea, watching the clock, thinking about when he would leave this place that had been his home for the past six months. Around four in the morning would be best, he'd decided, when everything was quiet, all the neighbors deeply asleep. His friend Jorge would come by at five-thirty or six to pick him up for a day of sea fishing, but he'd find the house empty, Thompson long gone. That was the only thing he regretted about leaving this way, not saying goodbye to Jorge.

So when the knock came he nearly jumped out of his skin. It was already past midnight, but it was much too early for Jorge. Was he hearing things? But there it was again, slightly louder this time. No question; someone was knocking at the door.

He got up slowly, heart racing, and walked to the door. "Who is it?" he said.

The reply was muffled, a man's voice, speaking quietly.

"Sorry, I can't hear you." He put his ear to the door but he still couldn't decipher the reply.

Maybe he doesn't understand English, Thompson thought. Carefully, he unlatched the door, leaving the security chain in place, and swung it open just far enough to see two men in dark clothing standing on his porch. As soon as he peered out one of the men shoved the door open with a massive push, ripping the security chain from the frame and knocking Thompson backward. The second man jumped in and pinned him down to the floor. It all happened so quickly he had no chance to react. Suddenly he was on his back with a knee on his shoulder and a hand over his mouth and a very sore head where the door hit him. He could see stars, and they weren't in the sky.

His eyes focused slowly on the man standing over him. He had very black hair and a small mustache, and he was holding a gun. It occurred to Thompson that he might be the man who had been questioning his friend Jorge about the house.

"Don't move, Thompson," the man said. "It will be easier for you if you stay still."

Thompson. The man had called him Thompson. He'd used his real name. How can that be? he wondered, still in a daze from the blow to his head. Nobody here knows who I am. Then his gaze shifted to the other man, the one who was still sitting on him, his knee grinding into Thompson's shoulder, his large hand clamped over Thompson's mouth. When he saw his face his eyes grew wide. He knew him. His name was Dimitri Andropov, and he was Russian. He'd only met him once, but the man had made a strong impression. Suddenly things that he hadn't understood became clear. "You," he croaked. It came out somewhere between a whisper and a groan. "I didn't know …"

Andropov cut him off. "Yes Thompson, we meet again. Listen carefully. I'm going to take my hand away from your mouth. But if you make a sound my friend here will show you what he can do with his gun. And I don't mean he'll shoot you; he's much too professional for that. Do you know about pistol whipping? He's an expert. Do you understand?"

Fear flooded through Thompson's body. He nodded as best he could. Andropov's hand was still clamped hard over his mouth, pressing his head against the floor.

The Russian slowly took his knee off Thompson's shoulder and lifted his hand away. He stayed there for a moment, one knee on the ground, his hand on the other, his face a few inches above Thompson's.

"Not a word, Thompson. If you cooperate everything will be fine. Just remember there are two of us and one of you and we know what we're doing. Trust me, you don't want to do anything foolish." Andropov got to his feet. "Now, stand up. Slowly."

Thompson got up, still groggy, and stood there swaying slightly. He was in shock but the adrenalin was coursing through his system and his brain was in overdrive. He had to find a way to escape this madness. His car keys were in his pocket and the car was outside, full of gas, waiting. He glanced over at Andropov's buddy, who was still holding the gun but no longer pointing it at him. To his right, just a few feet away, the door was still partly open.

Okay, Thompson said to himself, here we go. He deliberately buckled his knees and swayed sideways, almost losing his balance. "I don't feel very well," he said in a weak voice.

Andropov laughed. "Really? Okay, go ahead and sit down." He pointed to a chair.

Thompson took one hesitant step and then straightened out his left arm violently, catching Andropov full in the face. It was the last thing the Russian expected. The blow snapped his head back and he stumbled backward, surprised. Thompson bolted past the other man and through the door, pulling out his keys as he ran.

"Don't shoot," Andropov yelled to his partner as he scrambled to his feet, "we need him alive. Just stop him."

It was a brave move but Thompson didn't have a chance. He was just opening the car door when they caught him. Andropov's partner got to him first and grabbed him from behind in a choke hold. When he swung him around Andropov punched him hard in the stomach.

"You stupid prick," Andropov said quietly. Thompson couldn't breathe and in spite of the choke hold he doubled over. "Bring him back into the house," Andropov said to his partner.

They threw Thompson on the floor and this time they locked the door behind them. It took a few minutes before Thompson could breathe properly, and then he pushed up onto his hands and knees and retched. "Water," he said, his voice hoarse. "I need some water. Please."

Andropov ignored him. "Don't you understand, Thompson? I told you not to try anything stupid. And that really was stupid." He was thinking that he had underestimated the engineer. He had not expected any resistance; the first time he'd met Thompson he'd pegged him for a weak man, and everything that had happened since had confirmed that judgment. "I guess we'll have to tie you up. And don't try anything else because next time we won't be so gentle."

Andropov needed information, and he needed Thompson to be coherent, at least for a while. He nodded to his partner and they grabbed Thompson by the arms, one on each side, and dragged him into the kitchen. Andropov took a roll of heavy cord from his backpack and they sat Thompson in a chair and tied his arms behind him. Then they tied his ankles, each one to a leg of the chair. When they were sure he couldn't move, they stepped back.

"I'm going to leave you here for a few minutes, Thompson. Let you calm down and think about your situation. I want to take a look around this nice little place you have."

Jesus Christ, Thompson thought, it's like he's come over for a visit and wants a tour. He almost laughed at the thought; in spite of what was happening he could see the humor in the situation. But his neck was sore and his stomach ached where Andropov had punched him, and they'd pulled his arms back so tightly that his shoulders hurt. He wasn't sure what they wanted, and he had no idea what was going to happen next. Grit your teeth and endure it, he said to himself, get it over with and get out of here. Thompson had had enough deception, enough running. He was ready to go back to Canada and tell his story to … to whom? That was the question that still bothered him.

He thought back to the first time he'd met Andropov, almost three years ago now, at the Diatek mine in northern Canada. The Russian had flown in with the company's CEO and stayed for several days, and Thompson had found the whole visit odd. Andropov had been especially interested in how they kept the mine's ore processing system secure. Now he understood: he had been assessing the security system, and, Thompson thought to himself, he had also been checking me out.

Andropov and his buddy came back into the kitchen. "Got your bags packed, have you Thompson? Decided Ensenada is not the place for you?" They had seen his backpack and carryall near the front door.

"I thought I'd take a trip, drive south, do a little fishing," Thompson said, improvising. "I do that here, sometimes." He was frightened but trying hard to act unconcerned.

Andropov sighed and pulled up a chair. He turned it around and sat facing Thompson, his arms over the back. "That's not what it looks like to me. You've cleaned this place out; I don't think you were planning to come back. But it doesn't really matter. I'm glad I got here before you left, but I would have found you anyway. I don't like people who cross me. I always track them down eventually."

"Cross you? What do you mean, cross you?"

"You know very well what I mean."

"You mean because I left Diatek? I followed instructions and did what they asked for two whole years but then I just couldn't take it anymore and I panicked. It was stressing me out,

6

I was going crazy. I didn't know what to do. I had no idea you were involved."

"Does anyone else know?"

"Know what I was doing? Of course not. That's one of the reasons I was going crazy. I couldn't tell anybody."

"Are you sure?" Andropov said, and he nodded to his partner. The man took a package of cigarettes from his shirt pocket and lit one. He took a deep puff, then exhaled through his nose. The smoke curled up around his head and the sharp smell of tobacco filled the kitchen. Andropov reached out his hand and his partner passed him the cigarette. He took a short puff and blew smoke into Thompson's face. Thompson's eyes started watering and he shut them tightly.

Then Andropov took a longer puff and without warning reached forward and ripped Thompson's shirt open. He shoved the glowing cigarette into the engineer's chest. Thompson screamed.

"Shh," Andropov said, clamping his hand over Thompson's mouth again. "We don't want to wake the neighbors. If you can't keep quiet I'll have to tape your mouth shut."

Thompson was trembling. There was a searing pain in his chest where Andropov had burned him with the cigarette.

"I want you to tell me the truth," Andropov said. "Now, I'll ask you again: who knows what you've been doing?" He took a deep draw on the cigarette and held it in front of him.

"Nobody, I swear, nobody. I've never told a soul. That Irish guy, Brennan, the one who got me into this thing in the first place, he's the only one I met face to face. After that everything was done by phone or on the internet. I never said a word to anyone else."

Andropov drew on the cigarette again until it was glowing, then thrust it into the other side of Thompson's chest. This time the engineer's eyes were open and he saw it coming. He clamped his mouth shut and tensed his body and the scream that rose from his gut came out as a muffled groan.

"Good," Andropov said, "you're learning." He sat back. "You know, Thompson, I'm an expert in these things. I've studied ways to get people to talk. Sometimes the simplest techniques, the ones that have been used for hundreds of years, are the best. Your Canadian Indians, for example – what do you call them, First Nations? – they used to do just what I'm doing to you. They didn't have cigarettes, but they had tobacco and they would push their enemy's fingers into their pipes while they smoked. It didn't matter whether it was a French fur trader or an English soldier or someone from another tribe. And that was just the beginning. They would pull out fingernails, cut off skin …"

Thompson's face turned pale and Andropov said, "Don't worry, we won't cut off your skin. Fingernails, I don't know. It all depends on whether you tell me the truth. Not very pleasant to think about, is it? Those Indian braves, though, they were stoic. It was a badge of honor for them not to flinch when they were tortured. Right to the moment they died."

Thompson could feel the bile rising in his throat and he retched again. This time Andropov relented and brought him some water. "Open your mouth," he said, and poured water over his face. Thompson spluttered and coughed and hardly managed to swallow any.

"I'll tell you everything," he said. He was sobbing now. "Please stop. Please."

"That's better. I'm listening. We've got all night. I especially want to know what you did with the diamonds." Andropov smiled. "That was your big mistake. Did you think we were stupid? We were watching, we monitored the mine the whole time. If it hadn't been for that I might have fallen for your little ruse, thought that you really did drown. But the diamonds got me wondering and when they couldn't find your body I realized you must have planned the whole thing. To be honest you surprised me. I didn't think you had it in you."

Thompson slumped in his chair. He'd thought he was being clever, but they knew. "Okay," he said slowly, "I did take some. I needed money to get away. I sold most of them but there are still some left." He paused and caught his breath. He was feeling nauseous again. "They're in my bag – the ones that are left. But nobody knows what I was doing. I never said a word. That's the absolute truth."

"That surprises me." Andropov gestured to his partner, who lit another cigarette and handed it to him. "I've got lots of cigarettes, Thompson."

"Please, no, don't do that again. I swear, I didn't tell anyone."

Andropov's partner was rummaging through the bags Thompson had left by the front door, and he pulled out a bulky envelope and handed it to him.

"What's this?" Andropov read out the address. "Claire Thompson? Ontario?"

"Okay, I did write it down. What I did. It was for my daughter, in case something happened to me. I wanted her to know; I was going to mail it to her. There's a video in there too.

I set up my camera and videoed myself reading the statement so she'd know I was alive."

Andropov opened the envelope and took out a sheaf of papers. For several minutes the house was quiet while he read what Thompson had written. "I couldn't have described it better myself, Thompson. Your part of it, anyway, there's still a lot you don't know. And you never will." He laughed and turned to his partner and made a gesture Thompson couldn't decipher, and the man pulled out a small pair of pliers and walked around behind his chair.

"Are you sure there aren't copies of this somewhere?" Andropov said. "A man of your intelligence, I would have thought you'd make a few copies. Leave them in safe places."

"No, no, that's the only one. I just finished it last week. I haven't had time to make any copies." The words tumbled out, one over another.

"That seems strange to me," Andropov said.

Thompson shook his head. "It's the truth. The original is on my laptop but there aren't any other copies." His heart was thumping; he could sense Andropov's partner behind him but he couldn't see him. He felt something on his hand and then a searing pain shot through his arm and he started to scream. Andropov was ready and covered his mouth.

"Nine left, Thompson. One fingernail at a time. Until you tell us about the other copies."

Thompson was sobbing with pain again, and Andropov sat back. He still had Thompson's letter on his lap, and he noticed a yellow post-it note stuck on the front of the envelope. "What's this?" he said, picking up the envelope again. He peeled off the post-it note. "'Rick Doucet,' it says. Who's that?"

Thompson's head was hanging down, his eyes shut. He was blubbering quietly in pain, bubbles of saliva seeping from the corners of his mouth. He didn't reply.

"Fingernail number two, Thompson? Who is Rick Doucet? Did you send him a copy?"

"No, please God, no. Don't do that again." Thompson had reached his limit. He couldn't take more pain. "No, I didn't send him anything. I was just thinking about it. He doesn't even know I'm alive."

"Who is he? A friend of yours?"

"Yes, he's a friend."

"And where do I find this Mr. Doucet?"

"Please, he hasn't done anything. There's no need …"

Andropov stood up and pulled a large jackknife from his pocket. He unfolded it and held it under Thompson's chin. "Tell me Thompson. Where do I find Rick Doucet?" The knife was razor sharp and with a flick of his wrist he nicked the soft skin of Thompson's throat. A trickle of blood ran down his neck.

Thompson gulped and stifled another sob. "He's a geologist. At Diatek."

Andropov folded the jackknife and put it back into his pocket. He looked at Thompson for a moment and saw a broken man; he was reasonably sure he was telling the truth, and he didn't think they were going to get anything more from him. Amazing what a little pain will do, he thought, especially to someone who isn't used to it. Still, he'd have to do something about this guy Doucet. What they had going at the mine was too important to leave any loose ends.

"Okay," he said. He nodded to his partner, who was still standing behind Thompson, and handed him the knife.

"Are you going to cut me loose?" Thompson asked. "I've told you everything." He was desperate to be free.

Andropov didn't reply. He picked up the chair he'd been sitting on and carefully placed it back at the kitchen table.

The knife was so sharp Thompson barely felt the cuts. Two slashes on each wrist, expertly done.

Andropov turned back toward him and said, "It's the kindest way, Thompson. I don't know why I'm being kind after all the trouble you've caused me, maybe I just feel sorry for you. You won't feel anything."

It was more or less true. Thompson felt a stinging sensation in his wrists but the pain from the burns on his chest and the fingernail that Andropov's partner had pulled out was ebbing away. He felt something warm running down across his palms and wondered if he was dreaming. Soon I'll wake up. And soon they'll cut me loose. Maybe they already have, maybe that's what that guy was doing with the knife. But I'll just sit here for a while, regain my strength. He could see Andropov and his partner moving around the house, opening doors and talking to one another. He couldn't hear what they were saying; they seemed to be moving in a fog, their voices muffled. He thought about his daughter, and then about his wife. He could picture them clearly. They're going to be fine. And then he thought about Rick Doucet. I shouldn't have put his name on that envelope, he thought, I'll have to warn him. In case Andropov tries to find him.

Thompson was drifting, his eyes closed, when he heard the door slam. It took a minute to register. With an enormous effort he opened his eyes and looked around. The fog was still there and the house was quiet. He was having trouble seeing. He could tell Andropov and his partner were gone, though. The house was empty. Then everything went dark.

CHAPTER 2

In a way what happened to Bill Thompson that night in Ensenada – and the ripples that spread outward from it and affected the lives of many other people – had all started years earlier when two men met in a bar in Moscow. On the face of it, their conversation seemed innocent enough – although innocent was not a word usually associated with Vasily Gagarin. It might be more accurate to say that the consequences of what transpired that night were unintended, or at least unanticipated. Just a few words spoken and everything changed. As often happens.

It's a cold November night in 2009 and Moscow has just witnessed its first significant snowfall of the season. In the bar, Gagarin is talking to Dimitri Andropov; the two men come here often, especially when they want to speak privately. They always sit at the same table, in a shallow alcove away from other customers. Gagarin is one of the new rich, but he doesn't like Moscow's noisy nightclubs with loud music and disco lights, full of young Russian glitterati. This bar, in his opinion, is classy and discrete. The lighting is subdued and soft background music plays over the sound system, never so loud that it interferes with conversation. Gagarin knows the owner, and the girls who work here are very pretty.

Gagarin is not in a good mood. His teenage daughter Anna, a girl who has her father wrapped around her little finger, has been pressuring him to send her to London. "So I can improve my English," she told him. One of Anna's best friends is already there, at a private school, and the two girls stay in touch constantly by email. And recently they've been using some new internet program that Gagarin has heard about but doesn't understand called Facebook. From his point of view this only makes the situation worse. He doesn't want his daughter to go but he is incapable of refusing anything she asks, and he knows he'll eventually give in, which makes him irritable. He is not a man who gives in easily. His mood is not improved by the news he's heard tonight from Andropov. His right hand man has been telling him about the problems he's having with the diamonds they trade for arms in Africa. It is one of Gagarin's less savory enterprises, but with easy access to cheap Russian munitions the exchanges have been very lucrative. "It's a lot harder now," Andropov says, "we need to find new ways to launder them."

"Maybe you should just take the fucking diamonds to Canada," Gagarin says. It is an off-the-wall remark and he isn't even sure where it came from. Maybe it's the alcohol, which has loosened him up, maybe it's his foul mood, or maybe it's because his Canadian diamond mine has been on his mind lately. Maybe it's all of those things together, but it doesn't really matter. With Andropov he doesn't have to be discrete; he can say anything he wants. He trusts the man.

The Canadian mine has been on Gagarin's mind because of the protests. During the summer a group of environmental activists somehow managed to get to the remote site – the mine is in the far north, in the Northwest Territories – and set up a protest camp. It had all started when chemical waste leaked into a nearby lake and killed fish and migratory waterfowl. By a stroke of bad luck a journalist happened to be doing a story on diamond mining in the Canadian north at the time, and someone sent him photos of the dead birds. The next day he was at the mine, interviewing workers and taking pictures of his own, and the day after that he dumped his original story and wrote about the spill. Soon it was in the papers and all over the internet, and that was when the protests started. At first they were confined to the company's Vancouver headquarters, but then the hard core activists got to the mine itself, which generated even more press attention. The protesters claimed the company was run by greedy capitalists who were only interested in profits and cared nothing about the fragile ecology of the tundra. In reality it was not quite so simple, but never mind, the furor whipped up opposition to company policies and some of the native people who worked at the mine went on strike. Diamond production fell sharply, and that bothered Gagarin.

And why did Vasily Gagarin own a Canadian diamond mine in the first place? Vasily was one of those nimble Russians who emerged unscathed from the chaos that followed the break-up of the Soviet Union. More than unscathed: he emerged the owner of several formerly state-owned companies. Nobody – or nobody but Vasily – seemed to know how it happened. True, he had connections – in the military, in the government, and, probably most important, in Russian organized crime. It was also unclear where the money came from, if indeed he actually *paid* for those companies – something else that nobody seemed to know. But one thing was certain: Vasily now had more money than he knew what to do with. He couldn't spend it fast enough. That didn't keep him from wanting more, however. He was always looking for opportunities to extend his reach. And among other things he had a passion for diamonds. Why not buy a mine of his own?

In Russia, Gagarin's companies ran nickel and gold mines, but even he had found it hard to elbow his way into the country's thriving diamond industry, so when diamonds were discovered in Canada in the 1990s he followed developments closely. He had relatives over there who kept tabs on things for him and when a promising diamond prospect came up he pounced on it. Andropov, who was always weighing risks, told him it was a bad idea but Vasily wasn't deterred. He talked to the geologists and they told him that assays from the test drilling looked good. The long term projections for diamond recovery were favorable, they said; as long as diamond prices stayed high the mine would be profitable. Andropov was one of the few people in Gagarin's network of companies who could openly speak his mind to his boss and he told him he was crazy, that there were much better ways to use the money. Developing a mine would be hugely expensive. But for once Gagarin ignored his advice. He had good accountants; they knew ways to borrow the money and run it through so many offshore accounts that it probably wouldn't cost him very much anyway. At least he hoped so; he paid them enough.

Andropov was Gagarin's go-to man, his adviser, fixer and enforcer rolled into one. He had made himself indispensable, ready to go anywhere and do anything on a moment's notice. He'd initially got Vas's attention when he, Vas, needed someone who spoke Spanish well enough to negotiate a deal in Colombia. A deal that was … delicate; he couldn't send some soft-palmed guy in a suit. Dimitri was new then, he'd been hired in one of Gagarin's companies just a few months earlier. He was young but he'd spent three years in the Russian Special Forces and he spoke five languages, one of them Spanish. Vas talked to him and liked him so he took a chance and sent him down to Columbia. He was like that: impulsive. That was a decade ago. Dimitri got more out of the Colombians than Vas had ever hoped, and after that he moved up quickly. The man was still a bit of a mystery, even to Gagarin. But he got things done, God knows how, but he did. Gagarin – well enough versed in the darker arts himself – never pressed his associate about his methods. He didn't really need to know. But increasingly he turned to Andropov when he needed something, anything. He couldn't conceive of running his empire without him.

Even so, Andropov's doubts about the Canadian diamond project hadn't swayed him. Through an intermediary, and behind the screen of shell companies his accountants set up, he bought the mining rights to the diamond prospect from a small exploration company and founded a new company, Diatek Canada, to develop and operate the mine. It hadn't taken long to turn a profit. The land he'd bought was even richer in diamonds than the geologists had predicted, and in spite of the economic problems buffeting the world revenue from the mine rose rapidly. Newly rich Chinese were starting to believe they needed more and bigger diamonds, and even the Indians, who traditionally bought gold, were turning to diamonds. The best part was, the mine was producing high quality gems and the government certified every diamond coming out of the Northwest Territories. No blood on these diamonds. Customers could wear their jewelry with pride. And the business was completely legitimate.

The African diamonds, though, the ones they got in payment for arms shipments, were another matter. As far as Gagarin was concerned the Africans could buy all the arms they wanted. He didn't really care if they killed each other. The more wars raging in the Congo or Sierra Leone or wherever the merrier, as long as he got his diamonds. But now Andropov was finding it difficult to move them. And that was a problem.

"It's been a disaster ever since the U.N. got involved," Dimitri had said. "And that goddamned Kimberly Process. Nobody wants to buy diamonds now unless they're certified. Or, they'll take them, but they want a big discount."

The Kimberly Process was an international agreement that aimed to stop the trade in conflict diamonds; it obligated all participating countries to neither import nor export any diamonds that weren't properly certified, their origins accurately known. Andropov had found ways to circumvent it, but at a cost – both in money and in a huge amount of extra effort.

His complaint about the difficulties he was having had prompted Vasily's outburst about taking the diamonds to

Canada. "Just figure something out, Dimitri," Gagarin had said, and banged his glass down on the table. "Dammit, there's got to be a way to do it." He waved one of the girls over and asked for another drink. She nodded, then looked over at Dimitri. "You, sir?"

He lifted his glass and looked at it for a moment. "Not right now. I think I'll pass."

Vasily watched the girl as she walked back toward the bar, hips swaying with every step. "Jesus," was all he said.

The two men sat in silence for a few minutes and then Vasily started talking about soccer. Typical Vas, jumping from one idea to the next. "Maybe I should buy a club," he said. "Like Abramovitch bought Chelsea." Vasily knew Abramovitch but he didn't like him. It's just a prestige thing, Dimitri was thinking, he wants to one-up Abramovitch. I'll have to talk him out of it if he gets serious. Run the numbers and make him see sense. He was worried that Gagarin was losing his business sense, the very thing that got him to where he was today. I'll bet he wouldn't have bought a soccer club just to please himself ten years ago, Dimitri thought, even if he had the money.

But Vasily's comment about the diamonds kept echoing through his head. 'Take them to Canada' is what he had said. What did he mean by that? What good would it do to take African diamonds to Canada? And then it hit him. It was like magic, as though a puff of smoke had clouded his brain and then suddenly cleared away, revealing a breathtakingly simple scheme. If he could find a way to funnel the African diamonds through Gagarin's Canadian mine they'd come out government certified and squeaky clean. They'd sell at a high price.

The profits could be fed right back into Gagarin's companies. Afterwards, Andropov was never quite sure whether Gagarin had thought it all through or whether his outburst was just a random comment made in a moment of frustration. Either way, it would be a brilliant money laundering scheme. The challenge would be getting the diamonds into the mine without anyone knowing. But Andropov liked challenges.

By the time the two men were ready to leave the bar it was late. Vasily looked across the room and nodded, and two burly, thick-necked men sitting on identical chairs near the door stood up. They were his bodyguards; he might leave home without his American Express card but he didn't go anywhere without the bodyguards. In Russia, in 2009, it wasn't worth it for someone like him to be unprotected. One of the bodyguards brought over coats; the other took out his cell phone and called for Vasily's driver.

"Want a ride?" Vasily asked. He was staying at a company-owned apartment for the night and flying south the next day to his villa near Sochi on the Black Sea, where it was much warmer. And where he would find his wife and his teenage daughter, with her as yet unfulfilled wish to go to London.

"Thanks, but not tonight. I'll walk a bit; I need to clear my head." Dimitri didn't need a bodyguard and he certainly didn't mind the cold. It was part of his Russian blood, he always thought. The snowstorm that had swept through during the afternoon had blanketed the city and he was looking forward to walking the snow-muffled streets and hearing the snow crunch and squeak under his boots. It was something that recalled his childhood: the excitement of the year's first snowfall, going out after dark into a silent white world, tasting the snowflakes that landed on his tongue. A reminder of more innocent times.

He turned to Gagarin again. "But Vasily, you know, I think you're right. About Canada. I think I'd better pay a visit to that mine."

CHAPTER 3

Thompson first heard about the visitor in early December at the weekly meeting of senior personnel. Monday morning, nine o'clock, pitch dark outside. Not that daylight would have helped much; it was snowing and the wind whipped the snow horizontally across his face as he groped his way to the administration building. Near white-out conditions; thank God I'll be in Las Vegas by the weekend, he said to himself.

Sometimes he thought about moving on. In a few weeks 2009 would be history, and he would have racked up more than three years working at the Diatek mine. But move on to where? That was the problem. In spite of the isolation, he liked his job. A mechanical engineer with many years of experience in the mining industry, he'd been hired shortly after the company was founded and had started work when the mine site in the Northwest Territories was still a bleak piece of tundra real estate. Now he oversaw the complex machinery that transported ore from the mine workings, along conveyor belts, through crushers and sifters and sorters, past sophisticated laser-driven devices that singled out diamonds, and, eventually, to the super-secure building where few people were admitted and where – as if by magic – the diamond crystals, winnowed from tons of nondescript rock, dropped one by one, day after day, into small metal cups. He had been in that building and had watched the diamonds arrive, some clear and sparkling, others opaque and dirty looking, and he had marveled that it all worked. He knew, of course, that it should; he understood the theory and he had been involved in setting up every piece of the sorting equipment. When there was a problem, his team was called in to fix it. He knew the system like the back of his hand, but he could still be awed by how well it functioned. What an accomplishment: massive piles of raw rock from the mine pit at one end, a few tiny diamond crystals at the other, teased out of the ore with very little human intervention at all.

Thompson stamped the snow off his boots and took off his parka as he entered the building. It was warm and very bright inside – light was important, in the winter, so close to the Arctic Circle. He made his way to the conference room where most of the others were already gathered and poured himself a cup of coffee, then took a seat. The usual chatter continued until everyone was present and the mine manager knocked his fist on the table to get their attention.

"Okay gentlemen, we need to get started." He launched into a review of the past week's activities: the amount of ore processed, the number of carats of diamonds recovered, problems that had come to his attention, solutions proposed. Thompson's mind wandered; he really didn't like these meetings. He would much rather be out at the processing facility, taking care of his machinery.

It was funny how things happened. A decade ago he could never have imagined himself working at this remote mine. He'd had a good job in Sudbury, Ontario, a family, a bright future. But then personal problems overwhelmed him and all of that vanished, and when he emerged from a year of living hell he found himself without a job, alienated from his family, adrift. The Diatek job – he'd answered an ad in a trade publication – was like a lifeline thrown to a drowning man. A chance to leave his previous life behind and start over again. He soon found he wasn't alone; many others in the north were there for similar reasons.

From the beginning Thompson immersed himself in his work, trying not to think too much about yesterday, or tomorrow. And the pay was good. He decided that he would put most of the money aside for an as yet dimly imagined future; there was little at the mine site he could spend it on anyway. But then, on one of his breaks, he had gone to Las Vegas with another man from the mine, a geologist, single like himself. There could hardly be any place on earth more different from the mine site than Las Vegas: the weather, the casinos, the women. Like a sailor on shore leave, he went a little crazy, and since that first visit he had been back several times. And he'd be there again, soon. He liked the buzz, the adrenalin rush he got from gambling, and on his breaks he had started visiting casinos in other cities too. He'd gone north to escape the specter of an addiction in his past, but he wasn't yet ready to admit that if he wasn't careful he'd fall headlong into another addiction. In the meantime his nest egg for the future had begun to dwindle.

Thompson came to with a start. The mine manager was speaking to him, everyone around the table looking at him.

"Sorry, I must have been daydreaming," he said, flustered, reddening a little. "Not that you'd know it's daytime up here." Making light of it. A few people around the table chuckled.

It was his turn to give a brief report on his area of responsibility, a weekly ritual at these meetings. He looked down at the notes he'd brought with him, then launched into a discussion of a problem they'd had with one of the X-ray machines that were used in the final stages of separating diamonds from the ore – a minor problem, he said, it had to do with the power source for the machine and they had managed to get it up and running again in less than two hours. They'd had to shut down the conveyor system, but not for long. He'd never encountered a problem like this before, but he was looking into the possibility of installing secondary power sources that would switch in automatically if it happened again.

The mine manager nodded and made a note and asked about the cost. He grimaced when Thompson told him but he just said, "Okay, but keep me updated, eh?" He turned to the man sitting next to Thompson. "Anything Jim?" Jim was the geologist who had introduced Thompson to Las Vegas. He would talk your head off over a beer, but he was tongue-tied at the conference table with his peers. It drove the mine manager crazy but he tolerated it because Jim was so good at what he did. He solved the problem by meeting separately with the geologist, one-on-one. In those meetings, he was a different person.

Jim – as he usually did – said, "No, nothing this week," and turned to the pudgy man sitting to his right, shifting attention from himself to the Health and Safety Officer, who always had something to say. Thompson didn't like the Health and Safety Officer. He knew safety was important but in his opinion the guy was a prick. He had a certain amount of power and he could make life hell for anyone who didn't comply with his view of the regulations. Thompson had a different perspective on work at the mine; he paid attention to safety – mines are dangerous places – but he used common sense and he didn't much care for regulations if they got in the way of getting things done. As a result he'd had a number of run-ins with Health and Safety. The man was short and balding and chubby, and he wore steel rimmed glasses and spoke with a slight stutter which got worse when he was agitated. The men referred to him as H&S, and behind his back many of them made fun of him. This morning H&S went off on a long rant about hard hats and how some of the mine workers were far too cavalier about wearing them. He flipped through pages of densely scribbled notes as he talked, pointing out violation after violation. He was oblivious to the rolling eyes around the table.

The surprise, though, came at the end of the meeting. "Just a heads up before we go," the mine manager said. "We have a visitor coming later this week. I don't know a lot about it because I only got the message yesterday, but this guy is coming over from Russia, some kind of businessman with an interest in Diatek. Apparently he's fairly important because we're supposed to give him the kid glove treatment. It sounds as though he just wants a show-and-tell, so I'll be talking to some of you individually about that." He paused. "Okay, that's it until next week." He looked at Thompson. "Bill, can you stick around for a few minutes?"

It was not unheard of for high level visitors to come through the Diatek mine. They'd hosted a few dignitaries, both domestic and foreign, including politicians and the CEO of the South African Chamber of Mines. But such visits were rare, especially in winter, and they hadn't had any since the summer protests. The Russian visitor was staying for several days, which was also unusual.

"This visitor," the mine manager said to Thompson once the others had left the room, "he seems to be especially interested in how the ore processing system works, and how we manage security. The message I got was very vague, but it was from our CEO and he's coming too, so the guy must be important. I'll give him a general overview of our operations, but it would make sense for you to take him through the ore processing system, explain how everything works."

"When did you say he's coming? I have a break coming up, you know. I leave on Friday and I'll be gone all next week."

"I know, that's why I wanted to talk to you. Sorry, but you'll have to reschedule, it's just too important. The CEO said we have to do everything we can to impress this guy. His name is" – the manager leafed through the papers he was holding – "Andropov. Dimitri Andropov. He's coming straight from Russia; he gets here Thursday and will stay through the weekend – he'll leave on Monday, a week from today."

"Shit," said Thompson, "I already had to postpone my break because of the problem with the power source. I'm supposed to be going to Las Vegas for a little R&R in the desert. What a pain." Thompson was not happy.

"I'm sorry Bill, but all you have to do is push it back by a few days. You can leave early next week, just as long as you're around while Andropov is here."

"Strange this guy would want to spend a weekend in the Northwest Territories in December," Thompson said. "It's not what I would choose. If he's a bigwig like you said you'd think he could organize a better boondoggle. Or come in the summer, at least there's some daylight then."

"I agree. I have no idea what this is all about; you know as much as I do. I'll keep you in the loop, but make sure you treat Andropov well, eh?" The manager seemed anxious. "It's important that he sees everything working well, that he knows we're back to normal after the strikes."

Thompson nodded. "Okay," he said, "I guess I don't have much choice."

CHAPTER 4

By Thursday the weather had cleared and high pressure reigned. Thompson watched from the administration building as the helicopter carrying Diatek Canada's CEO and the Russian visitor landed just after noon. The men stepped out looking as though they were ready for an assault on Everest: bulky arctic clothing head to toe, parka hoods pulled over their faces, reflective sunglasses for the few hours of sunlight. Diatek was handling its important visitor with care. With the arrival of high pressure the thermometer had plummeted to -35 degrees Celsius and frostbite was a constant problem, and although the winter sun was just a few degrees above the horizon and its light weak, when it bounced off the snow-covered landscape that stretched to the horizon it was blinding. But even the CEO, who had met Andropov before, didn't know that his guest didn't need any coddling. For a man who had trained in Siberia with Russian Special Forces, the visit to the mine was a walk in the park.

The mine manager went out to greet the visitors. As the rotors slowed and stopped, the three men stood for a few minutes, looking around, the manager gesturing, pointing out different parts of the facility. But they didn't stand long in the cold. When they turned and made their way toward the administration building the one thing Thompson noticed was the way Andropov walked, fluidly, like an athlete. Even the bulky clothing didn't disguise the fact that he was lean and muscular. He walked like a cat, like a panther, smoothly and deliberately. Thompson had the odd feeling the man was ready to pounce. On what, he had no idea.

Thompson went back to work and he didn't see the visitors for the rest of that day, but there was a frisson in the air, something you couldn't quite put your finger on, everyone behaving just a little differently from normal. It wasn't every day the CEO visited. Who knew where he would pop up next? Better be ready.

He got a call from the mine manager at six that evening and went around to his office. "You're on for Saturday," the manager said, "around eleven. I have to meet with the boss then and go over all the things we're doing in response to the strikes – again. After that both of us are meeting with Hughes" – the mine manager rolled his eyes; Hughes was the health and safety officer – "so you'll be on your own with Andropov."

Promptly at eleven o'clock Saturday morning Thompson knocked on the mine manager's door. Inside, Andropov stood with the manager and the CEO, looking at the enlarged air photo of the mine site that hung on the office wall. They shook hands and when the introductions were over Thompson said to Andropov "Are you ready to start? I brought a few things that we should go over before we go outside. We can use the conference room; it's just down the hall."

"Fine with me." The Russian looked at the others.

"Go ahead," the CEO said, "we'll finish this when you get back."

Andropov picked up his parka and mittens from a chair. "Okay, see you later." He spoke with almost no accent.

"Your English is good," Thompson said as they walked down the hall toward the conference room, making conversation. "Where did you learn it?"

"Mostly in school. That and TV. We get English language channels in Russia now, CNN, BBC. And I like English movies, like the James Bond films. I think I've seen most of them." He laughed. "We're usually the bad guys, though, James Bond is always chasing Russians."

Thompson grinned as he opened the door to the conference room and switched on the lights. He turned and looked at Andropov. "Someone has to be the bad guy. Anyway it's all make-believe. I'm sure your Russian movies have American bad guys." He spread out his papers on the table. "Right. Have a seat. I'll start from the beginning, but if you already know this stuff just tell me, and we can skip ahead, okay?"

Andropov shook his head. "No, I need to hear it all." He pulled out a small notebook and a pen. "I'll make notes while you talk. I'll need to put together a report when I get back."

For whom? Thompson wondered briefly, but he didn't ask. He laid out drawings of the mine site on the table and talked the Russian through the ore processing operation. "It's good to have an overview in your head," he said. "That way it will make a lot more sense when we're out there. Besides, it's a hell of a lot warmer in here."

Andropov wrote quickly and kept interrupting with questions. Thompson had given briefings to important visitors before, usually to bored executives who feigned interest but didn't really listen. It was, he often thought, like talking to an empty room. But Andropov was different. He could feel he had the man's full attention.

"We're still in the open pit stage," Thompson explained. "These kimberlites ... you know about kimberlites?"

Andropov nodded. "I do. In my business you can get snowed unless you know what you're talking about." Thompson wondered again what Andropov's business was. Whatever the purpose of his visit, he was soaking up every bit of information Thompson gave him.

The Russian knew a lot more about mining than he let on. For years he'd been involved in Gagarin's mining ventures and he'd had many conversations with geologists. He'd learned that most of the world's diamonds come from kimberlites, a kind of volcanic rock. Nobody had ever seen a kimberlite erupt, the geologists had explained, but from decades of detailed mapping around diamond mines it was obvious that some of them had literally exploded out of the ground, maybe even at supersonic speeds. The reason, they told him, was that gases in the kimberlite magma expand tremendously when the molten rock nears the surface. Like the bubbles in champagne when you pop out the cork, except on a gigantic scale.

"Anyway," Thompson said, "most kimberlites, including the one we're mining here, are cone-shaped because of the way the magma expands when it approaches the surface. It's easy for us to mine the broad part of the cone from the surface, we just blast out the rock and cart it away. Eventually, once we get down to the narrower parts of the ore, we'll have to drive shafts for underground mining, but we haven't got there yet. So right now the mine is an open pit and we truck the ore over to the first of the crushing operations. That's a critical step – we have to crush everything to a manageable size before we can start winnowing it down, but we have to do it carefully enough that we don't actually crush the diamonds. They're very hard, but if you get it wrong you can crack or even break them and ruin a lot of gems."

Andropov kept asking about security. Thompson assumed he was concerned about workers stealing diamonds, a problem for diamond mines everywhere in the world.

"Oh, don't worry. You wouldn't believe the security we have. Actually, it's not a problem until around here." He pointed to a junction point on the flow chart in front of him. "This is where we start to get rid of some of the waste rock; before that there's no way anyone could find a diamond in the raw ore, let alone grab it from the conveyor. You don't actually start to see diamonds until right at the end of the sorting process, they're just too rare. That's true even for the richest ore."

"So, along the conveyor section after that first crushing there's no security at all?"

"Well," Thompson said, "to begin with the whole mine is secure. People can't just walk in off the street." He grinned. "Actually, there *aren't* any streets up here to walk in off. Hardly any people, either. We do have CCTV cameras along the conveyors, though, but they're for monitoring, to make sure everything is working properly. We check the monitors regularly, it saves us going out there. But no, we don't have anything in that area that's specifically for security. That comes later."

Andropov seemed thoughtful. "Okay," he said, "I just want to make sure I understand how it all works."

When they were finished in the conference room Thompson said, "Now we have to face the music." They donned their parkas and went out to walk through the processing system. At Andropov's insistence they started at the mine pit itself. It was an impressive scene: giant trucks with tires higher than a man crawling up and out of the mine with their loads of fresh rock, heading for the crushing facility. "In spite of the climate it rarely stops," Thompson said, speaking over the noise of the trucks. "Of course, in some ways it will be easier when it's all underground. Weather won't be quite such an issue. But it will be a lot more expensive."

It took several hours but eventually they reached the final, high security section of the facility where the diamonds, the ultimate reason for the existence of this strange patch of civilization in the middle of nowhere, arrived one by one, dropping from a funnel into small containers that reminded Thompson of the cups from his old stainless steel thermos. Here there were cameras everywhere, security guards at the doors. They had to pass through a tiny airlock-like room one by one to gain access to the inner sanctum where the diamonds arrived. The door locked behind them and a guard accompanied them everywhere. "Sorry, but no exceptions," he said.

They watched – and listened – in silence as the diamonds dropped into the containers, which were inside a kind of glove box. The guard invited Andropov to take a closer look, and he sat down and put his hands into the gloves. "Go ahead," said the guard, "pick one up. We'll check for holes in the gloves later." He chuckled and turned to Thompson. "It's amazing what diamonds do to people. We haven't had any problems here, but I've heard about cases where people tried to palm diamonds through a slit in gloves like these ones. There's something about handling diamonds that makes people do crazy things."

But Andropov wasn't one of those people. He picked up several diamonds, inspected them carefully, and put them down. "Nice," was all he said. He had handled a lot of African diamonds in his work for Gagarin, bags full of them, with no security at all. They have no idea, he thought, as he extracted his hands from the glove box and stood up. He opened his palms to the security man. "No diamonds," he said and laughed. "I think I've seen enough." He turned to Thompson. "Let's head back."

Both men were searched thoroughly on the way out – socks off, tongue out, flashlight behind the ears, clothes through the X-ray machine – this time by a different and slightly apologetic security man. "Sorry," he said, "but I have to do this. I can't make any exceptions; if I did I'd probably lose my job."

Thompson was ready to get back to work but as they left the secure area Andropov said, "If you've got a minute let's go over to the cafeteria – there are a few more things I want to ask you about."

Thompson really didn't want to spend any more time baby-sitting the Russian, but he said, "Sure. I could use some coffee."

His boss had told him to do everything he could to keep the visitor happy.

It was mid-afternoon and the cafeteria was nearly empty, just a few men sitting at a corner table playing cards and drinking coffee. Andropov got a large mug of tea and Thompson ordered coffee and a glazed donut – he couldn't resist donuts. They took a table at the opposite side of the room to the men playing cards.

"How do you like working here?" Andropov asked after they sat down.

"It's okay. I like the work, it's more interesting than what I did before. And the pay is good. The only problem, for me, is the isolation. It can be a bit lonely. I try to ignore it, and we have a pretty friendly community here, but it's not quite the same as living a normal life. We get plenty of breaks, though – I've got one next week; I'm going to Las Vegas."

Andropov raised his eyebrows. "Las Vegas? I've never quite seen the attraction, myself. Out there in the middle of the desert. I was there once, but I don't gamble so I was like a fish out of water. That's what you say, right?" Andropov's English was excellent but once in a while he stumbled over a colloquial expression.

Thompson nodded. "You got it."

"How about you? You do any gambling in Las Vegas?"

Thompson shifted in his seat. "Yeah, a bit. But I go for other things too, like the weather."

Andropov could tell from Thompson's body language that he was evading the question. He made a mental note, then took a sip of his tea and changed the subject. "Are you married?"

"I was. Past tense. For quite a few years, actually, but in the end it didn't work out. We got a divorce." It was a strange question. Why was Andropov asking him about his personal life? It was something he didn't usually talk about; even most of the men at the mine didn't know he was divorced.

Thompson had gone to work for a nickel mining company in Sudbury, Ontario, straight out of university, and he'd worked there for seventeen years. But his career came to a crashing end when a drinking problem – it had developed slowly, insidiously, over many years – began to affect his work. He started missing report deadlines and failing to show up for meetings and his bosses got concerned, but for a while he managed to cover up with inventive excuses. Eventually, though, his co-workers realized what was going on. The company had programs for employees with personal problems and he was encouraged to take advantage of them, but they were voluntary and Thompson was stubborn. It wasn't a serious problem, he said, he could handle it himself, thank you very much. Except that he really couldn't handle it himself. In the end they gave him an ultimatum – resign with a modest pay-out in recognition of his years with the company, or be fired. He took the pay-out.

His wife had found his drinking hard enough to take when he'd been going to work every day, but it was unbearable when he was at home all the time. And sometimes he just disappeared, for days at a time. At first she was frantic, calling the bars he frequented, driving him home when she found him. But eventually she gave up – it just wasn't worth the pain. One morning, six months after leaving his job, he came home after a three day binge to find she had changed the locks. He rang the bell and hammered on the front door and then tried the back door but there was no response. He'd had to call a taxi and check into a hotel and it shook him up so badly that he realized he needed to take charge, and checked himself into rehab.

He thought it would be a quick fix, that he'd be able to go back to his old life as soon as he got out. But his wife wouldn't have it. She didn't want him back and refused to talk when he called. She didn't even tell him she was filing for divorce, he found out from her lawyer. He didn't contest it, but on the day the divorce was finalized he decided he really needed a drink. He thought he could handle a rum and coke, or maybe even two, with no problem. He was deluding himself, and after a disastrous few weeks – he had little recollection of where he'd been or what he did – he resurfaced and staggered back to the rehab clinic. This time he knew his future was on the line. People said third time lucky but he doubted he'd ever get another chance. He had been sober ever since, almost five years and counting.

Andropov was sipping his tea and watching the engineer closely. His tour with Thompson had convinced him that it would be possible to launder Gagarin's African diamonds through the Diatek mine. But it would be risky, and he would need someone on the inside, someone with easy access to the ore processing system. Someone like Thompson. In Andropov's experience, money – accompanied by a few well-timed threats – usually worked. He wondered if the engineer would bite.

"Sorry to hear about the divorce," he said. "But I suppose a place like this gives you a chance to get away from it all." He paused. "Do you have any plans to move on?"

"You never know," Thompson said, "but I don't see myself leaving any time soon." He had come a long way from the depths of his addiction, but he still hadn't quite regained his old self confidence. And although he kept telling himself that the gambling wasn't a problem, deep down he knew it was – or would be if he didn't do something about it. He occasionally thought about looking for work somewhere that would give him a more normal lifestyle, but he wasn't ready for change, not quite yet. Besides, he knew he was appreciated at the mine. "Like I said before, I enjoy the work. As long as I can go to places like Las Vegas now and then I think I'll be around for a while." He drained the last of his coffee.

"Okay," Andropov said, "I'm sure you have work to do. And I need to get back over to the administration building. But thanks for your help. It's been very instructive." He stood up and held out his hand.

"No problem," Thompson said. "My pleasure. Have a good trip back."

Thompson watched the Russian walk to the cafeteria door, not knowing quite what to make of him, wondering again what kind of report he would prepare when he got back to Russian and who would see it. Andropov didn't fit the mold of the type of businessman that had come through the mine in the past, and even though he seemed to have some knowledge of diamond mining Thompson was pretty sure he wasn't an engineer or a scientist. He seemed to be mostly interested in security. And why all the personal questions? The guy is a bit of an enigma. He shrugged and went back to his office.

When Andropov left the mine he went straight to Sochi. It was a long haul: the company helicopter back to Yellowknife and then multiple flights and plane changes, but he wanted to talk to Gagarin face to face, and as soon as possible. He traveled business class but even so he got little sleep and by the time he arrived he felt as though he'd been traveling for weeks, although in reality it was little more than twenty-four hours. Gagarin was in a jovial mood – perhaps because Christmas was coming up and his wife and children were decorating the house accordingly – but all Andropov wanted to do was have a shower and go to bed. First, though, they needed to talk.

"You were right," he said to Gagarin. "What you said about taking the diamonds to Canada that night. Brilliant." Andropov didn't care whether Gagarin had really meant what he said that night in the Moscow bar. Getting Vas to think that it was his idea in the first place was the best way to persuade him to approve the plan he'd worked out during the long journey back from Canada. It was a tactic he had used before.

"We might lose a few diamonds in the processing – we won't have absolute control over them – but I think it would be worth it because when they come out the other end they will be government certified and we'll get much more for them than we do now." Andropov paused. "First, though, I need to get some information on a person who works at the mine. Alex could probably do it for us."

Alex Kalinin was one of Gagarin's cousins who had lived in Canada for many years, running protection rackets in the west of the country. He wasn't directly part of Gagarin's operation, but he was family and he had helped out a few times in the past when Gagarin's businesses needed something taken care of on the ground in Canada. It was Alex who had first alerted Gagarin about the availability of the diamond deposit that eventually became the Diatek mine. Andropov had met him once, and he liked him.

Gagarin was watching him with a bemused look on his face. "Sure. If you think it will work, go ahead." He turned and opened the refrigerator and took out a chilled bottle of his favorite vodka and poured two shots. "To diamonds," he said, and threw it back. Andropov did the same, and Gagarin poured another. "Just make sure Alex keeps it quiet. That mine is doing well, we don't want to spoil it."

"Don't worry," Andropov said, "Alex is good at that." He drank the second shot and raised his hand. "That's it for me. If I have another one I'll keel over. I have to go to bed. There are other things we need to talk about, but if it's okay with you they can wait until tomorrow."

Gagarin waved his hand. "Go, my friend. Get your sleep." As Andropov walked away he poured himself more vodka. I love that guy like a son, he was thinking. Laundering African diamonds through Canada. He shook his head. What an idea.

Over the quiet period between Christmas and New Year, an analyst for the RCMP, Canada's national police, noticed that one Dimitri Andropov had entered the country through Montreal's Trudeau airport a few weeks earlier. No flags had gone up when his passport was scanned at immigration, but the analyst had a confidential list that Immigration and Customs wasn't privy to.

It originated with the FBI and it was shared with the RCMP as part of their mutual cooperation in keeping North American borders secure. According to this list Andropov was a 'person of interest;' he was thought to be involved in illegal arms dealings for the Russian oligarch Vasily Gagarin, although nothing had ever been pinned on him directly. The Russians let him come and go from their country with impunity, but the Americans had been monitoring his movements for several years.

Andropov had been in Canada less than a week, the analyst noticed. He wondered if he should follow up, try to trace the Russian's movements within the country. But then he looked at his watch and realized he was due at a holiday party in half an hour and his wife would not be happy if he was late. What the hell, he thought, if someone thinks it's important I can always do it later. He annotated the file, sent it to his boss, and promptly forgot about it. Eventually the information got passed on to the FBI, but their focus was on Islamic terrorists, not Russian businessmen. The report was filed away, and the analyst never did get a request to dig deeper into Andropov's visit.

CHAPTER 5

Two years later …

London. What a city. Sarah could hardly believe she was living here. She was still finding her way around, and right now she was consulting her map, juggling her purse and umbrella and trying to stay dry. When she left her flat in Finsbury twenty minutes earlier the sun was out but now the rain was coming down hard, splashing up onto her shoes and the bottoms of her trousers. So much for exploring the city. The umbrella was pulled down over her head and she could see nothing but other people's shoes splashing along the pavement.

She had only been to London once before, when she was fourteen, and she had hated it. She had been on a family holiday, her father at a conference in Cambridge, her mother trying to keep Sarah and her younger brother busy. Maneuvering a punt along the Cam was fun, and so was exploring the town on a bike, but one day the three of them had gone down to London on the train. She still remembered emerging from the station on a hot July morning onto a crowded, noisy, and dirty road. The sun was relentless. Her mother dragged them down the street to the British Library where there was an exhibition she thought they would enjoy. But for fourteen year old Sarah it was boring; she sulked through it wishing she could be home in California with her friends. Later, waiting in a long line of tourists at the Tower of London, she and her brother quarreled endlessly – she couldn't remember now what it was all about – until their mother, exasperated, threatened to ground them both for a week when they got back home. At the end of the day they returned to Cambridge sweaty and exhausted, and, when her father asked her about the trip, Sarah said she never wanted to go to London again.

What a difference a few years make, she thought. Well, more than a few years, but still. Now she couldn't imagine not being in London.

She was looking for Holburn Street. That's where she would find the offices of Global Witness, the organization she had been placed with for her internship. "Can't miss it, luv," said a man selling newspapers when she asked. "Just keep walking this way and you'll come to it." She thanked him and thought, Why is it people always say that? It's easy enough for him to say you can't miss it, but I don't even know what I'm looking for. Holburn was marked on her map as a major thoroughfare, but she wondered if she'd recognize it. She wasn't used to street names changing every few blocks like they seemed to do here.

Sarah had come to London to do a Master's degree in international politics and human rights. Three years earlier, when she graduated from Stanford, she'd gone straight to work for McKinsey, the big consulting firm, without taking a break. But constant travel all over the United States and working sixty and seventy hour weeks had drained her, and when a friend told her about the program at the City University of London she checked it out and sent in an application. A month later she got a letter saying she was accepted into the program – they'd spelled it 'programme'. Quaint, she thought, I think I'll like it there. She gave notice at McKinsey, sublet her Chicago apartment, and bought a one-way ticket to London. It was late summer, 2011, and she was full of anticipation, ready to start the next phase of her life.

The program included a mandatory internship. She'd put Global Witness as her first choice; although she'd never heard of the organization before, when she researched all the possibilities on the University's list Global Witness seemed perfect: a nonprofit that investigated things like corruption and human rights abuses in industries connected with natural resources – mainly mining and forestry. Those were industries she knew little about, so she'd be learning something new. Besides, it would give her a chance to reconnect with the idealism of her undergraduate days at Stanford. And with the internship, a Master's degree, and her experiences at McKinsey she might even find a career in which she could do some good in the world.

Eventually Sarah found the address she was looking for – an imposing gray stone building – but most of the ground floor seemed to be taken up by a bank. No Global Witness signs that she could see. She shook off her dripping umbrella and went through a door and found herself in a small lobby. A bored-looking attendant sat at a low desk; when she asked about Global Witness he pointed to a list of building tenants on the wall. "Take the lift to the sixth floor," he said. "I'll call up and tell them you're coming." Uncharacteristically, Sarah was a bit nervous.

"Miss Patterson, is it?" asked a woman at the desk when Sarah walked into the Global Witness offices. "Welcome." She paused. "You're from America aren't you? I went to Florida last winter. It was fabulous."

Sarah acknowledged she was from the United States and told the woman to call her Sarah and said that she had spent a month in Miami a year ago for her job. "We were so busy that I didn't have time to see much of the city. I didn't even make it to the beach."

"How could you *not* go to the beach in Florida?" the woman asked, shaking her head. Sarah was about to explain that she had grown up near the ocean in Southern California and beaches were no big deal for her when the woman continued: "Anyway, I'd better introduce you to Zoe – she's the one you're going to be working with." She stood up and beckoned Sarah to follow. "Let's go through. She's expecting you."

Sarah had already corresponded with Zoe by email but she had no idea what to expect. When they walked in she was sitting at a desk covered with papers and stacks of file folders; even more papers covered most of the floor space around her. Zoe stood up and navigated through the piles of documents and stuck out her hand to Sarah. "Welcome to Global Witness," she said. "Didn't have any problem finding us? I hope you brought an umbrella; you never know when it's going to start raining here." Zoe wasn't wearing any makeup and she looked a bit disheveled. Stray tendrils of hair fell across her eyes whenever she turned her head and she kept pushing them away. She was wearing a wool sweater and jeans.

At least I won't have to worry about a dress code at Global Witness, Sarah thought. She'd brought most of her business clothes to London but it didn't look as though she'd need them, not for the internship, anyway. Wonderful.

"Let's get some tea," Zoe said, pointing across the hall to a small room where there was a sink and a kettle. "Unless you'd rather have coffee. I'm afraid we've only got instant though. This country runs on tea, as you'll find out. Although every time you turn around a new coffee shop has opened up. Have you been in London long?"

Zoe kept up a continuous patter; Sarah could hardly get a word in edgewise. But she managed to tell Zoe that tea was fine and that she had been in London for just two weeks and was still finding her way around, and she had settled into her flat nicely – she'd found it through a contact in McKinsey's London office. So far her classes were going well; it was a big change from the corporate world she'd been immersed in for the past few years.

"Yes," Zoe said, "well, Global Witness will be a big change too. It's not that we're *anti* corporate exactly, it's just that we're trying to expose some of the worst corporate behavior. And bad government behavior too. Especially when it comes to the environment, human rights, corruption … it's a long list. In the end a lot of it just comes down to greed." She took a carton of milk from a small refrigerator and poured some into her tea. "Milk?" she asked.

Sarah shook her head. "Black is fine."

Zoe looked at her. "Nothing like sweet milky tea. You should try it." She ladled two heaping spoons full of sugar into her own cup and stirred vigorously. "Let's go back to my office and I'll tell you about the project I have for you."

They settled into chairs on opposite sides of the desk and Zoe reached over and picked up a stack of paper from the floor behind her. She handed it to Sarah. "Do you know anything about the diamond industry?"

Sarah shook her head. "No," she said, "nothing at all. Most of the work I did at McKinsey was for financial companies, or insurance."

"Mm. I can't say that the financial industry has a very good reputation right now. But diamond mining … it might be even worse. It doesn't affect the global economy in the same way, but it *has* affected the lives of millions of people, and not in a good way. We've put a lot of effort into investigating the industry, especially in Africa. Did you see *Blood Diamond*? A lot of our research went into that movie."

Sarah raised her eyebrows. "I read about your work on conflict diamonds on the internet but I didn't know there was a connection with the film. It's a great movie."

"Mm. Those papers," – Zoe pointed to the stack of documents she had just handed to Sarah – "they're all about diamond mining in Canada. Have you heard about that?" Again Sarah shook her head. "No? Well, it's a really big deal in the diamond business. Canada has a lot of natural resources but they didn't mine diamonds until fairly recently, when someone discovered them in the far north of the country – really far north, up in the barren grounds, beyond the tree line. They opened the first mine there in 1998 and since then several more have started up. It's very lucrative; there are lots of diamonds and the quality is high and the mining companies are making a lot of money. So is the government, from the taxes, so they've got a vested interest in promoting mining. Problem is, the mines are on land traditionally used by native peoples. Also, the environment is very delicate up there."

It was hard to stop Zoe when she got going on something she was passionate about. "There are disputes about some of the treaties but the mining goes ahead anyway. A few groups of indigenous people have signed agreements directly with the mining companies; they get some money, but they're probably getting screwed, just like they are everywhere else. Several of the mines are right where huge caribou migrations go through every year. Who knows what effect that's going to have? The Dene Indians who live there still hunt and fish and they rely on the caribou, just like they have for thousands of years. And there'll be massive piles of crushed up rock left scattered around the landscape after the stuff is processed for diamonds. Not to mention the damage the mining may do to the lakes. So it's not a pretty picture."

Zoe paused for breath and drank some tea. Sarah asked if it really was possible to do anything about it if the agreements had been signed and the mines were already operating.

"You'd be surprised," Zoe said. "If there's new information, agreements can be modified or even canceled. A few well-written articles in the *New York Times* or the *Guardian* or the *Economist* can have a big impact. That's what we try to do – we lobby if we think it's necessary. The CEOs of those mining companies don't want their organizations to be seen as getting rich off the backs of poor natives even if that's actually what's happening. For us the important thing is to raise public awareness and lobby for change. We're not Luddites, but we are against exploitation.

"Those papers I gave you" – Zoe pointed to the stack of documents Sarah was holding – "there's background information in them about the Canadian diamond industry, and also summaries of the government treaties with the indigenous people. Most of them were negotiated a long time ago. I don't think we have many details yet on the more recent agreements, the ones that were negotiated directly between the First Nations and the mining companies. But that information shouldn't be too difficult to find. To be honest things are probably a lot better in Canada than in some of the other places we're working, but it still needs to be looked at. We're so stretched with other projects and the diamond industry over there has developed so fast that we just haven't had the manpower to dig into it. We've been accumulating these documents for several years now, but nobody's had the time to work on them. I haven't even read most of them myself. So my thought for the internship is that you could synthesize everything you can find out about the companies doing the mining in Canada, especially the impact they have on the environment and the First Nations people. Does that sound reasonable? It should be doable in the time you're here, and it would help us a lot."

Piece of cake, Sarah thought, although she didn't say so out loud. She didn't want to sound like a know-it-all American. But she was a good researcher; in her job at McKinsey she'd had lots of experience ferreting out company details and she didn't think it would be too difficult to do what Zoe asked. And she could look forward to learning more about an industry that was, for her, completely unknown.

"Sure," Sarah said. "That sounds fine. My adviser at City says it doesn't really matter what topic we investigate for the internship as long as it's serious research work. But actually what you've outlined sounds as though it would fit right in with what I'm learning in my classes. Plus I don't know anything about mining, so it would all be new, which is the whole point. It sounds perfect to me."

Zoe, still working on her mug of tea, was watching Sarah closely and considering her first impressions of the new intern. Articulate, she thought, and confident. Animated when she talks and she smiles a lot – and she has those perfect white American teeth. Zoe unconsciously closed her lips over her own tea-stained and not quite so regular teeth. And she has a *tan*. Not the disgusting orange-tinged spray-on tans that she saw on young women on the tube every morning when she came to work, but a real tan. Well, Zoe thought, she'll soon enough lose that over here.

"How do you want to do this?" Sarah was saying. "I can come in most any time except when I have classes – and I don't even *have* that many classes. After working at McKinsey being a student again almost seems like a vacation."

Zoe looked over at the calendar that was hanging on the wall beside her desk. She hadn't quite brought herself to use an electronic one; she liked to write in her appointments and activities by hand, and she liked the long term view the multi-month wall calendar gave her. By the looks of it she was busy:

almost every blank space was filled in with scribbled notes and appointment details. "If we can manage it, we should meet regularly," she said. "Once every couple of weeks at least. I'm free next week at the same time; we could meet then to see how you're managing. After that I'm away quite a bit, almost until Christmas. So we'll have to play it by ear. Why don't you go through the material I've given you and we can discuss it next week, then we'll go from there? In the meantime I'll try to arrange a desk for you. You should be able to do a lot of this work on your own even if I'm not around. I'm afraid we haven't got any spare computers, though."

"That's okay, I've got a laptop. As long as there's internet access it's not a problem."

They talked for a few minutes more and then shook hands again, and Sarah went back through the outer office, pausing to talk to the woman who had greeted her when she first came in. Then she took the elevator down to the ground floor and stepped out onto Holburn Street. The rain had stopped and the sun had come out and the city quite literally sparkled. She felt good about her talk with Zoe. The internship would be what she made of it, of course, but the topic sounded interesting and it looked as though she would be able to do her own research without too much direct supervision. That was the way she liked it. She walked away from Global Witness with a smile on her face, in her imagination floating through London like Mary Poppins with her umbrella.

She had mapped out a route back to her flat that took her through some of the old parts of the city and as she wound her way through small, uncrowded streets and passageways she felt a sensation of unreality come over her. Am I really doing this, she asked herself? Walking through the streets of this city I've heard so much about that is simultaneously modern and ancient? Again she marveled at the difference from that summer's day when she was just fourteen. How could she ever have hated the city? She had only been in London two weeks but already she was starting to feel possessive; she wanted to make London *her* city. And all those documents in the plastic carrier bag Zoe had given her to keep out the rain – well, they were an adventure waiting to happen. Who knows where they would lead? She was ready to dive in and use all the skills her three years at McKinsey had given her.

CHAPTER 6

By the time she got back to her flat Sarah had turned the project Zoe had given her over and over in her head and decided on a way to tackle it. She was in her element; she liked her classes but what she really loved was solving problems. This one didn't look too difficult, but she knew from experience that that could change. In an odd way she hoped it would; she loved a challenge.

She had picked up a latte from a coffee shop near her flat – she was already a regular there – and she poured it into a mug and warmed it up in the microwave. She didn't like drinking from cardboard if she could help it. And although she hadn't said so to Zoe, coffee was her drink of preference. Tea was okay once in a while, but she was convinced that she worked better with a cup of coffee in her hand.

She took out the documents Zoe had given her and organized them in piles on the floor. As far as she could tell they concerned four different companies that had active diamond mines in Canada. She made a note to do a search for any others that Zoe might have missed, then opened a spreadsheet on her laptop. At McKinsey her colleagues had teased Sarah about her obsession with spreadsheets. She used them for everything. Everyone has their own way of organizing things, she told them, spreadsheets work for me. As she leafed through Zoe's documents she typed in every detail she could find about the four companies, however insignificant. You never know what might turn out to be important, she thought.

She had printed out the spreadsheet and taped the pages together so that when they met in Zoe's office the next week it draped across her desk like a banner. Sarah led Zoe through the data company by company, focusing especially on the financial details – she'd accessed all the publically available financial reports she could find and summarized them in a way that was easy to understand. Finally I'm going to learn something from an intern, Zoe thought, instead of the other way around. Numbers were not Zoe's strong point.

"This one is interesting," Sarah said when she came to the last company on her list. "Diatek Canada. They've only been in existence for a few years, but based on their financial reports they've been quite successful. They're also the only Canadian diamond mining operation that doesn't seem to be part of a consortium. The other three all include large international mining companies like DeBeers. As far as I can tell Diatek is wholly owned by a holding company in Toronto, which makes it a little more difficult to figure out who is actually behind it, but I'm working on that. Some of my friends at McKinsey may be able to help.

"Something else that's interesting about Diatek is that they had an environmental problem at their mine a couple of years ago, and it caught the attention of Canadian environmentalists. They had a chemical spill at a lake near the mine, and it killed a lot of fish and wildfowl. Someone found out about it and before long there were newspaper articles and a lot of discussion on the internet, and that led to protests at Diatek's headquarters in Vancouver. It didn't last very long, but a few protesters even got to the mine – I don't know how they did that because there aren't even any roads up there. But it stirred things up enough that some of the workers went on strike, and that put a dent in Diatek's profits that year. They seem to have recovered pretty quickly, though."

"I don't remember anything about those protests," Zoe said, "although it's the kind of thing we usually track. But like I said before, Canada has been on the back burner because we're so stretched. I'm glad you caught it. It's good to have you doing this, Sarah." Although Sarah didn't realize it yet, that was about as close as Zoe got to praise.

"Yeah, well, I'm enjoying it. I'm going to spend some more time looking into this whole episode at Diatek. As long as you think that it's worthwhile, of course," she added.

"Definitely. It's exactly the kind of thing we should be doing." Zoe picked up some papers from her desk and then put them down again. "Look, Sarah, you seem pretty self-sufficient to me. Unlike some of the interns I've had, where I really had to hold their hands through a whole project. Which is good because I'm going to be doing a lot of traveling over the next few months. Two heads are always better than one and we should meet whenever I'm back in town and keep in touch by email when I'm not here so I know what you're up to, but mostly I'd say you should just follow your nose and see where it leads. And if you can drop by tomorrow I'll introduce you to Tim Galbraith. He's done a lot of our work on conflict diamonds in Africa and he's very knowledgeable about the diamond industry in general, so he's a good resource. Tim works from home a lot so he's in and out of the office but as long as you coordinate in advance I'm pretty sure he'd be happy to talk to you when I'm not here – or even when I am around. He'd be a good person to bounce your ideas off of. He'll be here all day tomorrow, so I hope you can make it."

"No problem. I'll come in after lunch. I'm free all afternoon."

Sarah quickly realized that her year in London would pass in a flash if she wasn't careful, and she was determined to make the most of it. As the weeks went by, whenever she had a little spare time, she would hop on a bus or take the underground and ride for half an hour, then challenge herself to get home without asking for directions. Whole districts became familiar, and she kept making discoveries: an ancient church hidden among skyscrapers, a tiny Victorian park with men in suits sipping their lattes on one bench and a homeless person on another, all enjoying a moment's peace. If she got completely lost, well, she always had her Oyster card.

Her British classmates gave her a blank stare or a shrug of the shoulders when she asked why they called it an Oyster card. "Don't get me started," one of them replied. "We've also got zebra crossings and toucan crossings and pelican crossings. They're names for different kinds of street crossings. Go figure."

By the middle of November the days were short; clocks had gone back to standard time and it was usually still dusky when she got up and very dark when she finished her day at the University. It was also getting colder, and it was perpetually damp. The weak sun, when it appeared, held little warmth and rose so low in the sky that it no longer reached some of the pathways she followed on her way to classes. Cobblestones, polished smooth by centuries of human traffic, stayed damp all day; they never lost their wet sheen. But when people asked if she missed the sun of her native California she realized – somewhat to her own surprise – that she was so immersed in her work that she hardly noticed the weather. She had also discovered a new passion: diamonds.

Her own work was focused on Canada but Tim Galbraith gave her a much broader perspective; he was a fount of information about almost every aspect of the global diamond industry. With his help she accumulated stacks of documents on everything from conflict diamonds in Africa to aboriginal claims on land mined for diamonds in Australia. She quizzed him about how conflict diamonds from Sierra Leone made their way to Charles Taylor's Liberia and from there into the world markets. He explained that diamond exporters sometimes obscured the country of origin by passing the diamonds through a country of convenience – like Switzerland, for example.

"Switzerland doesn't produce diamonds," he said, "it has no diamond mines – the geological conditions are just not right. But if a diamond shipment from another country transits through a free trade zone at a Swiss airport, well, when it gets shipped onward the papers can be changed to reference Switzerland as the country of origin." Galbraith got visibly angry as he told her this. "It shouldn't happen in the twenty-first century. The Kimberley process was supposed to change things, but even some of the governments that signed up occasionally turn a blind eye when it's convenient for them. It's still an uphill battle."

Zoe had found a desk for Sarah and put it in one corner of an open room at Global Witness. It wasn't perfect, but it was her own and with all the information she was collecting her little corner began to look just like Zoe's office: the floor was her filing cabinet, her desk surrounded by stacks of documents. She bought a small electric heater for warmth – when she stayed late or came in on the weekends the office was cold – and she brought in a desk lamp. She filled the wall above the desk with notes and newspaper clippings, and she felt right at home.

Sarah knew almost nothing about geology but she soon realized that to really understand the diamond industry she'd have to learn more. Tim Galbraith loaned her two geology textbooks, but they were too general – they didn't devote much space to diamonds, and if she was honest with herself she found them a little boring. Characteristically, she set up her own learning program, starting with the internet. She quickly began to understand why recovering diamonds in northern Canada required large operations and expensive mines – the diamonds there were still encased in the rocks that brought them up to the surface from deep in the earth's interior – while in some places in Africa or South America individual prospectors could scoop diamonds out of rivers and sandbanks with almost no equipment. There, time and weather had done the hard work, breaking down the rocks that encased the diamonds and freeing them to be carried and winnowed by rain and rivers and then, eventually, deposited far from their original source, like any other grain of sand. A bit like the mechanical processes that engineers had designed to separate diamonds from the ore at the Canadian diamond mines, except on a completely different scale, both in time and distance.

She visited the earth science galleries at the Natural History Museum and viewed the real diamonds on display there to learn more, and she went to the Tower of London to see the famous Koh-i-noor diamond. It was certainly beautiful, she thought, but as she joined the steady stream of tourists moving by she wondered what all the fuss was about. The Koh-i-noor's origins were so shrouded in mystery and legend that books had been written about it, but somehow it didn't quite live up to the hype. Sure, it was beautiful and it sparkled and gleamed, but after everything she'd read she thought it would bowl her over, and it didn't. Still, she was beginning to understand why diamonds had held such allure throughout history, why they had been fought over, stolen, and jealously guarded by everyone from kings and maharajahs to scrabbling prospectors trying to strike it rich. There was something about these little lumps of carbon from deep in the earth that cast a spell over people. She had never paid much attention to gems, but the more she learned the more her fascination grew.

Sarah also tried to dig deeper into the environmental crisis – if it really had been a crisis – that had sparked protests against Diatek Canada. On the face of it, the chemical spill didn't seem that serious – yes it had done local damage, but it had been limited to one lake. Had Diatek just been unlucky? As far as she could determine, none of the other companies she was researching had encountered similar problems or attracted the same kind of attention from environmentalists. The media coverage she was able to find was entirely from Canadian sources and it was all from a very short time period. The furor, it seemed, had erupted suddenly and died down just as quickly. But what had happened at the mine since then? Had Diatek taken care of its problems?

In trying to answer those questions she came to a dead end. She couldn't find any follow-up; it was almost as though the whole episode had never happened. She began to wonder if she was missing something, and one day she asked Tim Galbraith if he had any ideas about where she could look.

"Try to track down some of the people who were involved in the protests and talk to them," he said. "The serious ones, the ones who weren't just along for the ride, they might have kept an eye on the company even if the media weren't interested anymore. That's been a good source of information for us in other places."

Sarah smacked herself on the forehead. "Of course. Once in a while I have to remind myself that not everything is on the internet." She shook her head. "It's so obvious I didn't even see it. Thanks, Tim."

She went back through her accumulated documents and compiled a list of names - it was short, only six people in all, but each of them had been at the protests either at Diatek's Vancouver headquarters or at the mine, and they had been willing to talk to the media and give their names. Presumably they were the serious ones, to use Tim Galbraith's phrase. The question was, How could she locate them? An obvious first step was to check her list against people living in Vancouver; that was where the protests originated and even though several years had passed, some of them might still be there.

But there were only two matches, and when she found contact details and emailed them only one responded. She had a sinking feeling as she started to read his message. He didn't think he could give her any useful information, he said, he had moved on and was no longer involved in environmental issues. He had no idea how things had played out at the Diatek mine in the years since the protests. He went on to say he had always been a fan of the work being done by Global Witness and wished her luck on her project.

I need more than luck, she thought. But then, at the end of the message, he said he was still in touch with a few people in Vancouver who had been at the protests and might be willing to talk to her. He had attached a list with names and email addresses. Bingo. Sarah could feel the smile spreading across her face.

The next day she wrote to each of the former protesters, explaining how she had obtained their contact details and saying that she was currently researching environmental practices in the Canadian diamond industry. Would they be willing to do a Skype interview with her about their experiences at the 2009 protests at Diatek? She'd send them a few questions in advance as a guide to the kinds of things she was interested in, and she estimated the interview would take no more than half an hour of their time. Then she crossed her fingers and waited for replies.

Sarah's first term at City University was quickly coming to an end, Christmas less than a month away. She wondered where the time had gone; it seemed as though just yesterday she had had a whole year stretching out in front of her and now the first part of it was almost over. Suddenly she was swamped with work – papers for classes, an interim report on her internship, her ongoing research – and social engagements with her classmates. During her three years at McKinsey Christmas had almost been an afterthought. Here it seemed that the parties started by the end of November and just kept going.

And soon she would be going home to San Diego for the holidays. That too would be a novelty; it would be her first Christmas at home in three years. She had been tempted to stay in the U.K., especially because a classmate had invited her to her family home near Manchester for a few days over Christmas. But the University would be closed for a full three weeks and nobody she knew would be staying in London. Besides, she knew her parents would pamper her. And with all the airline miles she'd accumulated through her travel for McKinsey she could get a business class seat on a direct flight from Heathrow to San Diego.

In the meantime replies from the Vancouver protesters trickled in. With the press of things to finish before the holidays she'd decided to do the interviews when she was home in California; it would be much easier anyway because she'd be in the same time zone. Four people had agreed to be interviewed, which was better than she had hoped. Two were now graduate students at the University of British Columbia and one worked at a non-profit in downtown Vancouver. The fourth, according to his message, was temporarily unemployed.

And then, a few days before leaving for California, she noticed a Facebook post from her cousin Jennifer. Jennifer was the only daughter of Sarah's uncle Bruce, her father's twin brother, and in spite of growing up far apart the cousins were very close. 'Uncle Bruce' was an engineer who had taken a job in Toronto when he graduated from university, thinking he'd be back in the U.S. within a few years. But those few years stretched into ten, then twenty, and he no longer thought about moving back. Jennifer had been born in Toronto, and when she and Sarah were growing up they spent every summer together, alternating between Canada and California. They had been almost inseparable, the inevitable partings at the end of August always high drama. Now they saw one another only sporadically, but it didn't seem to matter. It always felt as though no time had passed at all.

And Jennifer had recently moved to Vancouver. Her Facebook post gushed about her new job and included pictures of the city. It was, she said, much nicer than Toronto. When she saw the pictures, Sarah froze. She already knew Jennifer had a new job in Vancouver, of course she did, but somehow she hadn't connected it with her research on Diatek. Why not stop there for a few days after the holidays, on her way back to London? She could see Jen, and she could do the interviews with the protesters in person. It would be so much better than doing them by Skype. With her elite airline status, changing her tickets wouldn't be a problem.

She also got a call from Peter Sutherland, one of her former McKinsey colleagues. Peter always seemed to be able to un-earth company details that no one else could find, and she had emailed to ask him about Diatek. It was the one company she was investigating for which she had no clear picture of who was ultimately in control. In particular she had asked Peter if he could find out anything about the Toronto holding company that owned Diatek Canada. Her own searches had found al-most nothing.

Interesting company, he said after they'd exchanged greet-ings and he'd asked how her course was going. Sarah knew that if Peter said a company was interesting it probably meant it had a very convoluted corporate structure.

"Obviously Diatek is a Canadian company," he contin-ued, "as is the holding company in Toronto. It – the holding company – is the sole owner of Diatek. The interesting thing is that it's registered in the Cayman Islands even though it's a Canadian company. And from what I can find out most of its financing comes from a private bank, also registered in the Caymans, that's controlled by one very rich Russian, a guy named Vasily Gagarin. He has mining interests in Russia so a diamond mining company would fit, although there's no direct link between him and Diatek except at arm's length through the bank. There are rumors that he's got connections with the Russian mafia. Apparently Putin sometimes stays at his villa on the Black Sea, so maybe that's why he's not in jail. Russia is one of those countries where the government, organized crime and legitimate businesses can sometimes all be in bed together."

"Wow. Peter, you've outdone yourself. Thanks."

He laughed. "No problem. I actually enjoyed it. So Sarah, bottom line is don't dig too deep into Diatek." Peter laughed again. "I don't want to wake up some morning and read in the paper that you've been shot by a Russian hitman."

"Yeah, sure … you still read the paper, Peter?"

"Actually I do, sometimes. Anyway, it's been nice talking to you but I've got to go. McKinsey is calling. And Sarah … just so you know, a lot of people around here would be very happy to have you back when you finish your course. Let's stay in touch, okay?"

They said goodbye and Sarah sat for a few minutes and thought about what Peter had said. It's nice to be wanted, she thought, but is that really what I want to do for the rest of my career? And then she looked down at the notes she'd written during their conversation. She had underlined the words 'Russian mafia.' Peter's imagination must be running wild, she thought, that can't be true. But however it turned out, Diatek was certainly the most interesting of the companies she was looking at. By comparison the others seemed positively boring.

Sarah hadn't lived in San Diego for many years. But as her mother drove her home from the airport it was as though she had dropped back into a parallel life that she'd never really left. It all seemed completely familiar. She woke up the next morning with the sun streaming through the open shutters, momentarily not knowing where she was. London had been gray for weeks; she couldn't remember when she'd last felt the warmth of the sun. But in spite of the sun her room was cold and she pulled the duvet close around her. She'd forgotten how chilly her parent's old and poorly heated California house could be on a winter morning.

Her two weeks at home flew past in a blur; a steady stream of old friends and neighbors dropped in to say hello, Christmas came and went, and on a few quiet mornings she took her coffee and wandered down to the beach to sit in the hazy seaside sunshine and watch the surfers. Her parents had bought the house in La Jolla before she was born, and when Sarah was growing up having the Pacific Ocean on her doorstep had seemed as ordinary as going to school. It was just there, part of her life. Now though, her perspective had changed. Maybe she should move back to California when she'd finished her Master's degree, she thought. As she sat on the rocks at Wind'nSea beach on those mornings the slow, steady beat of the waves breaking below her and the hiss of the sand as the water retreated – sounds so familiar from her childhood – lulled her into a trance. It was a delightful feeling, almost like suspended animation, her mind wandering in all directions. Usually though, her thoughts eventually came back to diamonds. Diamonds and Diatek and curiosity about what she would learn in Vancouver.

CHAPTER 7

"Sarah!" She heard her cousin before she saw her. Sarah had just stepped out into the airport arrivals hall and when she looked around she saw Jennifer waving her arms wildly, a huge smile on her face. Jen was hard to miss. She was tall, much taller than Sarah, and she had on a red and white wool hat with long, dangling earflaps. The two girls embraced in a bear hug and they both started talking at once. In spite of the difference in height they could have been sisters; they had the same coloring and a strong facial resemblance.

"My first visitor," Jen said, "it's so great you're here, I can't wait to show you around my new city. So how are you? How was Christmas? How are your folks?"

"It was good – pretty quiet, actually, and now I'm ready to get back to work on my thesis. How about you? You look good, Jen. You stayed here for the holidays?"

"Yeah, can you believe this was the first time ever I haven't been home at Christmas? But it was okay, I got invited for Christmas dinner by someone from work. They told me they always feed the strays." She laughed and gave Sarah another bear hug. "Let's go – we can talk in the car."

Jen was in IT. Ever since Sarah could remember, her cousin had been a whiz at puzzles and games. When they spent summers together at the lakeside cottage Jen's parents owned in northern Ontario the two girls would play cards and board games in the evenings, and Jen usually won. When she lost, Sarah suspected that she just wasn't trying very hard, making sure things didn't get too lopsided.

Jennifer had studied math and computer science at university and landed a job with a large international IT company when she graduated. But then she'd been headhunted for the position in Vancouver: "A dream come true," she told Sarah. "It's a young company and I think they're going to be very successful. I couldn't turn it down."

They turned into the drive of the modern apartment complex where Jen lived and she stopped the car and pointed across the water. "That's the city. Great view, eh? That's what I see from my apartment. Sometimes I have to pinch myself. What did I do to deserve this?"

Jennifer had talked her new boss into a day off and the next morning they went out for breakfast. They walked across a bridge to Granville Island and then through the covered market that sold everything from fancy cupcakes to live lobsters and ended up in a funky coffee shop that Jennifer liked. They sat down at a table looking out over the water; the sky was gray and even in the sheltered bay the wind was whipping up the waves and throwing spray against the shore. It reminded Sarah of the U.K.

"My transition back to gray skies," she said.

"Yeah, but at least it's not snowing. That's what they're forecasting for Toronto this week. But anyway, I'm still waiting to hear more about this work you're doing on Canadian diamonds."

"It's interesting," Sarah said. "It seems a little strange to be working on the Canadian diamond industry when I'm in London, but Global Witness is big on diamond mining – did you know they helped out with that film *Blood Diamond*?"

"No kidding. I saw it, it was a good movie. Leonardo DiCaprio was in it, right?"

"Yes, that's the one. Various people at Global Witness have looked at diamond mining all over the world, but not yet in Canada. Yours truly happened along just when they wanted someone to do that, so here I am. It's one of the reasons I'm in Vancouver. Besides seeing you, of course." She grinned at her cousin. "One of Canada's four diamond mining companies happens to have their head office here and back in 2009 some environmentalists organized protests against them. They'd had a chemical spill at the mine site, that's what started it all. I've been in touch with some of the people who were involved, and I'm hoping to interview them while I'm here. Which reminds me, I'll need to make a few phone calls when we're finished breakfast. I still have to confirm times with these people."

"As long as you keep the rest of the day free I won't complain," Jennifer said.

It took Sarah only twenty minutes to speak to the four people she planned to interview. "Done," she said when she put down the phone. "The first interview is at the university tomorrow morning. The guy is a grad student there. Then I've got someone downtown in the afternoon, and two more on Thursday morning. It shouldn't be too bad." She finished the second latte that Jennifer had brought while she was on the phone. "Say Jennifer, would it be possible to go by the Diatek office today? Just out of curiosity?"

"Sure. Where is it?"

"I googled it earlier." Sarah dug out a notebook and showed her cousin an address. "I think it's somewhere downtown."

"Yes, it is. I know that street – it's not too far from where I work. We can go by, but I don't know what you'll see – it's mostly just office buildings in that part of the city."

The Diatek headquarters were in a modern glass and steel building. They parked the car at a meter and walked down the street for a closer look. Sarah pushed through the glass doors into a spacious lobby and asked the uniformed man at the information desk about Diatek. "Fourth and fifth floor," he said, and went back to the newspaper he had open on his lap.

"Were you here during the protest?" Sarah asked.

"Huh? Protest? Not that I know of."

"It was 2009, there was a problem at Diatek's diamond mine …"

"Oh that, yeah, I heard people talking about it. But I wasn't here, I just started a year ago. I don't think it was too serious; they say it blew over pretty quick."

"Okay, thanks." Sarah looked around the lobby again. She noticed there were CCTV cameras in the corners and thought about what her friend Peter at McKinsey had said about Diatek. She shrugged her shoulders. Ridiculous, she told herself.

"Let's go, Jen. I'm ready to be a tourist."

The next morning Sarah's day got off to a rocky start. Jennifer showed her where to catch the bus to the university but it was ten minutes late and packed with students and she had to stand jammed against a huge guy who looked like an overweight linesman. Whenever he turned to talk to his friend his back-pack smashed into her shoulder. He said he was sorry but two minutes later the same thing happened again. Sarah willed him to stand still, but it didn't work. It was worse than the London tube.

It was a relief to pile off the bus but she was completely disoriented. As she stood there trying to figure out which direction to go a fresh-faced young woman came up to her. "Are you lost?" she asked.

"Sort of," Sarah said. "I'm supposed to be meeting someone at the Student Union Building. At Starbucks." She looked at her watch. "And I'm already late. Do you know which way I have to go?"

"It's not very far," the girl said. "I'm going over that way anyway. I'll show you."

She turned and started to walk away and Sarah fell in beside her.

"Are you thinking of going here?" asked the girl.

"What? Oh no, no." Sarah laughed. She didn't mind being mistaken for a prospective freshman. "No, my university days are over – well, they're almost over. I'm just here to meet someone."

"Where are you from?"

"Southern California. Originally, that is. Right now I'm living in the U.K. I go back on Saturday."

The girl's eyes widened. "I've never been to Europe. But I really want to go to England for my third year. On the study abroad program. My major is English. But I don't know if I can afford it."

Sarah figured she was probably only five or six years older than this young student, but the conversation made it feel like decades. "Go for it," she said. "even if you have to take out a loan. In a few years you won't even remember what it cost."

"Yeah, that's what people say, but I don't know. It's still a lot of money." She pointed to a building on their left. "That's the Student Union Building. Starbucks is down the stairs."

"Thanks," Sarah said. "And live dangerously, okay? Do the study abroad thing. You won't regret it."

The former protester's name was David Reitmann and he had told Sarah he was tall and had a ponytail and she wouldn't have any trouble picking him out. She spotted him as soon as she walked into the café. He was pacing back and forth near the entrance, his stringy hair tied back in a short ponytail, a heavy plaid shirt hanging out over his jeans. He had on hiking boots. Sarah almost laughed out loud. A stereotype if there ever was one.

She walked up to him and said, "David Reitmann?"

He turned and said "Yeah, that's me. Are you Sarah? You're late. I wondered if you were going to show."

Good morning to you too, she thought. "Yes, well the bus was late and I don't know the campus so it took me a little longer than I anticipated. Should we get some coffee?"

Reitmann got a large coffee and a Danish pastry and walked away from the counter, leaving Sarah to order her cappuccino and pay the bill. She took a deep breath. His behavior irritated her. It's only an interview, she said to herself, don't worry about it.

Reitmann had found a table and was stirring sugar into his coffee when she joined him. She decided to dispense with pleasantries and jump right in. "So," she said, "you were one of the people who protested at Diatek back in 2009?"

"Yeah, that's right." Reitmann was carefully cutting his pastry into bite sized pieces and he put one into his mouth, pausing while he ate it. "A bunch of us made signs and went downtown and stood around outside their offices. It was only a few years ago but I really didn't know what I was doing then. A friend of mine convinced me to get involved. I still think it was the right thing to do, though. All those bastards think about is money. They don't give a shit about the Northwest Territories or the people who live up there. Excuse my French."

Sarah started taking notes. "I hope you don't mind," she said.

"It's fine. I've got nothing to hide. Like I said, I went down there without knowing very much. My friend told me about all the fish they killed and I thought it would be fun to protest for a good cause. I'd seen demonstrations on TV but I'd never done anything like that before."

"And who were the organizers?"

"That I don't know for sure. I heard it was somebody from Friends of the Earth, but it seemed kind of spontaneous to me. There were people there from Greenpeace, Friends of the Earth, some other organizations too. Lots of them were UBC students. My friend tried to get me to go up to the Northwest Territories and protest at the mine, but it would have meant missing too many classes. And anyway I didn't have the money. You had to pay for it yourself."

"Who was your friend?"

Reitmann laughed. "Ron. Ah, my buddy Ron. We both graduated that same year, when we did the protesting. Would you believe he now works for an oil company in Houston? And here I am working on a PhD in biology and thinking I'd like to work for some environmental non-profit. Ron was the one who belonged to environmental organizations in those days, not me. Now he's on the other side as far as I'm concerned. I've completely lost touch with him."

"So what did your friend actually tell you about the issues? How did the organizers convince people to go downtown and demonstrate?"

"Oh, that was easy. It was all word of mouth, and there were emails going around and posters all over the university. I remember getting text messages about where to go to pick up signs and stuff like that. They told us this company was making a total mess of the environment, ripping up the tundra, and they weren't treating the First Nation workers very well either. For a bunch of UBC students that was like waving a red flag at a bull. It was a big deal for a couple of months and then it all faded away. I haven't heard anything about Diatek since."

Reitmann had relaxed a bit during their conversation and she realized that her first impression of him might have been wrong. The prickliness was probably because he was shy and maybe a bit insecure. As they were finishing up Sarah asked him if he knew of anyone else she should talk to about Diatek.

Reitmann thought for a moment, then his face lit up. "You know," he said, "there *is* someone. I'd totally forgotten about it until you asked, it seems such a long time ago, but there was this young guy that Diatek sent out to talk to us when we were walking around with our signs. I remember him distinctly; he didn't look much older than us, and he said he hadn't been working for the company for very long. There wasn't any violence or anything, but some of the people in our group were really agitated and when he came out they started shouting and calling him names but he just shrugged and told them to settle down, he wanted to hear what they had to say. He didn't try to justify what the company had done or anything. It was pretty impressive, I have to admit. He was calm and laid back and within about ten minutes we were having a reasonably civilized debate. I don't think it changed anyone's minds, but it's one of those things you remember, you know? He had a French name – what was it?" Reitmann closed his eyes and scrunched up his face, trying to remember the name. "Doucet," he said, opening his eyes. "I'm pretty sure his name was Doucet. I remember thinking he had the same name as the singer."

Sarah looked at him blankly.

"You know, Luke Doucet."

"Who is that?"

"You don't know Luke Doucet? If you don't you're missing something. He plays the guitar beautifully. Maybe he's related to the guy at Diatek, for all I know. Anyway it might be worth talking to him – the one at Diatek. If he's still there, that is. Personally I don't have much use for mining companies, but this guy seemed pretty cool. If you want to hear the other side of the story you should get in touch with him."

It was the longest answer Reitmann had given to any of her questions, and the only time in their short meeting when he showed much sign of enthusiasm. Sarah wrote down 'Doucet, Diatek' with a question mark after it.

"I hadn't thought about talking to anyone from Diatek," she said. "Good suggestion. Perhaps I'll try to get in touch with your Mr. Doucet." She thanked him and said she'd get back in touch if she had any other questions, and she wished him well on his PhD project. He actually blushed and shook her hand politely and said it had been interesting talking to her. Reitmann picked up his backpack and walked away and Sarah thought, What a change in half an hour. Amazing.

Riding the bus back into town she stared out the window but didn't really see anything. She was thinking about what Reitmann had said, wondering if she really should try to contact this person from Diatek. It wasn't such a bad idea. He would probably have a biased view of the issues, but then the people who did the protesting weren't exactly neutral either. She'd have to navigate carefully to get to the truth.

By the time she got off the bus she'd decided she would try to reach Doucet. Why not? She'd be finished with her interviews by noon tomorrow, and that left the afternoon and all day Friday free for Mr. Doucet. If he was still in Vancouver.

She grabbed a sandwich from a convenience store near the bus stop and took it up to her cousin's apartment. It was peaceful; Jen was at work and probably most of the other people who lived in the building were too. She sat down at the kitchen table, opened her iPad, and found the Diatek website. She'd looked at it before, but she hadn't paid much attention to the personnel section. There was a list of employees, alphabetical, and there near the top was Dr. Richard Doucet, PhD, Research Geologist. She was in luck; he still worked for Diatek.

She read the short bio: Dr. Doucet had an undergraduate degree in geology from a university in New Brunswick and a PhD from Penn State. He had worked for DeBeers in South Africa for a couple of years before taking a job at Diatek. It looked as though he'd joined the company not long after it was founded.

There was an email address, and a phone number. Sarah took a bite of her sandwich and looked out the window. Even from the kitchen the view was spectacular; she could see Granville Island and the bridge to the city, and in the distance high-rises silhouetted against the sky. She tapped her teeth with her fingernail, then started to write.

Dear Dr. Doucet: My name is Sarah Patterson and I'm working on a Master's degree at the City University of London (U.K.). I'm researching the diamond industry in Canada, and I wonder if you would be willing to meet with me and discuss some questions that have come up in my research. I happen to be in Vancouver visiting relatives and I would be available any time tomorrow (Thursday) afternoon or Friday. Sorry for the short notice but I would be very *grateful if you could spare the time for a short interview. I look forward to hearing from you. Sincerely, Sarah Patterson.*

She read over the message a couple of times to make sure the wording was right and then hit 'send.' She wouldn't hold her breath waiting for a reply, but even if she couldn't meet him in person she could probably correspond with him by email when she was back in London.

But to her surprise there was an email from Doucet that evening when she checked her messages before going to bed. No problem, he said, he'd be happy to meet up. Tomorrow would be fine. She laughed out loud when she saw where he suggested they meet: the same coffee shop on Granville Island where she and Jennifer had had breakfast the day before. Four in the afternoon would work for him, he said.

"Jen, what is it about coffee in this town? Every single person I'm interviewing wants to meet in a coffee shop."

"I know. Maybe it's the weather. It's like Seattle, except people say there are even more coffee shops here."

Sarah was already composing her reply. Four would be perfect, she wrote. She told him she had blond hair and would be wearing a blue coat. She wondered what he looked like. She'd never met a geologist before and she pictured a big, burly guy with a bushy beard. Or maybe with a ponytail like Reitmann.

CHAPTER 8

Sarah arrived at the café early and sat down at a table that gave her a good view of the entrance. When Doucet came in he didn't look anything like her imagined geologist, but instinctively she knew it was him. He was about her height, trim, with an athletic build and a small, manicured beard. He was wearing jeans and a North Face windbreaker and had on a baseball cap that he took off as soon as he entered the café. He hesitated for a moment and scanned the room, and she stood up and waved.

He walked over to her table. "Hi. Sarah Patterson?"

"Yes, that's me. You must be Dr. Doucet." Sarah stuck out her hand.

"It's Rick," he said, "Nice to meet you." He took off his jacket and put it over the back of his chair. "Can I get you something before I sit down? Coffee? Tea?"

Sarah said she'd like a mocha and Doucet went off to get their drinks. He returned with her mocha, a pot of tea for himself, and two muffins. "I can't resist the muffins here," he said. "They get them from one of the bakeries in the market and they're really good. I got blueberry and chocolate chip. Take your choice."

"I think I'll start with half. How about the blueberry?"

"Sure." Doucet cut the muffin and put half on a plate for Sarah.

"There you go," he said, taking the other half for himself. "So. You're over here from London? I was expecting you to be British, but it doesn't sound like it from the accent."

Sarah laughed. "No, I'm definitely not British." She explained that she was just in London temporarily, for her Master's degree, and that she was originally from Southern California. "How about you? Are you from around here?"

"Nope. I'm a transplant, I've only been here for a few years. I'm from the other coast, originally, Nova Scotia. But anyway, tell me about your project. You said you were working on the Canadian diamond industry? Seems like an odd thing to be doing in London."

"Yes and no. All of us in the Master's program have to do an internship with an organization in London, and the one I ended up with happens to have an interest in the diamond mining industry. It's been pretty interesting and it looks like the internship work will end up being the focus of my thesis."

"Huh. What organization in London is interested in the Canadian diamond industry?"

"Global Witness," she said. She hadn't mentioned Global Witness in her email and she watched Doucet's face for a reaction. Zoe had told her that they didn't have many friends in the mining business. Especially the diamond mining business. "Maybe you've heard about them."

"Mm, I have. I've heard a lot about them." He was thinking, oh shit, is she a tree hugger? He blew on his tea and took a sip. "They haven't exactly been kind to our industry. I have to admit they've done some good things on conflict diamonds but sometimes what they say about the mining industry is way overblown. At least it is from my point of view."

Sarah relaxed a little; he didn't seem too upset. "Six months ago I knew zilch about diamonds, except maybe for that awful phrase about them being a girl's best friend. Totally condescending if you ask me; it might have been okay for my parents' generation, or my grandparents', but not for mine." She looked at Doucet. "Sorry, I'm going off on a tangent. When I looked at the list of organizations we could intern with in London, Global Witness really appealed to me. It was totally different from what I'd been doing before – I worked for a consulting company for several years after getting my undergraduate degree. I thought maybe an internship with Global Witness would help expand my horizons. The Canadian diamond industry wasn't my idea, I didn't even know it existed. The woman I'm working with at Global witness has been collecting information on Canadian diamond mining for years but she hasn't had the time or the manpower to follow up, so she suggested it as a project for my internship. She wants me to focus on the environmental impacts of the mining, and the effects on First Nations people. I'm looking at some other things too, like the economics."

"Fair enough," Doucet said. "Just remember there's more than one side to every story. Mining can be a messy business; you're usually trying to extract a very small amount of something from a very large volume of rock. It wasn't true in the past, but I really believe that now most mining companies – the ones based in developed countries like Canada anyway – try pretty hard to protect the environment. But it's simply not possible to have zero impact, and also they need to make a profit. Otherwise they wouldn't exist. You have to dig out the ore, you create a lot of dust and dirt and waste, sometimes you use nasty chemicals. But if you didn't do all that, civilization as we know it wouldn't exist. The people who want to shut everything down are just being naive. We'd literally be back in the Stone Age. Think about it: almost everything we use every day comes out of the ground. All the metal in your car, or in the electrical wiring in this café" – he pointed to the ceiling lights – "or in your phone or your computer. Then there's plastic, and a lot of the material that goes into clothing: it all comes from petroleum. And stone for building material. The list goes on and on, it all has to be mined."

Sarah didn't entirely agree with what she was hearing, but she didn't want to get into an argument. So she simply said that it was good for her to hear about mining from a different perspective than that of her colleagues at Global Witness.

"You know, it's weird. I went into geology because I had this romantic idea about working outdoors, being out in the wilderness, mapping and exploring," he said. "It didn't work out quite that way because now I spend most of my time in the lab. And I work for a mining company. As somebody said, you never see the future until you get there. But I still love the wilderness. That's one of the reasons I like living here; you can be in the mountains or on a trail with almost no people very quickly. You're more likely to see a bear than a person. I don't want it messed up any more than you do. But you have to be realistic."

"Mind if I make some notes?" She looked briefly at her iPad – she'd been checking her email before Doucet came in – but decided to write in her notebook instead. "I have my own version of shorthand and it's pretty fast. Nobody can read it but me."

Doucet watched her write. She was very pretty; her skin was smooth and her face lightly freckled, and she had delicate ears and a small nose. Her eyeliner matched the blue of her eyes. From time to time he caught the faint fragrance of her perfume. Her blond hair shone in the light from the window and he had a sudden urge to run his hand through it.

Sarah paused and looked up at him and he wondered if she could read his mind.

"Um, I've got a few questions about Diatek, if you don't mind. And nothing from my notes will go into my thesis or a Global Witness report unless I run it by you first. Is that okay?"

Doucet cleared his throat. "Sure. I'll answer anything I can."

She started by asking him questions about the Canadian diamond industry: Why had diamonds only been discovered in Canada so recently? How had they been missed for so long? How had the industry developed so rapidly? And then she said she'd come across a few articles about protests against Diatek in 2009. "I've read everything I can find online, but I wanted to ask you what you know about them. Like how they started, who organized them, why the mine workers went on strike, that sort of thing. Most of what I've read is from the point of view of the demonstrators. There doesn't seem to be much out there from the industry side of things." Sarah didn't mention that she'd already interviewed some of the protesters.

"Well – it wasn't very pleasant for any of us, I can say that. I was here but I hadn't been working for the company for very long when the protests started. If you've read about them you probably know they started because of a chemical leak from one of the ore processing areas at the mine. Some nasty stuff drained into a small lake, and it killed some fish and a few ducks. Someone, maybe an employee, I don't know exactly, took pictures and gave them to a reporter who was doing a story on diamond mining in the Territories. It got picked up by several environmental groups and kind of snowballed from there. One of the First Nations groups got involved and they and some of the other mine workers used the situation to start complaining about working conditions – that's my take on it, anyway – and then they went on strike. The mine didn't shut down completely, but production went down for a while."

"You make it sound like it was no big deal."

"I'm not saying Diatek was blameless. In an ideal world the leak shouldn't have happened. But it was an accident, they didn't dump poison into the lake on purpose, that's for sure. It was all because of a faulty coupling on the waste pipes – it's something that probably should have been spotted, but nothing is perfect in a big operation like that. The guy in charge of doing the safety inspections was fired – somebody had to take the blame – and the problem was fixed. Like I said before, mining is a messy business and there are always going to be some environmental consequences. I just think they have to be balanced against the benefits. I don't have all the answers, but maybe in a country like Canada with a lot of wilderness you just have to put some regions off limits to preserve it, not allow any commercial activities. For the rest you have to accept that the environment won't be pristine forever."

"What about the working conditions? The people who went on strike, did they have a point?"

"Personally I don't think working conditions at the mine are that bad. I go up there once in a while and it seems to me they have it pretty good. I mean, it's isolated, so there is that part of it. It's like working on a ship or an oil rig; you can't walk down the street and go to a pub or a place like this. But for folks who like that kind of life it's okay. And they get paid well. Of course it's a business and management doesn't want to spend any more money on people or facilities than they have to, so I suppose it's not a bad thing to put a little pressure on them now and then. But as I said, they need to make a profit." He laughed. "If they weren't making a profit I probably wouldn't have a job. Anyway, after the strikes they started training pro-grams, especially for the First Nations workers – they're about half the work force. The idea is to help them learn skills they can take elsewhere. The mine will be there for a long time and some of those people will probably work there for the rest of their lives, but eventually it will be mined out. So it's good to have skills you can use in other jobs. And then there's all the associated work in places like Yellowknife, which is the nearest city. There are diamond cutting and polishing operations there now that didn't exist before the diamond discoveries, and those places also train and employ First Nations people. There's even a college course in Yellowknife that trains people in cutting and polishing diamonds. It's the only one in the world, and they've brought in experts from South Africa and other places to teach the courses. So it's not all about evil capitalists like some people want you to think."

Sarah scribbled notes in her personal shorthand as Doucet talked. She grilled him for almost an hour, asking questions and listening to his detailed answers. Finally she had run out of things to ask him.

"I think that's about it," she said. "Thank you. This is going to help a lot. Would it be okay if I get in touch if other things come up?"

"Of course, just shoot me an email. It's no problem." He hesitated for a moment. "Say, when do you go back to London?"

"Saturday. I've just got tomorrow in Vancouver and then I'm on my way. Why?"

"I was just wondering … would you be interested in seeing what a geochemist in the diamond business actually does? I'm heading out to the university soon – we rent time on one of their instruments when it's not being used by university researchers, usually at night or on the weekends. Tonight is one of my nights. I do mineral analyses out there on the samples we collected during the field season, and we use the data to plan our exploration program. You're welcome to come along."

Sarah had the feeling there was a little more to it than Doucet just being polite. But she and Jen had plans for the evening, and anyway the interview had already given her most of the information she needed.

"I'd love to, but I already have something organized for tonight with my cousin. Sorry." She stood up and put on her coat.

Doucet took the windbreaker from the back of his chair. She thought he looked slightly disappointed, or maybe it was just her imagination.

"Okay then, it was just a thought … it's been nice to talk to you, Sarah." They walked together to the door and he held it open for her.

"Let's stay in touch," he said. "Take care."

He stood by the door as Sarah went down the steps walked along the street. When she reached the intersection she glanced back. Doucet was still standing where she had left him. She waved, then turned the corner.

CHAPTER 9

About a month later ...

Doucet was working on a complicated-looking graph when someone knocked on his office door. He looked up and was surprised to see Bill Thompson, the chief engineer from the Diatek mine, standing there, a grin on his face.

"Hey. Bill Thompson. What are you doing here?"

They had met two years earlier when Doucet and several other Vancouver-based Diatek employees spent a week at the mine under a company program to foster better integration of the two operations. Although Thompson was considerably older than Doucet, the two men found they had shared interests and quickly became friends.

"Long story. I proposed putting in some new equipment on the sorting line – state of the art, it's just come on the market. The honchos want a formal presentation before they approve anything. It's expensive, but by my estimate it'll pay for itself in a year or so because it'll make the process more efficient. I guess they wanted me here in person so they could grill me about it – you know how they are about spending money. But I'm not complaining; it's good to get out, especially in the winter, and especially if I don't have to use holiday time. How's it going with you?"

"Okay," said Doucet, "I'm still working through last summer's field samples. It's interesting. Look." He turned the monitor around so Thompson could see the screen more clearly.

"What am I looking at?" All Thompson could see was a graph with data points in various colors scattered across it.

"I'm sure I've told you some of this before. This is a graph of my data for garnet crystals; the pickers sort them out by hand from the field samples and then I analyze them out at UBC. All kimberlites contain garnets, but the garnets from diamond-bearing kimberlites are special – they have a very specific chemical composition. So in principle my analyses can tell us which ones come from diamondiferous kimberlites, and then all we have to do is track them back to their source."

Diatek was using the same prospecting method that had led to the discovery of the first diamond deposit found in Canada's north. It worked because of the unique geological setting of the region: the glaciers of the last ice age scoured the landscape, scraping up rocks and gravel and dispersing the debris over great distances. When the ice flowed over an outcropping of diamond-bearing kimberlite rock, it scraped up bits of that too. But as the ice age ended and the glaciers melted back, all of this material was simply dumped on the land. Those glacial deposits still litter the landscape of much of Canada and the northern United States, and in some of them, mixed in with the other debris, are indicator minerals – grains of red garnet and bottle-green diopside that are abundant in kimberlites but not common in other rocks. The geologists call them indicator minerals because when you find them you can be sure that somewhere upstream, along the glacier's path, there is a kimberlite.

Chuck Fipke, the now-legendary geologist who discovered that first diamond deposit, crisscrossed the tundra for years, collecting bags of sand to take back to his home-made lab where he would sort through his samples, looking for the tell-tale indicator minerals. People mocked him; real prospectors didn't collect bags of sand, they said, they broke up rocks with their hammers. Soon – behind his back – Fipke was being called 'the sandman.' But the sandman knew what he was doing. Most of the prospectors in the Northwest Territories were looking for gold or copper and for that smashing up rocks with a hammer was the right thing to do. Prospecting for diamonds, though, was an entirely different matter. They are so rare that Fipke would never find them by simply breaking up rocks and looking inside. But he might find them indirectly by sifting through his sand samples searching for the indicator minerals, and, like a detective following clues, tracking them back to their source. In the end, after almost giving up in frustration, Fipke found his diamonds.

Diatek's exploration team used the same approach, but Doucet had taken the process a step further by measuring the chemical composition of the indicator minerals.

"See this group?" he said to Thompson, pointing to a tight cluster of data points on his graph. They plotted far away from the shotgun scatter of the others and he had highlighted the group in red so they would stand out. "Those are the ones we're looking for. Garnets with that chemical composition *always* come from kimberlites that contain diamonds. I don't know of any exceptions. So there have to be deposits out there that we haven't found yet. If we can locate the source rocks for those suckers we're almost guaranteed to have another mine. It's pretty exciting."

"You're telling me," Thompson said. He pulled up a chair to sit beside Doucet where he could see the screen better. "But it can't be that easy or everyone would be finding diamonds, right?"

"Absolutely. First you have to do brute force sampling, there's no way around it. You have to cover really large areas. Which means there are a lot of samples to analyze; that's why I'm still working my way through the ones we got last summer. And not everyone has the capability to do the kind of analyses we're doing – we're lucky to have the use of some pretty sophisticated instruments out at the university. I'm looking at trace elements in these garnets, things that are present at very low concentrations – a few parts per thousand at most, maybe just parts per million. It turns out that those are the elements that are the best indicators of whether the garnet comes from a kimberlite with diamonds or not. You have to have the right equipment to analyze things at that level."

Doucet owed his job at Diatek to the usefulness of the trace elements in indicator minerals. During his PhD research at Penn State he had perfected a method to classify complicated minerals based on just such analyses. It had been tedious work; he'd spent most of his time analyzing thousands of mineral grains from all over the world for the trace elements they contained. But then one weekend when he was compiling his data from the previous week he noticed that several of the garnets he'd analyzed displayed an unusual pattern of trace and minor elements. They were quite different from any other garnets he'd analyzed, and when he checked his notes to see where the mineral grains had come from he discovered they had been extracted from a piece of South African kimberlite rock. But that wasn't all: the kimberlite came from a diamond mine. His heart skipped a beat.

Still, he'd only analyzed five crystals, and they all came from a single rock sample. Without telling anyone what he'd found, Doucet went about amassing a collection of kimberlite samples from around the world. Some of the kimberlites were known to be diamond-bearing, others had no diamonds. He separated garnets from the samples as they came in and analyzed them for their trace element contents, hardly daring to look at the data until he'd finished. But when he finally put everything together and matched sample numbers with locations it was one of those eureka moments that happen only a few times in any scientist's life. He could still remember every detail of the room he'd been in, the time of day, even the gray squirrel, its cheeks bulging with acorns, that sat in the tree outside the window of the tiny graduate student office he shared with three others. He had discovered a chemical signature in the garnets that was specific to rocks containing diamonds, and the practical implications hit him like a freight train. He had always prided himself in doing basic research, but his discovery had the potential to radically change the way diamond prospecting was done. Soon it radically changed the trajectory of his career, too. As word of his discovery spread, he suddenly started to get job offers from diamond companies.

"Okay professor Doucet, that's pretty interesting." Thompson glanced at his watch. "I need to go and prepare for my presentation, but we should talk more. Have you got time for lunch tomorrow?"

Doucet was always happy to discuss his work. "Sure. I'll be here. Just knock on the door."

When the engineer showed up at noon the next day Doucet was more than ready. He'd been for an early morning run before coming to work, and he was hungry. They walked down the street to a nearby café; it was popular with people who worked in that part of the city and they had to stand in a line for a few minutes until a table became available. They talked about fishing; Thompson said he'd been ice fishing a few times in lakes near the mine, but the ice was really thick and it was hard to keep the holes open, they froze over so fast. Once they were seated and their order taken the talk turned to another of their shared interests, hockey; they had a friendly argument about whether the Vancouver Canucks would make the playoffs this year and how far they might go if they did, and about how good this year's new players really were. Then Thompson steered the conversation to Doucet's work.

"Tell me, how definitive are those trace elements you work on? Can you really be sure that when you get that pattern you were showing me yesterday there will be diamonds in the kimberlite?"

"The short answer is yes. If there are indicator minerals there will be a kimberlite, and if the indicator minerals have that pattern the kimberlite will have diamonds in it. We don't know how abundant they will be, or whether they'll be large or small or even if they'll be gem-quality. All of that is important for developing a mine. But in every case we know about, only garnets that come from diamond-bearing kimberlites have that unique trace element pattern. So it seems safe to assume that if we find the same thing in our field samples, those grains will lead us to a diamond deposit. Of course you still have to trace them back to their source, which is maybe the hardest part. And even then the deposit might not be economically viable. The ore might not be rich enough, or the diamonds might not be high enough quality. But they'll be there."

Thompson seemed lost in thought. He took a bite of his sandwich and looked up. "Can you do the same thing with diamonds instead of garnets? I mean, can you tell where a diamond comes from by analyzing the trace elements?"

"Good question. The problem is, diamonds are really pure. The garnets are different, they're like alphabet soup, they've got everything in them you can think of: iron, magnesium, aluminum, calcium, chromium, you name it. And all of those elements are there in high enough concentrations that you can measure them, provided you have the right equipment. But diamonds are almost pure carbon. There *are* other elements there, but the amounts are minute. The trace element contents are so low that I can't measure most of them accurately with the methods I use. It wouldn't make sense for exploration anyway.

Diamonds are just too rare; you never actually find a diamond in the sand and gravel samples we collect. At least we haven't found any at Diatek. Our pickers scan the samples using a microscope and take out the indicator minerals manually, with tweezers – they're easy to spot because of their colors: the garnets are red and the diopside crystals are bright green. There must be the occasional diamond in the glacial deposits, but we've never found one. I haven't heard of anyone who has, either. The ratio of indicator minerals to diamonds must be hundreds of thousands to one, or maybe even higher. So it doesn't make sense to work on the diamonds; it's much better to concentrate on the indicator minerals."

"No, that's not exactly what I meant. Say I gave you a diamond, could you tell me if it came from the Diatek mine, or some other place?"

"Unh uh. I couldn't, my technique isn't sensitive enough. Besides, there hasn't been much work done on trace element concentrations and patterns in diamonds, so there's no existing database for comparison. There are some people who claim they can tell where a diamond comes from just by looking at it, but I don't buy it. I know someone in California, though, who's been working on a really neat way to trace diamonds. He's been trying to develop a method for identifying conflict diamonds. It's a big problem because once they get mixed into a batch of legitimate diamonds you can't tell them apart. This guy discovered that there are microscopic bits of stuff from the environment left in the cracks and crevices on the surfaces of rough diamonds. Even if someone tries to clean them up by washing them in acid some of it remains. If you heat the diamonds up you can collect the minuscule amounts of water that get driven off from this surface residue, and the water has a very distinct isotope composition depending on where in the world it came from. It's complicated, but the isotopes are almost like a fingerprint. We actually sent him diamonds from DeBeers to test his technique. We knew where they came from but he didn't. It was a blind test, and his results were pretty accurate. He was able to pin down the locations for most of them quite closely. I haven't really followed his work in detail since then, though."

"Could he do an analysis on a random diamond if we sent him one? Find out where it came from?"

"We? A diamond from the mine, you mean? Actually that wouldn't work. The one drawback of this method – I didn't mention this – is that it's only valid for placer diamonds. Ones that have been sitting at the earth's surface for a while, in a river or a sandbank or something like that. Those are the ones that carry the local precipitation fingerprint he looks for. Not diamonds from an underground mine."

"No, no I didn't mean one from the Diatek mine. Suppose I had a diamond from somewhere else and I needed to know its origin. Could he do it? Even knowing if it's from a mine or a placer deposit would be useful."

"I guess, but … is this a hypothetical question?"

"It's not hypothetical. I have a diamond in my pocket."

"You're kidding me."

"No, seriously." Thompson had rehearsed this part carefully. "Six or seven years ago, before I started working for Diatek, I went to a mining conference in England and after the meeting a few of us flew over to Amsterdam for the weekend. We were already in Europe and it seemed like too good an opportunity to miss. I didn't know much about diamonds in those days, but they'd always fascinated me so I took a tour of the diamond district in Amsterdam. And afterwards I was just wandering around by myself, being a tourist, and I went into this little place that sold jewelry just to look at things and the guy sort of surreptitiously told me he could sell me a nice diamond, uncut, at a good price. I was a bit wary, I didn't want to get ripped off and I wondered if it even was a real diamond, but to make a long story short I bought it. It was probably more than I could afford at the time, but I bought it anyway." Part of the story was true; Thompson *had* gone to Amsterdam for a weekend with some of his colleagues and he had visited the diamond district. But he hadn't bought a diamond.

Thompson reached into his pocket and pulled out a small plastic box. He slid it across the table to Doucet.

"Whoa – this is it?"

"Yes. It's the one I got in Amsterdam. I had it valued by a jeweler when I got home, and it *is* a real diamond. He told me that it's probably worth more than I paid for it, which I found strange. I was planning to give it to my wife because we were having some problems and I thought it might help, but the right opportunity never came along and then we split up. So I've still got it. Go ahead and take a look."

Doucet propped his glasses up on top of his head and scrutinized the diamond through the lid. Thompson laughed and said, "It won't bite. Go ahead and open the box."

Doucet gingerly pushed up the lid and examined the diamond for what seemed like a long time. "Nice," he said, "very nice. I don't claim to be a connoisseur but for a rough diamond this is a beauty. From what I can see without a magnifying glass it's got nice crystal faces and no cracks or inclusions. And the color, that pale yellow color, it's beautiful, and it's pretty rare. You're jeweler friend was probably right; I think you lucked out. If you get this cut it will be a little smaller, but my guess is it'll be spectacular." He closed the box and handed it back to Thompson. "By the way, the color in diamonds comes from those trace components we've been talking about. There's maybe a few parts in a million of nitrogen in your diamond, that's what makes it yellow." Doucet grinned. "Pretty neat, eh? See why I'm so interested in mineral chemistry?"

Thompson put the box with the diamond down on the table beside his coffee cup. "Yeah, I do. Fascinating." But his mind seemed to be elsewhere. "Listen, if your friend in California analyzed this diamond would it have any effect? Would it mess up the crystal?"

"Well, he's not really my friend, I just know him scientifically. He's at Caltech; I know him by reputation and we've had some correspondence because we both work on diamonds. But to answer your question, no, you wouldn't know the difference. That's one of the things about his method, he doesn't have to take the samples to very high temperatures to get out the water from the surface layer. The diamonds are so robust nothing happens to them. Most of them, anyway, I guess if there was already a major flaw they might crack when they were heated. But I don't think it would be a problem with this one."

Thompson nodded. "Could you send it to him for me? As a favor? I'd really like to know where this thing came from. I'd be happy to pay for it."

"Jeez, I don't even know if he's still doing this kind of work. I guess I could get in touch and find out. If he did agree, though, I'm sure he wouldn't charge you. He'd just do it as part of his research. And he'd probably want to put the analysis in his database."

"That's not a problem for me. Thank you Rick, I really appreciate it. Is it okay if I leave it with you until you find out if he can do this? It's not a great idea to be carrying around a rough diamond when you work in a diamond mine. I'd have a lot of explaining to do if someone found it in my pocket."

Doucet laughed. "You're right about that. When I was working in South Africa I heard a story about a DeBeers mine in Namibia where the workers lived on site and whenever someone left they were thoroughly searched – really thoroughly, including all body cavities. It was such a hassle that most of them hardly ever left, they just stayed at the mine site. Then some of the workers started keeping pigeons, which everyone thought was fine, it was a good hobby, something for them to do in their spare time. But one day a security guard found a pigeon flapping around on the ground. He thought it was sick, but when he looked more closely he found a package of diamonds strapped to its leg. It turned out that a few enterprising workers were skimming off diamonds and sending them to their friends and families by homing pigeon. If someone hadn't been greedy and loaded down that pigeon with so many diamonds nobody would have been the wiser. After that the guards started shooting the pigeons."

"Amazing," Thompson said. "Human ingenuity never fails to surprise me, especially if there's money involved. But to come back to your friend, I guess even if I find out where my diamond is from I still won't know for sure if that jeweler in Amsterdam got it legally. That's the thing that's always bothered me, because of the way he offered it to me, and the price."

"No, you probably couldn't be sure, but it would narrow the odds. There are some places where there's a lot of trade in illicit diamonds and others where there's none." Doucet looked at his watch. "I didn't realize it was so late – I've got to run." He put a twenty on the table and stood up. "I'll take good care of this," he said, and put Thompson's diamond, still nestled in its little plastic box, into his shirt pocket. "Now you've got me interested. Even if I can't do it myself, I love it when you can use science to work out puzzles. I'll let you know when I hear from Caltech."

"Alright, but … can we keep it between the two of us? I don't want anyone else to know about this. I'll be back in Vancouver in less than a month – it's one of my scheduled breaks. We can talk about it then."

"Okay, sounds good," Doucet said, his thoughts already turning to the work waiting for him back at his office. He wondered briefly why Thomson wanted to be so secretive, but then the thought was gone. "Have a good trip back."

Thompson was in no hurry. He asked the waitress for more coffee and then he took out a pen and started making notes. He felt calmer now; talking to Doucet about getting the diamond analyzed was the first step in a plan he was formulating in his head, and getting started was always the hardest part. He was pretty sure what the analysis would show. Still, it would be good to know for certain. The next few months would not be easy, but at least he had started the ball rolling.

He left a generous tip and when he left the café he walked to the downtown bank where he had a safe deposit box. He signed in and took his box into a private, curtained cubicle, where he took an envelope out of his briefcase and added it to several others that he had stored away on previous visits to the bank. The envelopes were another part of his plan. He closed the lid and sat for a few minutes with the box in front of him, staring into space and not seeing anything, and then, with a sigh, he took the box back into the vault.

CHAPTER 10

That afternoon at work Doucet was acutely aware of the small plastic box in his shirt pocket. Had it not been for Thompson's comment about keeping the story of his diamond between the two of them he probably wouldn't have thought twice about it, but he couldn't shake the feeling that everyone must know he was carrying around a rough diamond. It was a relief to get home that evening and put it in a drawer.

He'd picked up Chinese take-out on the way home and after he'd eaten he sat down at his computer and sent a short email message to his Caltech colleague. They hadn't been in touch for several years, so he started off by saying he wasn't with DeBeers any longer, he was back in North America, working for a Canadian company. Are you still working on diamonds? he asked. And if you are, could you do an analysis for me? Just a single crystal this time, not a whole suite of diamonds like for the project we did earlier.

The answer came back almost immediately. No problem, the message said, we're running a batch next week. A couple of my students are getting them ready as we speak. Doucet looked at his watch and shook his head; it was after nine and they were still working. Just like when I was a grad student at Penn State, he thought. The geology building at the university had been quiet at night, but no matter what the hour there were always a few people around, working at their computers or taking care of an experiment. He had pulled his own share of all-nighters. But it hadn't been all hard work; they partied hard too and there had been a sense of camaraderie among the graduate students and some of the faculty, especially the younger ones.

Doucet sighed. Was he just remembering the good parts? Probably. Still, it had been a pretty good life. Not much money, but he'd been able to follow his curiosity with little pressure from anyone, and the only responsibility he'd had was for his own research. What would it be like to go back to academia in a different role, as a researcher or a professor? He liked his job at Diatek, but sometimes the constant demand for results got to him. Maybe he should keep his eyes and ears open, see what kinds of academic jobs were out there.

He shook his head again and brought his attention back to the message from Caltech. If he could FedEx the sample ASAP, it said, they would include it with the batch they were analyzing the next week. But it would have to reach them in the next couple of days.

He tapped out a quick reply saying thanks, he'd send the sample tomorrow. Then he wrote a message to Thompson. Just heard from Caltech, he said, all systems are go for your diamond. He paused for a moment and then went back and deleted the last part of the sentence. All systems are go. Period. No mention of diamonds, but Thompson would know what he was talking about.

Ten days later Thompson's diamond and a printout of the Caltech analysis were back. He found the package propped up against his apartment door – one of his neighbors had signed for it. Yikes, he thought, it's a good thing I shipped it as a 'geological sample for analysis.' A package sitting in the hall with 'diamond' written on it? That would be asking for trouble.

He tore open the envelope and read over the analysis and the hand written comments that were scribbled at the bottom of the page: as best they could tell, the diamond originated in the Democratic Republic of Congo, or possibly Angola. It had the same isotope fingerprint as several other diamonds they'd analyzed that had been dredged from the Kwango River in the DRC.

Doucet read through the analysis and notes a second time. If Thompson's diamond really was from the DRC, there was a strong likelihood that the jeweler he'd bought it from in Amsterdam had gotten it illicitly. Nobody had exact figures, but most of the people who tracked such things believed that the majority of diamonds from Angola and the DRC reach the world market in unconventional and often illegal ways. Many were sold by rebels or warlords, or even by the government, to fund conflicts. And if anything, that was even more likely around the time Thompson got his diamond than it was today.

He took out his hand lens and looked at the diamond again. It still looked the same. Of course it does, he said to himself;

blood diamonds look just like legal ones. That's why they're so useful to people who want to move money around the world, untraced.

He went to his computer and sent a cryptic message to Thompson, telling him about the results, again without mentioning the word diamond. He's got me acting like this a state secret, he thought. He picked up the box containing the diamond and put it on a bookshelf, right beside the bound copy of his Penn State PhD thesis. Why should I hide it? It can stay there until I hand it back to Thompson. He looked at his calendar: the engineer had said he'd be back in Vancouver the first week of March. Shortly after that, Doucet realized with a jolt, he'd be heading for Europe. He had been invited to give a keynote presentation at a meeting of the Society of Economic Geologists in Italy, and when the request came it had seemed far in the future and he'd replied that of course, he'd be happy to do it. There would be plenty of time to prepare, and the Society had said they would pay his plane fare. Why pass up a trip to Europe? But now the meeting was little more than a month away and time was flying by inexorably. He would have to start working on his talk soon or he wouldn't be ready.

Bill Thompson wasn't really surprised when he heard that the diamond probably came from the Democratic Republic of Congo. It confirmed his suspicion, and it reinforced his determination to stick to the plan he'd been putting together over the past few months.

When he got to Vancouver the first thing he did was visit his lawyer and have a new version of his will drawn up. Then he called Rick Doucet about getting together. "Officially I'm on a break so I don't really want to come into the office," he said. "There's an Italian restaurant where I sometimes eat not far from my apartment – the food's not bad. What about meeting there for lunch instead of downtown? My treat." Thompson didn't say that he wanted to be far enough from the Diatek building that he could be sure none of their colleagues would be sitting at the next table, overhearing the conversation.

Doucet grumbled; it would take him half an hour to get there and he was busy. But in the end he agreed.

Thompson had made a reservation and when they arrived a waiter led them to a table by a window that looked out into a small courtyard. It was unusually warm for the time of year, and outside there were a few people on benches, faces turned to the sun like sunflowers.

Thompson looked at them, then turned back to Doucet. "It was snowing when I left the mine," he said. "It'll probably be snowing when I go back. Sometimes it gets to you, although I'm inside most of the time so I suppose it doesn't matter. Summers can be nice, though, as long as you can stand the bugs."

"I know," said Doucet. "Usually I'm only up in the Northwest Territories in the summer." He paused. "By the way, I've got your diamond." He pulled a small padded envelope from his pocket and handed it to Thompson.

"Thanks. That was a fast turnaround – now I know where it comes from I've been trying to decide what it means. What's your take?"

Doucet shrugged. "It's hard to say. It could be that your guy in Amsterdam got it from somebody who was palming off conflict diamonds, or it could be entirely legal. You just can't tell. That's why diamonds have become the money laundering commodity of choice around the world. I wouldn't beat myself up about it – you ended up with a very nice diamond."

The restaurant was starting to fill up and a harried looking waiter came over and asked if they were ready to order. They hastily looked through the menu and ordered while he stood at the table, tapping his pen on his order book the whole time. When he left Doucet laughed. "A little obvious, wasn't he? No pressure from that guy. I wouldn't want to have his job, though."

"No kidding. Me neither. My wife – ex-wife – waited tables to make money when she was at university. She had some incredible stories about customers. After that experience she always left a big tip, no matter how bad the service was."

The waiter returned a few minutes later with lemonade and a beer. "Your food will be right up," he said as he put the glasses down. He didn't have to ask which of them had ordered which drink.

"Well," Doucet said. "He had a fifty per cent chance of being right about our drinks. Let's see how he makes out with the food."

"Yeah," said Thompson. He was trying to figure out how to turn the conversation to what he really wanted to discuss. "To change gears completely, there's something I wanted to talk to you about. A while ago I heard that an old friend of mine from university days had a heart attack. I know it sounds a bit morbid but it got me thinking, so yesterday I went over to see my lawyer about my will. How would you like to be executor?"

Doucet was completely taken aback. He had been about to take a sip of beer, but he put the glass back down on the table. "Me? Executor?" He shook his head. "There must be other people who would be better. I mean, we've only known each other a few years. And I don't have a clue what an executor does."

"I know this comes out of the blue, but don't worry, I'm not planning to pack it in any time soon, the will is just an insurance policy. And anyway the lawyer would do most of the work, you wouldn't have to do much. I know it may sound strange, Rick, but" – Thompson started checking off things on his fingers – "I'm not quite ready to trust my ex-wife with this, even though I think I'm still a little in love with her; my daughter is too young; I don't have any brothers or sisters; my father is dead; and my mother is in an old folks home and she's too old and frail to be saddled with this responsibility. Anyway I hope nobody will have to deal with this until long after she's gone. Most of my friends are back in Ontario and we've sort of gone our separate ways since I've been working at Diatek. I'm uneasy about turning over sole responsibility to my lawyer – he's good, but it would be just another job for him. I've watched you work on a couple of Diatek committees and I like the way you operate. We've known each other long enough that I trust you – I left this diamond with you, right? And now I've got it back." Thompson laughed. "Anyway, these things can always be changed down the line if you decide you'd rather not do it. What do you think?"

"Well," Doucet said slowly, "I'm flattered. I suppose I could be executor. It's just … well, okay, I guess I could do it."

The waiter arrived with their orders, and he got them right again, without asking. The two men were silent until he left.

"He definitely gets a good tip," Thompson said. "And thanks, Rick. I was hoping you'd agree. I'll give my lawyer your contact details before I go back to the mine, and I'll also have him draw up a power of attorney in your name. Just in case you ever need to access my safe deposit box or sign off on something. I'll get him to send you copies – both the power of attorney and will. Have you got a safe place to keep them?"

"Yeah, I do actually. I keep a safe deposit box at the bank because I have a few valuable things from my grandparents that I don't like to leave in my empty apartment when I go off to do fieldwork for long periods." Doucet laughed. "Some of it is jewelry from my grandmother. She's dead now, but she gave it to me when she was still alive and told me I was forbidden to sell it, I had to keep it for my wife, she said – my future wife. She was a tough old bird, my grandmother, and I wouldn't dare cross her, even now when she's no longer with us. I'd be afraid she'd conjure up a lightning bolt or something. But I don't see that jewelry leaving the safe deposit box any time soon."

"You never know, Rick. Your life can change in the blink of an eye. Trust me, I've been there." Thompson didn't elaborate. But, Doucet thought, he seemed genuinely happy, more relaxed than he'd been in a long time.

The two men finished their meal and ordered coffee and their conversation drifted to work and the Diatek mine. Doucet told Thompson about his talk at the meeting in Milan and said he planned to spend a few days in London on the way back. "When I was working in South Africa I always tried to come back to Canada at least once a year, mainly to see my folks. Most of the flights came and went through Heathrow so whenever I could I'd stop over in London for a few days. I love the city, there's always something to do there. So I'm going to do the same on the way back from Milan."

It was true, he did love London. But now he had another reason to stop there: Sarah Patterson. They hadn't communicated much after she'd interviewed him – she'd sent a short message thanking him for his time, and he'd replied saying it had been a pleasure – but he'd thought about her often. Something about her resonated with him. They had only met for a couple of hours and he wasn't even sure he could remember exactly what she looked like; sometimes he wondered if he was conjuring up some imaginary person in his head who wasn't really Sarah Patterson. But snippets of their meeting in the Granville Island café – little things she'd said or done – kept popping into his head at random moments. Then one day shortly before he made his travel arrangements for the Milan meeting he got a message from her: Would he be willing to review a draft outline of her Master's thesis, and give her feedback? Her advisors in London would read it through too, of course, but he was the only person she knew who had direct experience in the industry. He was busy and didn't reply immediately, but her message triggered the idea that he could stop over in London. It would be a chance to see her again.

Am I crazy, he wondered? She might not even be there. Or she might be busy. Or she might not want to meet with me. But she was the one who had asked for feedback, and if he stopped in London he could give it to her in person. So when he replied he said yes, he'd be happy to review her outline, and by coincidence he was going to be in London for a few days and they could discuss it then if that worked for her.

"Also," he told Thompson, "there's a student in London, an American, who's doing a Master's thesis on the Canadian diamond mining industry. Somehow she got my name and she was over here in January and interviewed me about Diatek. She seems like a really nice person. So I'm going to talk to her more about her thesis work when I'm in London."

Thompson smiled. "Sometimes, Rick, you're so transparent. You're stopping over in London and by the way this nice girl you met just happens to be there? You'd better be careful. Your grandmother's jewelry might not stay in your safe deposit box too much longer after all."

Thompson was teasing him and Doucet knew it but he said "Don't be silly, she's just someone I met and I'm helping her out with her thesis stuff."

"Right," Thompson said.

CHAPTER 11

He arrived in London late in the day and took the Heathrow Express into the city, then caught a taxi to his hotel. He'd found it on the internet after what seemed like interminable searching; he'd wanted something small, quiet, central and within his price range, and even though London seemed to have an endless supply of hotels it wasn't easy. The one he settled on was billed as a boutique hotel and he was pleasantly surprised when the taxi pulled up; he'd had mixed luck with London hotels in the past, but this one was on a short street with a grass median, and from the look of the exterior it was well maintained. He was even more pleased with the interior; it was spotless and comfortable, tasteful without being ostentatious.

After he checked in he walked to a nearby pub that the concierge had recommended and sat at a corner table nursing a beer and eating fish and chips and watching the ebb and flow of customers. What was it about British pubs? Funny, he could sit in a place like this, alone and not knowing a soul, and feel completely at home. Low ceiling, thick dark beams, benches and chairs with plush red upholstery. No TV screens, no rowdy patrons, just the low murmur of people talking and an occasional burst of laughter. Doucet went to the bar and got another beer. He was glad he'd decided to come to London, although unaccountably he was slightly nervous about meeting Sarah Patterson tomorrow. He'd told her where he was staying and suggested they meet there in the morning to talk about her thesis outline. Nine o'clock, in the hotel lobby.

She was just as he remembered. She paused when she came through the door, searching for him, and Doucet stayed still for a moment, watching her, then stood up and waved and when she saw him she smiled. She no longer had her California tan, but her cheeks were rosy from the walk over and she had her blond hair pulled back from her face. He noticed that he wasn't the only person in the room watching her.

"Dr. Doucet," she said, and put out her hand, "Good to see you again."

"Please, it's Rick. Seems like a long time ago when we met in Vancouver … do you want some breakfast? I waited because I didn't know whether you'd have eaten. I'm pretty hungry myself." Doucet had woken early and worked out in the hotel's exercise room.

"Oh, you really shouldn't have waited. I already had a bite before I came over." She glanced at her watch. "I don't have a whole lot of time today but sure, I'll have some coffee or something while you eat."

Doucet led the way into the breakfast room and they found a table. "Sure you won't have anything?" he asked. "It's buffet style, you can take whatever you want." The conversation felt stilted. He wondered if it was just him.

"I might take some fruit. Don't mind me, I'm not a big eater. Go ahead and get your breakfast."

When Doucet returned she burst out laughing. "Talk about a full English breakfast." Somehow it broke the ice.

"I'm making up for the past week," he said. "The Italians don't eat much for breakfast. Coffee, and maybe a roll. This is more my style." He spooned beans onto his toast and took a bite. "Mmm, that's good. So Sarah ... how's your thesis work going?"

"Pretty well, actually. Everyone here has signed off on my outline; they asked for a few changes but they're minor – it's still basically the same as the version you have. I didn't want to burden you with revisions. I'm anxious to hear what you have to say – I'm ready to get down to the actual writing."

"Nothing jumped out at me either. It's a good outline, it's thorough and it's comprehensive. It should make for a great thesis. I spent some time on it on the plane over here and I made a few notes, but they're mostly just suggestions about a few things you could add, and some ideas about organization. The diamond industry in Canada is still young so you've more or less got a blank slate, and as far as I know nobody else has done anything like this. If you get it right your work will be the primary source for everyone that follows."

"I guess I never really thought about it that way. I don't think I've got anything earth shaking, but you're right, nobody else has done quite what I'm doing. If they had, I'm sure I would have come across it because I've spent almost six months reading everything there is to read about the diamond industry in Canada. Putting it all together and writing it up is going to be hard work, but I like writing. My time at McKinsey was good preparation – I worked with some pretty smart people and they taught me a lot about writing reports. This will be different from a McKinsey report, but you need the same writing skills."

"You worked for McKinsey? The consulting company? I don't think you mentioned that before. No wonder your outline is so polished."

"Yeah, I did, for three years. I was lucky – I got the job right after I graduated. I learned a lot but it was pretty grueling. I didn't really have a life. We were always traveling. Staying in nice hotels sounds great until you have to do it all the time."

Sarah was being modest when she told Doucet that she was lucky to get a job at McKinsey. She had majored in Economics at Stanford and according to her professors her honor's thesis was one of the best in years. And after a little special pleading she'd been allowed to take a couple of courses in the graduate business school, unusual for an undergraduate. If anyone was lucky, it was McKinsey.

"That's impressive," Doucet said. "From what I've heard, McKinsey has pretty high standards. You must be good … not that I didn't already think you're good … well, it's just … it's impressive."

He laughed to cover his confusion. It had been a long time since he'd felt so awkward in front of someone else. He hoped it wasn't too obvious.

"What are you going to do next? When you're finished here?"

"Good question," she said. "The short answer is, I don't know. They liked me enough at McKinsey that I'm pretty sure I could go back there, but I really don't want to do that. Ideally I'd like to work for a non-profit. And I'd like to go back out to the west coast. So we'll see."

Doucet was still working his way through the food on his plate. Sarah poured herself another cup of coffee and glanced surreptitiously at her watch, but he noticed.

"Are we okay for time? Sorry I'm so slow – maybe I should just run up and get my notes and we can talk about your thesis outline in the lobby. There are some comfortable chairs out there."

"It's fine, take your time, I've still got almost an hour."

"No, really, I've had enough." Doucet pushed his chair back. "Let's go find a quiet place where we can talk."

He left Sarah in the lobby while he went up to his room to get his notes. He gave his teeth a quick brush and looked in the mirror. Not bad, he thought, and smoothed his hair with his fingertips. And then he stopped. Come on, Doucet, he told himself, get a grip. You'll probably never see her again.

They spent the next half hour huddled together in a corner of the lobby talking about her thesis, Sarah's outline spread out on the table in front of them. Doucet went through his comments point by point and Sarah took notes, and he told her again that it had the potential to make a great thesis. "And I'm not just saying that, it's true."

"I hope you're right. I can't thank you enough for taking the time to do this. Like I said before, no one here has the kind of industry perspective that you do, so it's a reality check. I really appreciate it. I'm just sorry I have to rush off – she looked at her watch again – but I really do have to go." She started to gather up her papers and put them in her handbag. "I hope you have a good stay in London. There's so much to do here."

Doucet really didn't want her to just walk away like that. "Um, Sarah, before you go … I usually try to get theater tickets when I'm here. I haven't even checked what's on yet, but would you be interested if I can get two tickets?"

She hesitated. He was a nice guy, but she was very busy and she tried to parcel out her free time carefully. She was already feeling that her time in London was limited. On the other hand he'd been really helpful both today and when she met him in Vancouver, and he was also in London on his own. Maybe she should make the time.

"It's short notice – for getting tickets, I mean. I don't know what's on right now; with my thesis and everything I just haven't been paying much attention. But sure, I'd like that. It would have to be tomorrow though, that's about the only day I don't have anything else scheduled. Why don't I give you my cell phone number and you can give me a call if you find something." She wrote down her number and handed it to him.

"Okay, I'll let you know."

"Thanks. And thanks again for all your help." She slung her bag over her shoulder and stood there for a moment, smiling, then turned and walked across the lobby and out into the street.

Doucet let out a long breath and went back into the breakfast room for another cup of coffee. Then he found the concierge and asked about theater tickets.

"It may be difficult on such short notice, sir, this being the weekend and all. But I'll see what I can do." In reality the concierge was adept at getting last minute theater tickets for hotel guests; he had contacts in the West End and with favors and money flowing in both directions he usually had no trouble. He made several phone calls and then put his hand over the mouthpiece and told Rick he was in luck.

"It appears I can get two tickets for a matinee tomorrow afternoon, sir," he said. "Very good seats, in the middle of the stalls. It's a musical, and I've heard it's good. Gershwin. One of your countrymen. What should I tell them?"

Doucet was used to being mistaken for an American and he let the comment go. "Okay," he said, "I'll take them."

They were the most expensive theater tickets he'd ever bought, but he didn't mind. He waited until later in the day to call Sarah – he didn't want to seem too eager – but she didn't answer. He left a message suggesting that they meet in front of the theater about fifteen minutes before the show started. He hoped she liked musicals.

It could hardly have been a better choice. When the show was over they spilled out onto the street with a throng of smiling theatergoers, humming familiar Gershwin tunes. "That's just what I needed," she said, "thank you so much for getting the tickets." She seemed much more relaxed than she had the day before.

"My pleasure," Doucet said. "Feel like some coffee? Or a drink?"

Afterward, Sarah could never quite decide whether it was the music, her mood, or Doucet himself, but to her own surprise she found herself saying, "Actually, if you'd like to see how a transplanted American lives in London you could come over to my flat and I could fix a bite to eat. We'd have to pick up a few things on the way, and it wouldn't be anything fancy, maybe just an omelet and a salad. What do you think?"

"Twist my arm. Yes, that would be perfect."

When they got to her flat Sarah took a bottle of wine from the refrigerator and poured two large glasses. "Cheers," she said, clinking her glass against his. "Why don't you just sit while I rustle up some food?"

"Can I help? I like cooking, it's a bit like working in the lab. Although just like in the lab I like to experiment, and my experiments don't always work out."

Sarah laughed at this. "I'm sure you're good. But this kitchen is so small that it's a real squeeze for more than one person. Why don't you just relax, it won't take me long."

Doucet walked around the room looking at books and pictures and asking Sarah how she liked City University and living in London. But she seemed distracted with the cooking and he sat down in a comfortable armchair and took out his phone.

"Do you have Wi-Fi? I should check my email."

"Yeah I do. Just a minute." She wiped her hands on a towel and came into the room where he was sitting and rummaged in a drawer. "Here," she said, handing him a slip of paper. "That's the password. You'll probably see lots of networks, just about everyone in the building has Wi-Fi. Mine is SarahBT."

The flat was quiet for the next few minutes as Doucet went through his messages and Sarah concentrated on her cooking. Then she heard a sharp intake of breath. "Oh shit," Doucet said.

"What?" Sarah turned to see him sitting immobile, his face pale. "Are you okay? What happened?"

"There's a message from our CEO," Doucet said. "One of our employees, a guy named Bill Thompson, was killed in an accident on Friday night. At our mine in the Northwest Territories. He's an engineer there and I know him. We had lunch together in Vancouver a couple of weeks ago."

CHAPTER 12

The news about Thompson put a damper on their meal. "I'm really sorry," Sarah said. She didn't know what else to say. "It must be a shock."

"You're not kidding," Doucet said. "It's not that we were best friends or anything, I've only known him for a few years. But it's still a shock, especially since I saw him so recently. He's based at the mine so he didn't get to Vancouver all that often. But when we met up he seemed pretty relaxed and happy with life." Doucet shook his head. "I wonder what happened. All it says is that he was killed in an accident."

Doucet thought back to the lunch he'd had with Thompson; it hardly seemed possible it was less than two weeks ago. He was about to take a mouthful of omelet, but he paused with his fork suspended between the plate and his mouth. He suddenly realized he would now be executor of Thompson's will.

"Are you okay?"

"Sorry, yes, I'm fine. It's just that I can't believe Bill Thompson is dead. And it's really weird because the last time we met he asked me to be executor of his will. He'd just been to see his lawyer and have it updated; it's almost as though he knew something was going to happen. I know that's impossible but you can't help thinking about it."

Sarah didn't say anything and they sat in silence for a few minutes, finishing their food. Then she got up and came around the table, her hand resting briefly on his shoulder as she picked up his plate. He could feel the warmth of it through his shirt.

"Are you up for apple pie?" she said. "I'm afraid it's not home made, but it's pretty good. You could probably use some comfort food right now."

"I never pass up apple pie," Doucet said. He watched as she moved around the kitchen, putting the pie in the oven to warm up, making coffee. Somewhere outside he heard a faint ringing of bells. He was in another universe, still reeling from the news about Bill Thompson.

When the coffee was ready Sarah poured two large mugs and brought them over to the table. "You know," Doucet said, as she sat down again across from him, "it's strange to be sitting here in your flat in London. A couple of months ago I'd never heard of Sarah Patterson. And Bill Thompson was very much alive, going about his business at the mine. But I guess that's life, eh?" He paused. "Sorry, I shouldn't dwell on Bill Thompson."

"No, no, it's fine. Don't worry about it."

The flat was quiet, only the coffee machine, still hissing and gurgling, broke the silence.

Sarah knew what he meant about life. A year ago she was working at McKinsey and now she was studying diamond mining and living in London. Sometimes she still couldn't believe it. And a few months ago she'd never heard of Rick Doucet, either. She looked at him and heard herself say, "I'm glad you came to London, Rick." When he met her eyes something passed between them.

Then the moment was gone. Doucet cleared his throat. "I know you've got work to do," he said. "I should probably be on my way."

"Yes," Sarah said, quietly. "I do have work to do."

Doucet got his jacket and walked to the door, Sarah just behind him. He stood there for a moment, one hand on the doorknob, not really wanting to go.

"Thank you for this afternoon," she said. "Let me know that you get home safely, okay? And I'm so sorry about your friend." To his surprise she reached out and gave him a hug.

"Thanks," he said, a little hoarsely, "it's okay. Bye now. You take care, Sarah."

Rick Doucet was not a particularly emotional man. But as he walked back to his hotel he could feel pinpricks behind his eyes. No tears, but the unfamiliar sense that they might start flowing at any moment. He shook his head vigorously. What's happening to me? he wondered.

Later, sitting in the armchair in his hotel room trying to read through the papers he'd brought back with him from the conference in Milan, he couldn't concentrate. His mind kept drifting back to his lunch with Bill Thompson and their discussion of his will, and powers of attorney, and what an executor had to do. It seemed unreal. And then an image of Sarah

Patterson would pop into his head. He'd felt at ease with her this afternoon at the theater, and during the walk back to her flat. And then the news of Thompson had hit like a thunderbolt, changing everything. What would happen now?

He'd had a long term girlfriend in South Africa, but they'd had a fractious relationship and when he was considering the job at Diatek she'd told him flatly that she wouldn't move to Canada with him. Since then he'd been wary about relationships and he'd buried himself in his work. Sarah Patterson, though ... he could imagine things being different with her. But it was fantasy, he told himself, complete fantasy. As long as she needed advice about her thesis she would probably stay in touch, but after that ... who knows?

When Doucet got home to Vancouver he was plunged back into the demands of his job with little time to think about anything except his work. He'd only been away a week and already the mineral pickers had accumulated piles of new samples for him to analyze. There were decisions to be made about the summer's field work and a ream of correspondence to take care of. Why do people expect instant answers, he wondered? It's only been a few days and they're already impatient. Maybe I really should start looking around for an academic job. Even though there would probably be just as much pressure in academia, only a different kind.

He also learned more about the accident that had killed Bill Thompson. Apparently the engineer had taken a snowmobile out on his own one night – nobody seemed to know why – and had driven out onto the lake. It was safe enough – the lake was still frozen solid – but he'd gone too close to an area where an outflow of warm water from the mine buildings had thinned the ice. Either he'd either ignored the warning signs or hadn't seen them in the blowing snow, and the snowmobile, with Thompson in it, had crashed through the thin ice. Heavy overnight snow had made reconstructing the accident difficult, but the snowmobile tracks appeared to lead straight to a place where the ice had cracked and buckled and where there was now an open hole with just a thin skin of new ice starting to form. There was no sign of either Thompson or the snowmobile. The lake was deep and the heavy machine would have pulled him down quickly into the frigid water, with little chance of escape. The company said they'd bring in divers to try to recover the body after the ice broke up, but that was still many months away.

Thompson's co-workers at the mine were stunned. He was well liked, but he had also been a very private person. Someone mentioned that from the way the accident happened it could have been deliberate, and a rumor that Thompson might have committed suicide spread quickly. One of the men who worked with him said he thought the engineer seemed to be on edge during the week before the accident, and that fueled the rumor. But others said he'd been his normal self right up to the night his snowmobile went through the ice. Doucet couldn't imagine Thompson committing suicide; when they'd met a few weeks before the accident he had seemed very content. There was no suicide note and the two RCMP officers sent to investigate found no other evidence that would suggest it was anything more than a tragic accident. But even though the suicide rumor died away almost as quickly as it had started, Doucet was left with one niggling question: Why had Thompson been so keen to update his will and appoint him, Doucet, as executor?

Bill Thompson's death was as much a shock to Dimitri Andropov as it was to Rick Doucet. But unlike Doucet, Andropov didn't care one way or another about the man; his main concern was the scheme at the Canadian mine. It had operated smoothly and profitably now for a couple of years and Thompson had played a key role. He had to find a way to keep it going.

"Shit," Andropov said when he saw the message on his phone. He was in Luanda, Angola, negotiating a deal to obtain more illicit diamonds, for cash, from a corrupt politician. He had just come from a long meeting with his contact, an aide to the Minister of Geology, Mines and Industry; the man had been coy, never mentioning his boss, and the agreement they reached had been entirely verbal, but Andropov knew that he would soon be getting a steady supply of Angolan diamonds – most likely stolen, but he didn't care – at a heavy discount. As long as he could launder them into the legal market – and the Canadian operation would be the most effective way to do that – they would command high prices. The profits would flow directly into Gagarin's companies. The aide and the Angolan minister would get rich, but they would also both be firmly in Andropov's pocket. That was the way he liked it.

He had patiently explained to the aide what would happen if he or his boss got greedy and tried to double cross him – it had happened before, he said, he had plenty of experience dealing with such situations.

"I remember one of those guys," Andropov told the aide, "they found him floating face down in a river, not that far from here. And then there was another one who jumped out of a helicopter. It was about a thousand meters up, just hovering. I don't recall exactly how it happened – it's possible someone gave him a nudge – but whatever, it was a long way down. Far enough that he probably had time to think about what he'd done all the way to the ground. I'm sure you get the picture."

With Thompson dead, he would have to rethink the Canadian operation. His initial instincts about the engineer had been right; for over two years he had delivered diamonds to the mine regularly and without a hitch. Money, and periodic reminders about what would happen if he screwed up – delivered courtesy of the Canadian mob run by Gagarin's cousin in Calgary – had kept him just where they wanted him. It was one of the most effective money laundering schemes Andropov had ever devised, and he wanted to make sure it continued.

"Shit," he said again, to no one in particular. At some point soon he might have to go back to Canada, and he didn't like it. He could travel many places without problems, but he was always wary about North America. The Americans were just too vigilant for his liking – he knew they were keeping an eye on Gagarin, and they probably monitored him as well – and they had pressured the Canadians to tighten up their borders. But first he needed Gagarin's Canadian relatives to take care of a few things for him, like checking out Thompson's apartment in Vancouver. It had to be clean. He had to be sure that no one would find anything there that might compromise the operation.

The man with the toque was called Igor, and he checked the address again and pointed ahead. "That's it, I think," he said, "the apartment building across the street. Slow down so I can make sure, then go around the block and come back."

The driver, whose name was Viktor, grunted. "No need, Igor. I checked it out on Street View and I recognize it. That's the right place. Thompson's apartment is on the ninth floor. Hang on." He made a sharp left turn across the street and drove down a ramp into an underground parking garage. "There should be an elevator in here. That way we can bypass the lobby."

There *was* an elevator but it required a key, which they didn't have. They could have jimmied the lock but that would have taken time and might attract attention, so they simply sat in the car until one of the residents drove in. They didn't have to wait long. A young woman driving a dark colored Honda Civic pulled into a spot close to the elevator. The two Russians looked at one another, nodded, and without a word stepped out of their car. But they were too late; the woman was out of her car and into the elevator with her shopping bags so fast that they were left standing in the garage watching the elevator lights tick off the floors as the woman went up to her apartment. "Fuck," said Igor. "Next time someone drives in we have to get out of the car right away and make sure we're close behind them when they get into the elevator."

Viktor nodded and they went back to their car. This time they had a longer wait, but then a Volvo station wagon pulled in and a family tumbled out: parents and two young children. They took their time getting their stuff out of the back and when they reached the elevator the two Russians were close behind. Igor – still wearing his toque – made a show of pulling a ring of keys from his pocket, but by then the family had already opened the door and stepped into the elevator. "Thanks," Viktor said, as he and Igor squeezed in beside them. There was a momentary elevator silence. The girl – the younger of the two children – was obviously tired and had her arms wrapped around her mother's legs. Her brother, blond hair hanging down over his forehead, stood erect like a little soldier, staring straight ahead. Viktor, smiling, said to him: "Young man, we're going up to the ninth floor. Do you think you could press the button for me?" Viktor's English was clear but strongly accented and the boy glanced at him quickly, then scanned the floor numbers and carefully pushed the button for the ninth floor.

"Good lad, thank you."

The boy blushed and gave Viktor a sly smile, and a moment later the elevator stopped at the sixth floor and the family stepped out. Igor jabbed the 'close' button impatiently and a few minutes later they had picked the lock to Thompson's apartment and were inside. It was dark and quiet and had the stale smell of rooms that had been closed up for a long time. Viktor crossed himself; it was just a job but he was superstitious about dead people.

The two Russians had worked together many times before and they moved through the apartment quickly, hardly exchanging a word. Igor swept several packages from the kitchen table into the sports bag he was carrying and then combed through the rest of the apartment, opening drawers and cupboards and throwing every paper and folder he could find into the bag. Viktor turned on Thompson's computer and plugged in the hard drive he'd brought with him. He was a computer geek and an expert hacker and it took him no time at all to break through the minimum security and copy all of the engineer's documents and emails. Then he wiped the computer clean. He wondered fleetingly why they were going to all this trouble, but those were his orders. The man was dead, he'd been told, but there might be sensitive information on his computer. Copy everything. Then make sure nobody else can access what was there. Viktor made sure.

CHAPTER 13

 One evening a few weeks after he returned from the meeting in Milan Doucet found a message from Thompson's lawyer on his answer machine. Could he return the call, please? There were things they needed to discuss in relation to Bill Thompson's will.

Here we go, Doucet said to himself. Just what I need right now, more things to do. He wrote down the lawyer's phone number and made a note to call him. He procrastinated for several days because he was sure dealing with Bill Thompson's will was going to put another large demand on his time, but when he finally called several days later he got a pleasant surprise.

"Really, I just wanted to say how sorry I am about Mr. Thompson, and to introduce myself and make sure I have your correct contact details," the lawyer said. "He had a lot of good things to say about you, Mr. Doucet – he was very happy you agreed to be executor. But I wanted to let you know that because of the circumstances we're more-or-less in limbo for the time being. I've never dealt with a case like this before – the problem is, because Mr. Thompson's body hasn't been recovered, no death certificate has been issued. And that means we can't proceed with the will – distribution of assets and so on. As I see it, we have two choices: either we wait – as I understand it the company will do a search for Mr. Thompson's remains during the summer, when the ice clears – or we can file for what's called a legal declaration of death. That would be straightforward, because there doesn't seem to be any possibility that Mr. Thompson could have survived the accident. I think it would be granted without any problem." The lawyer paused, but Doucet didn't say anything. "It's your decision, Mr. Doucet. But to be frank, my advice is that we should wait. The declaration of death requires a fair amount of paperwork and takes time. The divers should be able to get into the lake in a few months and do their search, so confirmation of Mr. Thompson's death may not be that far off anyway. It probably won't make much difference in when we can actually start working on the will. And in the meantime I can put together information on Mr. Thompson's assets so that when the time comes everything will be ready to go. But as I say, it's up to you to decide on which way to proceed."

Doucet was swamped with work and he didn't hesitate. "I agree with you," he said. "Let's wait until we know the results of the search. Hopefully we won't need to file for the declaration." He would probably still be swamped with work in the summer, but at least he could put off dealing with his executor duties for a few more months. "Eventually, though, you'll have to educate me about being executor. I've never done this before."

"Don't worry, it's not rocket science. You'll probably find it a bit tedious, but it's not difficult. I think you've made the right decision about waiting. I'll be in touch, Mr. Doucet. Bye now." The lawyer hung up.

Relieved, Doucet put down the phone and turned back to the data tables spread out in front of him. His work was crucial for planning Diatek's exploration strategy for the rapidly approaching summer field season, and he was feeling the pressure. His analyses of the previous year's samples showed that the 'right' kind of indicator minerals – the ones that always signified a diamond deposit – occurred in several geographically separated clusters, and when he backtracked on his maps to work out where the minerals might have come from he always ended up at the same spot, about a hundred miles northeast of the Diatek mine, close to the Arctic Circle. That's where he proposed to set up the base camp for further sampling. But other data, in particular the proprietary remote sensing data from a company that Diatek had hired to survey the region, showed no signs of kimberlites there. And the kimberlite rock was where they'd find diamonds. It was a puzzle, and Doucet didn't know what to make of it. But the indicator minerals didn't lie, he was sure of that.

Some of the others on the exploration team didn't agree, however. The remote sensing data, they argued, suggested that they should work further west, near where they had set up their field camp the previous year. Maybe Doucet's interpretation of glacier movements was wrong. Maybe the indicator minerals had actually been transported from the west, not from the northeast. But Doucet pointed out that the remote sensing data weren't infallible; the complex geology could be masking the kimberlite signature. It could be that there *are* kimberlites where the indicator minerals say they should be, he said, but they simply don't show up in the remote sensing data.

In the end he won the argument. He had the backing of the company's Chief Geologist, Tim Bailey, who made the final decision. Doucet knew there was a lot riding on it; if the summer was a bust Bailey's support of his work would evaporate and his job could be on the line. Diatek's exploration arm needed something to show for all the money they'd spent over the past few years.

The planning was carried out in complete secrecy. There was a frenzy of diamond exploration in the north now, and other companies, as well as independent prospectors, were hungry for any information they could get that might lead them to a diamond deposit. Even at Diatek only a few people knew exactly where the exploration team was headed until they departed for the field in early June. Doucet stayed in Vancouver for almost a month after they left so that he could finish his work in the lab, but then he joined them and spent several weeks at the camp in the tundra. It never got dark; for a few hours each night the sun dipped just below the horizon but a bright twilight remained. When the weather permitted, everyone worked more or less around the clock. In spite of the grueling schedule, punctuated by a few idle days when they were confined to their tents by fog or – once – unseasonable driving sleet, Doucet loved this aspect of his work; it was one of the reasons he had chosen a career in geology in the first place. When the helicopter dropped them off in a sampling area in the morning and whup-whup-whupped off into the distance, the silence was profound, the crunch of gravel underfoot or the sound of human voices magnified. The austere land had its own beauty, with muted hues that changed quickly in the northern light. Here and there splotches of color lit up the barren landscape: deep purple saxifrage flowers, pale yellow dryas, green patches of cotton grass with brilliant white puff balls of downy cotton swaying on their slender stems. Miniature arctic willows with spiny catkins grew everywhere underfoot, never reaching more than a few inches high. Doucet tried to find time each morning to walk away from the camp and spend a few minutes by himself, communing with the land, a world away from the concrete and steel and glass of Vancouver. It was a way to remind himself why he had chosen this life. At those moments even the mosquitoes didn't bother him.

By the end of July he was back in the city with a new hoard of samples to analyze. The plan was to make enough measurements to guide the final sampling push of the short field season in real time; if all went well his analyses would provide the information he needed to advise the sampling team on where to go next. He and several summer assistants – geology students who washed and sieved the field samples and then spent hours peering through a microscope and picking out the red and green indicator minerals for Doucet to analyze – worked flat out.

He spoke to the field team every few days on their satellite phone, bringing them up to date on his results, and as the data accumulated it looked more and more as though he had been right – the indicator minerals were leading them upstream along the path of ancient glacier movement as surely as Hansel and Gretel had been led home by their trail of dropped pebbles. The question he still had to answer, however, was, How far away is the source? Doucet examined the surface markings on the indicator minerals using the electron microscope and concluded that the grains had been transported over a long distance. Could they leapfrog ahead along the direction of glacier transport, saving time and money? "Your call," Tim Bailey told him. "So far you've been right."

To make sure he hadn't missed anything, Doucet shut himself in his office and went back through all his data. He double checked everything, but it all made sense. He couldn't see any flaws in his original arguments, and all the new measurements confirmed they were closing in on a potential diamond deposit. That night he called the field team and told them to move the base camp fifty kilometers north and set up a new sampling grid. He'd fly out and join them soon, and he'd stay through the first couple of weeks in September. By then the days would be short and the weather deteriorating, and they'd have to wrap up the field work for the season.

A week before he left for the field he got an email message from Sarah Patterson. He'd tried not to think about her too much since returning from London, but it was difficult. Meeting her was one of those chance encounters that happen in everyone's life, he told himself, get over it. In spite of that twinge he felt in his stomach whenever he thought of her, nothing was going to happen. It got easier as the months went by. But her message brought her abruptly into his thoughts again.

They'd corresponded once earlier in the summer – she'd asked if he was willing to read and comment on a draft of her thesis. In spite of his schedule he'd somehow found time to do it. But now she wrote that she was getting ready to hand in her thesis and leave London. She had two job interviews with non-profits in the States at the end of August, she said, one in San Francisco and the other in Seattle. She was thinking about driving up to Vancouver for the weekend after her Seattle interview, to visit her cousin. If he was going to be around she'd bring him a copy of her thesis and maybe they could meet for coffee.

Doucet sat back in his chair and read the message again. He wouldn't be in Vancouver at the end of August, he'd be in the field. It wasn't fair.

CHAPTER 14

Friday night in early September, the long Labor Day weekend ahead, and Ed Zelensky was working late. Not because he had to, but because he wanted to. Some of his colleagues thought he was crazy, but that didn't bother him. He loved his job and did some of his best work in the evening or on weekends when the building was quiet; he could think without being interrupted by the telephone or the demands of his coworkers. Heather, his wife, didn't like it at first, but she had long ago become used to his erratic schedule. Being married to a policeman required a certain kind of temperament, and over the years she had grown into the role. Besides, now that the kids had grown up and left home she had embarked on her own career with its own commitments. In some ways their separate lives brought them closer together; they had settled into a comfortable relationship in which he no longer felt guilty about spending so much time on his work.

Zelensky worked in a special unit of the RCMP in Vancouver, investigating organized crime. Lately a lot of his work had focused on Asian and Central American gangs operating in in the city, but recently he'd received an unusual request. It wasn't high priority and he'd only skimmed through the file when it arrived, not reading it in detail. But it had piqued his interest. Now, in the end-of-the day quiet, he had a chance to look at it in more depth.

The request had come from the central office of CSIS – Canadian Security Intelligence Service – in Ottawa, and it came to Zelensky for two reasons: first there was a Vancouver connection, and secondly he was fluent in Russian. He had learned the language from his grandparents, Ukrainian farmers who immigrated to Canada and built a farm on the prairies. They spoke Ukrainian and Russian fluently, and Ed – who spent a lot of time with his grandparents when he was growing up – had picked up the basics of both languages as a child. It was to have a profound influence on his life. At university he majored in Russian language and history, and with that background he was a natural for the RCMP. Within weeks of graduating he had enrolled. He had never been tempted to try anything else, even if operations with a Russian connection were now far less frequent than they used to be.

The request from CSIS was straightforward: take a look at some information that had been forwarded from the U.S. National Security Agency and see if there's anything there that Canada should be concerned about. The file he received was a collection of telephone call transcripts. In their ceaseless sifting through the billions of messages that crisscross the planet every day, the NSA computers at Fort Meade, Maryland, had singled out these particular calls – all of them in Russian. Zelensky had no idea why they were flagged, he knew only that the NSA, in its wisdom, had eventually decided there wasn't anything in them that might pose a threat to U.S. national security, so they had dropped their investigation. But because the calls had a Canadian connection they had notified CSIS.

The first thing Zelensky noticed was the dates on the transcripts – the calls had been made almost half a year earlier, in March and April. He wondered why he hadn't received the information sooner, but then he realized that once the NSA had decided they were no longer interested, all urgency would have evaporated. So they take their time and then almost half a year later someone decides to send them to Canada, he said to himself. As far as they're concerned there's no rush, this is now someone else's problem.

The transcripts were English translations of the original Russian but they were very clumsy and it didn't take him long to realize they must be computer generated, which probably meant they were not very accurate. The powers-that-be had sent the original audio files along with the transcripts; he would really need to hear them to evaluate the captured messages. But before he started he looked over the summary call log; it listed dates and locations – thank god for GPS, he thought – and it helped put the conversations in context.

The first burst of messages had bounced back and forth among several Russian numbers, one in Sochi, one in Moscow, and also a Russian cell phone that – according to the GPS data – had been in Luanda, Angola, when the messages started. Not long afterwards the cell phone, and presumably also its owner, were back in Moscow. Then came calls from the same Russian numbers to Canada, first to Ottawa and Calgary, Alberta, and a few days later to Vancouver. There were also numerous calls between the Canadian numbers. According to the log all of the telephone conversations were carried out in Russian.

That intrigued him. He knew there were a few Russian and eastern European gangs in the country, but not many, and he hadn't been involved in any cases concerning them for several years. He put on his headset and sat back to listen to the audio recordings, getting real pleasure from the sound of the language he knew so well. He rarely used Russian these days, but he had learned it so early that he had no trouble understanding the conversations. But unless he was completely missing something, he heard nothing in the phone messages that might have triggered NSA's interest. Most of the conversations revolved around business or family matters; there were a few raised voices in a couple of the calls, but nothing out of the ordinary. On the other hand it was possible that the NSA flagged the calls because of who the callers were, not what they said. And if that was the case the people who made the calls probably knew they might be overheard. That would make them careful about what they said, and it would be much more difficult to decipher their real meaning. That is, if there even *was* a hidden meaning … maybe he was reading too much into this, maybe they really were just innocent conversations. Zelensky shook his head. What he needed was to find out who the numbers in the phone log actually belonged to.

He took off his headset and sent an email request to CSIS, asking if they could send him any information they had about the phone numbers, then looked at his watch. He hadn't realized it was so late; Heather would already be home by now. She was on the board of a local charity and they'd had a dinner and auction tonight, the kind of event Zelensky disliked with a passion. He yawned and turned off the computer and decided that he'd come back and listen to the audio files again tomorrow, when he was fresh.

Tomorrow was Saturday, the beginning of the long weekend, and coming into work would be better than painting the spare bedroom, a job he'd been putting off for the past several months. Heather had been nagging him about it, but he didn't enjoy painting. At least he didn't enjoy the *thought* of painting, especially the thought of all the preparation beforehand and the cleaning up afterwards. When he was actually painting it wasn't so bad, and he always got a certain satisfaction when it was finished, when everything looked fresh and new. But now he had a legitimate reason for not tackling the bedroom. He needed to try to get into the heads of the speakers on those audio files and find out what they were really talking about. Correction, he told himself again, he needed to find out *if* they were actually talking about anything significant.

Saturday morning there was no alarm clock; that was a house rule. He and Heather slept a bit later than usual and then went out for breakfast: he had scrambled eggs and hash browns and really good back bacon, and Heather had French toast with a fresh fruit salad on the side. She told him about the previous evening's auction and said she'd bid on one of the big items – a week in Hawaii donated by a local travel agency. "I finally dropped out," she said, "It was amazing, the price just kept going up and up, and in the end it went for way more than the actual value. That was good for us, but I wouldn't have minded a trip to Hawaii ..."

It had been a busy week and a Hawaiian vacation sounded good to Zelensky too. Without really thinking, he said, "Why don't we go anyway? Early next year maybe, sometime after Christmas when I'm not so busy? Remember when we took the kids to Hawaii that one time? We had such a good time."

Heather smiled. "I'll remind you about it in a couple of months," she said. "I'll also remind you that it was your idea, not mine." She filed the suggestion away but doubted anything would come of it. She knew her husband too well. They talked about Hawaii for a while and then Zelensky said he'd better get to work. "I won't be late tonight, I promise."

Heather said she'd stay and have more coffee and read the newspaper. "Then I have some chores to do around the house." Zelensky was already standing up, putting on his jacket, not paying much attention. His mind was on the telephone conversations waiting for him in his office. Heather was watching with a bemused expression on her face. "And Ed, you are going to paint that room, aren't you? You know, before too many more years go by?" She wasn't angry; it had become something of a joke between them, but she liked to needle him about it.

"What? Oh sure, yeah, I'll get to it soon as I have a little time." He grinned. "I could do it in January instead of going to Hawaii. Like I said I shouldn't be so busy then." She gave him an exasperated look and he took out his car keys and blew her a kiss. "Bye hon. See you later."

The second time around Zelensky took detailed notes as he listened to the recordings. The quality was superb; even with his years in the business he was amazed at the crispness and clarity of the voices. How does the NSA do it, he wondered? It was like listening to a friend calling from two blocks away. The speakers' voices were clear; he could even make out background sounds – pop music in one, the voice of a young girl in another. He could tell that in the first few calls – the ones that bounced around between Moscow and Sochi and Luanda – the callers were dealing with some kind of business situation. There was a hint of urgency in their voices, but they seemed to be speaking in code. They didn't say 'someone shipped us one hundred right shoes and no lefts,' they just talked about their inventory and several times they mentioned a lake and a mine. They also referred to an engineer – in the abstract, no name attached. He wrote all these things down in his notes, but they still didn't make much sense to him.

To make real progress he would have to know more about the people behind the voices, and fortunately someone at CSIS headquarters in Ottawa had already answered his email about the phone numbers. Bless their souls, he said under his breath. He imagined an army of trolls ceaselessly mining data in some secret underground facility. They had managed to attach a name or organization to nearly every one of the phone numbers, and they'd annotated several of them with additional notes.

The numbers in Moscow and Sochi belonged to phones registered to a company owned by a wealthy Russian businessman named Vasily Gagarin. The Angola calls were from a cell phone belonging to one of Gagarin's close associates, a man called Dimitri Andropov. Neither name meant anything to Zelensky. He didn't recognize the names connected to the Canadian numbers either, even the ones in Vancouver.

According to the notes from the CSIS, the Americans had been monitoring Vasily Gagarin's activities for years because they believed he was involved in illegal arms trading, especially in Africa. He was one of Russia's wealthiest people – he regularly made the Forbes list of billionaires – and he had close ties to Vladimir Putin, who had recently been re-installed as President of Russia. On paper Gagarin's business empire was entirely legitimate, but the CIA and several other intelligence agencies had evidence that behind that bland exterior was a web of corruption and illegal activities. Andropov was his principle enabler, a shadowy man who seemed to be the major player in most of Gagarin's illegal businesses, including the lucrative sale of old Soviet Union military equipment to rebel groups around the world.

Zelensky stared at the notes for a long time. He was convinced now that the NSA had flagged the calls because of who these people were, not necessarily because of the content. But regardless of what they were talking about in those phone calls, he was interested in the connection to Canada. According to the notes from CSIS, Andropov was almost certainly involved in illegal activities. What was he doing calling people in Canada?

He circled 'Gagarin' and 'Andropov' and went down the hall to a door that was marked 'Restricted Entry, Authorized Personnel Only,' swiped his ID card, and went inside. He sat down at one of the secure computers, brought up a classified

RCMP database, and did a search for the two Russians. Their files came up immediately, complete with fuzzy photographs. He stared at the pictures for a while, trying to imprint the men's faces on his brain, and then read through the files carefully. There was a lot of background information, some of it useful and some not, but what he didn't find was any connection to Canada. Why did they make those calls to Ottawa and Calgary and Vancouver? he wondered again. There's still something missing here.

The only clue came near the end of the Andropov file, where there was a link to a spreadsheet documenting what was known about the man's international movements. As he scrolled down, one entry caught his eye: Andropov had been in Canada in December, 2009. He'd arrived in Montreal on a flight from Moscow, and left the country six days later on a flight out of Toronto. A comment in the file indicated that his movements within the country had not been monitored.

It might be nothing but Zelensky made a note of the date anyway. He sighed in frustration. Why is it always the information you really need that's missing? If they flagged this guy, why didn't they trace his movements?

He shrugged and turned to the other names on his list, but with one exception the database didn't yield any more useful information. The exception was one Alex Kalinin, a naturalized Canadian citizen born in Tomsk, Russia, who was known to the police in Calgary. Zelensky shivered involuntarily; he'd been to Tomsk once, a short stop on a winter trip in Siberia, and it was one of the coldest places he'd ever been. The heaters in his hotel room had been lukewarm, and when he got up in the morning the condensation on the windows had frozen to a sheet of solid ice.

According to the file Kalinin was involved in protection rackets targeting new immigrants in Western Canada, especially immigrants from Eastern Europe, and although the police had been watching him for years they'd never been able to pin anything on him. The word on the street was that he was ruthless. Nobody was willing to testify against him; it was healthier to pay the protection money and stay quiet. Apparently he had accumulated a significant fortune and had also cultivated friends in city government in Calgary, which helped keep him out of police hands.

When he'd finished, Zelensky went back to his desk and read through his notes, trying to find threads or connections, anything that might give him more clues to what the telephone conversations were really about.

Both Andropov and Gagarin had mentioned a mine several times; did that mean anything? According to the RCMP database Gagarin had mining interests in Russia so maybe they were referring to one of his businesses over there. Or maybe he wanted to invest in a Canadian mine – there was nothing intrinsically wrong with that, much of Canada's natural resource base was owned or run by foreigners. Zelensky couldn't think of any other reason they might be discussing a mine, so he moved down to the next section of his notes, which was punctuated with numerous question marks.

In spite of his excellent command of Russian, two words that he couldn't decipher had popped up several times during the recorded conversations. The automated translation was no help either; the computers had had as much trouble with these words as he had. In the transcripts they came out as 'die tech,' with question marks to indicate uncertainty. Zelensky went back to the recordings and listened to the words several more times. And he concluded that it definitely wasn't Russian, and it was one word, not two. Both he and the computer had gotten it all wrong. A single word; it could be a brand name, or perhaps the name of a place, although he'd never heard of anywhere called 'Dietek' or anything close to that. He turned to his computer. Okay Google, he thought, see what you can do for me.

Fifteen minutes later he was staring at the Diatek Canada website. Jesus Christ, he said to himself, could that be it? It's a mining company and its headquarters are right here in Vancouver. Could that be why they made those calls to Vancouver?

He kept reading. Diatek Canada operated a successful diamond mine in the Northwest Territories, and through its exploration arm the company was using cutting edge techniques to prospect for additional deposits. As he scrolled through archived news items he noticed several articles about an employee who had been killed in an accident almost half a year ago, in March. The man, an engineer named William Thompson, had drowned when the snowmobile he was driving broke through a patch of thin ice on a lake near the mine. Zelensky glanced at the date on the article and then did a double take. He grabbed the call log from the NSA and checked. The first few phone calls between Gagarin and Andropov were dated one day after the accident at the Diatek mine. And they'd talked about a mine and an engineer in those conversations.

He sat back in his chair and took a deep breath. It was possible that there was no connection, that these were random events that just happened to take place at the same time. But Zelensky had a knack for connecting the dots when many of his colleagues saw no links at all – and more often than not he was right. It was one of the reasons he had advanced so quickly in the RCMP. When it came right down to it, he didn't believe in coincidences, or at least he didn't trust them until he'd exhausted all the other possibilities. And he had just discovered several coincidences. But why would an accident at a mine in Canada trigger such a response from a very rich Russian businessman like Gagarin? It didn't make much sense. Still, even if he was being led on a wild goose chase he wasn't ready to give up quite yet. There were a few things he needed to follow up first.

CHAPTER 15

Z elensky picked up his phone and dialed the number of a woman who worked in the Organized Crime section of the Vancouver Police Department. They were friends as well as colleagues and they collaborated often. She was not married and she lived for her work and he was pretty sure she would be in her office on Saturday.

He smiled when she answered the phone on the second ring. "Helen, its Ed Zelensky. I was hoping you'd be in. Have you got a few minutes?"

"Hey, Ed. Sure, I'm busy, but for you I've always got time." Helen Williams was ten years younger than he was but they had formed a strong bond over the years they'd worked together. There were times when he thought he was a little in love with her, and he wondered what might have happened in another life, if he hadn't been married. But they'd always kept their relationship on a purely professional level.

"Any chance I could run a few things by you? Not on the phone, though. Over coffee, maybe? I could be over there in about an hour."

"Yeah, that would work. I've been here since early. I'm ready for a break."

Zelensky showed Helen his list of names. "It's a case I'm working on," he said. "I can't say more than that. Any of these people familiar to you?"

"Nope. I don't recognize any of them. Are they local?"

"They're all in Western Canada as far as I know, and at least a couple of them are here in Vancouver, or have been recently. Their cell phones received calls here, that's how we traced them. The guy who seems to be in charge works out of Calgary, his name is Alex Kalinin." Zelensky pointed out Kalinin's name on his list. "The police there keep an eye on him but they've never been able to put him away for anything. Apparently he has friends in the mayor's office."

Helen rolled her eyes. "One of those, eh? So what's this all about?"

"I can't say much except what I've already told you. I was hoping you might recognize one or two of these names because I know you keep your ear pretty close to the ground. Most of these people are Russian – have you heard any chatter recently about Russian criminal types in town?"

Helen shook her head. "No, nothing at all, not recently." She blew on her coffee, then put the cup down. "There is someone who might know, though. His name is Joey and he's one of my regular sources. He seems to know just about everything that's going down in Vancouver. He's a dealer, but he's not a big fish and we leave him alone as long as he feeds us information. He's in and out of jail but right at the moment he's out. We get along okay, for some reason he likes me, maybe because I've always treated him well … I give him a bit of respect. His mother ran off when he was four and he had a rough childhood." She laughed. "Me, the surrogate mother. It might be a long shot, but it's probably worth a try. What do you think?"

"If he can tell us anything about Russians moving into town or if he knows anything about the people on my list, then yes, I'd like to talk to him. I've got cash if he has anything useful. But only if it's useful. Don't tell him in advance that there's money in it."

"Ed. You know me better than that. Besides, Joey is a bit of an operator and if he senses there's something we really want he'll play it for all it's worth. I'll see what he has to say about the names on your list. If anyone can give you useful information it's Joey." She drained her coffee and put the list in her pocket. "Sorry, but I've got to get back to work."

They both stood up and Helen said "Thanks for the coffee, Ed. It's been too long. Take care, eh?"

"Okay, no problem. Let me know about Joey."

A few days later Helen called him back. "Joey says he doesn't recognize any of those names off the top of his head. But he did say he's heard quite a bit about someone called Viktor lately, a Russian, and there's a Viktor on your list. Joey doesn't know his last name but he'll ask around and see what he can find out."

"I think I'd better meet your friend Joey. Can you set it up?"

"Yes, it shouldn't be a problem as long as he knows I'll be there too. Joey trusts me, at least he trusts me as much as he'd trust anybody from the police. I'm not sure he'd agree if it was just you. Anyway, I'd like to hear what he has to say."

They met Joey at a small pizza place in the suburbs. "We always meet at night," Helen said, "and never twice at the same place." She smiled. "Pretty soon I'm going to run out of pizza joints. I have to wonder about people like Joey, he's not very smart but he really likes pizza and sometimes I think he talks to me as much for the free pizza as anything else. That and maybe the adrenalin rush." She turned serious. "It would be bad news for him if anyone found out he was talking to the police."

The restaurant was in an anonymous strip mall and as Zelensky pulled the car into a parking place Helen nodded toward a thin man pacing back and forth on the sidewalk. "That's him," she said. He had a cell phone to his ear and a cigarette in his free hand and he was gesturing wildly as he talked. Zelensky turned off the motor and they sat for a minute, watching. They were dressed casually but they were both carrying weapons.

"He's okay, is he Helen? Not shopping us to some of his buddies on the phone?"

"No way. It's worth too much to him, the money and the fact we go easy on him. *Especially* because we go easy on him, I'd say. And the pizza, of course," she added. "Only a couple of us know he's an informant and whenever he gets busted we try to smooth things out without making it too obvious. Usually it's just me who talks to him, but I told him you'd be with me tonight." She unbuckled her seatbelt and opened the door. "Come on, let's go."

The pizza place was generic, brightly lit with fluorescent lights, tables covered with red and white checkered tablecloths. Two families with kids were sitting near the front of the restaurant and Joey led Helen and Zelensky to the back, where he slid into a corner booth with a view of the door. Helen sat down beside him and Zelensky took a seat across from him. They watched one of the cooks throwing dough into the air, spinning the pizzas until they were the right size. Joey looked nervous. "This your friend, Helen?" he asked, not looking at Zelensky.

"Yeah, you can call me Ed." Zelensky extended his hand across the table and after a brief hesitation Joey shook it. "Pleased to meet you, Joey," Zelensky said.

They ordered pizza and when the waitress had gone Helen asked Joey how he was doing. "Okay I guess. I don't like snooping on those Russians though. I don't like Russians, period. They're trouble."

Zelensky raised his eyebrows. "They? Helen told me you'd heard about someone called Viktor. There are more?"

"Yeah, there are at least three or four Russians. They're moving in and making things difficult for some of the locals. People aren't happy. The one called Viktor, he's into computers. I still couldn't find out his last name. People say he's setting up computer scams."

"What about the others?" Zelensky said. "Are they all doing computer stuff?"

"No, I don't think so. I don't know what they're doing exactly but as soon as I started asking around I got some pretty bad vibes. People told me, you mess with these guys and you might get your tongue cut out so you can't talk. I got a couple of addresses, maybe it's where they live, maybe not. It's the best I could do. But don't ask me to do any more on this. Like I said, I don't like Russians." Joey pulled a crumpled piece of paper from his pocket, smoothed it out on the table and handed it to Helen. "Here they are."

"Good work, Joey." She glanced at the paper and handed it to Zelensky.

There were two addresses. He pulled out his cell phone and checked; they were both in Kitsilano.

"Thanks Joey, this is useful." Zelensky thought for a moment. "Ever hear of a company called Diatek? They're based here in Vancouver."

Joey shook his head. "No. Never heard of them."

"Okay," Zelensky said and pulled an envelope out of his jacket. He held it in front of him, fiddling with it, turning it over end for end. It got Joey's attention.

"I've got cash, Joey. This is a little advance for what you gave us and there's more where it came from. I know you said you want to drop it, but if you come across anything get in touch with Helen. There'll be something in it for you." He slid the envelope across the table.

But Joey wouldn't take the bait. He picked up the envelope without looking at it and put it in his pocket, all the while shaking his head slowly. "I don't think so," he said. "I hope you get rid of them, but I don't want to push my luck. They're in a different league from me. It's too risky."

Zelensky looked at Helen but she just shrugged and said, "All right Joey, let's leave it. But I'm always here if you change your mind. You should think about it."

"Okay," Joey said, looking around the restaurant, anywhere but at Helen and Zelensky. He drained the last of his Pepsi and glanced toward the door. "I'm outa here." He stood up abruptly. "See ya." He turned and walked to the door and out into the night.

"Joey is not one for lengthy goodbyes," Helen said. "Don't get up yet, we have a routine; he leaves first and I wait around for ten minutes or so before I go. He's paranoid about being seen with a cop. Actually I'm surprised he was willing to walk into the restaurant with us tonight. Usually he goes in by himself first to check things out."

"I guess I don't blame him for taking precautions; he's playing a dangerous game. But let's hope he has a change of heart about giving us more information." Zelensky looked around and lowered his voice. "Listen Helen, can we keep this under the radar for a while? At least for a couple of weeks? I can't say right now how I got these names but I'm pretty sure it's not because they're into computer scams. I'll have to think about it, but I might organize surveillance at these addresses, just to see what's going on. I'll keep you in the loop."

He wasn't giving her much. Helen liked working with Zelensky but usually it was a more equal partnership. And Joey was her source, not his. On the other hand she knew that Zelensky wouldn't keep her in the dark unless there was a good reason.

Reluctantly, she said "Okay, if that's how we have to do it, that's how we have to do it. But let's try to collaborate on this as much as possible, eh? If there are Russian gangs moving into town, I'd like to know about it."

"Don't worry, I'm not trying to cut you out, I swear, it's just that I don't have a choice on this one. It's one of those situations where I can't say anything more. When I can, I will. I promise."

That made her feel marginally better. If he can't say anything, it probably means whatever information he's got is classified, she thought. She looked up. "I guess I can live with it. By the way, what's with this Diatek thing you asked Joey? Or can't you say anything about that either?"

"Don't be so sarcastic." Zelensky grinned at her. "It's a mining company and it's based in Vancouver and I think there might be a connection with the names on my list. It's just one theory I'm working on. It was a long shot but I wanted to find out if Joey knew anything about the company."

"One more thing," Helen said. "Joey seemed pretty nervous tonight. Usually he tries to act like a tough guy even if he really isn't, so I think he must be really scared of these Russians. If you go after them make sure you work with a backup, okay Ed? Don't do anything silly." Zelensky had a reputation for being a maverick and a few times he'd followed a hunch on his own when he should have had a partner and had ended up in dangerous situations. So far he'd avoided disaster but there was always a first time.

"Okay mom. I'll be careful." Zelensky grinned at her again, then looked at his watch. "Our ten minutes are up. Actually, quite a bit more than ten minutes. Should we go?" He pulled out his wallet. "I'll get the pizzas."

CHAPTER 16

Mid-September and the sky was clear as the flight descended toward Vancouver International. Rick Doucet was sitting at a window and he looked down at the city below, spread out across the Fraser delta, the early autumn sun lighting up the mountains beyond. Geology at work. The endless cycle of the land eroding, the sediments being carried away by the rivers and dumped far away in a massive delta. It made him think of his indicator minerals, gouged out of the earth and transported far from their origins by glaciers and their meltwater streams.

He was happy with the progress the field team had made that summer. The weather had been good and they'd covered more ground than anyone anticipated. He had mapped out two broad swathes of territory for the team to examine, and they'd moved through both of them systematically, sampling every patch of sand and gravel they could find. Then, almost at the end of the field season, they'd stumbled across a sandbar chock full of indicator mineral grains. The sandbar was in a stream draining a small lake, and when they got to the lake they found the same thing. All along one side the beach sand was peppered with red garnets and green diopside crystals. Doucet had never seen anything like it. The whole exploration team was stunned by the discovery, and once they got over the initial shock they were like kids in a candy store, laughing and scooping up bags of the multi-colored sand. Doucet figured that the lake must sit right on top of a kimberlite; in this geologically old terrain, scoured by glaciers, it made sense that the soft kimberlite rock would form a depression. He immediately called Tim Bailey on the satellite phone and told him what they'd found, and asked him to book time for him at the university lab – he wanted to analyze the new samples as soon as he got back. In the meantime Bailey quickly organized a staking team; they'd need to stake out their claims before news of the discovery leaked out. Then Doucet grabbed several bags of the sand samples and took the helicopter back to Yellowknife, leaving the exploration team to finish their work. He was certain they'd found the source of the indicator mineral trail he'd been following for over a year, but he needed a few days in the lab to be absolutely sure. For the flight to Vancouver he'd put the samples in his carry-on bag, which was now wedged between his feet. He didn't want to let it out of his sight.

Doucet looked out the window again. The plane was banking to the left in a slow turn, lining up for landing, and when he looked straight down he could see the grounds of the university. If Tim Bailey had been able to book the time for him, he'd be out there tomorrow, analyzing his samples. And if the analyses turned out the way he thought they would, Diatek would have a second diamond deposit on its hands and the company's exploration arm would have earned its keep. Bailey would be very happy. If they'd followed the advice of the geophysicists and sent the field team in the opposite direction they would be going home empty handed.

The only thing Doucet wasn't looking forward to was the mountain of correspondence and commitments he knew would be waiting from him when he got home. In the field he'd been completely off the grid for a month, the only link to the outside world the satellite phone. Daily life seemed simple; the cook prepared their meals, the focus was on their work, entertainment was limited to reading or fishing or playing cards. He had turned on his cell phone in the Yellowknife airport but after watching for a few minutes as an endless stream of email messages downloaded he turned it off again. But once he landed in Vancouver he wouldn't be able to procrastinate any longer. He thought briefly about Sarah Patterson, and wondered if she had made it to the city while he was away.

The answer machine on his home phone wasn't as full of messages as his email account, and once he'd dumped his bags and made a quick tour around his apartment he quickly flipped through them. He stopped when he came to a voice he recognized immediately: it was a message from Sarah Patterson. It had been left a few days earlier and it was short: she wasn't sure when he was coming back from the field, she said, but could he give her a call when he had the time? There were a few loose ends from her thesis work that she wanted to talk to him about. She left her number and Doucet scribbled it down on piece of paper next to the phone.

There were other messages too, but most of them were either from people trying to sell something or charitable organizations asking for donations. He deleted them all. When he'd finished he looked again at the number Sarah had given him. It wasn't a British number – she must be back in the U.S. The area code looked familiar and when he checked he realized why: it was Seattle. Right next door, almost.

For the first few days after his return from the field he worked almost around the clock, spending his days at the Diatek offices and most of the nights at UBC analyzing samples. There were a few outliers but nearly all the grains he analyzed indicated that the field team had been successful: they had located a diamond-bearing kimberlite. Once he was sure, Tim Bailey told him he deserved a day off, and he went home and fell into bed and slept so soundly that he woke not knowing where he was. It was already dark; he'd been asleep for at least nine hours, but after two cups of coffee and several pieces of toast slathered with peanut butter he felt human again. He could relax; he didn't need to go back to the lab tonight. Finally he could call Sarah Patterson and find out what she wanted to talk to him about.

"It's a long story," she said when he reached her, "How much time have you got?"

"Until today I didn't have five minutes I could call my own," he said, "or at least that's what it felt like. I've been working night and day on samples I brought back from the field. It's completely confidential, but there's a good chance we've located another diamond deposit."

"Fantastic," she said. She sounded genuinely pleased. "That must feel good. Actually, I'd like to talk to you about work – about Diatek, anyway – that's why I left the message. There are a few things I found in my thesis research that still puzzle me. I'm just curious, I guess."

"What kinds of things?"

"Mostly financial, but a few other things too. It's stuff I didn't go into in my thesis, but it's still rattling around in my brain and I thought you might be able to help. For me, now's a good time to pursue it, while it's fresh."

"I'm no expert on company finances," Doucet said, "but I can always try." He thought for a moment. "What are you doing next Sunday?"

"Next Sunday? Nothing as far as I know. Why?"

"How about having brunch? I could drive down to Seattle and we could look at your questions together. We can talk about Diatek all afternoon if you want."

"But … that would be great, but I don't want to put you out. It's a long way to come for brunch."

"It's not that bad, actually, just a couple of hours. I've done it before, several times, and anyway I like driving. And I could forget about work for a day – well, sort of. I'd be happy to do it."

He put her address into Google maps and got to her apartment just after eleven. When she opened the door Doucet thought she was the most beautiful sight he'd seen in a long time. He was glad he'd decided to drive down here.

"Don't just stand there," she said, "come on in. How are you? You're the first visitor to my new apartment." She led him down the hall into a sparsely furnished living room. "My furniture is still in storage so it's a bit bare, but make yourself at home. Just give me a couple of minutes and then we can go. I'll be right with you."

While she was gone he wandered across the living room, which still smelled faintly of fresh paint and new carpets, and into the kitchen. He took a small package from his pocket and put it on a counter where he was sure Sarah would see it.

"A little housewarming gift," he said when she returned. He had wanted to find something different to bring her, and then he'd had an inspiration. He hoped she'd like it.

"Thank you – you didn't need to do that." She took off the wrapping paper and opened the box inside and pulled out a strange looking object. "It's beautiful," she said, "but what is it?"

"It's an Inuksuk. That's an Inuit word. They've become a kind of national symbol in Canada, you see them all over the place now. The real ones, though, originated in the far north and often they're just piles of stones out on the tundra, like cairns. They can be very big – this is just a mini version – and some of them are quite old. The Inuit use them as place markers or for directions because you can see them for miles. I got this one at the museum shop out at the university, where I go to do my lab work. I thought it would be appropriate – stones from a geologist." He laughed.

Sarah was watching him. "Thank you Rick Doucet. That was incredibly thoughtful of you. Once my furniture gets here I'll find just the right spot for him." She put the small stone figure down on the counter. "For the moment he can guard the kitchen."

The restaurant was a little over a mile from her apartment; Doucet said he'd drive but Sarah said no, they should walk, that after living in London for a year she was used to walking everywhere and she was thinking she might not even get a car in Seattle. Besides, walking is a lot better for you. She said the restaurant came highly recommended by people at work so she'd made a reservation, and when they arrived their table was waiting, festively decorated with small gourds and dried plants.

While they sipped coffee and waited for their food – Doucet had ordered the huevos rancheros breakfast and Sarah scrambled eggs with silver dollar pancakes on the side – she told him about her new job. Appropriately for Seattle it was with a non-profit organization that worked with coffee growers in Central and South America to bring fair trade coffee to U.S. markets. She waited until after they'd eaten to bring up the subject of Diatek.

"Like I said on the phone, there are some things about Diatek that still puzzle me." She took a thick stack of papers from her backpack and put them on the table beside her.

"If we're going to go through all of that," Doucet said, "maybe we'd better order more coffee. I hope it's not all financial data. The only part of company finances I pay much attention to is my paycheck."

Sarah laughed. "Don't worry, it's not that bad. But one thing that interests me about Diatek is that it's been a pretty successful company, more so than the other Canadian companies I looked at. Yes, your diamond production has gone up and down, but

Diatek has been consistently profitable almost since the day it started operating."

"That I do know something about. It's mainly a function of output from the mine coupled with world prices. DeBeers, where I used to work, has been pretty successful at keeping world diamond prices relatively high – they're kind of like an OPEC for diamonds; they have a huge reserve and at least until recently they've been able to release diamonds to the market in ways that keep the prices high. Obviously that's been good for Diatek. Our production went down this past spring – by quite a bit, actually – but we're still doing okay."

"Yes, most of that I know," Sarah said. "I've got graphs of diamond production from all the Canadian companies since they first started. And of world prices, although that's tricky because diamond pricing is so individual – at least for the more costly diamonds. But where I have a problem is with things that are less obvious. Here, let me show you."

She leafed through her stack of papers and pulled out several to show to Doucet. "These are spreadsheets I've put together from the publicly available financial data. It's a way of looking at company financials that a group of us devised at McKinsey, and sometimes it gives you a clearer picture of what's really going on – like details of things the company might not want to be too obvious. These spreadsheets are just for Diatek, but I've got similar ones for all the other Canadian diamond producers. For the other companies they're straightforward, it's just these ones from Diatek where I come up with a discrepancy."

For the next half hour she led Doucet through the numbers. It was unfamiliar territory for him and a few times he lost the thread of her explanations and just sat there watching and marveling at her total immersion in what she was doing. But even if some of the details escaped him, by the end he was convinced that she was right: some of the numbers literally didn't add up. When you looked at Diatek's diamond production, and then at the reported profits – and when everything else was taken into account – there were discrepancies. Some of them were large.

He shook his head. "I just don't know. When you lay it out like that it looks obvious. Is it possible there are errors in the financial statements? Clerical errors or something like that?"

"I doubt it. Not if the auditors knew what they were doing. So either Diatek had incompetent auditors, or somebody is cooking the books."

"I don't believe it," Doucet said. "I just don't believe someone is knowingly manipulating finances at Diatek. There has to be another explanation."

"That's what I thought too, but I've racked my brain for months and I can't think of any other reason for these differences. I might not have focused on it so much if it wasn't for something one of my ex-colleagues at McKinsey told me about Diatek. I don't think I mentioned this to you before, but he said it's possible there's a link between someone connected with Diatek and the Russian mafia. It's tenuous and word of mouth so of course I didn't say anything about it in my thesis. But I think it's colored the way I look at Diatek."

Doucet laughed. "Come on Sarah. The Russian mafia? You've got to be kidding."

"I must admit it sounds pretty far-fetched. But Peter – he's the one who told me about it – is a smart guy and I have a lot of respect for him. He's skilled at working out the intricacies of corporate structure. At the beginning of my research I found out that Diatek is wholly owned by a holding company – that's common knowledge, and it's not especially unusual, although it's different from all the other Canadian diamond miners. But Peter claims that the real owner might be a billionaire oligarch with links to the Russian mafia. He wouldn't tell me where his information came from, but he was serious."

Doucet shook his head. "Are you sure he wasn't just pulling your leg? It sounds like Alice in Wonderland to me. A Russian billionaire? Diatek is a Canadian company. I've never run into a single Russian there."

Sarah fiddled with her papers. "I know it sounds crazy, but I'm just telling you what he said. And then there's the financial stuff we've just been through." She looked up at Doucet. "Can I ask you to do something for me?"

"Depends what it is. But in principle, sure."

"It's just a thought I had and I'm a little uncomfortable asking, so please say no if you don't want to do it. The thing is, most companies have their own internal financial data that never sees the light of day – it's not in the public domain. It's what their financial people work with, and their accountants. I'm thinking that if I had that kind of data from Diatek I might be able to figure out what's going on. But obviously I can't just ask them for it – it's privileged information. And if there really is something funny going on they'd have even more reason not to give it to me."

"You want me to get you the data? Confidential financial information?"

"I don't want to pressure you. I totally understand if you don't want to do it. I just thought if I had that information it might help to get to the bottom of this financial puzzle …"

Doucet didn't say anything for a full minute. He was trying to process everything Sarah had told him. It was total nonsense of course, but she seemed to believe it. Maybe if he got her the information she wanted she'd let it go. But where would he find it? And if it was proprietary and he gave her copies would it be tantamount to stealing from his own company? He could sense Sarah watching him from across the table, waiting for an answer.

"I don't even know where I'd find that kind of information."

"I'm sure it would all be in a secure electronic database. Everyone keeps their financial data that way now."

"I guess it might be on our internal network – that's where I store all my mineral analyses," Doucet said. "You have to access it from an office computer; even with a password I can't log in from my laptop at home. It's a pain sometimes, but they wanted to keep the data secure. I only use the geochemistry part of the site. There's lots of other stuff I've never looked at; I guess I could check and see if they have financial data there too."

"Thank you, Rick. You've made my day."

Doucet was in no hurry to get back to Vancouver so they took his car and drove to a park that Sarah had heard about but hadn't yet been to; it overlooked Puget Sound and it was breath-takingly beautiful. They walked for miles through the woods and then along a sandy beach, and they watched the sun sink into the western horizon before hurrying back to the car in the near dark, the air turning colder. On the way back they stopped for hot chocolate and pastries and when Doucet dropped Sarah at her apartment building they said their goodbyes. It had been a good day, but for Doucet it had gone by too quickly. Before he knew it he was winding his way through Seattle suburbs toward the interstate and back to Vancouver.

As he drove he kept thinking about Sarah's request for financial data from Diatek. It was one thing to hand over publicly available information, but she had that already anyway. It was quite another to look for confidential data. But he could already feel himself being pulled into something that his better judgement told him wasn't an especially good idea; he knew that in the coming days he would almost certainly search through Diatek's internal network and he also knew that if he found the kind of data Sarah had described he would probably copy it for her.

As he turned these things over in his head, not paying too much attention to the road – traffic was light and he was making good time – he suddenly noticed brake lights flashing on far ahead. He abruptly brought his attention back to the highway and reduced speed, and within a few minutes he came to a dead stop behind a long line of cars. He could hear sirens in the distance and then, on the shoulder, a fire truck and a police car went by, emergency lights flashing. So much for the easy two hour drive. He would not be home until late.

By the time he got past the accident – an SUV had sideswiped a tractor trailer, and the truck had jackknifed – and then through the border controls, he was hungry. He stopped at the first Tim Horton's he saw and ordered two chicken sandwiches and coffee.

"Do you want a drink to go with the second sandwich?" the woman at the counter asked.

Doucet grinned. "They're both for me. So one coffee is fine."

After the frustration of sitting in stop-and-go traffic for more than an hour the food and the lingering memory of his afternoon with Sarah cheered him up. He was still feeling good when he arrived home, but that changed the moment he opened the door and turned on the light. He stood stock still in the doorway trying to comprehend what he was seeing. It was as though a hurricane had passed through. The bookshelves had been emptied and his books strewn across the floor. The coffee table was turned over. His TV was on the sofa, lying on its side.

Oh shit, he thought, I've been robbed. Then a whole series of thoughts flashed through his head. How could this happen? They'd have to get in the front door, and then through the locked door of the apartment. Why did they pick my apartment? It's not even on the ground floor. Did they use the elevator? Did anyone see them? He had a momentary panic: maybe they're still here. But the lights were off and the apartment was quiet; they were probably long gone.

Still, he didn't go in. He took out his cell phone and dialed 911.

By the time the police arrived Doucet had relaxed a bit, but he had still not gone into his apartment. He met them in the lobby; there were three officers, two men and a woman, and the woman took out a notebook and wrote down details and then they all crowded into the elevator and rode up to the apartment in silence.

Every room except the kitchen was a mess: drawers opened and emptied, clothes thrown out of closets, sheets pulled off the bed. Papers everywhere. The room Doucet used as his office was especially bad. Journal articles he'd collected as reference material for his PhD thesis had been dumped out of their boxes and his filing cabinet had been emptied, its contents scattered around the room. He felt violated.

"They were looking for something," the female police officer said, surveying his office. "Do you keep anything valuable in here, anything someone might want to steal?"

"Not really," Doucet said. "I'm a scientist. I keep some stuff from work here but it's not like it's trade secrets or anything."

The officer wrote in her notebook again, then looked back at the previous page. "Downstairs you said you're a geologist, right? You work for a mining company? I don't really know what geologists do, but did you have mineral samples in here? Gold, silver, anything like that?"

Doucet almost laughed. "Nope, nothing." He thought momentarily about Thompson's diamond; it had been sitting on one of his bookshelves for a few weeks back in February but then he'd given it back. "I have a few mineral samples that I've collected over the years but they're not particularly valuable – certainly not valuable enough for someone to break in looking for them." He picked up a lump of rock from the floor and showed it to her. "Like this one." It looked very ordinary, but when he turned it over she could see a beautiful blue crystal projecting out of the rock. "Beryl," he said. "I got it in Italy." He put it down on the desk. "What a mess."

One of the officers who had been checking the other rooms came in. "I don't know what all was in here, but they didn't take the TV or the stereo or the computer. There's a twenty dollar bill in plain sight on the kitchen counter and they didn't even take that. It doesn't look like an ordinary robbery to me. Have you noticed anything missing Mr. Doucet?"

"No, not really. I'll have to look around carefully, but I don't see anything obvious." Doucet was baffled. "It beats me," he said. "I have no idea what they could have been looking for. Maybe they broke into the wrong place. What happens now?"

"I'm afraid we can't do much," the female officer said. She seemed to be the one in charge. "We'll dust the hard surfaces and see if we can get prints, but I'm guessing we won't find much that's useful. We'll take some pictures and file a report, but if there's nothing missing and no one's hurt we can't really do anything else. You'll want to get in touch with your insurance company though. I'd take some pictures if I were you, to show them what happened. It makes it easier. And you can refer to our report."

After the police left Doucet sat down on his sofa and looked at the disaster around him. He felt helpless. He had grown to like his apartment; he'd taken a lot of care with the furnishings and over the several years since he'd moved in he had decorated the walls with photographs – many of them his own – and prints. The place had a comfortable feel to it – *did* have a comfortable feel to it, he reminded himself, before this happened. He wondered what it would be like after he cleaned up.

He stood up with an effort. Okay, he said to himself, stop feeling sorry for yourself. He looked at his watch: it was almost three a.m. Suddenly he was very tired. He could sleep for a few hours and still get to his office in reasonable time in the morning. He had a very busy week coming up; he would have to deal with his apartment later.

CHAPTER 17

Ed Zelensky wasn't happy with progress on what he now thought of as his Russian case. He'd organized surveillance on the addresses Joey had given them, but after two weeks of watching the houses in Kitsilano he wasn't any further ahead and he was considering calling it off. It required a lot of manpower and some of his colleagues were complaining. Zelensky could live with the complaints if he was getting results, but so far he wasn't.

The men who lived in the houses under surveillance came and went at random; they didn't appear to have regular jobs, at least not jobs that followed a schedule, but so far they hadn't done anything to arouse suspicion. They spent a lot of time inside, which made sense if what Joey had said about them working on computer scams was true. Still, nothing serious enough to justify around the clock surveillance. If they were criminals at all they appeared to be low level criminals. However, the intercepted phone calls that he'd been forwarded from the NSA linked them to Alex

Kalinin, the protection racket boss in Calgary, and ultimately to the Russian billionaire Vasily Gagarin. Gagarin was definitely not low level. Zelensky couldn't shake the hunch that he was missing something. He needed a breakthrough.

It came when his phone rang on a Monday afternoon.

"Hello, Zelensky here."

"Ed, it's Helen. How're you doing?"

"I'm fine I guess. But I'm frustrated. I haven't gotten anywhere with those guys your friend Joey told us about. Has he come up with any more information?"

"No, I haven't heard a peep from him. I would have let you know. But I've got something that might interest you."

Zelensky brightened. "Oh? What is it?"

"When we talked to Joey, you mentioned a company called Diatek, right?"

"Jesus, Helen, you've got a good memory. Yeah, I did. I'm surprised you remember."

"Part of the territory, Ed. I file away every detail, you never know when it might come in useful." Helen paused. "So you want to hear the rest?"

"Yes, of course. What have you got?"

"I have a colleague here by the name of Sue Parker. Do you know her?"

"No, it doesn't ring a bell."

"Well, she and I have become pretty good friends. For one, we're both female, and there aren't that many of us on the force. She was on duty last night and she came in early this afternoon, and we just had coffee together."

"Okay," Zelensky said.

"Yeah, well anyway we were talking and she told me about a strange break-in she got called out to last night. Guess what? The guy who was robbed works for Diatek. She just mentioned it casually, she said he worked for a mining company here in town called Diatek and asked me if I'd ever heard of it. I thought it sounded familiar but I just shook my head no, and then later I remembered that it was the company you asked Joey about. It's probably a coincidence but I thought you should know."

Zelensky grabbed a pen and wrote 'Diatek' on the pad on his desk, and circled it. "Where was the break-in, Helen? Do you have the address?"

"Yes, I asked Sue if I could have a copy of the report – she didn't ask why I wanted it, and I didn't volunteer anything, but I'll send it over if you like. I've got it right here … hang on for a second." She read out the address to Zelensky. "The guy is a geologist; Sue remembered that because he showed her some of his mineral samples. She said they were really beautiful. The strange thing is, whoever broke in didn't take the minerals or anything else. Sue said they really trashed the place, she figures they were looking for something specific and maybe got a bit frustrated when they couldn't find it. The guy's name, the one who got robbed, is Richard Doucet. Dr. Richard Doucet, actually, he's got a PhD. He told Sue he had no idea what they could have been looking for."

Zelensky wrote 'Richard Doucet' on his pad and drew an arrow between the geologist's name and Diatek. "Can you send me over a copy of that report right away? I'd like to take a look at it. I might go have a talk with this Mr. Doucet. I owe you one, Helen."

"No problem. Just keep me in the loop, okay?"

Zelensky sat back and thought about what he had just learned. He looked again at the address he'd written on his pad and had a glimmer of recognition. It was vaguely familiar. He took out the weekend surveillance log and started to leaf through it. There it was: Sunday night one of the guys from his team had followed two men from one of the houses in Kitsilano to the very same address. They had been wearing backpacks, the report said, and although the watcher was some distance away it looked as though they had tried several buzzers before the doors finally opened. They were in the building for over an hour and they still had their backpacks on when they left. They went straight back to the house in Kitsilano, and the surveillance team didn't see them again until the next morning.

Well, well, Zelensky said to himself. This gets more and more curious by the minute. Maybe I'd better keep that surveillance going for a while longer.

He looked at the pad on his desk where he'd written 'Diatek' and 'Richard Doucet.' There were other connections too, he realized, quite a few of them. Writing things down always helped him visualize links, and he picked up his pen and began to jot down everything he could think of that might be related: Alex Kalinin. Calgary. Moscow. Gagarin. Andropov. Luanda. Accident. William Thompson. Vancouver. Break-in. He didn't understand it yet, but in one way or another all of those things were somehow linked to Diatek. Some of the connections were tenuous, but they were there. There was no way it could all be coincidence.

He picked up his phone and called Helen.

"Hi Helen, it's Ed."

"That was quick. What's up?"

"I think I know who broke into that apartment where the Diatek guy lives."

"Tell me."

"I've had a team watching those addresses Joey gave us. On Sunday night one of my guys followed two people from one of the houses, and guess where they ended up? The same apartment complex where the geologist from Diatek lives. I can't be absolutely sure they're the ones who broke in because my guy obviously couldn't follow them inside, but it just can't be a coincidence. They spent a little more than an hour in the building altogether."

Silence on the other end of the line. Then Helen said, "Wow. Do you want to talk to Sue about it?"

"Maybe eventually, but not yet. I want to keep watching these guys for a while and the fewer people who know the better. I mean, as far as your friend Sue's concerned, she's probably filed her report and considers the case is closed, right? So can we keep it between the two of us for now?"

"Alright, but let me know when you change your mind. I feel funny not telling her."

They said goodbye and Zelensky turned to his computer. He had bookmarked the Diatek web page and he brought it up and found a short bio for Dr. Richard Doucet. The website highlighted the geologist's stellar academic record and research achievements and noted that he had worked for DeBeers in South Africa before joining Diatek. No hint of a Russian connection. Zelensky scratched his head. I think I need to go talk to him.

He didn't want to walk in on him at work, that would be too public. It was already five-thirty and he decided that if he waited a bit he might be able to catch Mr. Doucet at home. But when he got there just before seven and rang the bell there was no answer. A couple who lived in the building arrived and opened the door while he was standing there, and they asked Zelensky if he wanted to come in. Trusting souls, he thought, and shook his head. "Thanks, but no, I don't think the person I'm looking for is home. Do you know Mr. Doucet? Richard Doucet?"

The couple looked at one another and shook their heads simultaneously. "No," the woman said. "But it's a big apartment building. There are lots of people here we don't know."

"Okay, thanks," Zelensky said. He turned to go, then turned back. He couldn't resist being a policeman. "It's not a good idea to let strangers into your building," he said. The couple stopped in the doorway and looked at him. "You can never tell," he said. "If you don't know them, don't let them in."

The man shrugged and shut the door, and Zelensky went back to his car shaking his head and drove home. The next evening, though, he was back and this time he was in luck. Doucet buzzed him in and when he knocked at the apartment door it opened almost immediately – but only a crack. Doucet kept the security chain in place.

"I'd like to see some ID please."

Zelensky held up his badge and the geologist examined it carefully before he unlatched the chain and let him in. He looked younger than Zelensky expected, a trim man with a small, neat beard.

"Rick Doucet," he said, and held out his hand. Zelensky shook it. "A week ago I probably would have just let you in, no questions asked. But this," – he gestured vaguely around – "this has made me extra cautious." Doucet had cleared out a small space in the middle of the room, but there were books and papers scattered everywhere.

"I understand. A burglary will do that to you." They were still standing near the door and Zelensky said, "Mind if I sit down? I'd like to ask you some questions."

"Oh, sure," Doucet said. He shut the door and the two men sat across from one another, Zelensky on the sofa and Doucet in an armchair. Doucet wondered why the RCMP was interested in the burglary, but he didn't say anything.

Zelensky cleared his throat and then told Doucet that he was doing a follow up to the initial police investigation. "I'll probably ask some of the same questions, but don't worry about it. We do it all the time because sometimes it brings out an overlooked detail, something you've just remembered, that could be important. Let's start with motives. Have you discovered anything missing since the police were here? Or have you had any thoughts about why someone would want to break into your place?"

"No, that's the weird thing. There's nothing missing that I can see. I think that policewoman was right, they must have been looking for something specific because they turned the whole place upside down. But I have no idea what it could be.

The only thing I can think of is that they made a mistake and broke into the wrong apartment."

Given what he knew Zelensky didn't believe it was a mistake, but he didn't pursue it. "Where were you when all this happened?"

"I was gone all day Sunday and got back late – I drove down to Seattle to see a friend."

"Okay. Who knew you'd be away? And could you give me your friend's name and address? I didn't see it in the original report."

Doucet thought for a moment. "I don't think anyone knew I'd be gone. Except Sarah. I mean I was just going to be away for the day, I didn't mention it to anyone at work or here in the building."

Zelensky nodded. "Sarah is your friend in Seattle? Have you known her long?"

"Yeah … I haven't known her too long actually. Less than a year, I guess. I've been helping her out with some research she's doing." Doucet colored slightly and Zelensky noticed. He was very good at reading people's moods and emotions.

"Her address and contact details?"

"Oh, right." Doucet got up and came back with a laptop. "I keep everything on here," he said, and gave Zelensky Sarah's address.

When he'd finished writing it down in his notebook Zelensky said, "The police report says you're a geologist."

"Yes, I'm a geochemist if you want to be precise. I work on the chemistry of minerals."

Zelensky didn't know what that meant but he let it go and continued. "Is there any way this could be connected with your work? Anything you do that someone might want badly enough that they'd break into your place?"

"They asked me the same thing the other night. There are things we don't want our competitors to know, but that stuff never leaves the office. I don't have any confidential information here, it's all stored in the company's internal computer network." As he said it Doucet thought about Sarah's request for confidential Diatek financial data. But that was completely different. It couldn't have anything to do with the break-in at his apartment.

"Did you want to add anything?" Zelensky had seen a flicker of doubt cross Doucet's face, as though he was about to say something.

"No," Doucet said. "I was just thinking … it's nothing."

Zelensky closed his notebook and put it back in his jacket. "Well, if you do think of something, give me a call. Anything at all, even if you don't think it's important. Sometimes the most unlikely information helps." He handed Doucet his card.

At the door Zelensky paused. "Geologists travel a lot, don't they? Go to all sorts of exotic places to study rocks?"

Doucet grinned. "Yes, it's one of the things that attracted me to the field in the first place. Why?"

"Have you ever worked in Russia? Nothing to do with this," – he gestured around the room – "I'm just curious. My grandparents were from Russia – well, actually from Ukraine, but it was part of the Soviet Union in those days – and I studied

Russian history at university, so I'm always interested to talk to people who've been there."

"No," Doucet said, shaking his head. He thought it was an odd question. "I've worked in lots of places, but never in Russia. They have plenty of their own geologists, actually, because of all the natural resources."

After Zelensky left Doucet looked around his apartment and shook his head. He couldn't bring himself to start sorting things out, and besides he'd come straight back from work just before the policeman arrived and hadn't had anything to eat since lunch. His refrigerator was almost empty and the apartment was depressing. It seemed like a good night for pub food. And there was an Irish pub half a mile from his apartment that he could walk to; they served Guinness and Murphy's and Irish stew, but they also served burgers. Thick, juicy burgers with home cut fries. Somehow that seemed appropriate tonight.

It's like developing a photograph, Zelensky thought as he drove home. Solving a case like this is just like developing a picture in a darkroom; you start with nothing and gradually it gets clearer until finally you see everything.

Zelensky's father was an amateur photographer, a good one, and as a boy Zelensky had often helped him in the tiny basement darkroom that his dad had built. Of course now his father was quite old and if he took photos at all he used a digital camera and printed them from a computer, but Zelensky had fond memories of the time he'd spent in that little darkroom: the peculiar smell of the chemicals, the darkness lit only by the feeble red safelight, and especially the magic of an image gradually appearing on a blank sheet of photo paper as his father swirled it gently in a pan of developing solution. Later he learned about the chemistry behind the process, how the salts in the photographic paper got reduced to the tiny black grains of silver that made the image, but even then he liked to think there was a bit of magic involved. Magic and skill, getting the timing and temperature and all the other parameters just right to produce a perfect photograph.

I could use a bit of magic right now, he thought. I'm not seeing the whole picture. What role does Doucet play? He was about to say something back there, I'm sure of it. Is he hiding something? Does he know what those guys were looking for in his apartment? Zelensky sighed and rubbed his hand across his eyes. Let it go, he told himself. Think about something else, let your subconscious work on it. Maybe the answer will float up, unbidden. It wouldn't be the first time it had happened.

CHAPTER 18

Alex Kalinin had never hesitated to help out his Russian cousin. But this whole thing with the diamond mining company was turning out to be more than he had bargained for, and it wasn't bringing him any revenue. In fact, it was costing him. Kalinin was very sensitive about his cash flow. Still, helping out bought him the goodwill of his cousin, and Gagarin had become such an important figure in Russia that Kalinin had long ago decided not to complain. Who knows when the shoe would be on the other foot, and he'd be the one asking for a favor?

But now his two guys in Vancouver, Igor Petrov and Viktor Churkin, had messed up. He'd sent them out to Vancouver a year ago – nothing to do with his cousin's interest in Canadian diamonds but just to get the lay of the land, to see if he should expand his operations to the coastal city. They were two of the best he had and they complemented one another; Victor was a magician with computers and Igor was a thug who could hold his own in any situation. Until now Kalinin had been happy with the way things were going in Vancouver. So when he heard about their mistake he was surprised. And angry.

It was yet another operation connected with his cousin's Canadian diamond enterprise. Dimitri Andropov – Kalinin rarely heard directly from his cousin – had asked him to find out if a Diatek employee named Doucet, who worked at the company's Vancouver headquarters, had received any communications from the engineer William Thompson. Do whatever it takes, Andropov had said, and make sure that Doucet doesn't talk about it afterwards. It's possible Thompson sent him a document and a video; if he did, destroy them. Kalinin had passed on the instructions to Viktor and Igor.

But they had been sloppy and broke into Doucet's apartment without first confirming he was at home. So they couldn't question him, and they didn't find anything from Thompson, either.

"Jesus Christ," Kalinin said when they told him, "what the fuck were you thinking? You should have made sure he was there before you went in. Now you'll have to do it all over again. Track this guy down, rough him up a bit, find out what Thompson told him. If he has a video or a statement make sure you get every copy that exists. Scare the shit out of him so he'll never mention it to anyone. And don't let him see your faces," he added.

But they had done one thing right. It was Viktor's idea, he was the technical one. He'd left two bugs in the apartment, one in the phone in Doucet's bedroom, the other concealed in a small cavity on the underside of a coffee table in the living room. He hadn't heard much from the bug in the phone;

like a lot of people Doucet used his cell phone for most of his calls. But the one in the living room was proving useful. It was powerful and Viktor had been able to follow most of what was said between Doucet and the police officers immediately after the break-in. And he had no trouble with the conversation between Doucet and another police officer two days later, either. Nothing Doucet said gave any indication that he knew about Thompson or any papers or video. All the same, to satisfy Kalinin they were going to have to grab the guy and push him around a bit. Igor thrived on that kind of thing, but Viktor didn't like it.

Meanwhile, Doucet was having a difficult week. The break-in had thrown him; he found it difficult to focus on his work. He usually went to his office or the lab looking forward to whatever challenges the day might throw at him, but not now. Other things kept intruding. The insurance company was giving him the runaround about sending out an inspector, Bill Thompson's lawyer wanted to meet with him about filing for a legal declaration of death – in spite of an intensive search, the divers Diatek had brought in hadn't recovered a body, so they'd need the declaration before they could proceed with the estate – and then there was the Diatek financial data he'd promised to get for Sarah. On top of it all the RCMP officer, Edward Zelensky, had called him twice asking if he'd thought of anything else that might relate to the break-in. He hadn't, and he was a bit annoyed at the man's persistence.

By Thursday morning he still hadn't done anything about the data for Sarah. He had been procrastinating – what if someone came up and looked over his shoulder just as he was downloading sensitive information? But he steeled himself. It's no big deal, he told himself, just do it. Take a look at lunchtime when there aren't many people around.

As it turned out, almost everyone went out. "Sorry," Doucet said when they asked if he was coming, "I've got too much to do; I'll have to take a rain check. Can you bring me a sandwich? Roast beef on a baguette if they have it? With horseradish."

When they were gone Doucet exhaled in the silence and looked around. Hardly anyone was left, even Tim Bailey had gone out. He logged into the Diatek system and started his search. The database was supposed to be an internal resource organized so that authorized employees could quickly get the information they needed for their work. In principle it couldn't be accessed from outside, but Doucet wondered how secure it would be for an experienced hacker. If they could hack into the Pentagon they probably wouldn't have much trouble accessing Diatek's supposedly secure data. So if he wasn't able to download the information Sarah needed, maybe she could hire a hacker. Doucet shook his head at the thought. What am I thinking? he wondered.

The database was set up in sections; the ones he usually worked with, the geochemistry and geophysics sections, were by far the largest. They contained reports, geological maps, reams of remote sensing data from aeromagnetic surveys, and hundreds and hundreds of Doucet's own chemical analyses. He knew the contents like the back of his hand. The other sections, though, were virgin territory for him.

He clicked through the administration and HR sections just to see what was there and discovered that access to personal data was restricted and required further passwords. Fair enough, he thought, better to keep personal information confidential. Then he turned to the financial section. It was neatly organized, with headings and sub-headings and sub-sub-headings. Just as you would expect from accountants, he thought. And there were a lot of files. He looked at his watch. Probably not enough time to pick and choose; I'll just download everything and look at it later, he decided. He took a new thumb drive from his desk and started copying, watching the file names flash across the screen as the data was transferred. Then, suddenly, the whole process came to a stop and an 'Access Denied' message appeared. "Dammit," Doucet said under his breath.

One whole block of financial data was locked, protected by another layer of security. Access required additional passwords. Trying to get in would be asking for trouble, Doucet realized. He didn't want anyone to know he was nosing around, and he guessed he might leave electronic traces if he tried to break in. He skipped over the protected folders and continued copying the rest of the data, then logged out and slipped the thumb drive into his pocket. Not too difficult, he thought – and his pulse rate was still normal. He'd send what he had to Sarah and think about how he might be able to retrieve the restricted data later.

When Doucet's colleagues got back from lunch he was working on his geochemical data. "The sandwich is on me," Tim Bailey said and plunked a brown paper bag down on Doucet's desk. "Since you're working so hard."

If he only knew what I was doing while he was eating lunch, Doucet thought. But he looked up and grinned. "Thanks, I appreciate it. I'll probably be staying late tonight too if you want to buy me dinner ..."

"You wish," Bailey said and went back to his office.

By eight-thirty that night Doucet was ready to go home. He had been sitting at his computer for hours and he'd had enough, but before shutting down he stood up and stretched and walked around the office for a few minutes. The thumb drive with the data he'd downloaded for Sarah was still in his pocket. But how was he going to access those files that required another password? Then he stopped and stood still. Probably all the financial data Sarah could ever want would be on Jim Mulroney's computer. Mulroney was the CFO; his office was on the next floor. It was late and almost certainly he'd already gone home. *Everybody* on that floor has probably gone home, Doucet thought, they're all administrators. They watch the clock.

He took the stairs up one level and slowly opened the door into the hall. As far as he could tell it was deserted – except for the cleaner. He could see her cart down at the end of the hall, one of the office doors open, light spilling out into the corridor. That could be a problem. He didn't want her to see him sneaking into Mulroney's office. But then he had an idea. He took a deep breath and headed toward the open office.

"Hi Gabriela," he said, poking his head around the door.

"Oh ... Mr. Doucet, you scared me! I didn't know anyone was here."

"Yeah, it's just me. I'm here late as usual. Sorry if I startled you."

Doucet knew the cleaner well. She was a friendly Portuguese woman who came in every night to clean the Diatek offices, and because he was often still at work she would sometimes stop to chat with him. She'd proudly shown him pictures of her daughter and two grandchildren.

"How are those grandchildren, Gabriela?" he asked.

She beamed. "They're good, Mr. Doucet. The older one, he just started school this year. He's going to be a good student. Maybe a doctor, or a scientist like you."

Doucet nodded. "Great. Say, Gabriela, could you do me a favor? Mr. Mulroney – he has one of the offices down the hall here – he was supposed to give me some papers before he left, but he forgot. I called him at home and he says they're still in his office, but I don't have a key. Could you open it up for me?"

"Sure Mr. Doucet, no problem." She put down her mop and took out a bundle of keys. "Which one is it?"

"Here, I'll show you," Doucet said, and they walked down the hall together toward Mulroney's office.

"You shouldn't work so hard, Mr. Doucet. You should get married, have some kids. That would be good for you." She laughed. "Have you got yourself a girlfriend yet?"

"Not really. I did meet a nice girl though, only trouble is she doesn't live in Vancouver. She's down in Seattle. So I don't know how that's going to work out."

Gabriela sighed. "You young people, you're always all over the place." She opened the door to Mulroney's office. "Here you go Mr. Doucet. You can leave the door open when you're finished. I'll be down here to clean in a little while anyway. Have a nice weekend."

"Thanks Gabriela. You too."

Doucet turned on the lights and waited until she'd gone and then walked over to Mulroney's desk. Am I really doing this? he asked himself. The computer was on standby and when he turned it on a login screen came up.

"Okay, first problem," he said under his breath. "What's his password?" Everybody writes down their passwords somewhere, he thought. He opened the drawer in Mulroney's desk: pens, elastic bands, several hand calculators, a few coins. No passwords. He leafed through the papers on the desk; still nothing. Then he noticed a yellow post-it note stuck on the side of the printer. It had the name of Mulroney's boat - *SevenSeas* - written on it, and below that a long string of letters and numbers. Aha! That has to be it, Doucet said to himself. He typed in the boat's name and the password and hit enter and the screen filled with a picture of Mulroney's boat, a wooded island in the background. It was beautiful, but he didn't have time to admire the image. He knew Gabriela would be working her way down the hall and he wanted to be finished before she reached Mulroney's office.

He didn't even need to log into the Diatek network because Mulroney kept everything on the hard drive of his office computer. There were hundreds of files, maybe even thousands, and Doucet didn't know which ones were important and which he could ignore. He decided to start at the beginning and copy everything. He probably wouldn't get it all tonight, but he'd get as much as possible and come back another night or on the weekend and keep going. He might even need another memory stick. He wrote down Mulroney's password on a piece of paper and put it in his wallet.

When he heard the sound of Gabriela's vacuum in the next office he stopped and turned the computer back to standby. He put the memory stick into his pocket and straightened up the papers on the desk and took one last look around – everything looked just as it had when he came in. He turned off the light and went out into the hall. Gabriela was just coming out of the office next door.

"Still here Mr. Doucet? Did you find what you needed?"

"Yeah, thanks Gabriela. Took me longer than I thought, but I found it. Goodnight. Take care."

"Goodnight Mr. Doucet."

This time Igor and Viktor didn't make a mistake. Kalinin had sent them a photograph of Doucet from the internet and they waited for him at his apartment building, standing in the shadows when he drove into the parking garage. He was still thinking about the files from Mulroney's computer and he didn't even notice the two Russians. He got out of the car and started to walk toward the elevator and the next thing he knew someone had grabbed him from behind, an arm around his neck and a hand clamped on his right arm. It was so unexpected that his reaction was completely reflexive. He swung his briefcase back against the attacker and twisted violently, breaking the hold on his neck. Adrenalin coursed through his system and he broke free, but he stumbled and went down on one knee. As he scrambled up he didn't even see the fist; it hit him hard on the right side of his face and then glanced across and smashed into his nose. His brain registered the crunch of fist hitting cartilage and he thought in surprise, he's broken my nose, and then he was falling in slow motion and everything went black.

"Shit," Igor said, looking around. "I shouldn't have hit him so hard. We can't take him up to the apartment like this, someone might see us. It wouldn't look good, he's out cold and he's bleeding like a stuck pig. Let's throw him in the back of the van. Quick."

Igor grabbed Doucet's arms and Viktor took his feet and they lifted him into the van like a sack of flour. "Get a blindfold on him," Igor said. "And prop up his head." He laughed. "We don't want him to suffocate. He won't be able to breathe through his nose for a while, that's for sure. I think I might have broken it. And get a cloth or something to stop the bleeding."

Viktor got in the back and Igor shut the doors behind him and climbed into the driver's seat. For a few moments he sat there, thinking. Then he turned to Viktor. "I think we'd better do this somewhere else, where we won't be disturbed. Any ideas?"

"What about that place we went with the mountain bikes? Out by the university? Remember where we parked at the head of the trail? It's off the road and nobody's going to be there at night."

Viktor never seemed to forget anything. "Good thinking," Igor said as he started the van. "Keep an eye on our patient, okay?"

Twenty minutes later they pulled into a very dark and secluded parking lot. It was surrounded by tall pine trees that muffled the sound of passing cars. "I think he's coming around,"

Viktor said. Doucet had started to moan as they bumped down the rutted road.

"Good. Let's do this outside, the fresh air will wake him up. We can sit him at that table over there. Make sure the blindfold is secure, okay? We don't want him to see our faces. And stay behind the flashlights just to be sure."

Doucet moaned again when they picked him up and carried him to the wooden picnic table. "What's happening?" he said. His words were slurred; he was still very groggy. Neither Viktor nor Igor said anything. They set him down and tied his hands together behind him and looped the rope over the seat and around his ankles. When they were satisfied he couldn't move Igor emptied a large bottle of water over his head.

It was cold and he gasped at the shock and jerked upward, gulping in air through his mouth. He couldn't breathe at all through his nose, and his whole face ached. "Shit," he said and shook his head and then stopped because it hurt so much. "Shit," he said again, "it hurts."

"Yeah, it probably does," Igor said. "If you cooperate I won't have to hurt you again."

"Where am I?" Doucet asked. "I can't see anything? What do you want? You can have my wallet, there's about a hundred dollars in it." He was very uncomfortable; they had propped him up awkwardly and something hard was digging into his back. His whole face ached and when he tried to move the rope cut into his ankles.

"We don't want your wallet. What's your name?" Igor was sure they had the right person, but he didn't want to screw up again. Kalinin would have their heads.

Doucet noticed the accent. It wasn't strong, but it was there. Not French or German or Spanish, but maybe eastern European. A vaguely Slavic sound. He filed the information away.

"My name? What the … Doucet. My name is Rick Doucet. Why do you want to know?"

Igor just grunted. Then he said, "You know William Thompson, right? The engineer Bill Thompson?" This time Kalinin had written out a series of questions for them to ask Doucet. Victor was supposed to write down the answers, in Russian.

Doucet was so stunned it took him a minute to answer. "Bill Thompson? The mining engineer at Diatek? I knew him, yes, but he's dead. He's been dead for six months."

Igor and Viktor looked at one another. Kalinin had told them the whole story but unless Doucet was faking it sounded as though he didn't know about Thompson. Still, they followed the script and kept asking him questions.

"Did he ever give you any papers about his work at the mine? Or a video?"

This is surreal, Doucet thought. Am I dreaming? But the rope on his ankles and wrists felt very real, and he could feel a cold wind on his face. Occasionally he heard the whine of car tires; they must be close to a road. He clearly wasn't dreaming.

"A video? Bill Thompson? I've got a copy of his will, that's all." Although his face was throbbing with pain Doucet was starting to think more clearly. He had no idea what they were going to do to him, but he forced himself to memorize everything that was happening. That RCMP officer had told him that sometimes a little detail was really important. He was going to store everything he could in his memory.

The questions went on for another ten or fifteen minutes, Doucet couldn't be sure exactly how long, but eventually his captors seemed to run out of steam. It was almost as though they were losing interest. Eventually one of them said, "Okay, Doucet, we're going to take you back now. But a little bit of advice. This ride tonight didn't happen. Nobody asked you any questions. *Nothing* happened, you just went home from work. Okay, maybe you walked into a door and hurt your nose if anyone asks. But nothing else. Understand?"

Doucet nodded, slowly.

"We know where you live and we'll be watching. One word, to anyone, and we'll find you again. Next time it won't be so pleasant." It wasn't entirely true, they couldn't spend their time monitoring Doucet. But Alex Kalinin had taught Igor about threats. Keep it simple, he'd said, don't be too specific. Let them use their imagination; they'll imagine the worst. In the protection rackets, that had usually worked.

Doucet could feel them untying the rope and then they pulled him up, but they'd left his ankles and wrists bound together so he couldn't walk. One of them grabbed him under the arms and the other took his legs and they hoisted him up into some kind of vehicle. They drove for about twenty-five minutes, he estimated, then went down a ramp and stopped.

"We're going to untie you now and walk you over to your car," one of the men said. Doucet realized they were back in the parking garage at his apartment. "Act normal, and don't touch the blindfold or I'll make sure your face is in even worse shape than it already is." The ropes came off and Doucet flexed his hands and feet, trying to get the circulation back. They pulled him roughly from the van and guided him, unseeing, to his car. "Just sit here and relax for a while and think about what we've said. Don't get out and don't take off that blindfold for at least fifteen minutes. Okay?"

Relax? Are they trying to be funny? "Okay," he mumbled, and they shoved him into the car and slammed the door.

CHAPTER 19

Doucet sat still for several minutes and then he started to shake. For most of his ordeal he'd stayed calm, but now he couldn't control it. Shock, he thought, or maybe I'm just cold. He could feel his teeth chattering. Once, several years ago, he'd taken an Indian geologist into the field with him in the Northwest Territories. The geologist had spent most of his life working in a hot climate, but in the far north it never really got warm, even in the summer, and the man had been perpetually cold. Whenever Doucet asked him how he was he'd say, "Rick, my teeth are typing." Doucet grinned at the memory and clamped his mouth shut. Can't have my teeth typing, he thought. He grabbed the steering wheel hard and forced himself to breathe deeply. Inhale slowly, exhale, pause. Inhale again ... it was something he'd learned from a classmate in graduate school who often got nervous and tensed up before a presentation. It had amazed Doucet how quickly simple breathing helped his friend relax, and he'd started using it himself. Now it was working again. Gradually the shaking receded. He let his jaw slacken and his teeth stopped chattering.

He had not been paying attention to time, but he was sure his captors were long gone. To be sure he continued his deep breathing for a few minutes, then reached up and took off the blindfold. He'd been in total darkness for so long that even the dim light of the parking garage was a shock and it took his eyes several minutes to adjust. He sat there, blinking, his whole face aching and his stomach sore where they had punched him. What do I do now? he wondered. He reached up and touched his nose; it felt like it was sitting at a strange angle and when he looked in the rear view mirror a stranger looked back at him. His nose *was* at a strange angle; it was bent sideways, almost certainly broken. His face was bruised and smeared with blood. If I don't want to have a permanently bent nose, he thought, I'd better go and get this fixed.

His best option was Emergency at the Vancouver General. Although his face was puffy and his right eye was partly shut he could see well enough to drive so he started the car, half expecting someone to jump out and drag him away again. But nothing happened. Twenty minutes later he was at the hospital.

The woman who checked him in took one look at his face and said, "Oooh. What did you run into, dear?" She had a broad Scottish accent.

"I know. I can't look at myself in the mirror. I had a stupid accident, is all." His voice sounded very nasal.

The woman raised her eyebrows. "Not drinking, were we?"

"No, but a few drinks might make it feel better."

She laughed. "Well, we'll have to get this straightened out. So to speak. Have a wee seat, dear. It shouldn't be too long."

Doucet looked up too quickly and a wave of pain surged through his face. "Ouch. I keep forgetting to move my head slowly." He paused. "A wee seat? That's one I haven't heard before."

She grinned. "Aye, it's what we say. Now just go and sit down. They'll be with you soon."

In spite of the woman's optimism, though, it was a long wait. Doucet sat and watched as other patients were rushed through the waiting room on stretchers, paramedics and doctors tending them as they went. He couldn't begrudge them the attention – at least he was upright – but that didn't stop the ache in his face. He tried to distract himself by going over everything that had happened tonight. Unbelievable that just a few hours ago he was driving home from work, a normal evening, no inkling of the reception that awaited him. He was completely baffled by what had happened. First someone breaks into the apartment, throws things around but doesn't take anything. Then a couple of guys beat me up, don't want my money, but they take me off somewhere and ask questions about Bill Thompson. It's totally bizarre. Does it have something to do with the will? He shook his head in frustration and winced as the pain shot through his face again.

It was after midnight when they let him go. They had been concerned when he said that he'd been knocked unconscious, but he wasn't nauseous and he answered all their questions and told them he felt fine except that his whole face hurt, so they gave him painkillers and told him to go home and take it easy for a few days. If he had any dizziness or blurred sight, they said, or if he started to forget things, he should see his doctor.

By the time he got back to the car he was hungry, probably a good sign, he thought. He hadn't eaten anything since the roast beef sandwich Tim Bailey brought him at lunchtime. He thought for a minute and then turned south. There was a twenty-four hour Tim Hortons not far away. Tim Hortons was his go-to restaurant when he wanted coffee and food in a hurry.

A few people were sitting at tables drinking coffee but there was no lineup and the woman at the counter did a double take when Doucet walked up. "My goodness, what happened to you?"

Part of his face was now covered in white bandages, and where skin showed under his eyes it was turning an ugly yellow-green color. The doctor had washed away the blood but there were still red blotches on his shirt. He tried to make light of it. "There's a nice face under the bandages," he said, "I had a freak accident, that's all. He ordered a sandwich and a donut and a large coffee and took it to a table by the window. As he sat eating and staring out at the parking lot he realized he really didn't want to go back to his apartment. Maybe in the daylight things would be different but right now he was still on edge. He just couldn't face it, not tonight. Maybe he should check into a hotel.

He finished his food and got another coffee to take with him, still unsure about what he was going to do. He reached into his pocket for the car keys and when he pulled them out he was holding both the keys and a memory stick in his hand. *The* memory stick, the one with Diatek financial data on it. He had completely forgotten about it. The guys who mugged him hadn't searched his pockets, hadn't wanted anything from him except to ask questions. He would have to send it to Sarah.

He got into the car and sat there staring out into the darkness. Or, he thought. Or, he could *take* it to Sarah. Instead of checking into a hotel here he could drive to Seattle. Somehow being in another country, even if it was only the United States, seemed a lot safer than going back to his apartment. He looked at the gas gauge; the tank was almost full, he wouldn't even have to stop for gas. Why not? he thought, and then wondered if he was crazy. Or still in shock. Or was it just that he desperately wanted to see Sarah Patterson again? He took out his cell phone and sent a short text to Tim Bailey. A freak accident at home, he wrote, I broke my nose. I'm okay but I won't be in Friday.

Except for the occasional tractor trailer the highway was almost empty, and the drive south was even easier than he thought it would be. He had a momentary panic when he realized he'd need his passport to cross into the U.S., but then he remembered it was still in his briefcase where he'd left it after last weekend's visit to Seattle. And the briefcase was in the back seat, where he'd thrown it when he left work. That seemed like years ago.

When he got to the border the American immigration people made him get out of the car so they could check his face against his passport photo.

"You don't look much like your photo," the officer said. "What happened?"

Doucet told him he'd had an accident but he had a friend in Seattle and he was sure she'd look after him. The officer laughed and handed back the passport. "Sounds like a plan," he said. "Drive carefully."

It was three-twenty when he pulled into Sarah's street. Every window in her building was dark and the street was very quiet. He'd seen two motels near the exit when he pulled off the interstate and he'd slowed briefly but kept going. *I really am crazy,* he thought as he took out his cell phone. *What is she going to think?* He dialed her number and let it ring, and after what seemed like an eternity she answered.

"Hello?" She sounded half asleep.

"Sarah, it's me, Rick. Rick Doucet."

"Rick ... what in the world? ... What time is it? ... Is something wrong? Your voice sounds funny."

"Yeah, I'm okay. Sort of. I got that financial data you wanted from Diatek."

"Oh, great ... that's great ... but you didn't need to call in the middle of the night. Are you sure you're okay?"

"This is going to sound weird. Something happened, and I'm actually in Seattle. I'm parked right across the street from you. Can I come in?"

"What? You're *here*? Of course you can come in."

She was standing with the door open as Doucet got off the elevator. When she saw him she gasped and put both hands to her face. "What happened?"

"It's a long story," he said, looking at her. Sarah had thrown on a robe and her hair was tousled. She had no makeup on. "I know I probably look like a casualty from MASH but I wanted to bring you this." He took the memory stick from his pocket. "It's the financial data you wanted. I just managed to get it today – or maybe it was yesterday. It's all a blur. I had this urge to bring it myself, right away, before anything else happened. I think I might still be in shock. Sorry to wake you up."

He was swaying on his feet in the doorway and a look of concern came over Sarah's face. "You'd better come in. I'll make some tea."

"No, it's okay, I just wanted to give you the memory stick. I'll check in at one of those hotels by the freeway and we can talk in the morning."

"You're not going anywhere like that," she said and took his hand. He let her lead him to a sofa in the living room. "It's new," she said as he sank into the soft cushions. "They delivered it yesterday. Just in time."

Doucet suddenly felt very tired. He'd been running on adrenalin and caffeine for hours, and now it was catching up with him. He put his head back and shut his eyes. He could hear Sarah saying something from the kitchen, but he couldn't quite make it out. The next thing he knew she was sitting beside him, rubbing his arm. Her hand was warm and it felt good on his skin. He opened his eyes and saw the worry in her face. "You can do that for as long as you like," he murmured.

"You've been out – asleep – since you sat down," Sarah said. "I was worried."

"I'm fine, I'm just tired. Did you already make tea?"

"Yes, a while ago, it's right here." She handed him a mug. "You don't look fine to me. What happened?"

So he told her everything: the break-in at his apartment on Sunday night, the mugging in the parking garage, the interrogation. "I decided there was no way I was going back to my apartment tonight – last night – so I came here. I hope you don't mind…" His voice trailed off and he shut his eyes. Sarah got some blankets from a closet and covered him, then turned off the lights.

When he woke, Doucet had no idea where he was. He was lying on his side and all he could see was a wall and a window. But everything was wrong. The color of the wall, the shape of the window – it wasn't his apartment. And then he remembered. The drive down from Vancouver, Sarah's apartment. How could he have done that? What was he thinking? His face was aching again; the painkillers had worn off. He touched his nose and flinched. Carefully, he rolled over onto his back and stared at the ceiling. It had seemed so simple last night, just get in the car and drive. But now what?

He could hear noises from the kitchen and he thought he could smell coffee, but his nose was completely blocked and it might just be his imagination. How could you smell things if you couldn't breathe through your nose? He slowly pulled back the blankets and sat up, his whole face throbbing every time he moved. He felt stiff and sore all over. He still had on the clothes he'd gone to work in yesterday morning. When he hobbled into the kitchen Sarah looked him up and down for a moment without saying anything.

Then: "The invalid. Sit. I've made coffee."

He sat down and took the cup she handed him. "Sarah, I …"

"Shh. Just enjoy your coffee. We've got plenty of time to talk. I already called my boss and told him I couldn't come in today. I didn't say why, but he's okay with it as long as I do a few things from home. So we've got all day."

CHAPTER 20

Sarah found an old sweat suit and a spare robe for him to wear while they washed his clothes. They barely fit but he struggled into them and when he came out of the bathroom she laughed. "You're quite a sight," she said, "I think you're going to need some new clothes."

She'd been out to the bakery earlier and she put a basket of fresh pastries and rolls on the table. "Cereal? Eggs? What would you like?"

Doucet sat down and she poured more coffee. "I'm fine. This is just right." He took one of the pastries. He seemed distracted. "I can't believe I'm here. I don't know what came over me last night. When I reached into my pocket and found the memory stick I just had the strongest urge to deliver it personally." He shook his head. Gently.

"It's okay. I must admit it was a shock when you appeared in the middle of the night – especially because you looked like you'd just come from the casualty ward. You can stay until you're feeling better, but I really think you should report this to the police. The sooner the better. Do you have any idea who attacked you – or why?"

Again Doucet shook his head. "No clue. I thought maybe the break-in was a mistake, but this mugging definitely wasn't. Those guys knew my name – they were looking for Rick Doucet. They even asked me, to make sure they had the right person. And they kept asking me about Bill Thompson. It was bizarre. He's been dead for half a year, and they wanted to know if he'd sent me a video. A video! I don't understand it. The only remote possibility I can think of is that it has something to do with his will, since I'm the executor. I need to go see his lawyer when I get back."

"It *is* bizarre." She picked up her coffee cup and then put it down again. "To totally change the subject, that memory stick … how did you end up getting the data?"

He told her how he'd logged into the company's internal network and discovered he couldn't access some of the financial data, but then it occurred to him that it was probably all on Mulroney's computer. When he checked it out his hunch turned out to be right.

"Rick – I don't believe it. You copied stuff from your CFO's computer? I didn't mean for you to do anything like that."

"It was kind of weird; I felt like a spy from a le Carré novel. And I only got part of what's there because the cleaner was about to come into his office. Unless you know a good hacker the rest will have to wait until I get another chance to use Mulroney's computer."

He said it in jest, but Sarah looked at him and said, "Actually, I think I might. Know a hacker, that is. There's a woman I work with whose son is obsessed with computers. She's worried about him, she was telling me that all he and his friends do is sit at their computers. He's in high school, I think he's about sixteen. He told her they don't do anything malicious, they just do it for fun. Apparently they put jokes on people's websites and stuff like that, so he must be pretty good. I told her he'll probably be the next Bill Gates, but she's still worried."

Doucet was feeling reckless. "I've got Mulroney's password, it's just a matter of getting through the firewall and into the company's internal network. I don't know how to do that, but maybe your friend's son could do it for us. What do you think? I've gone this far, why not give it a try? Do you feel like giving him a call?"

"I wouldn't want to get him into trouble," Sarah said.

"Me neither. But nobody needs to know he was involved. I'll take the blame if anything goes wrong. Just don't tell his mom what you really want him to do."

Sarah called her friend and said she had a computer problem and wondered if her son might be able to sort it out. She'd pay him by the hour. "I'm not feeling very well today so I'm working at home," Sarah said. "I'll be here all day. He could come over after school. Or tomorrow, if the weekend is better."

An hour later Sarah got a text. He'll be over this afternoon, her friend wrote. Thank you, Sarah. This is what he needs. It will be really good for him to make a little money doing something he likes.

Sarah didn't know what to expect, but when he arrived he looked like any other Seattle teenager, gangly, sloppily dressed, a baseball cap on backwards and a skateboard under his arm.

"I'm Chris," he said as she opened the door for him, "Mom said you had a computer job for me?"

"Hi Chris. I'm Sarah, and this is my friend Rick. Come on in."

Chris's eyes lingered for a moment on Doucet's bandaged face and then he came in and Sarah shut the door behind him. "Your mom told me you're a computer whiz so I thought maybe you could take a look at something for us."

Chris put his skateboard down by the door. "Okay if I leave this here?"

"Sure. The computer's in the other room. Rick can tell you about the problem."

They trooped into the spare bedroom that Sarah used as a makeshift office and storage room, and Chris sat down at the computer.

"Here's the deal," Doucet said, "I need some data from a computer at work but I don't know how to access it remotely. I've got the password and everything but there's a firewall and I don't know how to get in from outside. Is there a simple way to do that? My office is up in Vancouver, so it's not like I can just drive over and get what I need."

"Cool," Chris said. "I've been in Vancouver a couple of times with my parents. I like it there." He grinned at Rick. "So you want me to hack into your company's system?"

"Uh, I guess so, yeah. If that's what you have to do."

"If there's a firewall, that's what I have to do." Chris took off his jacket and put it over the back of the chair. He had on a black sweatshirt with 'Foo Fighters' written across the back. Rick looked at Sarah and raised his eyebrows. Or tried to raise his eyebrows. Once again a sharp pain shot through his injured nose. How long before my brain stops me from moving my face? he wondered.

Sarah shrugged. "What's Foo Fighters?" she asked.

"You don't know? They're a band. From Seattle, and they're really good." Chris turned back to the computer. "Okay, first I need to go to your company's web site. What's it called?"

Doucet told him and Chris brought up the Diatek web site and then plugged in a flash drive he'd brought with him and hunched over the keyboard for several minutes, completely oblivious to everything except what he was doing. Occasionally he'd sit back and scratch his head or say something to himself and then he'd go back to work. It was as though Sarah and Rick were not even in the room.

Then he turned and looked at them with a big smile on his face. "Okay," he said, "I'm in. Looks like there are a bunch of networked computers. Which one do you need?"

"Amazing," Doucet said. He looked at the list on the screen and found the CFO's computer. "This one," he said, pointing, "this is the one we need to log into." He gave Chris the CFO's password.

"Nobody's logged into that computer at the moment, which is good. It's on standby, but I can wake it up."

"Yeah, it's Friday afternoon, the person who uses that computer has already left." Doucet hadn't thought about what might happen if Mulroney was on his computer when they tried to hack in. But he knew the CFO was taking his boat out for the weekend, and that meant he had probably left the office early. His computer would be on standby until Monday morning.

Chris typed in a few more commands and suddenly they were staring at the contents of Mulroney's computer.

"Fantastic," Doucet said, shaking his head. "The files I need are in the financial section. I'll show you." He took the mouse and highlighted a group of folders, and Chris started downloading them.

But after a few minutes a message appeared on the screen: permission denied.

"There's more security for some of these folders," Chris said. "Do you want them too?"

"Yes, but I don't have that password with me."

"No sweat. I have a neat little program that can hack almost any password. Just give me a minute."

A few minutes later they had access to a whole new series of files.

"You are a genius," Doucet said when they had finished copying.

"He's right," Sarah said. "You've got a lot of talent, Chris. You should set up a business doing computer stuff. Do you want some tea? Or a Coke or something?"

Chris seemed a little embarrassed by the praise. He was just having fun, he didn't think of it as work. "Thanks, a Coke would be great."

When he was putting on his coat and getting ready to leave Rick handed him a hundred dollar bill. "This is for you, Chris. What you did is definitely worth it."

Chris's eyes widened. "That's way too much," he stammered. "It only took me about half an hour." He tried to hand the bill back.

"No, you keep it. It's worth it to me. If you hadn't done that I would have had to go back to Vancouver to get that information. So you saved me a lot of money. And a lot of hassle."

After he left Sarah and Rick looked at one another.

"I'll never believe my computer is secure again," Sarah said. "Imagine. He's only sixteen." She shook her head.

"Yes," Doucet said, "thank goodness for teenage hackers. As far as I can tell that's everything from Mulroney's computer that has anything to do with Diatek finances. I hope that gives you what you need."

"The thing is, I don't really know what I need," Sarah said. She was already thinking about how to approach the problem. "I think the best thing would be to take a quick tour through all the files and make an inventory. Then make a priority list of the ones that look most interesting, and start going through them in detail."

She looked over at Doucet. "My God, Rick, you don't look so well." The bruises on his face had turned an ugly blue-black color and the swelling had gotten worse. His eyes had been reduced to slits. "Why don't you lie down? There's no need for you to sit here while I do this."

"Mm. I do feel pretty thrashed. I don't think I'd be much help anyway." He walked to the sofa and lay down, and was asleep almost instantly.

When he woke he was again momentarily disoriented. Then he remembered Chris the hacker and downloading files from Mulroney's computer. It was dark outside, but he had no idea what time it was, and he was sure he could smell the aroma of cooking. Good, he thought, my nose can't be *that* bad.

With an effort he pushed himself up and walked into the kitchen. He had always prided himself on being fit, but now he felt like an old man, his shoulders and hip joints stiff.

Sarah was taking dishes out of the oven. "Well hello. How are you feeling?"

"Decrepit. I think it's all catching up with me. How long was I asleep?"

"A couple of hours. I ordered some Chinese takeout. It's been in the oven to stay warm. Are you hungry?"

After they'd eaten Doucet said he'd considered driving back to Vancouver tonight but didn't think he could do it, he was still exhausted. Would it be okay if he stayed over another night?

"Of course," Sarah said. "I didn't expect you'd be in any shape to go yet anyway. I changed the sheets on my bed, you can sleep in there tonight where you won't be disturbed. I'm going to keep working on those files."

"Sarah, you didn't have to …"

"No arguments. It's fine, just go and sleep when you're ready. You need it."

The next morning Doucet was feeling much better. He gently touched his face around the edge of the bandages; it was still puffy but not as painful as it had been the day before. The sun streaming through the bedroom window helped his mood and he lay on his back for a long time, thinking about the events of the past week, and what he needed to do next. When he heard the door open he turned to see Sarah peering into the room.

"Just checking to see if you were conscious," she said. "Stay there, I'll be right back."

She returned a few minutes later with a tray and two steaming mugs of coffee. Self-consciously he sat up and pulled the blankets around him. Sarah sat on the edge of the bed cradling her mug in both hands.

"I feel like an invalid," he said. "But I could get used to this. Thank you."

"My pleasure Mr. Doucet. But I only do room service for the sick and wounded. Just so you don't get any ideas." She laughed, an infectious laugh, and Doucet started to laugh too.

"Ouch," he said, and stopped. "It still hurts."

"When you're ready," she said, getting up, "there's breakfast stuff in the kitchen. And I've got a few things to show you. I think you'll find them pretty interesting."

After a long shower and breakfast Doucet felt almost normal, except for his face. It still looked awful and it still hurt, but he could sense the improvement. He took a chair from the kitchen into Sarah's makeshift office, where she was sitting at the computer.

"The rest of my furniture is on the way," she said. "It should be here sometime next week. Then things will be a bit more comfortable."

Doucet pulled up his chair and sat down. "So, what is it you wanted to show me?"

"Are you ready for a little tutorial on Diatek's finances? Some of it you probably know and some of it was in my thesis, but before I show you what I found last night I think we should go over it so we're both on the same page."

Doucet nodded.

"Okay. First of all, Diatek is structured differently from any of the others I looked at for my thesis. It's quite complicated. It's a Canadian company, obviously, and it's incorporated in Canada. And it's a wholly owned subsidiary of WorldWide Mineral Enterprises, the holding company in Toronto. So far so good. But here's the interesting part about WWME: they have their office in Toronto, but the company is registered in Grand Cayman."

"Grand Cayman? I didn't know that. Are you sure?"

"Yes. Grand Cayman as in the tax haven. I got that information from my friend Peter, the McKinsey consultant, the same one who told me about the possible Russian mafia connection. It doesn't mean Diatek or WWME is doing anything wrong; all sorts of international companies are registered in the Caymans for tax reasons and WWME is probably registered there to minimize Canadian taxes. Believe it or not there are more companies registered in the Caymans than there are people. So it's not necessarily a problem, but for me it sets off alarm bells. But," she said, "take a look at this." She turned the monitor so he could see it better.

"What is it?" Doucet asked. The screen was full of columns of numbers.

"A spreadsheet. A very large spreadsheet, full of information on wire transfers. Hundreds of them; it goes on for pages and pages. And this is just one file. There are more; it looks as though each one covers a calendar year."

"Okay. But is that unusual? Aren't they just normal business records?"

"Yeah, of course, the transfers may be completely legitimate. But when you look at them carefully there are some unusual things. First, they all go into just a few accounts. Some of the money goes to Canadian suppliers, as you would expect, but most of it is transferred to Cayman Islands accounts. The rest goes to accounts in Switzerland and Russia."

"How do you know that?"

"Oh, that part is easy. The receiving accounts are listed here." She pointed to one of the columns in the spreadsheet. "There's a universal protocol for international financial transactions – every account has a unique code that identifies it. For example every account in a Cayman Islands bank has 'KY' in the code. Swiss banks use CH as the country code, Russian banks RU, and so on. So it was easy to figure out what country the transfers go to. With a little bit of research I could find out exactly which branch of which bank the accounts are held in."

"Okay." Doucet drew out the word: ooo..kaay. "But Diatek does get services and equipment from other countries. Not the Cayman Islands, but I know there was discussion about a contract for mining services from a Russian company. Russia has a big diamond mining industry, so it would make sense. Maybe they were the lowest bidder, I don't know."

"Sure, you're right, and I'm not saying there are problems with all of these transfers. For example some of them are loan repayments to an account in the Caymans, and even though

I've highlighted them – I'll get to that in a minute – as far as I can see they're perfectly legal. From what I've been able to figure out, most of the initial funding for Diatek was in the form of a loan from a Cayman bank to WWME International. WWME probably got government incentives for investing money in Canada – that's speculation on my part, but it's the kind of thing that happens all the time – but also Diatek can write off the interest on the loan, even though the money is actually being paid to a bank in the Caymans and not staying in the country. The only reason I flagged the interest payments is because of the interest rate – it's really high. Maybe the lender thought it was a risky loan, but a high interest rate means two things: first, Diatek gets a big write off, and secondly, the bank that loaned the money in the first place makes a big profit as long as Diatek pays off the loan. It's legal, but the only people who win are Diatek, WWME and the banks – everyone else loses, especially the average tax payer. Furthermore if WWME decides to sell Diatek some fine day they won't have to pay taxes on any profits they make because they're registered in the Caymans where there's no capital gains tax. When corporations avoid paying taxes all of us end up paying more. Or we get fewer government services."

"You sound like you're on a campaign."

"Maybe I am. Working at Global Witness tuned me in to the abuses that are endemic in tax havens. It's an issue that has already come up in my job here in Seattle, too, because we work with individual farmers and small companies in developing countries. Some of them have competitors in their own countries that are big enough to run their accounts through tax havens, and when they do that they basically suck a huge amount of money out of the country. Something has to give, so either taxes go up on the little guys – who don't have access to tax havens – or government spending on things like infrastructure suffers. Either way, the small companies we work with get hit hardest. The U.S. and some other countries are starting to pay attention, but there is a long way to go."

"Okay, so maybe you don't approve of what Diatek is doing, but there's nothing illegal, right?"

"I'm reserving judgement. There's more."

She closed the spreadsheet they'd been looking at and opened a graph. "Here's the Diatek production data – it's the red line – the number of carats of diamonds recovered each week. I'm sure you're familiar with that."

"Very. It's our bottom line."

"Okay. The other line on the graph, the blue one, is production costs. That's based on Diatek's financial statements, and then I added some data last night from the files you brought on that flash drive and the ones Chris got for us. The costs aren't broken down week by week so you can't exactly compare production and costs, but I think it gives you the general picture. Tell me what you see."

"They're correlated. When production goes up expenditures do to, and vice versa. Isn't that what you'd expect?"

"That's the thing. To some extent you *would* expect it – say the company hires more people and they process more ore, so you recover more diamonds. But you also have higher costs because of the additional employees. So there's a correlation. But the details of those wire transfers are what did it for me. Look at this" – she pointed to the screen – "about two and a half years ago, in early 2010, there was a huge jump in the amount of diamonds recovered, about thirty percent. And what happens to the cost of producing all those diamonds? It goes up by thirty percent too."

Doucet scratched his head. "Yes, I remember the production increase. It was sudden and nobody anticipated it; everyone just figured we got lucky and hit a patch of high grade ore. And diamond production stayed high and pretty steady until this spring. Then it dropped again."

"You just proved my point. It corroborates what I figured out last night. I didn't know for sure whether or not the production increase was a case of processing more ore at a higher cost. But you say it must be because you were just tapping richer ore. The means the company didn't have to hire more miners or scale up operations, so the production cost shouldn't have gone up at all. But they did. And who did Diatek pay those additional costs to?" She tapped the keyboard and brought up her spreadsheets again. "Most of the money was sent to a couple of accounts in the Cayman Islands. These are the wire transfers from around the time when diamond production went up in 2010. I haven't had time to plot this data, but I'm sure if I did you'd see that the amount of money transferred to these accounts in the Caymans would track the production. As far as the company's financials are concerned, these are expenditures, the cost of doing business. But why should production costs be paid through accounts in the Cayman Islands? Unless there's some very circuitous accounting that I don't understand, I think someone is cooking the books."

Doucet looked at the rows of numbers on the screen, not really seeing them, trying to find an explanation for the scenario Sarah had just laid out. He could sense her watching him. Finally he shrugged. "I don't know what to say."

"What I'd really like to do is trace those accounts," Sarah said. "Find out exactly who owns them. It's not peanuts. If you add it all up it's tens of millions of dollars. But I don't know how to do that because places like the Caymans are just too secretive. Probably even the IRS would have trouble finding out. But I'll bet your CFO knows. I don't see how he *couldn't* know. I've only looked at a fraction of the stuff that Chris downloaded from his computer. I haven't seen anything yet, but I'm hoping that there will be some clues in there somewhere."

CHAPTER 21

Sarah continued to work on the downloaded files most of Saturday. Doucet helped for a while – she asked him the occasional question about how things were organized at Diatek – but she was totally absorbed in what she was doing and he felt like a spare wheel on a bicycle, not very useful. "Sorry," she said. "I hope you're not too bored. It's just that I love doing stuff like this and I get totally sucked in. I don't really know why, but I can't help it. It's just me." Eventually he got up and wandered into the kitchen for more coffee; Sarah hardly noticed.

More from boredom than anything else he turned on his cell phone. He had turned it off when he arrived at Sarah's on Thursday night; he had already emailed Tim Bailey saying he wouldn't be in on Friday, and he really didn't want contact with anyone else. He still didn't, not really, but he checked his voicemail anyway and scrolled through his messages. Nothing demanded immediate attention. There was one text message, though, that he came back to. It was from a number he didn't recognize and he was tempted to delete it, but it was addressed to him as Dr. Doucet and said it was urgent and concerned his work at Diatek. That was too much information for it to be a random junk message. He noticed that it had been sent by one Jorge Vasquez. He'd never heard of Jorge Vasquez. The message contained a phone number and said he should call ASAP and ask for David Brown. All very strange, but then his whole week had been strange. The phone number was foreign and he didn't recognize the country code.

"Sarah," he said, walking into her office, "any idea what country has '52' for their telephone country code? I got a text message asking me to call a 52 number."

"What was that?" Sarah was still immersed in her work on the Diatek files and it was an effort for her to turn away.

He explained again and she stood up and stretched. "Sorry, I was a bit distracted. I should get up and walk around for a few minutes anyway, I've been sitting here too long. Here, let me see."

Doucet handed her the phone and she read the message. "I have a feeling 52 is Mexico, but I'm not sure. You could check on the internet. The name fits: Jorge Vasquez. But these things are usually scams. I wouldn't call back if I were you."

"Yeah, that was my first reaction too. I don't know anyone called Jorge Vasquez, or David Brown for that matter. I almost deleted it, but they got my name right, and they know I work for Diatek. I'm curious."

"Well, I guess there's no harm as long as you don't give them your bank account details." She grinned and stretched again and walked around the room a few times. He could tell her mind was on other things. "Use my phone if you want, I've got an international calling plan so it won't cost much."

Sarah had been right; when he checked he found that '52' was indeed the country code for Mexico. He picked up her phone and dialed the number.

After several rings a woman's voice answered, in Spanish.

Oh shit, Doucet thought, of course, it's Mexico. He desperately tried to remember what little Spanish he knew and mumbled a few words. Apparently it was enough. "Yes, just hold on for a minute, I'll connect you to Mr. Brown," the voice said in perfect English.

"Hello?" A man's voice, weak and tentative.

"Hello, this is Rick Doucet calling. I got a message to …"

"Rick! Thank goodness you called." The voice was stronger now and there was something about it that sounded familiar. But Doucet couldn't place it.

"I hope you're sitting down. It's" – the voice dropped to a whisper – "it's Bill Thompson."

"What? But that's impossible." Doucet was stunned. He swung one of the kitchen chairs around and sat down heavily.

"It may sound impossible, but it's true. In spite of what you may think I'm very much alive. I'm calling from a hospital in Ensenada, Mexico. It's a long story and I can't say much on the phone, but we have to talk. Can you come down here for a couple of days? It's really important."

Doucet couldn't believe he was talking to Bill Thompson.

"Are you still there Rick?"

"Yeah, I'm here. I just find it difficult … is there something you can tell me that only you would know? So I can be sure this is

Bill Thompson I'm talking to? Too many weird things have been going on lately."

"No, it really is me, I can assure you. How about that day we had lunch and I asked you to be executor? Or even better, how about that … the sample we sent to Caltech. Nobody else knows about that."

He was right, no one except the people at Caltech knew about the diamond they'd had analyzed. And they didn't know the context, or who Bill Thompson was. "Okay … but I can't get my head around this. I've got so many questions I don't know where to start … like who is David Brown?"

"Not now, Rick, the place I'm in is too public. Besides I don't even trust this phone. I don't trust anything anymore. We have to talk face to face, and there isn't much time. And you need to watch your back."

That got Doucet's attention. The guys who mugged him had asked about Thompson. Somehow it was all connected.

"You should have told me a week ago. Why can't you just come back here?"

Thompson didn't catch the sarcasm in his voice. "Believe me, if it was that easy I would. But I can't, not without help, and you're more or less my only hope. You've got to come down here, Rick. Please."

Doucet could hear the desperation in his voice. He was tempted to say, okay, I'll come, but instead he said, "Give me a little time, I'm still trying to process this. I'll call you back in a few hours, okay? Same number?"

"Yes, same number. Same David Brown. I'll explain."

They said goodbye and Doucet hung up the phone, his head still reeling from the news that Thompson was alive.

Sarah had come into the room without him noticing. "You're looking thoughtful," she said. "Did you get through to that number in Mexico?"

"Mm. I did. Do you know where Ensenada is?"

"Sure. Was that an Ensenada number?"

"Yes. It's complicated, but I think it might have something to do with the people who did this." He pointed to his bandaged face. "And I think I might have to go down there. Like tomorrow. Where exactly is it?"

"Tomorrow? Wow, that's a bit sudden. Ensenada is in Baja. We used to drive down there for the day when I was a kid. It's not that far from La Jolla. I don't remember much about the place except for the blowhole; it's like Old Faithful, huge sprays of water going up into the air. Something to do with ocean waves getting compressed in a cave. My dad explained it but I've forgotten the details."

Doucet laughed. "You got it right, more or less. That's basically how blowholes work. I've never seen a blowhole in the flesh. Maybe I really will take a trip to Ensenada."

It took him a while to work it all out, but with help from Sarah he was able to organize his trip south: fly to San Diego, take the tram to the border, then pick up a rental car in Tijuana and drive to Ensenada. He left Seattle the next morning and by the time he found the hospital it was late afternoon, and when he walked in the receptionist took one look and tried to direct him to a nurses' station. He looked at her in confusion and then remembered the bandages on his face; he'd become so accustomed to them that he was only barely aware they were there. He touched his face and laughed. "Oh, no, I'm just a visitor. I'm here to see one of your patients. Mr. Brown, David Brown."

Her English was limited and Doucet wasn't sure she understood everything he said. But she had a list of patients and when he pointed out Brown's name she broke into a broad smile. "Three," she said, holding up three fingers. "Floor three. By elevator." She pointed across the room to the elevators.

"Gracias," Doucet said, and she smiled again.

He had no idea what to expect when a nurse showed him into 'David Brown's' room. One glance, however, left him in no doubt that it really was Bill Thompson. The engineer was asleep and he looked gaunt, much thinner than Doucet had ever seen him. His complexion was pale and he had a full beard tinged with gray. But it was him.

Doucet sat down in a chair by the bed and looked around. The room was small but it was clean and bright with a large window on one wall. One of the first things Doucet noticed was that there weren't any flowers. He had never been a patient himself, and he hadn't spent much time visiting people in hospitals, but his strongest memory of hospital rooms was of flowers. Lots of flowers. It's what friends brought to cheer you up. Thompson, it appeared, didn't have friends in Ensenada who brought him flowers. But then the engineer didn't have many friends in Vancouver either, as far as Doucet knew. That was probably why he was executor of Thompson's will. And also probably why Thompson had called him, not someone else, when he needed help. Doucet looked over at frail figure on the bed and realized that he knew very little about the engineer beyond his work at the mine and the common interests they'd talked about when they met, hockey and fishing mostly. Once or twice Thompson had mentioned something about his life in Ontario before he came to Diatek; Doucet knew he was divorced and had a daughter. But that was all. Beyond that his life was a mystery.

As though he somehow sensed his past was being analyzed, Thompson moved his head and slowly opened his eyes. When he saw Doucet he smiled and pushed himself up into a half-sitting position, leaning back on his elbows. "You made it," he said, his voice hoarse with sleep. "I was having a nap. I seem to sleep a lot in here." He propped up two pillows against the head of the bed and sat up. "That's better." He looked over at Doucet and his eyes widened in alarm. He had just registered the bandages. "What happened to your face?"

"I had a little accident – we can talk about it later. How about you? How are you doing?"

"I'm okay, but we can't talk here." He pointed to the open door and lowered his voice. "There's no privacy. I can't wait to get out of here. Have you got a car?"

"Yes, I got a rental in Tijuana. But you don't look in any state to leave."

"Nonsense. I lost a huge amount of blood and they gave me massive transfusions, so I'm a little weak, that's all. I just need to eat and get my strength back and I'll be fine. The doctors have cleared me to leave – they said I could stay a few more days if I want, but they left it up to me and I definitely want to go." He paused and looked around, and again lowered his voice. "It's so good to have someone here who knows who I really am; I don't have to pretend to be someone else."

Thompson buzzed a nurse and rattled off something in Spanish. "I asked her to bring the paperwork I need for checking out," he told Doucet. "It's the one constant in the world. It doesn't matter where you are, there's always paperwork."

When the nurse came back it appeared that the main thing the hospital was interested in was payment. Without some assurance they would be paid, Thompson couldn't be discharged. "Shit," he said, "I don't have a credit card. The only way I can pay that much money is to call the bank and get them to transfer it."

"I can put it on my card if you want."

"Thanks, but it's okay, it will just take a little time, that's all," Thompson said. "I'll explain when we get out of here."

It took Thompson several hours to arrange the payment from his bank, but finally Doucet was allowed to take him out in a wheelchair. He was weak but in good spirits and as Doucet helped him into the car he said, "I can't believe how good it feels to breathe fresh air. And to be alive."

Doucet grunted a reply. "I'm sure." I hope I don't have to play nursemaid for the next few days, he thought. He climbed into the driver's seat. "Where to?"

Thompson guided him out of town, looking around as though he'd never seen the place before. He was savoring his freedom. Then he told Doucet to turn into a small road that wound through a new development and eventually came to a street with a row of identical houses on one side. "Mine is the blue one," Thompson said. "Pull into the driveway." Doucet could hear the crash of waves on the beach somewhere in the darkness, behind the houses.

The street was well lit, but Thompson's house was in darkness. "I have no idea what we'll find inside," he said. "They carried me out on a stretcher, I don't remember any of it. Jorge – he's the one who found me – told me there was blood all over the place. I've kind of blocked out everything that happened." He shivered.

"You okay?"

"Yeah, I'll survive. I just want to get that bastard Andropov."

"Who's he?"

"He's the one who tried to kill me. I'll tell you about it later."

They went inside and Thompson turned on the lights and looked around. "Home sweet home," he said, and laughed." It was the first time since they left the hospital that Doucet had seen a smile on his face. "It doesn't look much different. That's the kitchen," he said, pointing to a door. "I'm not sure I want to go in there, that's where they tied me up." He sat down in a chair. "Do you think you could make some tea? There should be some in the cupboard."

Doucet opened the door to the kitchen and wrinkled his nose. The smell was disgusting and the room was a mess. Two chairs, tipped over, were lying on their backs near the table, and there was a large reddish-brown stain on the floor, covered in dead flies. Dried blood. Pieces of rope and plastic littered the floor and someone had stepped in the wet blood and left tracks around the room. Doucet skirted the table and opened the back door and two of the windows. He shuddered when he thought of what must have gone on in here. It was no wonder Thompson wanted to stay out of the kitchen.

He found teabags in a cupboard and boiled water and took two mugs of tea back into the room where Thompson was waiting, closing the kitchen door behind him. "Have you got a mop or something?" he asked. "The kitchen needs a bit of cleaning up."

"I'll bet it does. But don't worry, it can wait."

"No, I think I'd rather clean up now," Doucet said. "It's really not very pleasant in there."

Thompson shrugged. "Okay, if you really want to, be my guest. There's cleaning stuff in the hall cupboard. Or there should be, unless those bastards took that too." He gave a bitter laugh.

It took Doucet almost an hour to get the kitchen habitable. The blood was the worst; it was caked and still sticky and he had to keep rinsing out the mop and adding more cleaner to the bucket. But he felt much better when he was finished. Aired out and cleaned up, it looked like an ordinary kitchen again.

When he went back into the living room Thompson was asleep in his chair, his mug of tea still half full beside him. Doucet sat down on the sofa, uncertain now if he should have agreed to bring the engineer home from the hospital. He didn't look very well. But the doctors had agreed to release him; they couldn't have been too concerned. Still, whatever had happened, it was going to take a while for him to recover. He looked around the room and wondered how long Thompson had been here, and why he had ended up in Ensenada. It was a long way from the Northwest Territories.

Thompson stirred and opened his eyes. "Sorry, I drifted off," he said when he saw Doucet. He straightened himself up in the chair. "I've got a lot to tell you, Rick. Once I was conscious in the hospital it's all I thought about. I have an idea about why all this happened" – he waved his hand vaguely around the room – "and once I figured it out I had Jorge send you that text message. I hope you can stay for a couple of days because it's going to take that long to get everything organized. In the meantime we'd better go out and get some groceries or we'll starve. I pretty much cleared the place out just before Andropov and his friend arrived."

"Bill, you're talking in riddles. I have no idea who these people you're talking about are. Until a couple of days ago I thought you were dead."

Thompson managed a hoarse laugh. "Yes, well that was the idea. To bury Bill Thompson and start a new life. But it hasn't quite worked out that way."

On the way to buy groceries Thompson stopped and withdrew cash from an ATM. "They weren't interested in money," he explained. "They took everything from my wallet except a little cash and this bank card. These guys are very thorough, Rick, and they're careful. My bank account here is in the name of David Brown, and that's what it says on this card, so they left it in my wallet. But they took everything with my real name on it – driver's license, passport, my Canadian credit cards. They made sure that nobody called Bill Thompson had lived here in Ensenada. It's ironic because that's exactly what I was trying to do too, be anonymous, or at least be someone else. Now I no longer have any ID that actually identifies me. I don't really exist." Thompson laughed his hoarse laugh again.

When they got back to the house Doucet made sandwiches and more tea. What he really wanted was a beer, but there were none in the fridge. Then he remembered that Thompson didn't drink.

"Okay Bill," he said when they were finished, "So far I've restrained myself. But I have to know. Who the hell is this person Andropov you keep talking about?"

"Like I said, he's the guy who attacked me. Andropov and someone else, someone I don't know."

"You know Andropov?"

"Well, in a way, yes. I met him at the mine about ..."

"You met him *where*? Jesus, Bill."

"Yeah, I know. It's complicated. He was only at the mine for a couple of days, and it was a few years ago. I spent several hours with him, walking him through the ore processing system. Nobody was quite sure exactly why he was there. Apparently – or this was the rumor going around – he was some kind of important Russian businessman, and he'd come straight to the mine from Russia ..." Thompson noticed a strange look come over Doucet's face. "What?"

"Russian. That's it, I'm sure now. This," Doucet pointed to the bandages on his face, "I told you I had an accident. But actually it was more than that, I was mugged, two guys, and they asked me about you. I was totally confused because at that point I was sure you were dead. But both of these guys had accents. They spoke English pretty well, but both of them had accents I couldn't quite place. I'll bet they were Russian. In fact I'm sure of it."

"Jesus Christ," Thompson said quietly. "These people are everywhere. I didn't think they'd act so quickly. I'm sorry you got dragged into this, Rick. It's my fault. I got involved in something I shouldn't have and I'm beginning to understand that it was more ... more serious than I thought, and everything that's happened since is because of that. Andropov found your name on some papers of mine when he was here. That's probably why you got mugged. I'm sorry. I'm just starting to put it all together; I honestly didn't know Andropov had anything to do with what was happening at the mine until he showed up here. Or that there was a Russian connection. I was so ignorant about what I was doing for them that they probably didn't need to kill me – or try to kill me – but obviously they wanted to make sure I wouldn't be around to tell anyone about it." He laughed his weak laugh again. "The irony is I probably would have kept quiet if they hadn't shown up and tried to kill me. Their mistake was leaving the house before I was actually dead. They were so confident I'd bleed to death that they just left."

CHAPTER 22

The next morning Thompson seemed much stronger. Doucet, already awake and making coffee in the kitchen, heard him taking a shower and then he walked into the kitchen. He looked around anxiously. "Bad vibes," he said. "I keep having flashbacks about what happened in here. At least my clothes are clean." He patted his shirt. "This shirt was covered in blood when they took me out of here, but Jorge got everything cleaned while I was in the hospital. But this is it, these are the only clothes I have left. They cleaned the place out, they even took my car. Last I heard from the police they hadn't found it yet. I don't even really care anymore." Thompson poured himself coffee. "Come out back when you're ready. It's one of the things I love about this place – being able to sit out on the deck. I've got a lot to tell you."

There was no wind when Doucet stepped outside and the air was still slightly cool. He noticed a distinct and unfamiliar smell, a delicious blending of the sea and the scent of dry chaparral. He pulled a chair into the sun and sat down. It was surreal. The soft, humid air, the sound of the waves on the beach – he had to remind himself that he wasn't on vacation. He looked over at Thompson, a man who, until a few days ago, he'd thought was dead, and he noticed again the thick bandages wrapped around both of the engineer's forearms and several fingers of one hand. Instinctively he put his own hand up to his face and felt the bandages on his nose. "I'm listening, Bill," he said.

Thompson sat back in his chair. "You know, in a strange way I feel completely liberated. Almost dying, then lying in that hospital bed with time to think – not to be too philosophical about it, but it gave me a new lease on life. It made me very happy just to be alive. That's something that I haven't even thought about for a very long time."

Doucet didn't say anything. In spite of what had happened, Thompson did seem serene. He hoped the engineer wasn't going to recount some kind of religious experience he'd had in the hospital – he'd heard about it happening to people who had near death experiences. Doucet had little use for religion.

It was as though Thompson had read his mind. "But you probably don't want to listen to me talking about how great it is to be alive. I'll start from the beginning and it's going to take a while because it's a long and complicated story, and sometimes I find it hard to believe myself. But it's all true as best I can remember. I'm telling you because I want someone to know what happened, and you'll understand it because it all has to do with Diatek. I really want to go back to Canada and tell the police or someone in authority, but I can't just jump on a plane and do that."

"Why not?"

Thompson shook his head. "Wouldn't work. I'd probably be arrested. Or else nobody would believe me – when you hear what I have to say you'll see that the whole thing sounds pretty crazy, even though it's the absolute truth. Also I'm worried that Andropov or whoever else is involved in this would get to me before I had a chance to explain everything. That's one of the reasons I wanted to tell you first – coming from you the story will have some credibility. I'm hoping that once you hear what I have to say you'll help me get back and get this out in the open."

Here we go again, Doucet thought. Why is it people are always asking me to do things for them? It had happened before, both at grad school and when he was working for DeBeers in South Africa. Several times colleagues had poured out their personal troubles to him and asked for advice. He sometimes thought he should have been a psychiatrist. Who am I to tell them what they should do, he wondered? But he had trouble saying no. Usually they ended up doing whatever it was they wanted to do in the first place anyway, they just needed a little reassurance that it was okay. It sounded as though Thompson didn't need reassuring, however; he'd already made up his mind. He just needed some practical help from Doucet to do what he'd decided to do.

"Most of what I'm going to tell you, Rick, I wrote down as a kind of affidavit. I also made a video of myself reading the affidavit, with a local newspaper beside me to date it – like you see in the movies. I hadn't decided what to do with it yet when Andropov showed up, and he took the only hard copy I had, and he took the video too. And my computer, so I don't even have the original files. I'd been seriously thinking about sending you a copy – that's how Andropov knew about you, your name was on the hard copy of the affidavit. It's too bad I didn't send it to you, then there'd be at least one copy floating around. But it's all still pretty fresh in my memory so I'm sure I can reconstruct nearly everything."

"So that explains the break-in."

"What?"

"I said, that explains the break-in. It's something I haven't told you about. But a few days before I got mugged someone broke into my apartment and turned the place upside down. They didn't take any money or valuables, they just trashed the place. The police figured they were looking for something specific, but as far as I could tell nothing was missing. They were probably looking for your affidavit. Or the video."

"Jeez, Rick, I'm sorry all over again. I never imagined … when you start something like I did you have no idea about the consequences. I thought I would be the only one affected, but obviously not."

"Well, nobody has a crystal ball. You can't predict the future. It's done; as far as I'm concerned it's water under the bridge. So what is it all about, Bill? I know a bit more than I did yesterday or last week, but not much."

And so Bill Thompson started to tell his story. It was as though a tremendous weight had been lifted from his shoulders. For the past two and a half years he had been carrying around knowledge that he could share with no one else, and now he could pour it all out. At first what he had done seemed like an adventure, a little risky but exciting just the same. Then, gradually but inexorably, he began to feel as though he was being dragged down into a whirlpool, his life and his future spiraling out of control. And when he'd tried to regain control, he had almost succeeded. Almost, until Andropov finally tracked him down.

"It started with a woman," Thompson said. "Doesn't it always? Actually, it probably started before I met her, that time Andropov came to the mine. It was in 2009, December, I can picture him now, getting out of the helicopter with our CEO. But what drew me into it was a woman named Lea. I never did learn her last name; I realize looking back that she was very cagey about that. She kept saying we should just keep it as Bill and Lea for a while. Maybe Lea wasn't even her real name. Anyway, it was sometime early in 2010 and I was in Vancouver on a break." Thompson told Doucet how he'd been sitting in the Starbucks near his apartment, minding his own business, when a woman sat down at his table and struck up a conversation. "She was very attractive. There aren't many women at the mine site, and it was just nice to talk to a pretty woman." Thompson looked a little wistful.

Doucet didn't say anything. He had decided that it was best to let Thompson talk without too many interruptions.

"She was a complete stranger, I'd never seen her before in my life. But she must have known who I was. She must have known a lot, actually; obviously she knew that I went to that Starbucks for breakfast when I was in town. It's spooky, these people are good, Rick, and they must have a lot of resources. I'm trying to join up the dots and the only answer I can come up with is that it all comes back to Andropov. He has to be the key.

He had been at the mine not long before I met Lea – or she met me, I should say. He knew exactly what I did there. They got me to walk him through the ore processing system, and the whole time he kept asking about security. At first I thought he must be some kind of security consultant, but after a while I realized he actually didn't know that much about how our security was set up, which seemed strange. By the end of his visit, though, he must have realized I was the perfect person to carry out his scheme. He even took me to the cafeteria one day, just the two of us, and asked me a lot of questions, we even talked about my personal life. He was very smooth, it just seemed like a couple of people shooting the breeze over coffee. It was only when I was lying in that hospital bed playing it all over in my head that I realized he was gathering as much information about me as he could. And somehow most of that got passed on to Lea so she could identify me. That and more; there were also things she knew that I'm sure I didn't tell Andropov. I doubt she knew why she was doing it, though; I think she was pretty far down the chain of command."

Thompson seemed to be savoring the fact that at last he had an audience. It was, Doucet realized, a kind of catharsis.

"I'd already been at the mine for several years when I met Lea – you're pretty isolated up there, and I must admit my social graces, if I ever had any, had gone into decline. I'm a fairly private person anyway so I was actually a little annoyed when she sat down at my table. I was probably a bit rude to her. But she persisted and eventually we started talking and after a while I started to think it wasn't so bad to be having a normal civilized conversation with a very attractive woman. To make a long story short, we met up several times after that first encounter and I grew to like her – I liked her a lot. And I think she truly liked me, although maybe that is just wishful thinking. We … she even spent a night at my place once. But then she just disappeared without a trace; her cell phone number didn't work, and I never saw her again." Thompson paused and looked out into the distance. "But by then they'd hooked me."

The sun had already risen high in the sky and the morning chill was gone. They moved their chairs into the shade of a large deck umbrella.

"Anyway, one morning – this was just before she completely disappeared from my life – we agreed to meet for breakfast. I was due to go back to the mine in a couple of days and I thought it would be a nice quiet breakfast, just me and Lea. But when I got there she was sitting with this guy I'd never seen before. She introduced me and said he was a friend; I didn't like him from the beginning. It was one of those things, you make an instant judgement about someone, and then everything that happens afterwards confirms your judgement. Perhaps it was just my annoyance that there was someone else with Lea, but I think there was more to it than that. His name was Brennan, and from his accent he was Irish. A red-headed Irishman. He wasn't really obnoxious, but he had a kind of nervous and shifty manner, always looking around as though someone was watching. It was weird. I couldn't see him and Lea as friends, they didn't have much in common and they didn't say much to one another during breakfast. The whole situation was very awkward for me, there were things I wanted to say to Lea because I was going back to the mine, but then suddenly she stood up and said she had an appointment and had to leave. So I found myself sitting there with this person I didn't know and didn't really like." Thompson gave a wry laugh.

"At that point I wasn't sure quite what to do but I'd finished my breakfast, so I told him I had to leave too. I wanted to get out of there as soon as possible. He just looked at me and then he put his hand on my arm and said, 'No, stick around for a few more minutes. I've got something I want to talk to you about, and I think you'll find it interesting.' He said this in his Irish accent, and the funny thing is I actually kind of liked the accent, even though I didn't like him. He was persuasive in that Irish way and he got the waiter to bring more coffee and suddenly I found myself stuck there with him. Stuck until he'd finished telling me whatever it was he wanted to tell me.

"I should have walked away right then, and none of this would have happened. I'd probably still be happily working at the mine. But obviously I didn't. Brennan said he'd heard from Lea that I worked at the Diatek mine, and that was why he wanted to meet me. By a total fluke, so he said, some people he did business with wanted to hire someone from Diatek. It sounds far-fetched now, but I guess I didn't think so at the time. I bought it; I actually thought maybe he was going to offer me a job. And he did, in a way, but it wasn't what I thought. He said these people wanted someone to take stuff to the mine periodically, things that needed to be hand carried and not shipped in the usual way. He said that from what Lea had told him he understood that I was back and forth from Vancouver pretty often, and I said yes, that was true, and he said if that were the case I'd be perfect for the job. When I asked him what was in these packages that had to be hand carried, he said his clients hadn't told him, it was confidential, but they had assured him it wasn't drugs or anything like that. He trusted these people, he said, and he never did anything illegal. The kicker was that they'd pay me for delivering the packages, quite a bit of money, actually." Thompson paused. "I thought the whole thing was totally bizarre, but I'd been gambling a bit at the time and I needed the money, and also there was Lea. Brennan was Lea's friend, so I thought if I did something for Brennan maybe that was a way to stay in touch with Lea. Little did I know.

"Brennan said I could think about it but he needed to know soon, and he gave me his telephone number and asked me to call before I went back to the mine. I couldn't sleep that night trying to decide what to do, but I kept thinking about the money and my gambling debts and I decided there was nothing to lose, so I called him the next morning and said I was in. I'd take the packages to the mine for him. But what was I supposed to do with them? Don't worry, he said, he'd tell his clients that I'd agreed and they would be in touch with me. That was the last conversation I had with Brennan. Both he and Lea simply disappeared. When I tried to call Lea I got a message saying her number was no longer in service. Ditto with the number Brennan gave me. Brennan had said he was a private investigator and later on, when I was in Vancouver on one of my breaks, I visited just about every PI office in the city, but I couldn't find him.

"So the next time I went back to Vancouver from the mine there was a stack of FedEx packages in my apartment. One of the concierges at my building, an older Chinese guy I trust, has a key to my place and he takes up my mail when I'm away. Sam – that's his name – asked if I had a new hobby because all of the packages came from a hobby shop in Ottawa. At least that's what the return address said. I also got anonymous phone calls, telling me exactly what to do with the packages. The calls weren't friendly. They were vague about what would happen if I didn't do as instructed, but it was clear it wouldn't be pleasant. It didn't take me long to realize that I'd gotten in over my head. But I couldn't see any way out."

"That's crazy," Doucet said. "So you started taking this stuff back to the mine? What was it?"

"Three guesses. Every FedEx box had a whole bunch of smaller packages inside – little gray bags, sealed up, that felt like they were full of sand. They told me to drop them into the ore stream at regular intervals, every day if I could. One a day, like vitamin pills. In with the raw ore, before it goes into the crushers. That was when it clicked."

Doucet was staring at Thompson, a look of disbelief on his face. "You've got to be joking. You were taking diamonds *into* the mine?"

"Yeah, unbelievable, isn't it? Because I was there all the time monitoring the conveyor system, it was easy enough to do. And Andropov knew that. I had shown him the whole ore processing system and I'd told him we didn't worry about security before the ore gets to the crushers. He knew that I was part of the landscape and no one would give me a second glance. I got so used to it that eventually it seemed perfectly normal. Except that I was always nervous someone would find out. But when I think back on it now I realize how incredible it was. It's a perfect money laundering scheme, Rick.

"Those little gray bags were not very strong – they never broke in the FedEx packages but they wouldn't last long tumbled around in the ore stream. They probably burst as soon as I dropped them in, but if not the crushers would tear them to shreds. You know that diamond we sent to Caltech? I took it from one of those bags. I just slit it with a razor and it was like cutting butter with a hot knife. I'd had warnings about what would happen if I opened them, but even though I was sure the bags had diamonds in them I had to be certain. And I decided that there was no way they – whoever they were – would know if a diamond or two was missing. How could they tell? The sorting system is good, but it's not one hundred percent. Or maybe a diamond goes into the crusher the wrong way and gets shattered.

"When I brought you that diamond I had to make up that story about buying it in Amsterdam. I suspected all along that the diamonds were illicit – otherwise why would somebody go to all that trouble? – but for me that analysis confirmed it. Probably all the diamonds I took into the mine were blood diamonds. Think about it. What better way to launder conflict diamonds than to have them come out of the Diatek mine, certified as genuine Canadian diamonds?"

Thompson had lived his double life at the mine – engineer and diamond smuggler – for several years, and he made it sound normal. For him it *had* been normal, and he told his story as calmly as though he was talking about last night's trip to the grocery store. Nothing unusual. But Doucet was dumbfounded. And the wheels were beginning to turn in his head.

"When did you start taking diamonds to the mine?"

"It was 2010. Around late February or early March. Just a few months after Andropov had been there."

Doucet thought about the graph Sarah had shown him a few days ago. It showed a thirty percent jump in diamond production from the Diatek mine in March 2010 and an equivalent decrease two years later, around the time when Thompson was supposed to have drowned.

"Our diamond production increased right around that time. By a lot, around thirty percent. Are you telling me that was because of the diamonds you were bringing in, salting the ore? We all thought it was luck, that we'd hit a rich part of the kimberlite."

"That's right. They fed me a lot of diamonds."

Doucet was shaking his head. "It's incredible. But who is laundering the money? How does this guy Andropov get anything out of it?"

"I've been thinking about it a lot. There must be people at Diatek involved, and somehow they must have connections with Andropov. Who they are and exactly how they benefit I don't know. When Andropov visited the mine that time he came with the CEO, so at least they must know one another. What I was doing brought a lot of extra money into the company and it must have gone into someone's pocket. When I got to the point where it was all getting too stressful and I couldn't take it anymore, I thought about going to someone at Diatek. Someone at the top, confess and tell them what was going on and try to end it. But then I wondered, What if they are in on it? So I ended up not saying anything. When I faked the accident I was pretty sure I could get away and leave everything behind. I thought it would give me time to figure out what to do."

Doucet had heard many stories about the diamond industry, stories about corruption and betrayal, about scams and get rich schemes. Diamonds seemed to have a malign influence on some people; they were beautiful, very valuable, and at the same time small and easy to conceal and transport. But he had never heard anything like Thompson's story. Smuggling diamonds *into* a diamond mine. It was – almost – beyond belief. But obviously it had happened, and Thompson, sitting there in front of him, had lived it.

CHAPTER 23

Thompson talked all day and into the evening. Not just about what had happened at the mine, but also about his life before Diatek, when he worked at a nickel mine in Ontario. Doucet learned more about the engineer than he really wanted to know.

The next morning they started again. "So, where were we?" Thompson asked. "I think I was telling you how paranoid I became, how stressed out I got. I was constantly looking over my shoulder, wondering if someone was watching. And the phone calls. They got more and more disturbing. They left me imagining the worst. I think I did a pretty good job of not letting it show but by the end I was a mess, on the inside at least. I got headaches and stomach aches and I had trouble sleeping."

"You certainly hid it well. That last time we met in Vancouver I remember thinking you were pretty happy. More upbeat than I'd seen you in a while."

"Yeah, by then I was feeling a bit better because I'd made the decision to get out, come hell or high water. That's why I asked you to be executor, just in case something happened and I didn't make it. But a little earlier it had been really bad."

"Did you know that someone at the mine started a rumor that your accident was actually suicide? A couple of people said you hadn't been yourself before it happened, but others said they hadn't noticed any difference, so the rumor died away. And there wasn't a suicide note."

"I thought about writing a suicide note, but I didn't want my daughter to have to live with the thought that I'd killed myself. I actually did think about suicide a few times when I was really down, but it was one of those things that just comes into your head and then you dismiss it. I don't think I could do it anyway, I like being alive too much." Thompson laughed. "I also had a little ace in the hole. I'll tell you about that later."

Doucet raised his eyebrows. The engineer was full of surprises.

"So I decided the only way out was to make everyone think I was dead. But how do you do that if there's no body? Then one day I was watching someone on a snowmobile and I thought to myself, that would be perfect. If someone goes through the ice on a snowmobile and drowns, you probably don't find the body. At least until summer, when the ice is gone. The main problem I had was getting away from the mine without anyone knowing. I didn't want to risk going out with the truckers on the ice road – it would be too slow and there was too much of a possibility that someone would see me. Besides, if there was a thaw I could be stuck. So I started talking to some of the pilots who flew in the cargo planes – not telling them what I wanted to do, just getting to know them. One guy in particular I liked, he was quiet and professional and I figured he might do it and keep quiet if I gave him some money. So one night when he came in late I bit the bullet and grabbed him and asked if he'd take me out on his plane the next day, no questions asked, for five hundred dollars. Part of the agreement, I told him, was that he couldn't tell anyone. That was a weak link in the plan, but I didn't see any other way to do it – whoever I went out with would know I was still alive, and I'd just have to trust them to keep their mouth shut. This guy seemed to be okay, he didn't ask any questions, he just said if I wanted to sneak away it was no skin off his back, and he wouldn't tell anyone. He bargained a bit and I ended up giving him eight hundred. He was taking off at six the next morning and I figured it was my best chance. Fortunately it was snowing that night, which I realized would help cover up my footprints, so I took out one of the snowmobiles and when I got close to the thin ice area I got off and pointed it straight ahead, put it in gear, and walked back along the tracks. No sweat. The snow covered up everything so nobody knew the difference. I hid out in the plane overnight and nearly froze to death, but I was so happy to be leaving the place that I didn't care. We landed in Calgary and when I got out of that plane I just walked away. It was one of the best days of my life."

"There was a lot of discussion at Diatek about why you went out on the snowmobile so late at night, especially in a storm. People figured you probably ended up on the thin ice because you got disoriented by the snow."

"Oh, I knew exactly where the thin ice was. I'd been checking it out for weeks. The snow was a lucky break."

Doucet shook his head. "It's mind boggling, stranger than fiction. How did you end up in Ensenada?"

"That's a long story too. I'd been to Ensenada once before, a long time ago. It was not long after I got married; Sharon and I came on a holiday with some friends, another couple from back east in Ontario. It was winter, February I think, and we thought we'd died and gone to heaven, the climate was so perfect. We rented a camper van and drove all the way from Tijuana to Cabo San Lucas, and along the way we camped on the beach for several days not far from here. We got to know an American couple who were renting a house here for the winter. They were from somewhere in the Midwest, they were both retired, and they told us they came down here every winter to escape the cold. They invited us all over for a drink one night, and their place was one of the houses on this street – just a few houses down from here. It seemed like paradise to us, and my wife and I vowed we'd come back some winter, but of course we never did. It was one of those things that sticks in your memory, though. It seemed like a good place to hide while I sorted thing out. And it has been."

"It can't have been very easy to get here, crossing borders and everything."

"Yeah, that was the nerve wracking part, especially going into the U.S. As soon as I got off the airplane in Calgary I took the quickest bus route I could to the U.S., straight south to Great Falls, Montana. I literally held my breath when we crossed over because there was nothing I could do except use my real passport. But it was soon enough after the accident that no alarm bells went off. Somewhere, though, there must be a record that I crossed the border shortly after I was supposed to have died." Thompson laughed. "It sounds funny now, but it sure wasn't at the time.

"I'd been planning the whole thing for quite a while and I'd gradually built up a supply of cash – U.S. dollars – so I didn't have to use a credit card. I stayed in a cheap motel in Great Falls and then for the next few days I took buses and zigzagged around a lot to make sure nobody was following. But as soon as I was sure I was in the clear, I came straight here. It wasn't difficult to cross the border at Tijuana, I just walked over with the tourists."

"How in the world did Andropov find you? Or I guess a better question is how did he figure out you're still alive? No one else seems to know. Your lawyer even called me the other day and said we should file for a formal declaration of death because there didn't seem to be any chance now that your body would be recovered."

Thompson laughed again. "A formal declaration of death? That sounds pretty macabre. Well, now you can hold off for a while because I'm determined to come back. Back from the dead." He shook his head. "I don't know for sure how Andropov tracked me down. I thought I'd covered my tracks well enough that even if someone *did* suspect I was still alive they wouldn't be able to find me. I've been really careful here; as far as anyone knows I'm David Brown, a bachelor from Chicago who likes the sun and has enough money to rent a place like this on the beach for a year. The only thing I can think of is that Andropov or whoever he works with somehow got to the pilot who flew me out. He's the only person who knew I was still alive, I'm sure of that. It always worried me because on the flight to Calgary we were talking, just shooting the breeze, and at one point he asked me what I was going to do when I got off the plane. I was keyed up and so happy to get away from the mine that without thinking I said I would probably go south and sit in the sun in Mexico. I almost bit my tongue as soon as I said it, but of course it was out there and I couldn't take it back. So if they found him and got him to talk, it might have pointed them in this direction. Although Mexico is a big country. How Andropov knew I was in Ensenada is anybody's guess. With everything I know now I'm actually not that surprised. I almost got away again, though, because my friend Jorge told me that someone had been asking around about who lived in this house, which scared me, so I decided to clear out. I was going to leave that same night Andropov arrived. A few more hours and I would have been gone."

Thompson got up and started to pace back and forth across the deck. "Speaking of which, I'm worried now too. Obviously he figured out that I staged the snowmobile accident, and once he knew that he tracked me down. If he did it once, he can do it again, and I'm afraid that somehow he'll find out that I survived his attack. That's one of the reasons I asked you to come down here. I really need to get away, soon, and go back to Canada.

"Like I said before, I can't just get on a plane and go back that easily. Besides, I don't even have a passport anymore, or any other ID for that matter. They wouldn't even let me on an airplane. But on the other hand I've got detailed information about serious fraud at Diatek. That should give me some leverage. If I can convince the police that the information is genuine and I'm not just some crackpot, the situation would be entirely different. Does that make sense?"

"Yes, I think you're probably right. But how do you convince the police?"

"Well, I'm hoping you'll be an intermediary. We've worked together at Diatek, you know I'm really Bill Thompson and you know I'm still alive. You've seen these" – he indicated his bandaged wrists and hand – "and you've seen where Andropov and his sidekick tortured me with their cigarettes." He lifted up his shirt so Doucet could see the burn marks. "I think that would get their attention. I wouldn't want you to give them everything I've told you, not until we've worked out some kind of agreement. But if you told them in a general way about what I know I think they'd be ready to listen. So if you go back and contact the police I'm hoping it will pave the way so I can leave soon. In the meantime I asked Jorge to get me a gun, just in case. And I won't open the door to anyone I don't know."

"You've got a *gun*?"

"I'm getting one. Jorge said it shouldn't be a problem. This time I want to be prepared. If Andropov or any of his friends show up again they won't find it so easy. Last time I wasn't expecting them and even if I'd had a gun I'm not sure it would have made much difference."

"I'd like to meet this Jorge."

"Yeah, he's a good friend to have. He knows just about everybody in town, and if I ever need anything he's the first person I ask. I really lucked out when I met him, he's about the only local I know. I was wandering around at the harbor one day not long after I got here, looking at the boats and the scenery, and I started talking to him about fishing. Jorge is in real estate but he's also got a really nice boat and he takes people out deep sea fishing. It's more of a hobby than a business, I don't think he makes any money on it, just enough to keep the boat in good shape and pay for fuel. Once I got to know him we'd go out fishing regularly, just the two of us. He's the one who found me after Andropov left; we had decided to go out fishing that morning and even though I'd made up my mind to leave I didn't dare tell anyone – even Jorge. He came by earlier than we planned – he told me later he couldn't sleep and figured he'd just come and wake me up. It was a lucky break. I'm convinced I would have bled to death if it hadn't been for him. Andropov and his buddy had no way of knowing Jorge would be coming so soon after they left. It was their big mistake.

"When Jorge got here and I didn't answer the door he went around the back and looked in the kitchen window. That's when he saw me tied to the chair, and he called the police and told them they'd need an ambulance. He knows most of the police in Ensenada, so they came right away."

Doucet couldn't get over how calmly Thompson talked about his ordeal. "I think I know who I could talk to in Vancouver," he said. "A couple of nights after the break-in at my apartment an RCMP officer showed up at the door and asked me a bunch of questions. Just a follow up, he said. It seemed odd because when I called 911 it was Vancouver police who came, not the RCMP. I still don't know why they got involved. But he gave me his card." Doucet pulled out his wallet and found Zelensky's card and handed it to Thompson.

Thompson looked at it for a minute. "Another lucky break," he said. "I wasn't sure how to do this, who to go to, because if you just make a cold call or walk into the police station and tell them some incredible tale, who's going to believe you? But if you already know this Mr. Zelensky it's a whole new ball game. Will you do that Rick? Call him as soon as you get back?"

CHAPTER 24

Ed Zelensky was surprised when he saw the text message from Rick Doucet. He'd tried to contact the geologist a couple of times the previous week about the break-in at his apartment, but he had not replied. Now he wanted to meet, ASAP: there was something important they needed to talk about. The message had been sent on Saturday but Zelensky hadn't seen it immediately because Heather had talked him into taking a few days off before the cold weather closed in, and on Saturday morning he'd turned off his Blackberry and they'd driven up to the Sunshine Coast for a long weekend. Now it was Monday night. He typed out a reply: Sorry, I was away and just saw your message. Come in any time tomorrow. He gave Doucet directions to his office. Maybe the geologist had remembered something relevant to the break-in.

Doucet had spent most of the weekend at the lab, catching up on work he'd had to put aside after the mugging and his trip to Seattle and Mexico. He'd been away for just over a week; after deciding to go to Ensenada he'd texted Tim Bailey and said he had to go back east for a family emergency and would have to be away from work, probably for the whole week. It was a little white lie, but he couldn't tell Bailey the truth. Doucet had been worried about taking the time off, but Bailey replied that it wasn't a problem. After your work this summer, he said, you deserve some rest. I hope it's nothing serious.

Doucet realized he could probably ask Bailey for almost anything and his boss would give it to him. His exploration team was still basking in their success and his own star was on the rise within the company. Diatek had staked a large area around the lake where they had found the abundance of indicator minerals, and plans were already underway for test drilling. If the assay results were positive, they'd have a second diamond mine.

But other things were not going as smoothly. Especially he was concerned that Zelensky hadn't replied to his message. In spite of the praise his work was getting, the conflicting demands of his life – Diatek, taking Thompson's story to the RCMP, his career – were weighing on him, and he wanted to get the business with Thompson behind him. And then there was Sarah. He'd spent the night at her apartment on his way back from Mexico, and he'd told her everything about his trip to Ensenada. They'd talked until late, and in the morning, both of them tired, she'd walked with him to his car. She was going to work, he was driving back to Vancouver, and as they stood saying goodbye he felt something pass between them. He didn't know what it was but he was sure she felt it too, he could see it in her eyes. It had happened once before, in her flat in London, just after he'd learned about Thompson's snowmobile accident. For Doucet it was like a jolt of electricity and without thinking he reached out pulled her to him. She didn't resist and for a long moment they stood there, pressed together, her head on his shoulder. He could feel her breath on his neck. In that instant something changed, and now he couldn't stop thinking about her.

So when at last he saw a message from the RCMP officer on Monday night he breathed a sigh of relief. He'd have to take a few more hours off work, but the sooner he told Zelensky about Thompson, the sooner he'd be rid of that responsibility. He replied immediately, saying he'd come by the next day, in the afternoon.

He got to the RCMP building just after three. In his briefcase he had a statement Thompson had written out and signed, describing, in vague terms, what he had to offer: information about serious fraud in the Canadian diamond industry that he'd be willing to divulge in return for safe passage back to Canada. He wrote that he was currently in Mexico and that someone had already tried to murder him to prevent him talking about it. He was, he said, still in fear for his life. Doucet hoped that between the statement and his own account of his encounter with Thompson in Ensenada, Zelensky would be able to do something.

He had to go through security and then he was directed through a maze of hallways to Zelensky's office. "Come in," a voice said when he knocked on the partly closed door, and he walked into a small, cramped office with books and papers everywhere. Zelensky was sitting at his computer and got up when he saw Doucet. "Welcome Mr. Doucet," he said, "we meet again. Sorry about the chaos; we're getting ready to move to new buildings so I'm sorting through a lot of old paperwork and the place is a bit of a mess. Like your apartment when I came to see you, as I recall." He smiled, then did a double take. "What happened to your nose?"

Doucet instinctively put his hand up to his face. He'd been to the doctor earlier in the day and the large bandages were gone, but there were two smaller ones across the bridge of his nose and his face was still reddish and slightly puffy. "Uh, I had an accident. It's one of the things I need to talk to you about."

Zelensky looked at him quizzically. "Okay," he said. "Have a seat. I got your message, obviously. What's so important you needed to talk to me right away?"

"I'm not sure where to start. Things have gotten more complicated since that night you came to my place. A lot more complicated. Probably the best thing is for you to read this." Doucet opened his briefcase and pulled out Thompson's statement.

The room was quiet while Zelensky read it through. It didn't take him long, and when he finished he looked up at Doucet but didn't say anything. Then he read it again. Finally he put the paper down on his desk and leaned forward on his elbows. "Is this for real?"

"Yes," Doucet said, "it's for real. It was written by someone who used to work at Diatek – that's the company I work for – at our mine in the Northwest Territories. The information he refers to there has to do with something that happened at the mine. I can't say any more than that, but believe me, it's mind-blowing. The whole thing is almost beyond belief. All of us thought he was dead, and I got the shock of my life when I got a message to call a number in Mexico, and it was him. He was in a hospital and I went down there last week, took him home, and talked to him for a couple of days. He wants to come back and tell his story to the authorities."

"William Thompson," Zelensky said, looking again at the statement. "Isn't he the one who drowned in the snowmobile accident?" His face was expressionless but all the neurons in his brain were lighting up. This could be the break he'd been looking for.

"You know about that?" Doucet was surprised. The accident hadn't exactly been headline news and outside the Diatek community few people had paid much attention. "Yes, that's him, except obviously he didn't drown. He faked the whole thing and got away without anyone realizing it. Then someone caught up with him and almost killed him. He was very lucky to escape."

"And you're absolutely sure it's Thompson?"

"Oh yeah, no question. I've known him for several years. He's thinner and he's grown a beard but it's him."

"Why you? Why didn't he come to us himself? Does anyone else know he's in Mexico?"

"Good questions. I don't think anyone else knows he's alive. He's divorced; his wife and daughter are back in Ontario and I know from what he told me that they have no idea. He didn't do this for insurance or anything like that; all I can say is that he got deeply involved in something before he really understood that it was illegal and dangerous. The snowmobile accident was an act of desperation, it was the only way he could think of to get out. As for why me, I don't really know except that Thompson doesn't seem to have many close friends. I only know him through work, but we get along well and earlier this year he asked me to be executor of his will, so I think in his mind I was the logical person to turn to. He's been living incognito in Mexico and right now he doesn't even have a passport. It wouldn't be easy for him to come back here without some help."

Zelensky was writing notes and he looked up when Doucet mentioned the will. "What's happened to his estate?" he asked. "Has anything been distributed yet?"

"No," Doucet said, "nothing at all. We couldn't, because there was no death certificate. I guess as far as the law is concerned, he isn't officially dead – they've never found a body. His lawyer told me recently that we need to file for a legal declaration of death so things can go ahead."

"Mm. Can you tell me a little more about this 'serious fraud' he mentions in his statement?"

"No, I can't. I gave him my word."

Zelensky stopped writing. "But he told you? It would be very helpful if you gave me something, Mr. Doucet. I can't go off investigating every problem someone brings me if I don't know what it's all about." He spoke calmly but there was a hard edge to his voice. Doucet realized there was a lot more to the policeman than his friendly exterior revealed.

"Um, well, that puts me in a tricky position. He really wants to come back but I promised I would leave all the details to him. From what he told me, though, it was – it is – a major scam, and he has detailed knowledge about it that he's willing to hand over. Mainly he wants to be sure he'll be taken seriously if he comes back. Like he says in the statement, he's convinced his life is in danger. He knows enough that they tracked him down and tried to kill him in Mexico, he's just lucky to be alive and he's convinced they'll try again if they find out he survived. He thinks one of the guys who attacked him is a Russian he met several years ago at the Diatek mine. As I said, it's mind-blowing."

Zelensky froze. He tried to keep his expression neutral. "Russian? How does he know that?"

"Well, as I said, he'd met the guy before, at the mine. He had a Russian name: Andropov. I don't think Thompson would mind me telling you that. He recognized him because he'd spent a day with him, showing him around the ore processing operations. That's Thompson's specialty. Apparently this guy had come over from Russia especially for the mine visit. But you really should hear the story yourself."

Again Zelensky struggled to keep his face blank. It had to be the same Andropov, it couldn't be a coincidence. "What did you say the Russian's name was?"

"Andropov. Thompson talked about him a lot. Not someone I had ever heard of at Diatek."

Zelensky wrote 'Andropov' in his notebook and circled it. He made a decision.

"Listen, Mr. Doucet," he said, looking up. "If Thompson has the kind of information you say he has we might be able to put him in the witness protection program. I have to tell you that that doesn't absolve him from responsibility. If he's committed a crime he'll have to answer for it, but if he's cooperative there might be some leniency. Do you think he'd be interested?"

"I think he'd be very interested. From what he told me, he'll do anything he can to help you bring those people to justice. And he understands that even if he cooperates it won't give him a free ride."

"There are some practical things I'll have to take care of before he can come back – first of all I have to get approval to put him in the program. I wish I could simply wave a magic wand but this place is a bureaucracy and I'll have to jump through quite a few hoops. I don't think it will be a problem, though. If all goes well it shouldn't take more than a few days. Does that sound okay?"

"Yeah, I think so, the sooner the better. Thompson is sure these guys will come back for him when they find out he's alive. He told me he was going to get a gun from a friend so he could protect himself. Just in case. At least he'll be prepared."

"I hope he knows how to use it. If he doesn't he might be better off without it. Anyway, why don't you tell him what's happening and as soon as I get the necessary approvals I'll let you know. From that point on I'll take over all communications and make the arrangements for him to come back."

Doucet nodded his assent.

"Oh, and Mr. Doucet? Why don't you tell the lawyer to go ahead and file for that legal declaration of death." Zelensky was already working on a strategy. "I think it's best if everyone still believes Thompson is dead. Especially the people who tried to kill him in Mexico, but everyone else too, including the lawyer. So don't tell anyone. Not even your mother." He smiled. "Before you go, any more thoughts on the break-in at your apartment?"

"Possibly," Doucet said. "Apparently the guys who attacked Thompson in Mexico found my name on some papers at his place. They were documents connected to the scheme he wants to tell you about, so when they ransacked my place they may have been looking for copies of those documents that I didn't actually have. That would explain why nothing was taken. And then a few days after the break-in somebody mugged me." He pointed to his face. "That's the reason for these bandages; they broke my nose. But that wasn't a robbery, either. They didn't want money, they just asked me about Thompson. At the time I didn't understand it, because as far as I knew Thompson was dead. Now I'm pretty sure it's all connected."

Zelensky looked across the table at him. The pieces of the puzzle were starting to come together. "Mr. Doucet, you've made my day. I'll be in touch as soon as everything is in place for Thompson to come back. I might need to speak with you again."

CHAPTER 25

When he left Zelensky's office on Tuesday afternoon, Doucet checked his phone and found a short message from Sarah. Call me tonight, she said, it's important. It was barely more than twenty-four hours since they'd said goodbye in Seattle, but already he missed her. He almost didn't care what she had to say, he just wanted to hear her voice.

He worked late at his office then called her as soon as he got home. "I got your message," he said, "What's up?"

"A lot, Rick. It's dynamite, but I'm not sure you'll be happy to hear what I have to say. I've gradually been working my way through the files that Chris downloaded from your CFO's computer, concentrating on the company financials. Then for some reason I decided to take a look at a folder he'd labeled 'personal.' I did it on a whim, I didn't think there would be anything important in there, but boy was I wrong. I got so excited I almost called you at midnight."

Doucet could hear the excitement in her voice now, but he didn't say anything.

"Are you there?"

"Mm. I'm listening."

"Okay, so I didn't call at midnight; I thought better of it. But I hardly slept all night. Your Mr. Mulroney appears to be one very bad apple. Fortunately he's also a neat and tidy guy who keeps records of everything. He keeps maintenance records for his boat and his cars, records of how much gas and electricity he uses, you name it and he's got a file on it. But he also put some Diatek stuff in with his personal files. Things that are very confidential – I think he was probably trying to hide it in plain sight. It's a lesson in why you shouldn't keep sensitive material on a networked computer if you don't want someone to see it. None of us think someone is going to break in, but you saw how easy it was for Chris to get the information."

Doucet could picture her, sitting in her makeshift office or maybe on the sofa in her living room. "Mulroney always struck me as being very organized," he said. "He always has things lined up in neat little piles on his desk. What did you find in his files?"

"Where do I start? There's so much it's hard to digest all at once. I'll make a summary and send it to you when I get through everything, but I had to call – there's no one else I can talk to about this, and I just can't stay quiet. First, there are more details in Mulroney's files about how WWME International is structured. We talked before about how it's registered in the Cayman Islands, but it turns out to be a lot more complicated than that. WWME has three Directors, each of which is a company – it's not completely unusual to have a company listed as a Director, but my guess is these are just shell companies – and each of *those* companies is solely represented by a single individual. Those three individuals are also Directors of the bank that issued the original loan to purchase the Diatek mining property. I'm guessing, but I bet these three people make out like gangbusters financially. Either that or they're Cayman residents who get paid handsomely for being just-on-paper Directors and someone else makes the real money. Complicated arrangements like this are always done for money. Does all this make sense so far?"

"It's convoluted, but I think I follow. My head is spinning, though."

"That's the whole point. It's supposed to make your head spin, and confuse the authorities. As we talked about when you were here, Diatek writes off the interest on the loan in Canada, and the bank in the Caymans doesn't have to pay taxes on the interest it earns. So those transactions are essentially tax free. It's a very cozy setup. And that's not all. I had noticed earlier that the interest rate on the original loan was high, but when I looked at it carefully I found that it's way higher than the going market rate at the time the loan was made. Mining is a risky business but even when you factor that in, the rate is higher than it needed to be. They could have gotten a better deal elsewhere, but they didn't. And here's the kicker. The Caymans bank that made the original loan is a small private bank owned by the Russian oligarch Vasily Gagarin. He's the guy my colleague at McKinsey claimed had connections with Diatek."

"Yes, I remember you told me about that. I didn't really believe it. I'm still not sure I believe it, the Russian mafia part, anyway."

"But it's there, it's in black and white in those files." Sarah sounded exasperated. "I don't know about the mafia, but there's a direct connection between Gagarin and Diatek through his bank in the Caymans. Surely you can see that."

"Okay, okay. Yeah, of course, I do. It's just … it's hard to believe. Diatek is a great company and I've never heard anything about Russians being involved. Suddenly Bill Thompson gets attacked by a Russian and you're talking about the Russian mafia – it's like they're the flavor of the month."

"Exactly. They seem to be all over this thing. There's more, too. You know all those wire transfers to the Caymans we looked at? A lot of them get split three ways once they arrive at the bank, and the money gets transferred to the three companies listed as WWME Directors. And the company accounts are all held at Mr. Gagarin's bank. Again I know this courtesy of Mr. Mulroney's record keeping. That's why I said that either those three WWME Directors or others behind them are making a lot of money." She paused and then laughed. "Hard to believe, but I'm actually having fun doing this."

"I get it, Sarah. I don't like it because of what it implies about Diatek, but I get the satisfaction. It's like me tracing my indicator minerals. When you find the answers you're looking for, that's all the reward you need."

"Uh-huh, my sentiments exactly. By the way, the name Gagarin also pops up in another one of Mulroney's files – it's in a note he wrote in 2010. A memorandum about setting aside a million dollars to open an account for one A. Gagarin at a private bank in London. A million dollars! No explanation, no justification. The money was routed through the bank in the Caymans but as far as I can tell it ultimately came from Diatek operating costs."

"This is turning into a total nightmare, Sarah. A couple of weeks ago I was on such a high after we found that new diamond prospect, and now all this. It's going to take time to process. Like, do I even want to work for Diatek if all this is true? There are a lot of good people here, and so far it's been good for me personally, better than DeBeers …"

"Sorry to be the bearer of bad news, but it's better you know now rather than later. I doubt it's the company as a whole anyway, that would be too obvious. It's probably just a few people, maybe even just Mulroney, although it's hard to imagine he could do it all himself. Remember Enron? It was a case study for us at university. A small group of people manipulated the accounts so it looked like the company was making a ton of money. Nobody else knew what they were doing. Enron was the darling of Wall Street; even the outside accountants were fooled, or maybe they just looked the other way. By the way, if I remember correctly, Enron had almost seven hundred subsidiaries registered in the Cayman Islands and they passed a lot of money through them. It was so complicated nobody could figure it all out, but even the guys who were manipulating things couldn't hide the fraud forever and eventually the company collapsed. Most of the money they claimed to be making wasn't even real, it was just an artifact of their bookkeeping. And it was all down to just a few guys. Most of the others who worked for Enron were good people."

"I'm thinking about Mulroney – even he seems like a good guy," Doucet said. "He's super smart, I know that. He can be a bit arrogant at times but it's hard to believe he's a crook."

"You can never tell, Rick. The Enron people called themselves the smartest guys in the room and their colleagues believed them. They didn't know that in reality they were crooks. But I'm getting distracted. I found even more surprises in Mulroney's files. For instance, diamond sales. There are notes about selling rough diamonds to a cutting and polishing company in Yellowknife. But if you read between the lines it's clear that it's only being done for PR – you know, supporting small local industries. Most of the diamonds are actually shipped out of the country, to New York or Antwerp or India for cutting and processing and only a very small fraction of the total production stays in Canada for processing. And on paper at least, the ones that get shipped out of the country are first sold to WWME – at a low price. On a per carat basis Diatek gets less for those diamonds than for the ones they sell to the company in Yellowknife. Maybe it has to do with quality, but I doubt it, because WWME then sells them on at a much *higher* price. Are you following?"

"Yeah. But it still makes my head spin."

"It's a classic tax haven ploy. They call it 'transfer mispricing' in the business, and it's a sleight of hand to confuse the authorities. Diatek in Canada gets an artificially low price for the diamonds they sell to WWME; they may price them to make a small profit or maybe they make a loss, but either way they keep their Canadian taxes low. WWME is the company that makes the big profit, but it doesn't get taxed because the onward sale of diamonds takes place in the Caymans, where they're registered. Or at least that's what it looks like on paper; in reality the diamonds go straight from Diatek to India or wherever, it's only the money that goes through the Caymans. The problem – or if you're from WWME the beauty of it – is that it would be pretty hard to prove that they are actually mispricing the diamonds. It's not like buying and selling light bulbs or shoes or bananas because the price of diamonds is entirely based on quality, and from what I've read the quality of rough diamonds varies tremendously. Not even the experts always agree on the quality."

"That's true," Doucet said. "The diamonds have to be cut and polished before they're sold to consumers, and you never know what will happen. It's not so bad with small diamonds, but the cutters have to have nerves of steel when they're working on large ones. You hear stories about diamonds shattering into pieces when they start to cut them. It must be very scary. No minerals are perfect; when they grow they incorporate things like tiny gas bubbles or small grains of other minerals. They're referred to as inclusions, and in diamonds any obvious inclusions lower the quality." Finally there was something in the conversation Doucet could talk about knowledgably. "And then there are what we call lattice imperfections. Diamonds are made of carbon, right? But no diamond is one hundred percent pure carbon, there are always other elements there, even if they are present in minute amounts. Those other elements are a different size from the carbon atoms, so they distort the crystal structure, and if there are enough imperfections or inclusions they create zones of weakness that you can't see, even with a magnifying glass. People think of diamonds as being hard and indestructible; well, they're hard, that's for sure, but when they start cutting one of these little crystals that has been sitting around underground for hundreds of millions of years it's suddenly stressed by the pressure of the saw, and it's also heated up by friction from the blade. That can be enough for it to fracture along one of those zones of weakness."

"There you go, Rick. You get your kicks from geology, I get mine from finances." She was quiet for a moment. "The question is, who should all this information go to? It wouldn't be right if it just got swept under the rug."

"I think I know the answer," Doucet said. "When you sent your text this afternoon I was sitting with an RCMP officer, a guy named Zelensky, telling him about my visit to Ensenada. My impression is that he's pretty good, and he seems very interested in this case. He's planning to bring Thompson back to Canada and put him in the witness protection program, probably in the next few days. I didn't say anything about what you've been doing, but it's starting to look as though it's all connected. I could pass your summary on to him. Assuming it's okay with you."

"That's fine with me. But I won't put my name on it. I don't mind if you tell him I wrote it, but I'd rather keep it anonymous as far as the official record is concerned. For the time being, anyway."

CHAPTER 26

Zelensky moved quickly. He had to call in favors from several of his colleagues but three days after Doucet brought him Thompson's statement he had the authorization he needed to put the engineer in witness protection, and he had arranged to keep him at least temporarily in a safe house in Vancouver. As soon as he'd made the arrangements he left for Mexico to accompany Thompson back to Canada.

They arrived at Vancouver International on a commercial flight, Thompson unrecognizable with his beard and dark glasses and the baseball cap that Zelensky had insisted he wear pulled down over his forehead. The last thing the RCMP officer wanted was for someone on the flight to recognize the engineer. It was unlikely they'd encounter anyone who knew him, but he didn't want to take any chances. If word got out that he was alive it would blow Zelensky's plan out of the water. He'd spoken to the police in Ensenada, and they in turn had spoken quietly to the hospital staff, and now both police and hospital records showed that one David Brown of Chicago had died in the Ensenada hospital of injuries sustained during a brutal and unsolved attack, probably connected to drug trafficking.

On Zelensky's authority he and Thompson bypassed immigration and customs and went directly to a waiting car that took them to the safe house. During the journey the engineer had been tense, but now that he was back on Canadian soil he relaxed and started to thank Zelensky effusively.

The policeman cut him short. "Don't thank me yet, Mr. Thompson. This isn't a holiday; I can more-or-less guarantee you'll have some rough times ahead." Zelensky wanted to keep his distance until he got to know Thompson better. He also didn't want the engineer to think this was going to be easy.

The safe house was an anonymous two story home that looked no different than the other houses on the tree lined street. Zelensky took Thompson inside and introduced him. "You're completely safe here," he said, "there's always someone on duty and nobody who isn't authorized gets in. There's food in the kitchen and you can help yourself but if you need anything just ask. Tomorrow is Sunday, but we'll start anyway – I'll be back first thing in the morning. It's likely to be a long day so get some sleep tonight if you can, okay?" He turned and went out the door, not waiting for Thompson to reply.

Zelensky was true to his word; he got to the safe house early Sunday morning. He had skipped breakfast and stopped at Tim Hortons for coffee, and after a moment's hesitation he bought a box of Timbits to take with him. He knew he shouldn't – he'd noticed recently that his belt was uncomfortably tight, and he'd had to slacken it another notch – but it was going to be a long day and Timbits were so good. He was sure Thompson would appreciate them; there were no Tim Hortons in Ensenada.

The engineer was showered and ready for him, and he looked better than he had the day before. It had taken him a while to settle down, he said, but he'd slept well. "It's good to be back here," he said, "even under the circumstances. I like Mexico but I couldn't live there forever."

Zelensky set up the recorder and made sure it was working properly. He had conducted many interrogations during his career but he had a feeling that this was going to be one of the most interesting. Thompson's statement hadn't revealed much but as soon as Rick Doucet had mentioned Andropov he had started to connect the dots – to the phone calls intercepted by NSA, to the Russians in Vancouver, to the break-in at Doucet's apartment, and now, apparently, to fraud in the diamond industry. The case was beginning to look like a set of Russian dolls – every time he opened one he found another one inside.

"Before I turn on the recorder I just want to say that when we formally begin this interview," – Zelensky always called them interviews, not interrogations; he'd found it made a huge difference in the way people answered his questions – "I will tell you, on the record, that you don't have to provide evidence if you think it might incriminate you. Personally I don't really like it; I'd much rather hear everything you know. But it's the law and I have to explain it to you. Okay?"

But Thompson waved his hand and said he wouldn't hold anything back. "I've made that decision," he said, "I'm ready to live with the consequences."

"Good," Zelensky said. "That will make my life easier." He turned on the recorder and told Thompson formally that he had the right not to incriminate himself, and then they started. He began slowly, wanting to establish some kind of rapport with the engineer. But he was surprised at how quickly Thompson opened up to him. He's been on his own in Mexico for six months, Zelensky realized, with hardly anyone to talk to. Now he's making up for it. After a few questions about his background, all the policeman had to do was sit back and listen. Thompson spent the whole morning telling him about growing up in Ontario, how he'd always liked to build things when he was a kid and how that led him naturally – in a mining town like Sudbury – to take up mining engineering at university. Nickel capital of Canada, they called Sudbury; he'd been hired by the mining company as soon as he graduated and until he moved out west, he said, he'd spent virtually his whole life there. He told Zelensky about his problem with alcohol and how it had wrecked his career and led to his divorce and was ultimately the reason he ended up working at a diamond mine in the Northwest Territories. But he got through it, and he'd been on the wagon ever since.

Thompson kept talking and at noon Zelensky said they both needed a break.

"The guys downstairs will get you some lunch," he said. "I have a couple of things I need to take care of back at my office." He told Thompson he'd be back around two o'clock.

By midafternoon they got to what really interested Zelensky: the fraud Thompson had written of in his statement. Once again it was like turning on a tap; Thompson needed little encouragement to spill it all out. Now, though, Zelensky stopped him frequently, asking him to go back through details multiple times. It was tedious and at times Thompson got visibly frustrated. Zelensky didn't think the engineer was making things up, but he wanted to get it right.

"It's not that I don't believe you," he said when Thompson complained. "It's just that your memory can play tricks on you. Sometimes going through it several times makes it clearer. Or you remember details you missed the first time."

Zelensky had been flying under the radar on this case; he was senior enough that he had a lot of leeway in what he did and he hadn't yet briefed his superiors in detail. He knew bringing Thompson back from Mexico was a risk, but his intuition told him it would be worth it. By the end of that first afternoon questioning the engineer he knew for sure he'd made the right decision. If half of what he'd heard from Thompson was true, this case was going to be a major breakthrough. More than once in the periodic RCMP training seminars he attended he had heard speakers talk about the potential for the fledgling Canadian diamond industry to be targeted by organized crime. It hasn't happened here yet, the experts always said, the industry has multiple built-in safeguards. Still, we have to be vigilant, we have to think outside the box and anticipate problems. Organized crime has made inroads in most other countries with diamond industries because diamonds are fundamentally untraceable; they're a money launderers dream.

Well, Zelensky thought, this will really shake them up. If Thompson is right someone is bringing diamonds *into* the country, not smuggling them out. It's the criminals who are thinking outside the box, not us; they've figured out that they can use our safeguards to their advantage.

On his way home that night Zelensky called Rick Doucet and asked him if he could come to his office early the next morning, before he went to work. He didn't tell Doucet why he wanted to see him because he wanted to ask his questions cold. Assuming Doucet and Thompson hadn't cooked up some elaborate story, which he thought unlikely, the geologist should be able to verify some of the things Thompson had told him – or not. He was pretty sure Thompson was telling the truth, but he'd been fooled before. Before he went much further he wanted to be absolutely sure.

The RCMP building was still quiet when Doucet arrived, not many people were in yet, but Zelensky took him down the hall to a small cubicle where he already had coffee brewing and poured Doucet a cup. It was very strong and Doucet had to add milk and stir in several spoons full of sugar before he could drink it. When they got back to his office Zelensky closed the door and told him to take a seat.

"Thanks for coming in on short notice. This shouldn't take long, I just have a few questions for you. And I'd appreciate it if nothing I say gets repeated outside this room, okay?"

Once again Doucet noticed the hard edge to Zelensky's voice, something in the tone that made him realize the policeman was someone you wouldn't want to cross.

"No, of course not. And I was going to call you anyway, because I've got something I think you should see …"

Zelensky raised his eyebrows. "For me? Okay, but let's get these questions out of the way first. They're straightforward, I just want to confirm some details about Bill Thompson and the chronology of everything that's happened." He spent the next fifteen minutes quizzing Doucet on what he knew about Thompson's life at the mine, how often he came and went from Vancouver, the details of what Thompson had told him about the attack in Ensenada.

When they were finished he said, "Good. What you say fits with what I already know." He hesitated for a moment. "Thompson is here, in Vancouver. I spent most of yesterday with him and I wanted to double check some of the things he told me."

The surprise showed on Doucet's face. "He's here already? That was fast."

"Yeah, well sometimes it happens. Everything went smoothly and fortunately the Mexicans were cooperative. Officially David Brown died in that hospital and there never was a Mr. Thompson in Ensenada. I think we can keep the lid on it, at least for a while. The weak link is probably the hospital staff, because he was there for a while and some of them know he walked out with you. They've been warned, but you never know. It would be good if no one at Diatek knew you were down there in Ensenada."

"They don't. As far as they know I had to go back east for a family emergency."

"Okay, try to keep it that way." Zelensky glanced at his watch. "I have to go soon. What was it you wanted to show me? Can we keep it short?"

Doucet reached into his briefcase and pulled out Sarah's summary of her research into Diatek's finances. She'd sent it to him the night before. "This is pretty complicated. Maybe you should read it when you have more time and then we can talk." He handed the papers to Zelensky.

The policeman glanced through it, three densely written pages. "What is it?"

"It's a long story. It's based on work a friend of mine has been doing on the Canadian diamond industry. But this is kind of an offshoot of her research – it's about financial irregularities at Diatek. I think it's connected with what Thompson was doing."

Zelensky looked at him sharply. "Really?" He turned again to Sarah's summary and for several minutes the room was quiet as he skimmed through it. Finally he looked up. "Where did your friend get this information?"

"Uh, various places. Some of it is internal company data." He paused, wondering if he should tell Zelensky about hacking into Mulroney's computer, then decided against it. "But there's something else you should know about. It's not in those papers, she only told me last night when she sent me this summary. First of all, when Thompson started taking diamonds into the mine several years ago, diamond production at Diatek went up because of the smuggled diamonds. Sarah thinks she has evidence that the profits from that increased production got skimmed off by somebody. And then when Thompson had his 'accident' and stopped taking in diamonds, production went back down to normal levels. The thing is, Sarah told me last night that it looks as though the same thing is happening again. Diamond production went way up again this summer. And once again the increased profits that you'd expect don't show up in the company's bottom line. She thinks the money is somehow being skimmed off again."

Zelensky looked at him incredulously. "Are you telling me that this has started up again? That someone else is now smuggling diamonds into the mine?"

"I don't know, but it's a possibility. Sarah is convinced that's what's happening. She knows the whole story because I told her most of what Thompson told me. I guess I have to agree with her because it's just too much of a coincidence. And the increase in production is big. She did an estimate of the extra profits, and it's a huge amount of money. I think whoever is behind this had such a good thing going they didn't want to stop, so they've recruited someone else."

Zelensky shook his head. "Mr. Doucet, I thought I had seen everything, but this one just keeps getting stranger by the minute. This friend of yours, Sarah, who is she? Is she the one you were visiting that day your apartment got broken into? Does she want to join the RCMP?"

Doucet chuckled. "Yes, that's her. She lives in Seattle; I'm sure I gave you her contact details that night you were at my apartment. I doubt she'd want to join the RCMP though, she's not even Canadian." He wasn't ready to discuss his relationship with Sarah with Zelensky. He wasn't even completely sure himself where the relationship stood.

"Yeah, I was just kidding. But I will study these." He waved the papers he was still holding. "And also I'm going to ask something that I normally wouldn't: Do you have time to sit in on some of my discussions with Thompson?"

"Jeez, I don't know. I've already taken a lot of time off work lately."

"What about nights? Weekends? It would be really useful because you know so much about Diatek. And also the financial stuff your friend Sarah found. Plus Thompson might be a little more comfortable having you around when we talk, because he already knows you."

"Well, I spend some of my nights and weekends doing analyses at a lab out at the university, but I guess I could work around that."

"Great," Zelensky said. "Walk with me to the parking lot, okay?" He stood up and took his jacket from the back of his chair "How much of the financial stuff does Thompson know?"

"As far as I know, nothing. *I* didn't even know all the details when I talked him in Mexico. Sarah's had suspicions for a while, but she didn't have hard evidence until very recently."

"Mm." Zelensky seemed lost in thought as they walked to the parking lot. "Could you make it tonight?"

"Tonight? To meet with Bill? I suppose, I haven't got anything else planned."

"Good. Give me a call when you leave work and we'll take it from there."

Zelensky got into his car and drove off, and Doucet stood there wondering if the policeman ever took a break.

CHAPTER 27

Each time he had gone to work since coming back from his week in Seattle and Ensenada, Doucet had felt unsettled. Everything looked the same, the people were the same, they were doing the same things they usually did, and the work he did himself was familiar, but he now looked at the company through very different eyes. He had knowledge that no one else had. He knew that Bill Thompson was alive, not lying at the bottom of a lake in the Northwest Territories; he knew that diamonds had been smuggled into the Diatek mine and passed off as genuine Northwest Territories gems; and he knew that Jim Mulroney, the CFO, was almost certainly corrupt and fiddling the company's finances. Who else might be involved he didn't know. He had to keep telling himself that most of his colleagues knew none of this. *He* hadn't known any of it until recently either; some of it he had only learned in the past few days. Even so, every time he spoke with one of his colleagues a voice would whisper in his ear: what do they know? And after his discussion with Zelensky this morning he felt even more schizophrenic.

He tried to focus on his mineral analyses but his mind kept drifting back to Thompson. He had thought that his life would return to normal once the engineer was back in Canada, but now Zelensky wanted to include him in talks with the engineer. Tonight. When was it going to end?

For someone who usually found himself wondering where the time had gone, the day passed with agonizing slowness. Glacial slowness, Doucet thought to himself as he looked at his watch, then laughed at the metaphor. Glaciers were part of his life, they were the agents that had scattered his indicator minerals over the landscape of northern Canada and made his work possible. But still the day dragged. He kept looking at his watch; the hands seemed to be stuck in place. Eventually, though, five o'clock rolled around; he forced himself to stay for another fifteen minutes and then turned off his computer and left. He could feel the eyes of some of his colleagues on him; usually he was one of the last to leave, but tonight he didn't care. When he got to his car he called Zelensky.

The officer sounded tired. He's human after all, Doucet thought to himself. "Can you be at the RCMP building in about twenty minutes?" Zelensky asked.

"No problem," Doucet said, "I'm already in my car."

"Good. I'll meet you there and drive you over to the safe house. In principle you're not supposed to know where it is, but I'm not going to blindfold you. You can close your eyes."

Doucet grinned. He was beginning to realize that Zelensky was one of those people for whom following the rules to the letter was not a high priority. He did whatever was necessary to get things done, and Doucet liked him for it.

It took them about twenty-five minutes to reach the safe house. Doucet didn't close his eyes and it seemed to him that Zelensky took a very roundabout route. Once, when he was sure they were driving down a street that they had already been down before, he looked over at the policeman. He didn't have to say anything.

"Just being careful," Zelensky said. "I'm not trying to confuse you, I'm just making sure there's nobody following us. But we're clean."

When they eventually parked Zelensky led Doucet up the steps of a nondescript house to a small porch; he rang the bell and after a long pause – Doucet assumed they were being checked out on some kind of surveillance system – they were let in by a short, muscular man with a military style crew cut.

"Hi Frank, I'm back," Zelensky said. "This is Mr. Doucet." He turned to Doucet. "We tend to use first names around here, do you mind? It's Rick, right?"

"Yes, Rick is fine."

Frank nodded to Doucet and closed the door behind them. "Denise is upstairs. She got here a few minutes ago." Doucet looked at Zelensky, expecting an explanation, but he got none. Instead, Zelensky turned to Frank and asked him to order pizzas for all of them. "Pizza okay with you?" he asked Doucet. "Any special requests?"

Doucet shrugged. "I'm not fussy," he said. "I eat most anything."

"Okay then, get the usual, Frank."

They went upstairs and Zelensky led him into a room furnished with a large oval table surrounded by chairs. There was a small sofa at one end of the room and a single shaded lamp hung low over the table casting a warm, yellowish glow. Thompson was sitting at the table talking to a young, dark haired woman with glasses, and he jumped up when they came into the room. What a difference a week makes, Doucet thought. Thompson was dressed in new jeans and a loosely fitting sweatshirt and although he hadn't shaved off his beard – Zelensky's orders – his face had started to fill out again and he had lost the gaunt look he had when Doucet last saw him. He came around the table and grabbed Doucet by the shoulder as they shook hands. He was evidently happy to see him.

They had just started to talk when Zelensky said, "I don't want to break up the reunion, but we need to start. I'm not recording tonight but Denise is going to take notes." They sat down and he turned to address her. "Denise, for the record this is Rick Doucet. D-O-U-C-E-T. Rick is a geologist at Diatek." Doucet nodded to her and she started writing in her notebook.

Zelensky looked at Thompson. "I don't normally bring in a non-RCMP person at this stage of an investigation. I haven't even cleared it with my boss – you can leave that part out of the notes, Denise," he said, turning to her – "although he'd probably approve. But you two know one another and also Rick brought me something this morning that puts a whole new light on what you were doing at the mine. If it's true it's explosive." He picked up the copy of Sarah's summary that was lying on the table in front of him and looked at Doucet. "I've read this statement, Rick, a couple of times. But I'm assuming Bill doesn't know most of it. Why don't you go over it for us?"

Doucet took a deep breath. "I'd better start at the beginning," he said.

For the next hour he led them through everything Sarah had discovered about Diatek, starting with her Master's thesis research in London. "It's all purely by chance that I know any of this," he said. "She happened to be in Vancouver last year just after Christmas and someone happened to mention my name so she interviewed me about Diatek. It's spooky. Otherwise we might not know anything."

He told them that she had had questions about Diatek's finances almost from the start, but because financial affairs weren't the main focus of her thesis she had put her doubts aside. And then, her thesis behind her, she'd decided to look at the issue again, just to satisfy her curiosity.

"She's persistent," Doucet said, "and she wouldn't let it go. We stayed in touch and occasionally she would ask me questions about Diatek. I was skeptical that there was anything funny going on, I guess because I work there and I think it's a good company. When she told me she had information that Diatek was somehow connected to a shady Russian billionaire named Vasily Gagarin I just laughed. Who's laughing now?"

"Hold on," Zelensky said. "I hadn't heard about Gagarin before. His name isn't in this thing she wrote up." Zelensky knew from the intercepted phone calls and the RCMP files that Andropov worked for Gagarin, but he didn't know the extent of Gagarin's involvement in what had happened at the Diatek mine.

"No, not by name, but he's the Russian businessman she mentions there who owns the bank in the Caymans."

Zelensky turned to Thompson. "Did you ever hear anything about Gagarin? From Andropov or anyone else?"

"Gagarin? No, never, and that's something I would be sure to remember. When I was a kid I was fascinated with rockets and I read everything I could about space travel. Yuri Gagarin was one of my heroes." Thompson noticed the blank look on Denise's face. "Before your time," he said. "He was the first man in space. He orbited the earth in 1961."

Doucet continued, explaining Sarah's findings about Diatek's complicated corporate structure, about the probable deliberate mispricing of Diatek diamonds to avoid taxes, about the wire transfers to the Caymans, and about everything else she had found. Zelensky knew most of it from reading Sarah's summary, but Thompson looked stunned.

"Rick, where did you get all this?" he asked.

"Not me, Sarah. Most of it is from her research. She's the expert on finances. But I have to admit" – he looked around the table at the others and reddened slightly – "I did download some stuff from Jim Mulroney's computer to a flash drive one evening after he'd gone home. And then we – Sarah and I – hacked into his computer and got more data. Actually we didn't do the hacking part ourselves, we had the help of a teenage computer whiz." He turned to Zelensky, who was shaking his head. "Mulroney is Diatek's CFO."

"You *what*?" Zelensky said. "You've got to be joking."

"No, I'm serious. Sarah kept asking me questions about Diatek's finances that I couldn't answer, and at first I thought that if I got her the right information it would prove there was nothing wrong, and then it sort of snowballed from there. Otherwise we wouldn't know most of this."

There was a knock on the door and Frank came in with a stack of pizza boxes and cans of soft drinks and Zelensky put the conversation on pause while they ate. Part way through the break he cornered Doucet. "Depending on where this goes I might want to talk to your friend. Sarah. Do you think that's possible?"

Doucet shrugged. "I can't really say. That would be up to her."

"Yes, of course. Could you ask her for me? Not for a definite commitment, but just whether she'd be willing in principle?"

Doucet said he would, next time they talked.

Later in the evening Doucet got to Sarah's bombshell about the fact that Diatek's diamond production had shot up again during the summer and what it might mean: that diamonds were again being smuggled into the mine. Zelensky already knew about it from their conversation that morning, but Thompson's jaw dropped.

"You mean they've got some other poor bastard taking their diamonds in now? Jesus. Although from what you say about the money it brings in I guess I shouldn't be surprised."

Zelensky asked Thompson if he had any ideas about who it might be.

"I really couldn't say, except that it would have to be someone with access to the conveyor system, like I had. That narrows it down a bit, but it's still quite a few people."

By ten o'clock Denise was yawning every few minutes. She had said little all evening but she'd scribbled notes in her book the whole time. Zelensky seemed remarkably fresh, more energized than when they started, but he called the meeting to a close and asked Doucet if he could come back again tomorrow night. To his own surprise, Doucet had enjoyed the evening and said yes, he'd like that. Leaving aside the possibility that he might be putting together evidence that would bring his own company down – a possibility that might leave him without a job – it was the thrill of the challenge, the satisfaction of solving a puzzle, piece by piece, that appealed to him. And watching Zelensky work was a pleasure. He knew how to ask the right questions.

But Doucet wasn't quite ready for what came next. As they drove back to the RCMP offices where Doucet had left his car, Zelensky said he had a favor to ask. "You don't have to do this," he said, "but it might just give us the information we need. I don't think it would be dangerous."

Doucet didn't say anything. How could this possibly get more complicated? he wondered.

"Could you find an excuse to go up to the mine for a few days? A legitimate geological reason?" Zelensky glanced over at him then brought his eyes back to the road.

There was a long silence. Doucet wanted to help, but this was getting impossible. How was he supposed to do his real work when he was always getting sidetracked like this?

"It's possible, I suppose, but I'm not sure it's something I want to do. For one thing, I'd have to convince my boss that it was something worthwhile, something that would help our exploration efforts. He's very sharp and I'd have to have an iron-clad story or he'd see right through me. And who knows? Maybe he's involved in this thing himself, and then he'd be even more reluctant to let me go."

Zelensky didn't reply and Doucet continued. "I guess you're thinking it would be good to have eyes on the ground, so to speak. To see if we can figure out who has taken over for Thompson."

"You got it. Obviously it can't be me or some stranger, it has to be someone with a legitimate reason to be there for a few days. If you went nobody would think twice about it. Thompson mentioned that it's probably someone who has easy access to the conveyor system." Zelensky chuckled and glanced at Doucet again. "I've learned a hell of a lot about diamond mining in a couple of days. It's one of the things that makes this job interesting to me; you're always learning new things. Anyway, with Thompson's knowledge of what people do at the mine we could narrow down the possible suspects and you could keep an eye on them for a few days. Hang around the conveyor system, maybe. What do you think."

"Couldn't you simply look at CCTV footage or something? There must be cameras."

"Yes there are. I quizzed Thompson about how he avoided being detected. He says the cameras in that part of the system are not really for security, they're for monitoring the machinery. Apparently he always made sure he dropped the diamonds in where there are gaps in the video coverage. If the next person isn't so careful the videos might help. But there's the problem of how we get them; we can't request them officially through the RCMP or the cat would be out of the bag. Maybe when you're up there – if you're up there – you could find a reason to look at them. Let's sleep on it and talk again tomorrow night."

Zelensky let him out at his car and Doucet climbed in and turned on the radio and sat there listening to music and thinking for a long time. How do I get myself into these situations? he wondered. Talk about feeling schizophrenic. If I go up to the mine it will be even worse. I'll be actively spying on my own company.

CHAPTER 28

Doucet had a dream that night; when he woke all he could remember was a series of disjointed images. Bill Thompson, lying in a hospital bed swathed in bandages, Sarah Patterson calling to him from the other side of a river. At some point he was running, running for his life in the dark with two men chasing him and then Ed Zelensky pulled up beside him in a car and opened the door. He jumped in and they sped away, safe. But when he opened his mouth to tell Zelensky what had happened, no words came out. Try as he could, he couldn't speak.

What was that all about? he asked himself as he got ready for work. The images kept playing in his head, over and over. Then, cleaning his teeth and looking in the mirror, he came to a decision. "I'm going to tell Zelensky I'll go up to the mine," he said out loud. He still had the toothbrush in his mouth and toothpaste sprayed all over the mirror as he spoke. He laughed and picked up a towel and wiped the mirror but he only succeeded in making it worse. I'm already in this up to my neck, he thought, and if I can help Zelensky find out who's behind it, I will. If I don't, I won't be able to face myself in the mirror.

Tim Bailey, a cup of take-out coffee in his hand, was just coming in when Doucet arrived at work. He looked preoccupied. "Can I have a quick word?" Doucet asked.

"Sure, come down to my office. What's on your mind?"

They walked together down a hall and into Bailey's office. He had obviously been there early this morning; the lights were on and Doucet could see a document open on his monitor.

"I'd like to do a little research project on the side. It's something I've been thinking about off and on, and now seems like a good time. I'm busy, sure, but I've almost caught up from being away last week. The only thing is, I'd have to go up to the mine for a few days." He explained to Bailey what he wanted to do. "It would involve taking samples of ore along the conveyor system in a systematic way, maybe every few hours over several days, then I would bring them back here for analysis."

"Mm." Bailey nodded and Doucet wasn't sure if his boss had really been listening. But he had.

"You could get someone up there to do that for you," he said. "You don't need to go yourself."

Doucet wasn't ready to give up so easily. "Yeah, I suppose I could. But it's never the same, you know that. I'd be asking myself forever if the sampling had been done properly."

Bailey still seemed preoccupied. "Yes, I suppose you're right. I guess if you really want to do it and it's not going to affect your work here you should go ahead." He grimaced. "I'm sure we'll have to fill out a form. Send me whatever paperwork you need and I'll approve it." Bailey was an old school field geologist and he hated paperwork.

"I'd like to go as soon as possible," Doucet said, "I'll try to get the forms to you today."

"What? Hell, don't worry about it, if you can't find me just go. I'll sign them when you get back if it's necessary. And send me a report when you're finished, okay?" He sat down and turned to his computer and Doucet knew the meeting was over.

He let out a long breath. That wasn't so bad, he thought. I caught him at the right moment; he had other things on his mind. He wanted to call Zelensky right away, tell him he was cleared to go up to the mine, but he resisted. He'd talk to the policeman after work.

Viktor Churkin called Alex Kalinin, his boss in Calgary, as soon as he had finished listening to the recording. Actually, he had played it twice because he wanted to be sure, but then he crossed himself and silently thanked God that he'd left bugs in the apartment. He had developed a ritual; each morning he would scan through the previous day's recording, skimming through the quiet parts, listening when there were voices. But until today he hadn't heard any of the things Kalinin had asked him to listen for, and he was getting increasingly irritated that he had to spend so much time on what seemed to be a fruitless task. Doucet was hardly ever at home anyway; mostly what he heard on the recordings was silence. The man had disappeared for a week after he and Igor had mugged him, which worried them for a while – they had no idea where he was – but then he was back and now everything seemed normal again. He left for work each morning and returned late in the evening, and after he got home the only thing Viktor ever heard on the recordings was music. And he didn't like Doucet's taste in music.

Last night's recording was different, however. For once Doucet didn't put on his lousy music and a few minutes after he came in he called someone on his cell phone and talked for almost an hour. Viktor could hear only one side of the conversation, but it was enough to make him realize that it was something Kalinin would want to hear. Neither Viktor nor Igor knew all the details of Kalinin's interest in Doucet – their boss had told them to search the apartment for those papers, and later to rough up Doucet and ask him questions about the engineer Bill Thompson, but he hadn't explained why it was so important. When Viktor told Kalinin he'd bugged the apartment, though, he'd been very happy. He said if Doucet talked to anyone about Bill Thompson, or about diamonds or Diatek, to let him know immediately. On last night's recording Doucet had talked about all of those things. At the end of the conversation he said he was leaving for the Diatek mine the next day to conduct some experiments; he'd be back in a few days.

Viktor played the recording over the phone for Kalinin. His boss was quiet for a few moments when it ended, and then he said, "He knows too much. He needs to disappear. You know what I mean Viktor?"

Viktor knew what he meant. He'd never been directly involved in the violent side of Kalinin's operation, but he was only too aware of it. He'd been hired for his computer expertise; he was very good, which is why Kalinin had re-cruited him in the first place, and during the time he'd been in Vancouver he'd been content to let Igor take the lead whenever violence was required. As long as he had his computers, Viktor was happy. But getting rid of someone – even if Igor organized it – went far beyond anything he'd been involved in before.

"What about this person he was talking to, Sarah?"

"That can wait. Deal with Doucet first, as soon as he gets back. And make sure it's clean, okay? No screw-ups this time. Make sure nobody can trace it back to you two."

Doucet caught the regular supply flight from Yellowknife to the mine on Friday afternoon. He'd made arrangements with the mine manager to be there four or five days, depending on how his project went. He explained that he wanted to take random samples from the ore stream every few hours so that he could examine the proportions of the various indicator minerals in the rocks and how they changed from sample to sample. No one questioned his plan.

It was only mid-October and winter had not yet set in, but when the plane came down through the low clouds Doucet was greeted by a bleak, gray landscape stretching to the horizon. He loved this country in the summer but now, at least from his bird's eye vantage point, there seemed to be no life, no color reflected in the dull light. Was it really just over a month ago that he'd left the field camp, barely a hundred miles north of here? Below him only the twinkling lights of the mine buildings and the airstrip broke the monotony. It *looked* cold. In places he could see a dusting of snow. No wonder Thompson had been happy in Mexico.

By that evening, with the help of Thompson's replacement – a gruff, taciturn mining engineer named Helmut with a German accent who told Doucet he'd worked in northern Scandinavia before coming to Canada and he didn't mind the cold – Doucet had set up his sampling plan. It required periodic visits to the open part of the conveyor system, but these didn't take very long and he soon realized that he would have a lot of time on his hands. On the second day of his visit he asked Helmut, as casually as he could manage, about the CCTV system. "I know it's there mainly to monitor the machinery," he said, "but it must give you a pretty good view of the ore, too, right? I wouldn't mind taking a look at it, just to get a sense of the variability of the ore. I've got a lot of time with not much to do, and it would be a lot more comfortable to look at a video than to stand out by the conveyor." Asking straight out like this was a risk; it was always possible that Helmut was the person now slipping foreign diamonds into the ore.

Helmut just grunted and shrugged his shoulders. Doucet had the distinct feeling that the engineer didn't think much of his request, couldn't see why anyone would be stupid enough to sit and watch videos of rocks being carried along a conveyor belt. He didn't seem at all alarmed, though, which might mean he wasn't following in Thompson's footsteps in all respects. Helmut took him into a room with several TV monitors and said he was welcome to watch them any time.

"And the old ones, the past records, are they available too?" Doucet said.

Again Helmut looked at him with an expression that said he thought he was crazy. He pointed to a computer monitor and said, "They're all on the computer. We only keep them for a week, and then they're automatically deleted. Otherwise we'd run out of memory. There are four cameras along the system and each one has a separate record. The files are organized by camera and date, so it should be easy enough to find what you're looking for. Help yourself."

That night, after he'd eaten, Doucet went back to the video room. No one was there. For a while he watched the live feeds and it didn't take him long to understand Helmut's reaction to his request: it was truly mind-numbing. Even if you were looking for something specific, like he was, peering for hours at grainy black and white footage of a jumble of rocks moving along a conveyor system would drive you crazy. Not only that, but after a while he began to feel queasy. The constant movement of the images was starting to make him seasick.

Doucet turned away from the monitors and shut his eyes for a few minutes, waiting for his stomach to settle. Maybe it was the greasy food he'd had in the cafeteria, he thought. Then he turned back to the computer and found the stored CCTV records. He started with the oldest one, from exactly a week ago. That was before the mine manager or anyone else knew he would be doing experiments along the conveyor system; in fact it was even before Zelensky had asked him to visit the mine. He found that by running the video at high speed and not sitting too close to the monitor he could quickly scan through a lot of footage without feeling nauseous. After an hour and a half, though, he'd had enough. He'd only managed to get through a portion of the week's record from one of the cameras, but he had to stop. He realized that he'd have to do this in small batches, and he probably wouldn't be able to get through the accumulated records from all four cameras in the short time he had at the mine. Still, he'd do what he could.

In the videos he'd viewed tonight, human figures had appeared several times. Each time he'd stopped the playback and gone back to the point where the men first appeared, then watched their actions closely at normal speed. He didn't see anything that looked even vaguely suspicious. Once he recognized Helmut, pointing toward the conveyor and gesticulating as he talked to another man. But none of the other figures were familiar.

Three days and hundreds of hours of video later he wasn't any further ahead. His eyes were sore and he was sick of watching the speeded-up walks and jerky steps of the mine personnel who flitted in and out of camera range. They reminded him of characters in an old Charlie Chaplin movie. When he slowed the videos down and looked at what the characters did, it was clear that none of them had thrown anything into the stream of rocks on the conveyor belts, except for the occasional cigarette butt. He had also wandered along the length of the conveyor system each time he took a sample, but again he'd seen nothing suspicious. It looked as though he was going to return to Vancouver with no better idea of who was smuggling diamonds into the mine than they'd had a week earlier. It was disappointing, to say the least. He did have his samples, which would be shipped out later on a supply flight, but that was little consolation. To keep up the charade he would have to process them and carry out the experiments he'd proposed to Tim Bailey. He'd delay it as long as possible, but if he didn't eventually do the analyses his boss would wonder what was going on. In the meantime, they were no closer to finding out who had taken over Thompson's role as a diamond smuggler.

It was just past eight in the evening when Doucet arrived back in Vancouver. Because he had nothing new to tell Zelensky and Thompson his mood was subdued, but hovering somewhere at the back of his brain he had a feeling that perhaps *not* finding anything was also evidence about what was going on. It was an elusive idea and he couldn't flesh it out, but he was sure there was something to it.

He called Sarah from the taxi on his way home – since that impulsive hug as he left Seattle just over a week ago he'd thought about her all the time and more than anything he wanted to hear her voice again. She asked him how the trip had gone and he said he hadn't found anything and then he told her about his hunch that maybe that in itself was important.

Sarah was quiet for a minute and then she said, "You might be right. Maybe you're on the wrong track. Maybe you shouldn't bother trying to catch someone red-handed and just follow the money." He could hear the pitch of her voice marching higher; she was getting excited. He had noticed it happen before when she had a new idea.

"Follow the money how?"

"I was just thinking. It's like before, like when I was trying to figure out the wire transfers. Not exactly the same, but it's the same principle. Follow the money. Don't look for people, look at bank accounts. I'm sure the RCMP could do that."

"I still don't get it."

"Thompson did it for money, right? Isn't that what he said?"

"Yes, at least that's how he got sucked into it in the first place."

"Okay, so if they're paying some new person you might be able to find them by looking at bank accounts. Check the mine employees, look for unexplained deposits. It might work."

"Sarah, you're a genius."

"I don't know about genius, it's just common sense."

"Zelensky will love this. When I gave him your summary he asked me if you wanted to join the RCMP. He was just joking around, but when he hears this you might get a job offer."

Sarah laughed. "No thanks. I'm sure the RCMP does good work, but I'm happy where I am."

CHAPTER 29

Igor Petrov rubbed his hands together when he learned from Viktor that Alex Kalinin wanted Rick Doucet to disappear. Viktor might be happy sitting at his computer all day, but Igor thrived on action. And as far as he was concerned there hadn't been enough action since Alex had sent them to Vancouver. He was bored.

"How do we do it?" Viktor asked. "I've never done anything like this before." He was nervous. Roughing someone up was one thing, but killing them …

Igor thought for a minute. "Easy," he said. "We go to his apartment, or maybe we wait for him in the parking garage, like before. Then we knock him out with a sedative and throw him in the van and drive to somewhere remote. Take him into the forest and bury him. End of story. No one will find him, it will be like he disappeared off the face of the earth."

"I hope you're right." Viktor didn't have Igor's blind faith in their ability to scoop up Doucet and get rid of him without something going wrong. But Igor had the experience and he would have to follow his partner's lead, like it or not. "Alex was pretty upset about the phone conversation, he said this guy Doucet knows way too much. But he was talking to someone, a person named Sarah, so she must be in the loop too. Alex said to worry about her later, but maybe we should try to find out who she is from Doucet. You know, before …"

Igor grinned. "You're good, Viktor. I'd like that." He rubbed his hands together again. "Put a little pressure on the guy."

The two Russians had no idea that for weeks their movements had been watched by a RCMP surveillance team. So they also had no idea that Zelensky had pulled the team a week earlier, once he had Thompson in protective custody. The stake-out had caused grumbling among Zelensky's colleagues because it was so expensive, and it hadn't yielded much useful information. In the overall scheme of things the two Russians were pretty low on the totem pole, so the policeman had decided to discontinue it. For Viktor and Igor it was a lucky break that they didn't even know they'd been given.

Viktor didn't know exactly when Doucet would be returning to Vancouver – in the recorded phone conversation the geologist had only said he'd be gone 'for a few days' – so he began to monitor the recordings from Doucet's apartment closely for signs that he was back. Meanwhile Igor, bored and with little to do, drank even more than usual. It was the Russian malaise, and it worried Viktor, who rarely took more than a shot of vodka with his dinner. Igor, though, downed glass after glass. On the evening Viktor finally heard noises from the bug in Doucet's apartment and went to tell his partner that the geologist was back from the mine, Igor had passed out on the sofa.

It took several slaps on the face and a glass of cold water to wake him up, and even then he was barely coherent. It was obvious he was in no shape to go to Doucet's apartment that night. "We'll have to do it in the morning," Viktor said. Igor mumbled something but his speech was so slurred that Viktor couldn't understand him. He shook his head in frustration. "We need to be ready to leave at seven," Viktor said. "Understand?"

Igor nodded and stumbled into the bedroom and collapsed onto the bed, fully clothed. Moments later he was snoring. But by morning he was ready for action. He still reeked of alcohol, his eyes were red and his voice hoarse, but he downed a glass of orange juice and two cups of strong tea and told Viktor to hurry up, they needed to get going. In a small satchel he had two syringes and several ampoules filled with sedatives.

Viktor drove. They found Doucet's car and made themselves inconspicuous behind a nearby truck. Their main concern was being seen by other residents, but the garage was empty. Then Doucet stepped out of the elevator and walked to his car and just as he started to unlock the door Viktor stepped up behind him, silently. "Mr. Doucet?"

Doucet, startled, began to turn and Viktor pinned him against the car while Igor plunged the needle into his thigh. Doucet yelled out in pain and started to say, "What the …" and then Igor clamped his hand over his mouth and the two men dragged him across the garage toward their van.

The drug wasn't instantaneous but Doucet could feel the numbness creeping up his leg and he began to feel dizzy. He looked around wildly and out of the corner of his eye he saw the display over the elevator light up. Someone was coming down; he hoped against hope they were coming to the parking garage. But Viktor saw it too and nudged Igor and they started to drag him even more quickly toward the van. They were almost there when the elevator door opened and a man stepped out. Doucet knew him; he was a neighbor who lived one floor below him, a professional hockey player. But he was looking at his phone; he had no inkling of the drama playing out just a short distance away. Doucet was helpless, Igor's hand still clamped across his mouth.

Then he had his chance. It only lasted a few seconds, but it was enough. Igor took his hand away to open the door of the van and Doucet yelled with every ounce of strength he could summon, "Gerry, help!" Then the hand was back over his mouth. But the hockey player reacted instantly. He looked up and saw two strange men struggling to lift Doucet into the back of a van and he roared at them and sprinted across the garage like a charging bull. Gerry was big, over six feet, and Viktor was terrified. He let go of Doucet and jumped into the van, reaching for the keys. Igor, his reactions still slowed from the previous evening's alcohol, hesitated, and because of that he took the full force of the hockey player's charge. Momentarily stunned, he released Doucet from his grip and shook his head, then he too scrambled around the van and jumped into the passenger seat. Doucet slid down to his knees, barely conscious.

"What the hell's going on?" Gerry said.

"Trying ... kidnap me," Doucet said. He fumbled with his jacket and took out his phone. "Call Zelensky ... number's in the phone." Then he passed out.

"Jesus," Gerry said, putting his coat under Doucet's head. The van's tires screeched as it careened away from them and he looked up and registered the license number. He pulled out a pen and wrote it down, then called 911.

Doucet woke up slowly. It was like crawling out of a deep cave; first there was a faint light behind his eyelids, then it got brighter and he started to hear noises, then finally he opened his eyes. He was surprised to find himself in a brightly lit room, a nurse standing at the end of the bed, Zelensky sitting beside him.

"Where am I?" he asked.

"Vancouver General," Zelensky said. He looked at the nurse and nodded and she left the room. "They figure you must have been drugged. Something to put you out cold for a few hours. Do you remember what happened?"

Doucet frowned. "I think so. It's a bit hazy. I was on my way to work and somebody grabbed me and tried to throw me into a van. There were two of them."

"You're lucky, Rick. One of your neighbors happened along just at the right moment. Otherwise I don't know what would have happened."

"Oh yeah, it's coming back. It was Gerry Clarke. It's a good thing it was him. Nobody wants to tangle with Gerry Clarke."

"He called me on your phone right after he called 911. He also got the license plate on that van. I've got a trace on it as we speak."

Doucet turned to look at Zelensky. His neck hurt and he was still groggy and something was bothering him. Something he should tell Zelensky. He couldn't remember what it was, but he knew it was important.

"Wait," he said, "that's it."

Zelensky looked at him. "What? What's it?"

"Sarah. What she told me yesterday. Last night, when I was coming home in the taxi."

"Slow down," Zelensky said. "Take it easy and start from the beginning. I don't think whatever they gave you has worn off yet."

"I didn't see anything at the mine. Sorry. It was a waste of time."

"Damn."

"Yeah, that's what I thought too. But then I started to wonder if not finding anything was actually useful in itself. Know what I mean?"

"Not really. Tell me."

"Well, suppose we're barking up the wrong tree. Maybe they've found some other way to get the diamonds into the mine. On the way back from the airport last night I called Sarah, and when I mentioned it to her she agreed. She said we should just follow the money. If they're paying someone to smuggle diamonds we should look at the bank accounts of mine employees for unexplained deposits."

"Holy shit," Zelensky said. "Why didn't we think of that before? Rick, I really have to meet this friend of yours."

Doucet grinned. He was beginning to feel a little better. "I'm sure that can be arranged. But right now I need to get out of this place. When can I leave?"

"Take it easy. They want to keep you in for observation, just to make sure everything's okay. Twenty-four hours, they said, so until tomorrow morning."

Doucet groaned. "I guess I'd better call my boss and tell him I won't be in."

"Already done. I worked the phone a bit while I was waiting for you to wake up. I told them at Diatek that you'd been robbed and injured on the way to work and you'd probably be in the hospital for a couple of days. And just in case, I've requested a guard on your door. He won't let anyone in except me or the nurses."

"Jesus. So what happens when I go home?"

"I had an idea about that too. You'll still have the guard, twenty-four seven, until all this blows over. I've already arranged for that. He'll be as inconspicuous as possible. But actually I don't think you should go home. Bill Thompson's apartment is empty, and he agrees it would be fine for you to stay there. All his bills are still paid automatically from his bank account through the lawyer handling the estate, so there's no problem there. I'll have someone go in and clean the place up and stock it, and when you're feeling better you should go back to work and act as normal as possible. Hopefully all this won't last too long."

Zelensky went straight to the safe house after leaving the hospital. He told Thompson about Sarah's suggestion that they should follow the money and asked how they could get a list of mine employees.

"Easy, it's on the website." He went to the computer and used Rick Doucet's login details and ten minutes later they had two printed copies of all of Diatek's current mine employees.

"Okay," Zelensky said, "let's go through this one by one and highlight anyone who wouldn't be out of place along the conveyor system. I'm counting on your knowledge of what people do at the mine."

"I don't know everybody, but I know most of the people who work in that area. How be we start by scratching off the ones I'm sure *wouldn't* have easy access?"

"Good idea." Zelensky said. His appreciation of the engineer's practical intelligence deepened day by day.

Working on the pared down list, Thompson identified fourteen people whose jobs gave them easy and regular access to the open sections of the ore stream, where he himself had dropped in hundreds of those small gray bags of diamonds over almost two years. He shook his head when he thought about it and said it seemed like another life. "It's hard to believe that someone else is doing that now. It could be any one of these people."

Zelensky nodded. "Okay, let's concentrate on them. That's not bad; it narrows things down a lot. We'll need addresses, social insurance numbers, whatever we can find, before I can get warrants to access their bank records. How many of them do you actually know?"

"Basically all of them. The only one I don't know is Helmut Oster, the guy who took over my job." Thompson looked down the list again. "There are a few other people that might be worth including – they work in more secure areas so it would probably be more difficult for them but not impossible. But as Rick said, they might have changed tactics. As long as they can get the diamonds mixed in with the ones that actually come from the mine it wouldn't matter where they do it."

Zelensky agreed, and they added five more names, bringing the total up to nineteen. Thompson told Zelensky everything he knew about each of them: where they were from, whether they had families, where they had gone to school, whatever he could remember. By time they were through Zelensky was confident he had enough information to apply for warrants for most of them.

"When I started out," he said, "this kind of thing took weeks, sometimes months. Thank God for computers. If there aren't any glitches we should have the bank data by the end of the week." Maybe even sooner, he thought. He didn't mention it to Thompson, but he planned to claim that the warrant requests were part of a national security investigation. It was stretching the truth a bit, but this case had started with the NSA phone interceptions, and if that got the warrants processed faster, he'd use it.

Zelensky stood up and rubbed his eyes and stretched. "I need to get more exercise," he said. "Too much sitting around rooms like this and too much fast food." He patted his stomach. "Anyway, I think we're done for the time being. I'm going to be mostly in my office for the next few days, but if anything important occurs to you just call me. I'll be back when the bank records start coming in because you're the one who knows these people and we'll need to look at the records together." With that the policeman picked up his briefcase and started for the door.

It was a shock. Thompson had been in the safe house for ten days now and Zelensky had been with him for a good part of all of them. They had gradually developed a good working relationship – at least Thompson thought about it as a working relationship, although he knew it was really something different – and he hadn't really considered what would happen when Zelensky no longer needed information from him. He paced around the conference room aimlessly for several minutes. It was fine when there was something to do, but what would happen now? He'd only been outside twice, both times after dark and both times with one of the minders at his side. Twenty pounds lighter than when he worked at the mine and sporting a bushy beard, Thompson was sure that none of his few Vancouver acquaintances would recognize him, but Zelensky wasn't taking any chances.

What he really wanted to do, though, was to go over to his apartment, but he knew it wouldn't happen. If you want something, Zelensky told him, we can get it for you. But it wasn't really things Thompson wanted, he just wanted to *be* at the apartment. Not cooped up in this safe house, which was nice enough but made him feel like a prisoner. Which in a way he was. Zelensky had been vague when he asked him how long he would be there. "Until we crack this open and you testify and we get some convictions," he'd said. "At this point I have no idea how long that will take."

CHAPTER 30

Viktor Churkin didn't blame his partner to his face for the botched attempt to grab Doucet, but it festered inside him. If Igor hadn't been so drunk they could have gone to the apartment as soon as they knew Doucet was back, and they could have overpowered him easily. There wouldn't have been anyone to interrupt them like that giant who exploded at them in the parking garage. He thought about telling Kalinin, but decided against it. He had to live with Igor, at least for a while; there was no sense antagonizing him. When they talked about it he told Igor it was just bad luck. If it hadn't been for that animal who stepped out of the elevator just as they were bundling Doucet into the van everything would have been okay. They'd have to try again, and next time they would do it somewhere other than the parking garage.

But as the days ticked by they began to wonder if there would be a next time. Doucet had disappeared. Kalinin was livid; they'd screwed up for a second time and he told them to drop everything else and take care of Doucet. Viktor monitored the bugs every few hours and heard nothing but silence. They watched the apartment building, but Doucet didn't appear. His car stayed in the same parking place. They staked out the Diatek building mornings and evenings but saw no sign of him.

What they didn't know was that Zelensky had whisked Doucet from the hospital and installed him in Thompson's empty apartment in a different part of the city. And when Doucet went to work he and the bodyguard parked half a mile from the Diatek building and took a circuitous route, entering from a back alley through a service door. It was stressful, but at least he hadn't been attacked again.

In the meantime, from the license number Gerry Clarke had supplied, Zelensky learned that the men who had tried to abduct Doucet had been driving a van registered to one Viktor Churkin. The same Viktor who was on the list of names generated from the NSA phone transcripts. The same Viktor that Helen's snitch, Joey, had fingered, and who lived in one of the houses in Kitsilano. It would have been easy to pick him up, but it wasn't Viktor he wanted and he couldn't let the Russians know he was closing in on them. Instead, he regrouped his surveillance team and had them start watching the house again. Watchers watching watchers.

Zelensky was now spending all his time on the case; everything seemed to be happening at once. His warrant requests had been approved and bank account information for the mine employees was trickling in. When he had what he needed for all but three of the nineteen men he called Thompson and told him to get ready, he was on his way over. They divided the work between them and he and Thompson sat on opposite sides of the conference room table, poring through the details of other people's bank statements. Most of them were perfectly ordinary: salary deposits, mortgage and credit card payments, the financial records of a normal life. Thompson noticed that most balances came close to zero just before the next paycheck. He was beginning to feel a bit like a peeping Tom, peering into other people's financial lives. It didn't seem to bother Zelensky.

One of the sets of statements in Zelensky's pile was different, however. He read through the statements twice, then handed them to Thompson. "Take a look at these and tell me what you think."

They covered three years and for most of that time they looked like the others: regular paychecks and withdrawals, the balance rising and falling predictably. But beginning early the past summer there had been several large cash deposits and suddenly the balance in the account was higher than it had ever been.

Zelensky had blocked out the account holders' names on all of the statements, mainly so that Thompson, who knew most of these people, wouldn't be biased. "Whoever this is," Thompson said, "either he won the lottery or …" He didn't have to finish the sentence.

"Exactly. It's number twelve on our list. That's … hang on a second … that's someone named Sullivan. Thomas Sullivan. Do you know him?"

"Tom Sullivan? Sure, I know him. He's one of the security guys. He's kind of surly, I never …" Thompson stopped in mid-sentence. "It's him, isn't it? I had always assumed they'd get someone to put diamonds into the ore like I did, but Rick was right, they've changed tactics. And Sullivan would be perfect. He works in the secure areas, he's one of three people who transfer the rough diamonds to the vault for storage. They search all those guys thoroughly when they're finished work but not when they start. They're worried about people stealing diamonds; they've never thought about someone taking them *in*. He could walk in with a whole pocket full of diamonds and mix them in with the rough from the mine before taking them over to storage and nobody would be the wiser."

Zelensky grinned. "Don't get too excited. You may be right but I don't want to jump to conclusions; all we've got so far is the cash payments. That and the fact that Sullivan works in an area where he could bring in diamonds." Zelensky circled Sullivan's name and put a star beside it. "What do you know about Sullivan?"

"Well, he's an older guy and he once told me he has grown up kids. I never did like him much, there was something about him that put me off. He was kind of … I guess he was sort of full of himself in his role as a security person. I think he's one of those people who like to have a little power over other people that he probably doesn't have in other parts of his life. He's got a house in Calgary; I'm pretty sure that's where he goes on his breaks, but I have the impression that Sullivan is happier at the mine than at home."

"If we end up deciding he's worth a closer look, how would I find out when he's going to be on a break? When I might find him at home in Calgary?"

"That's easy," Thompson said. "There's a duty roster on the website. They update it every weekend; it shows everyone's working schedule for at least a month in advance. It's in the employee part of the website, you need a password to log in, but we can use Rick's."

Two days later Zelensky had received bank statements for the three remaining people on his list. It was Friday, and at the end of the day he took the new records to the safe house and he and Thompson sat together checking through the accounts. When they'd examined them Zelensky said, "I didn't see anything, did you?"

"No, nothing. Sullivan's statements are the only ones with anything unusual."

Zelensky looked tired. He *was* tired. "I think I'd better pay Mr. Sullivan a visit. I already checked the website and he's on his break right now, due to go back to work at the mine on Monday morning. I hope to hell he's at home in Calgary for the weekend." He picked up his phone and called the travel desk and asked them to book him a seat on the first flight to Calgary in the morning. Then he opened his laptop and typed in Sullivan's name. "There's one more thing I should check," he said to Thompson, "see if we already have anything on Sullivan."

But there was no criminal record, only a couple of minor incidents from more than a decade earlier when Sullivan had been involved in brawls at a Calgary bar. Zelensky closed his laptop and stood up. "I'll see you in a couple of days," he said as he left.

Sullivan lived in the suburbs on the eastern outskirts of Calgary, in a squat one-story house with a postage stamp lawn in front and a pickup truck in the driveway. An overweight woman with stringy gray hair answered the door and looked at Zelensky suspiciously. "What do you want?"

Zelensky had his badge ready. "RCMP," he said. "I need to talk to your husband. Is he home?"

"What's he done now?" she said, and turned away, her hand still on the door handle. "Tom," she yelled, "Tom. Someone to see you."

A moment later Sullivan appeared behind her. He was short but broad across the chest and shoulders, obviously very fit, his muscles bulging under a tight fitting T-shirt. A weight lifter, Zelensky guessed, it's probably what he does in his spare time at the mine. Built like a fire hydrant.

"Okay if I come in? I'd like to have a word with you, Mr. Sullivan. You are Thomas Sullivan, right?" The woman who had opened the door still stood with her hand on the doorknob, the door only part way open. Zelensky was holding his badge up for both of them to see.

"Let him in, Anne, it's alright." Sullivan had a curiously high-pitched voice. "Yes, I'm Tom Sullivan. You want to talk to me? What about?"

Zelensky stepped into the hall and put away his badge. "It's private, Mr. Sullivan." He looked at the woman called Anne. "Sorry Mrs. Sullivan, but I need to talk to your husband alone. Is there someplace we can do that?" Without a word she led them down the hall and pointed to an open door.

"The den," she said. "I'll be in the kitchen if you need me."

For the next hour the door to the den remained firmly closed. Anne Sullivan, who always wanted to know what was going on in other people's lives, felt her curiosity growing by the minute until she was ready to explode. What did the police want with her husband? He was hardly ever here; had he done something at the mine? Occasionally she could hear the sound of his squeaky voice raised in excitement or anger, she couldn't tell which, and then the low pitched reply of the RCMP man. Once she knocked on the door and opened it a crack to ask if they'd like coffee or tea; the men immediately fell silent and the RCMP officer told her they were fine and would she please close the door. He spoke with such authority that in her haste to get the door shut she slammed it with a crash.

Eventually, though, she heard the door to the den open and the two men came out. She was sitting in the kitchen drinking her third cup of coffee, and she stood up so abruptly that she knocked it over, slopping coffee across the table. She didn't bother to wipe it up. When they came into the room she looked from one man to the other; her husband was pale and subdued, but the RCMP man had a satisfied look on his face.

"Thank you, Mrs. Sullivan," Zelensky said. He shrugged on his coat and went out into the hall, Sullivan following. "I'll be in touch, Tom," he said as he went out the door.

"What did he thank me for?" Anne grumbled after Zelensky left. "He didn't even want coffee. Tom, he called you? You're on first name terms with the RCMP? What were you doing in there?" Her questions came tumbling out.

"I can't say, Anne, it's between me and him."

"What do you mean you can't say? I'm your wife, aren't I? I deserve to know what's going on."

Sullivan turned abruptly and left the room without replying. A few minutes later he was back, wearing his coat, a bag in his hand. "I'm going to the gym," he said.

Zelensky, back in Vancouver after a long day, had a dream that night. He had been chasing a tall figure across a snowy landscape in dim, wintry light, desperate to catch up. He didn't know who it was or why he was chasing him, but in one hand the man held a bag that glowed with a brilliant light and suddenly Zelensky realized the bag was full of diamonds. Just as he seemed to be gaining on the man the ground under his feet turned to jelly and he couldn't move; it was like trying to run in quicksand. The man turned and opened his mouth wide in laughter, and Zelensky recognized the face: it was Dimitri Andropov, the man in the RCMP database, the man who Thompson said had tried to kill him. Zelensky, mired in the glue-like substance that engulfed his legs, watched helplessly as Andropov disappeared into the distance, the light from the diamonds fading to a small dot and then disappearing altogether.

When he woke, Heather was already up; he could smell the coffee. He lay in bed trying to remember what else had happened in the dream, but nothing came to him. I'm too wrapped up in this, he thought, I need a break. But even as he said it to himself, his thoughts slipped back to the dream. "I'll get you, Dimitri Andropov," he said out loud, "even if I have to run through quicksand to do it."

Zelensky didn't give himself much of a break; by the middle of the afternoon he was back at his computer. He fleshed out his notes on the conversation he'd had with Sullivan and read them through a second time to make sure he hadn't missed anything. Then he composed a message to the man he always considered his mentor, an RCMP officer who had seen something in Zelensky when he first joined the force as a young recruit, and who had nurtured him in his early years as a policeman. Over the years they had become good friends as well as colleagues. Zelensky had advanced rapidly and Phillip always told him it was through his own talents, but Zelensky knew it didn't hurt to have someone like Phillip as an advocate.

He didn't often ask for a favor, but this time he thought it was justified. Phillip had officially retired from the RCMP several years earlier and he was currently acting in some kind of senior advisory capacity to Security Intelligence Services – Zelensky didn't know exactly what he did, but he knew he had influence. He worded his message carefully, explaining that CSIS had earlier forwarded him NSA intercepts from several phones in Russia, and that recently there had been some interesting developments related to the calls. Could Phillip use his connections to request NSA records from the same phones for the next several weeks? And would it be possible to receive them in real time? I won't burden you with the details, Zelensky wrote, but it's important. It's worth a bottle of good single malt next time you're out in Vancouver.

Phillip was a whisky aficionado. He'd taught Zelensky to buy only single malt Scotch, and to leave out the 'e' when he wrote 'whisky.'

CHAPTER 31

On Monday Zelensky called Doucet and asked if he could come to the safe house that evening after work. When they had gathered around the table he brought Doucet up to speed on the search through the bank records and told him how they'd found things in Sullivan's account statements that looked suspicious. "Please thank your friend," he said to Doucet. "That was a brilliant idea."

He told them that he'd been to Calgary on Saturday and met Sullivan face-to-face, but he didn't say what he'd learned. "Listen," he said, "I'd love to tell you everything, but I can't. It's already very unusual for us to be working together like this; I sometimes think of you two almost as part of my team. But I can only bend the rules so far and it's for your benefit and mine that as few people as possible know all the details. What I can say is that partly due to the work the two of you have done, I have a plan. Things are in motion that I can't tell you about, and we're at a crucial stage. If everything works out the way I hope, it should all come together soon. So for the moment you'll just have to grin and bear it. I know it's hard, but it's their move now."

Thompson and Doucet looked at one another. They could only guess at what Zelensky's plan might be. Who, exactly, were 'they'? If this goes on much longer, Thompson thought, I'm going to start screaming.

Zelensky put on a brave front with them but he wasn't as confident as he appeared. The message to his mentor had brought results; Zelensky was now getting the daily NSA files for all the telephone numbers he had requested. But so far he hadn't heard anything in the audio files that even tangentially related to Diatek, and the days were slipping by. His plan depended heavily on Sullivan. Had he misread the guy? He didn't think so, but if something didn't happen soon he might have to start all over again.

The waiting was harder for Thompson than for Doucet or Zelensky. He had time on his hands, and he spent most of it thinking about his life and his future. He kicked himself for getting seduced by Lea; he'd been stupid and greedy but when you looked at it rationally, what had he done wrong? He hadn't stolen anything, he hadn't bribed anyone, all he'd done was slip diamonds onto a conveyor belt. It hadn't been his idea; he was just the instrument for someone else's scheme. After he staged the accident and disappeared they recruited someone else in his place. He hadn't even benefited much aside from the relatively small amounts of money they'd paid him – although he did have his private insurance policy; that was something he'd have to talk to Doucet about. And he had certainly suffered. And now he was cooperating. If they charge me, any smart lawyer could get me off, he told himself.

Still, as the days went by without progress he became more and more apprehensive. For the time being, under witness protection in the safe house, he could sleep soundly at night. But he couldn't live the rest of his life like this. He was already getting cabin fever. It was much worse than being at the mine; there he had lived in isolation too, but at least he'd had had his work to keep him occupied.

Unlike Thompson, Doucet could go to work each day, but even so it didn't feel real; he drifted through the days waiting for something to happen, and sometimes he'd find his mind miles away from whatever he was supposed to be doing. He was living a double life, hidden away in Thompson's apartment with a bodyguard trailing him everywhere he went, sneaking into the Diatek building through the rear entrance. When he looked around at his colleagues he would think, they have no idea. He wondered what they would do if they knew what was going on just across town at RCMP headquarters and at the safe house. He was sure now that when the revelations about diamond smuggling and financial fraud came out a tsunami would sweep through the company, and he worried about what he would do. The only person he could talk to about it was Sarah.

"If you're concerned," she said one evening when he called, "start looking around. You told me once that you were happiest when you were working on your PhD. So why don't you take a look at what's available in academia? I know the salary wouldn't be as good, but money isn't everything. I don't get paid as well here as I did at McKinsey, even with an extra degree. But I'm reasonably happy. You shouldn't lose sleep over Diatek; if it's going to collapse when all this stuff comes out there's not much you can do about it. Prepare for it. Think about it as an opportunity."

"It sounds simple enough, but it would be a major change for me … your organization doesn't need a geologist, do they?"

Sarah laughed. "Not that I know of. But seriously Rick, you're good at what you do. Take advantage of it. Decide what you'd really like to do and make them come to you. Make them think it was their idea in the first place."

Doucet knew it wouldn't be easy, but he also realized that Sarah was right about being prepared. It made no sense to sit around doing nothing when the future at Diatek looked so murky. Good academic jobs were hard to come by, and he knew it would be even more difficult for him because he'd spent his entire career so far in the mining industry. He'd had no university work experience since his days in graduate school.

Doucet had not been to the safe house for almost a week. But tonight Zelensky wanted him there, that's what the bodyguard said when Doucet met him as usual at the back service door as he left work. They drove in silence. The man was even more careful than Zelensky, doubling back frequently, constantly checking the mirrors, and Doucet wondered how much longer he would have to endure this surreal, clandestine life.

The first thing he noticed when he saw Thompson was the engineer's appearance; it had steadily improved since that day he had found him in the Ensenada hospital, and now he was almost the old Thompson he remembered from … was it really only seven or eight months ago? Was it only last winter they had met and talked about Thompson's will and the diamond he wanted to have analyzed? It seemed like a lifetime away.

Zelensky didn't have much to tell them. He said he wanted to touch base, let them know everything was going according to plan, they just had to be patient. But he looked tired and for the first time Doucet thought the policeman seemed worried, as though – in spite of what he said – things actually *weren't* working out quite the way he had hoped. Zelensky had ordered in Chinese food and the three of them sat around eating and making desultory conversation and then he looked at his watch and said he had to go.

After he left Thompson and Doucet looked at one another across the table. "What was that all about?" Doucet said.

Thompson shook his head. "Beats me. But I'm glad you're here because it's good to have someone other than the minders downstairs to talk to. They're nice enough but we don't have a lot in common. And it's good that Zelensky is gone because there's something I want to talk to you about privately. I need you to do me a favor."

Oh no, Doucet thought, what now?

"When we talked in Ensenada, I'm pretty sure I mentioned that I have a little insurance policy. Do you remember that?"

"Yes, I do, vaguely. I wondered what you were talking about."

"It's something I set aside for later – for after I finished what I was doing at the mine. The problem is, it's in my safe deposit box and obviously I can't just go over and get it. But I'm worried about what's going to happen when all this stuff about Diatek blows up, what my status will be. So I'm thinking it should be moved, as a precaution. Could you do that for me? You've still got Power of Attorney, it shouldn't be a problem."

It was complicated because the only key to the safe deposit box was at Thompson's lawyer's office, in an envelope with the original of his will. On his way to work the next morning, the bodyguard/chauffeur driving – something Doucet thought he could get used to very easily – he called the lawyer and asked if he could drop by his office on his lunch break. There are a few things I'd like to check in the will, he said.

"That shouldn't be a problem," the lawyer said, "although unfortunately I have a lunch meeting with a client. But I'll leave the will with my assistant, and she should be able to answer any questions you have."

Perfect, Doucet thought. He asked the bodyguard to pick him up in the alley at noon, and when he arrived at the lawyer's office the assistant gave him a large envelope and showed him into a conference room. "Everything Mr. Thompson gave us is here," she said. "I'll close the door and leave you to it. Let me know if you need anything."

Doucet dumped the contents of the envelope onto the desk. Along with the will and some other papers was a small envelope with a number written on it, just as Thompson had said there would be. Doucet opened it, found the key, and slipped it into his pocket. He sat there, idly leafing through the will; he didn't want to leave too quickly. This is crazy, he thought. But he waited for a few more minutes and then gathered up everything and returned it to the assistant. "Thanks," he said, "I got everything I need."

As soon as he finished work that afternoon Doucet had the bodyguard drive him to Thompson's bank. But getting permission to access the safe deposit box took longer than he expected; the bank staff didn't know him and although he showed them the Power of Attorney papers they asked him a series of questions and wanted multiple pieces of ID. They didn't appear to know anything about Thompson's accident and presumed death and Doucet didn't volunteer any information; he knew it would make things even more difficult. Finally, though, they were satisfied and let him sign in and take out the box.

It was a large one, and it was heavy. Doucet carried it into a booth and drew the curtain shut behind him. Thompson had told him what was inside, but even so he wasn't prepared for what he found in the leather pouch that took up more than half the space in the safe deposit box. He almost fell off his chair when he opened it; he had never seen so many diamonds. There were hundreds of them, a small fortune's worth, maybe even a large fortune's worth. Thompson had said they were his insurance policy and now Doucet understood why. They would keep him secure financially for a long time.

Thompson had told him that as soon as he realized what was in the packages he was taking into the mine he started slitting open some of the small bags and taking out a diamond or two before putting the rest into the ore. He had reasoned that there was no way whoever was sending them to him would know. "It was a risk," he said, "but a small one. They couldn't track individual diamonds and the day to day fluctuation in diamond production was large enough that they wouldn't notice if a few were missing. I thought it was a really sloppy way for them to do it, actually, but I didn't mind. Every time I came back to Vancouver I'd put the ones I'd taken into my safe deposit box. The only mistake I made was near the end, when I'd already decided to get out. I got greedy. I didn't even take the last few packages up to the mine, I just kept them. I figured they wouldn't know, but I was wrong. It's what tipped Andropov off that I wasn't really dead."

Doucet's thoughts were interrupted by a knock. "Are you almost finished, Mr. Doucet? We're getting ready to close up. We'll need to shut the vault soon."

"Okay," he said, "I'll only be a minute." He picked up the leather pouch – it was quite heavy – and hesitated for a moment before putting it in his briefcase. Should he really walk out onto the street carrying a fortune in diamonds? But he'd walked around town hundreds of times carrying a briefcase and never had a problem. Why should today be any different? He would be the only person who knew what was in the briefcase. Still, he hugged the bag tight to his body, his arms wrapped around it, as he stepped out onto the street, and it wasn't until the next day, with the diamonds safely stowed in his own bank, that he relaxed.

CHAPTER 32

Almost two weeks after Zelensky's conversation with Sullivan in Calgary the phone intercepts still hadn't yielded anything useful. He was getting more and more concerned. He'd thought it would start with Alex Kalinin, the local in Calgary, and work its way up to Andropov or maybe even Gagarin. Was he missing something? Were they using other ways to communicate? Patience, he kept telling himself, but he couldn't wait forever. It was Friday afternoon, another week gone by, but at least the NSA files would keep coming over the weekend. The computers didn't take time off, they kept working day in and day out, and probably a lot of the analysts did too. Zelensky knew that he would be in his office tomorrow, and Sunday, waiting for something to break.

On Saturday afternoon he sat at his desk watching the rain lash against the windows. The building was quiet, almost empty, and he could hear the wind sighing over the low hum of the heating system; the first really big Pacific storm of the season, barreling down from Alaska, was forecast to hit Vancouver that evening. The weather matched his mood. Bringing Thompson back from Mexico and hearing his story, and especially finding Sullivan, had given him a high. Now, after almost two weeks of no progress, he was beginning to lose his confidence.

The NSA files were routed through CSIS in Ottawa, and they typically arrived in Vancouver mid-afternoon. Today there were only a few phone conversations from the Moscow-based phones, covering Friday night through noon on Saturday, Moscow time. There were also calls to and from Kalinin's phone in Calgary. Zelensky put on his headphones and clicked through them. Most of the calls were in Russian; he'd requested originals because they could be sent through immediately. That was the beauty of knowing the language – if he'd wanted translations he would have had to wait.

But when he'd listened to everything he took off his headphones and slammed them down on the desk in disgust. "Dammit," he said out loud. "Dammit, dammit, dammit." Another day with nothing to show for it.

He was so disappointed that he almost didn't look at the text messages. The intercepts swept up texts as well as voice messages, but none of the Russians were heavy texters and everything Zelensky had seen in the texts so far had been completely innocuous. But for completeness he decided he should scan through them before he went home. If he hadn't done that he would have missed it: late Friday afternoon – yesterday – Alex Kalinin had received a message that said only 'meet me.' But below those two innocent sounding words was a British Airways flight itinerary: Moscow to London Heathrow, then a connecting flight to Calgary. The message had been sent from Dimitri Andropov's cell phone in Moscow.

Zelensky exploded out of his chair, a huge smile on his face, and pumped his fist into the air. "Gotcha," he said out loud. There was no one around to hear him, and he sat back down and wrote out the flight numbers. The first leg had left Moscow early this morning and the flight from Heathrow was due to land in Calgary at five-twenty, local time. It had to be Andropov. There was no name on the itinerary, but it had been sent from Andropov's phone. It had to be him. Zelensky's watch read four-thirty and Calgary was an hour ahead; if the flight was on time it was already on the ground. He would have to act fast.

It took him less than ten minutes to set up an emergency three-way conference call with one of his colleagues at RCMP's Alberta headquarters in Edmonton and an officer with the Canadian Border Services Agency at Calgary airport. "Let's keep the lines open, okay? This is important. And don't turn on your speaker phone if there's anyone within earshot. We have to keep this between the three of us. There's a serious national security angle on this." That always got people's attention.

Zelensky was thinking fast and scribbling down a list of everything he'd need. "First, can you get me a passenger roster for BA103, today's flight? It was scheduled to land a few minutes ago."

"Shouldn't be a problem," the CBSA agent said. "Give me a minute, I'm going to put the phone down."

There was silence on the line. Zelensky drummed his fingers on his desk, watching the clock. Then the agent was back.

"Got it," he said. "By the way, that flight was delayed by about half an hour. It's on approach right now, but it hasn't landed yet. Anyone in particular you're looking for? We can hold them when they get off the plane."

"It's just one person, a Russian male, but don't do anything. We don't want this guy to know we're watching him. Can you email me the passenger list right away?" Zelensky read off his email address.

"Sure." Again the line was silent while the CBSA agent put down the phone and sent the list. It arrived moments later and Zelensky scrolled up to the top, looking for the 'A's. But it wasn't organized alphabetically. "Got the list," he said. "Thanks. Give me a minute while I check the names." He had to force himself to slow down and scan through systematically, reading each entry in turn. But Andropov wasn't there.

"Is this final?" he asked. "The name I'm looking for isn't here."

"That's definitely the final list. Every passenger who went through the boarding gate at Heathrow is there."

"Shit," Zelensky said. "He must be using a different name. I'm sure he's on that flight." He was quiet for a moment. "Okay then, we'll go with plan B. If I send you a photo, can you get it to the immigration agents before he gets to passport control? And Jim," – Jim was Zelensky's Edmonton-based RCMP colleague and they knew one another well – "if we find him, can you organize a tail from the airport?"

Jim didn't reply immediately and the CBSA agent broke in. "I'm monitoring the flight for you," he said. "It's just touched down. It'll take a while for him to taxi to the gate. If you need a little more time we can organize a delay. Don't tell anyone from the airlines I said this, but we can tell the pilot the gate isn't ready, or there could be a glitch with the jet bridge – lots of possibilities. What do you think?"

Zelensky laughed. "You've got my vote … what did you say your name is?"

"Craig."

"Okay Craig, let's do it."

"You've got it. I'll be away from the phone for a few minutes but I won't disconnect. In the meantime send me the pictures."

"Jeez, Ed, we need more people like him." It was Zelensky's Edmonton colleague; Craig had already put the phone down.

"Tell me about it. What do you think about the tail?"

"To tell you the truth I was gonna say I couldn't guarantee anything. That was before our friend from CBSA reminded me how we should work. So I'm going to say yes, I'll get you a tail. Just remember it's Saturday and there'll only be a skeleton crew on duty. I assume it should be someone who knows what they're doing so your guy doesn't spot him. Will he be watching?"

"I don't know, but he may be. I don't think he'll be expecting anything, but at the very least he'll be alert. From what I know about him, being alert is something this guy does well."

"Okay. Forward me those pictures if you haven't already. I'll keep the line open but if we get cut off just call me back. I'll have to go to the other room to do this."

Zelensky sent the pictures he had downloaded from the RCMP files. He'd cropped them so that they showed only Andropov's face.

Enlarged, they were grainy, but unless Andropov had altered his appearance they would be good enough to identify him. Then he turned on his speaker phone and got up and stretched. There was nothing more he could do now except wait for answers from the others. He walked over to the window and peered out into the gloom. No question the storm was getting worse; across the parking lot he could see the trees bending in the wind, their last remaining leaves being stripped off and whirled away. He paced around the room, his eyes on the big clock on the wall, wondering what Andropov was doing, imagining him walking into the Calgary airport. Unsuspecting, he hoped. Come on, he said under his breath, willing something to happen.

"It's me, Craig." Zelensky was standing close to his desk and he jumped when he heard the voice, then he grabbed the phone.

"Zelensky. What's happening?"

The CBSA agent sounded as though he was out of breath. "BA103 is parked at the gate but they're having trouble with the jet bridge. One of the wheels on the bridge is jammed and they can't get the thing lined up with the airplane door. If it doesn't get fixed soon they may have to tow the airplane to another gate. Strange how these things happen, eh?" He chuckled. "Actually, it wasn't that difficult to arrange. So your guy is probably sitting there fuming, like all the other passengers. And the immigration people have the photos. I told them to keep them out of sight but to check them against every male who came in on flight 103. If they think there's a match they'll buzz me. I'll be watching too, from our observation room. What do you want us to do if we spot him?"

"Just keep an eye on him. Jim is trying to get someone out to the airport soon, so it's best you liaise directly with him. The tail will need a good description of this guy, what he's wearing and what he's carrying. It's likely that someone will be at the airport to pick him up. The best of all worlds would be if Jim's people get out there fast enough to follow him into town. If he actually shows up I'll come to Calgary with two of my own surveillance people as soon as I can, and we can take over when we get there."

It was Zelensky's lucky day. There were two undercover officers at Calgary police headquarters and neither of them had pressing assignments. Twenty-five minutes later they were at the airport being briefed by Craig Hill, the CBSA agent. He gave them copies of the photos Zelensky had sent and the three of them stood in the observation room looking out over the immigration hall, which was rapidly filling up with passengers streaming in from several recently arrived flights. Hill had been monitoring the status of BA103; passengers had begun to disembark but none of the passport control officers had yet processed anyone who resembled Andropov.

One of the undercover officers nudged Hill and said quietly, "Look, over there, the tall guy. I think it's him." She pointed to the left and they watched as Andropov, in jeans and a leather jacket with the collar turned up, walked across the hall searching for the shortest passport line. He had a black carryall bag slung across his shoulder and when he stopped he put it down and looked up and they got a good view of his face.

"You're right, it's definitely him," Hill said, glancing from the photo to Andropov. He went over to the desk and picked up the phone. "It's Craig again. Are you still there Zelensky?"

"Yeah, I'm here. What's happening?"

"We've got him. He's in one of the immigration lines, ten or fifteen meters from where I'm standing. Waiting to have his passport checked. It's definitely him. Looks a bit older than in the photo and he hasn't got as much hair now, but it's the same person. The two undercovers are here with me, do you want to talk to them?"

Zelensky said yes and Hill handed the phone to the woman. "Wilson here," she said.

"Hi, it's Ed Zelensky. Has Craig filled you in? I'm RCMP in Vancouver. This person who came in on the flight from London, we don't want him to know we're watching. Can you tail him from the airport and find out where he goes without being spotted? I'm coming out there with two of my surveillance people ASAP and we'll take over, but in the meantime don't let him out of your sight." There was a pause. "Do you have a first name?"

"It's Terri. Terri with an 'i'. Don't worry, we won't lose your guy. And he won't know we're there."

"Okay Terri with an 'i'. And thanks. I appreciate what you're doing."

Zelensky was so happy to have Andropov in his sights that he could hardly contain himself. He called Michael Foster, the best surveillance man he had, and told him to pack his bags.

"Get out to the airport ASAP. We're going to Calgary."

"What?" Michael was used to getting calls from Zelensky at odd hours, but usually they involved something in Vancouver, or occasionally a nearby town. "Calgary? Right now?"

"Yes, right now. We'll need another body too, so pick a partner and get them out there as well. Your choice about who you bring. We'll take a military flight if we have to, but we need to get to Calgary as soon as possible. It's a long story but we need to watch someone who just landed there. And probably arrest him. He's Russian and he has links to those guys you were watching at the house in Kitsilano. I'll tell you about it on the way. He's important; we can't let him slip through our fingers."

CHAPTER 33

A s soon as Zelensky got off the phone with Michael Foster he called Air Canada and got three seats on the last flight to Calgary. Economy was almost full but because it was the weekend there were lots of business class seats available and he used his RCMP status to get them bumped up. They wouldn't arrive until after midnight, but at least they'd be there.

Craig Hill from CBSA greeted them when they got off the plane. He was a younger man than Zelensky expected. "Officially I finished work a while ago," he said, "but I thought I'd stick around and talk to you in person. Come on over to my office. I've got something to show you." While they walked through the terminal he gave them an update on Andropov's whereabouts. "The undercover people said he was met by someone in a Mercedes. They got his plate number, so you can track it, but get this: one of them recognized the driver. Someone known to Calgary police, apparently. They can give you the details. They tailed the car to a downtown hotel and parked across the street. Probably in front of a fire hydrant in their unmarked police car." Hill laughed. "Parking is really expensive downtown. Anyway, one of them stayed in the car to watch the entrance, that's where he is now. The other one went into the lobby."

"Did they see Andropov check in?"

Hill looked at him. "Oh, so that's his real name, is it? You didn't say before. Yes, he checked in and they got his room number." They had reached his office and he unlocked the door and ushered them inside. "He's traveling as Mr. ..." He searched through some papers on his desk. "Mr. Magnusson. Eric Magnusson. Here's a copy of the passport he used. It's Swedish, issued three years ago in Stockholm, and it didn't raise any flags when he came through immigration. The picture is pretty close to the one you sent us. Whoever did this passport is good."

"Andropov has enough resources that he can get most anything he wants," Zelensky said. "My guess is that Eric Magnusson is a real person who died at birth forty years ago, or at least is no longer with us. Andropov will probably use the passport once and dump it. But if I have my way he'll be in jail before he can do that."

Hill called the undercover police, who were sitting in their car across the street from Andropov's hotel. He handed the phone to Zelensky.

"I'll be there as soon as I can," Zelensky said. "There are three of us; we can spell you off when we get there. In the meantime, don't let him get away."

"Don't worry, he won't go anywhere without us knowing. Terri went into the lobby and watched him check in and take the elevator up to his room. The guy who picked him up at the airport went with him; we know him well, his name is Alex Kalinin – we can fill you in when you get here. Kalinin came down after about twenty minutes, by himself, and he left, and now we're just watching. My guess is your friend is asleep – he came in from Europe, right? You probably won't see him until breakfast."

Zelensky and his team rendezvoused with the undercover agents an hour later. They told him that they were pretty sure Kalinin hadn't seen them when they followed the car to the hotel, but even if he had it wouldn't have raised any alarms. They often tailed Kalinin, they said, and he knew it. Flaunted it, actually. The guy was a known criminal but he was rich and he spread his money around and had a lot of friends in the city. It was frustrating because they hadn't been able to take him down for anything yet.

Zelensky didn't tell them he knew all about Kalinin and that he had been expecting him to pick up Andropov.

They gave Zelensky Andropov's room number and a physical description of Kalinin so that he and his team would be able to recognize him. He thanked them and asked them to keep the operation under wraps, at least for the next few days. "I don't want Kalinin to know we're watching his visitor," he said, "or that anyone except the Calgary police are interested in him. The fewer people that know about this the better. If he has as many friends here as you say, it would just take a word to the wrong person and he'd know."

Zelensky and Michael Foster took the first shift, sitting in the car across from the hotel where they had a good view of both the main entrance and the exit from the parking garage. When the sky started to lighten on Sunday morning, Foster went into the lobby. He wanted to make sure he spotted Andropov when he came down for breakfast. They'd sent Dominic Fournier, Foster's partner, down the street to a different hotel to get some sleep. The two men had decided that he and Foster would switch off later in the morning. Zelensky said he didn't want to sleep; he'd catnap in the car but he wanted to be there for the whole operation no matter how long it took.

The car was cold and Zelensky wrapped his bulky coat around him and stuffed his hands into his pockets. He'd already been up for more than twenty-four hours and he was having trouble staying awake. He pushed the seat back and pulled his woolen toque down over his eyes. He had just dropped off to sleep when Dominic knocked on the car window, and he opened his eyes and jerked upright. When he saw who it was he opened the door. "I'm going in to relieve Michael," Dominic said. "But I've got a bad feeling about this. I just talked to Michael and he says Andropov hasn't shown up yet."

"Shit," Zelensky said. He looked at his watch; it was just after nine. "Let's give it another half hour. He came straight from Moscow after all. Tell Michael to come out here to the car."

Nine-thirty came and went and Dominic called to say he'd still seen no sign of the Russian. Zelensky was wide awake now, and he was starting to worry. "Okay," he said, "stay there. I'm going to call his room." He turned to Michael. "What's the room number?"

"It's five-three-four. It's imprinted on my brain; I've been watching the elevators like a hawk every time they stop at the fifth floor. But he never showed, I'm sure of it."

Zelensky dialed the hotel and asked for room 534. The room phone rang for a long time but there was no answer and eventually it went to voicemail. He ended the call and looked over at Michael. "Something's wrong. Stay here. I didn't want to do this, but I'm going to have a chat with the manager." He walked across the road and through the lobby, giving Dominic a glance that said "sit tight." They'd worked together long enough that he didn't have to say anything. There were two young women at the check-in counter and one of them turned and asked Zelensky if she could help. He showed her his RCMP badge and asked if he could speak to the manager. She looked startled.

"Of course, just hold on for a minute." She went through a door behind her and was back a moment later with a man about Zelensky's age, dressed in a suit.

"I need a word with you," Zelensky said, "in private."

The manager led him into his office and as soon as he had shut the door behind him Zelensky said, "I'll get right to the point." He told him what he needed. Ten minutes later he was standing at the end of the corridor watching while one of the cleaning ladies knocked on the door to room 534. "Housekeeping," she said, "may I come in?"

There was no response. She knocked again, and again there was no response, and she looked down the hall at Zelensky. He nodded, and she opened the door and went inside. A minute later she came back out, shaking her head. "Shit," Zelensky said to himself and walked down the hall.

"It's empty," she said, "It doesn't look as though anyone's been in the room. No one slept here, anyway; the bed's still made up. Are you sure this is the right room?" She was flushed with excitement. She'd never met a real RCMP officer before. Although this one didn't look anything like the ones she'd seen on TV in their red uniforms and Stetson hats – in fact, he looked a little scruffy and he obviously hadn't shaved. Still, he wasn't *that* bad looking …

"Yes, this is the right room," Zelensky said. He went inside and looked around – as the housekeeper had said, it was undisturbed. He checked the bathroom. A bar of soap had been unwrapped and one of the towels had been used. So he was here, he thought, but not for long. He looked in the closet but Andropov hadn't left anything. The room safe was open. The Calgary undercover officers had watched Kalinin and Andropov get into the elevator and ride up to the fifth floor, and then they'd seen Kalinin leave, alone, twenty minutes later. How the hell did Andropov get out of here without being seen? Was he just being careful, or does he know we're watching?

He thanked the housekeeper for her help and asked her not to say anything about their little adventure and then he went back down to the lobby and had a brief conversation with the manager. He told Zelensky that Mr. Magnusson's reservation was for three nights and he hadn't said anything about changes to his stay when he checked in. And no, he did not have a rental car reserved in the parking garage. Zelensky gave the manager his card and asked him to call if Magnusson reappeared. He also asked him not to say anything to anyone about a visit from the RCMP. But he wasn't happy. He could swear people to secrecy until he was blue in the face, but he knew human nature and he knew how difficult it was to keep a secret. Under the circumstances it couldn't be helped, but already too many people knew about his interest in Andropov.

When he got back to the car he found Dominic drinking coffee and Michael curled up in the back seat, napping. He was ready for a nap himself, but there was too much to do. He woke Michael and the three men huddled to plan their next steps. Timing was crucial. He knew in broad outline what they had to do, but they would have to improvise as they went along. First up, though, he had to decide what to do about Tom Sullivan. He had spoken with the security guard regularly after their initial meeting, but he had heard nothing from him for several days. That worried him.

Two weeks earlier, when he had confronted Sullivan with the evidence of unexplained deposits into his bank account and asked him if they were linked in any way to his activities at the Diatek mine, he had seen a flicker of fear cross the man's face and he knew immediately he had the right person. Zelensky was a skilled interrogator and it had not taken long before the man began to tell his story, reluctantly at first but then, with some gentle encouragement from Zelensky, more and more forcefully. He had been getting ready for retirement, Sullivan said, he'd always planned for the work at the mine to be his last job. Then this possibility came along, a way to get extra cash for a little sleight of hand. It would be easy money, like a gift from heaven. Besides, it wasn't so bad, was it? He wasn't stealing from the company or anything like that.

Zelensky had assured him that it *was* pretty bad, and that he had a choice: he could look forward to spending his retirement in jail or he could cooperate. If Sullivan could help them find whoever was behind this scheme he could expect leniency. The RCMP were more interested in catching the big fish, Zelensky said, than putting Sullivan in jail. And then he outlined his plan. He'd been thinking about it ever since they realized that the diamond smuggling operation had started up again. Based on what Thompson had told him, he had a good idea of how the Russians worked. He thought he might be able to bring them out into the open – if he could get Sullivan to cooperate. To some extent, Zelensky was flying by the seat of his pants, but he was good at it and as far as Sullivan knew it was an elaborate plan hatched by a team of RCMP experts.

"You have a contact number, right?" Zelensky said.

"Yeah, I do, although usually they call me, or send a text, not the other way around. I think I only called them once, when one of their deliveries didn't arrive before I had to go back to the mine. Sometimes when they get in touch they threaten me – you know, what will happen if I don't do what they say." Sullivan laughed. "I don't pay much attention to that. I've been in this kind of job all my life, I've been a bouncer and a security guard and I can take care of myself."

If only he knew, Zelensky thought, but he didn't say anything. He had an image of what Andropov had done to Thompson. "Here's what I want you to do. First, cancel your trip back to the mine. Then send your boss an email or a text or whatever and tell him you're tired or stressed or something and you just can't face coming back next week, and you're thinking about retiring. Keep it as simple as you can and do it all by text or email, don't talk to him in person. That way you can control it and not get flustered by an unexpected question. Get your wife to answer all your phone calls. Can you do that?"

Sullivan sat forward. "But I can't just …"

Zelensky cut him off. "Sure you can," he said. "Maybe your retirement will start a bit earlier than you expected, but if you want to stay out of jail you can do it. Once you've written to your boss, send a text message to that contact number. Keep that one short and simple too. Tell them you can't do this anymore, you're stressed out, you're going to retire from Diatek." He reached into his coat pocket and pulled out a cell phone and a pen. "These are for you," he said. He handed Sullivan the phone. "It's secure, and my number's there, there's no name, just a number. It's the only contact listed. You can call me any time, but don't use this phone for anything else, okay?" Then he gave Sullivan the pen. "And this, as you can see, is a pen." He grinned. "It actually writes, but it's also a micro recording device. When you press down the button on top the nib comes out like a regular pen, but it also starts recording. It's got a tiny memory card inside. The battery is fresh and it'll record for hours. Believe it or not, it's made in Russia." Appropriate, Zelensky thought to himself. "They're good at this sort of thing."

Sullivan turned the pen over in his hand and clicked the button a couple of times. "I've heard of these things but I've never seen one," he said. "Expensive, I bet." He looked at

Zelensky and the policeman nodded. "So what am I supposed to do with it?" Sullivan asked.

"It's backup. Just in case you actually end up talking to any of these people face to face. I don't think that will happen, but if it does, just click the button and turn on the recorder. It's sensitive, it will pick up the conversation even if the pen is in your pocket. That would be tremendously valuable for us." Zelensky was bending the truth a bit. He actually thought there was a good possibility that someone would confront Sullivan face to face, and considering what had happened to Thompson it could turn out to be unpleasant. But Sullivan was better equipped to handle a situation like that than Thompson had been. And besides, Zelensky told himself, I'll have enough warning to get back here to Calgary before anything happens.

And now Andropov was in Calgary, and Zelensky was sure he was here to confront Sullivan. The smuggling scheme was just too valuable to the Russian for there to be yet another disruption; he would try to convince Sullivan, or more likely force him, to go back to the mine.

Zelensky turned to his men. "I'm worried that we haven't heard anything from Sullivan."

"Maybe he didn't have a chance to call," Dominic said. "What if Andropov and Kalinin went to his place last night and surprised him?"

"It's possible," Zelensky said. "Andropov certainly went somewhere. It's one reason I don't want to call Sullivan on that phone I gave him, just in case Andropov is there. Michael, you and I better drive out to Sullivan's place and do a reccy.

Dominic, I have a feeling that Andropov isn't going to show his face at the hotel again, but for the time being I want you to stay here and watch. If he shows up call me right away."

CHAPTER 34

Foster drove while Zelensky navigated – he had an almost photographic memory, and he had driven out here himself just two weeks ago. And when he wasn't quite sure he checked the GPS on his phone. Sullivan's street was quiet: Sunday morning, an occasional car driving by, a few kids on their bikes. It all looked very normal. They drove past the house and Zelensky noticed that the pickup truck he'd see in the driveway when he was here before was gone. The house itself was quiet. He told Foster to pull around the corner at the next intersection and park. They'd have a good view of the house but they wouldn't be conspicuous.

They sat watching for about forty-five minutes but there was no sign of activity. Foster checked in with Fournier at the hotel but nothing was happening there, either. Then the front door of Sullivan's house opened and a woman stepped out. She had on boots and a padded jacket and had a scarf wrapped around her head, but Zelensky recognized her as Tom Sullivan's wife, Anne. Behind her, on a leash, she trailed a small black Scottie. "We're in luck," Zelensky said to Foster. "That's Anne Sullivan."

He got out of the car and walked to the corner, intercepting her as she passed.

"Hi," he said, and she stopped, uncertain. "Please, just keep walking." He bent down to pat the dog but the Scottie barked and he straightened up and walked along beside her. "Not very friendly, is he? Remember me? From the RCMP? I came to see your husband a couple of weeks ago. Is he home today?"

She scowled at him. "You startled me. Why didn't you just knock on the door?"

"Doesn't matter. Is he around?"

"No, he went out in the truck a few hours ago."

"Do you know where he went?"

"Not a clue. I hardly ever know where he's going – he never says. Besides, this morning some guy I'd never seen before came and got him. It was early; Tom was already up but I was still in bed when I heard the doorbell. They had an argument at the door, I didn't hear what they said, but then Tom came and got his wallet and his coat. And he put on his hunting vest, you know, those ones with all the pockets? I don't know why he did that. He said it was someone from work and he was going out with them. Maybe it's something to do with retiring. He told them last week he was going to retire, you know? You could have knocked me over with a feather. I thought he'd be going up to that mine forever. I'm not sure what I'm going to do with him moping around the house all the time."

"One guy or two?" Zelensky asked.

"What? Oh, you mean at the door? There was only the one. I suppose there could have been someone else in the car. I didn't see."

"And he didn't say anything about where they were going?" Zelensky kept pressing.

"I already told you. He never tells me anything."

"Okay. Just one more question, Mrs. Sullivan, then I'll stop bothering you. This person who came to your door this morning, was your husband expecting him?"

"Not that I know of. He hadn't said anything about it to me, anyway." Suddenly she smiled. "He's very organized you know, and he has a calendar next to his computer where he writes down appointments." She looked at Zelensky. "I took a look after he left and he didn't have anything down for this morning. So I guess it wasn't something he'd planned on."

"Okay, thanks. Have a nice walk." He turned to go, then stopped. "Mrs. Sullivan – could you get him to call me when he comes back? He has my number." She paused for a moment but didn't say anything, then she jerked on the leash and started walking again. The Scottie trotted along obediently behind her.

Zelensky jogged back to the car and flopped into his seat, out of breath. "I need to get more exercise," he said, panting. "I probably couldn't pass the physical right now."

"You're always saying that," Michael said.

"Mm. I think we may have a situation." He told Foster what Anne Sullivan had said. "See if you can get a license number for Sullivan's truck. It's a brown pickup, looks a bit beaten up. I don't know the make. Registered to Thomas Sullivan, or possibly Anne Sullivan."

"Okay, I'm on it." They switched seats and Zelensky sat there thinking, drumming his fingers on the steering wheel while Foster worked his phone.

Ten minutes later Foster said, "Got it," and handed Zelensky a slip of paper with the license number of Sullivan's pickup scribbled on it.

"Fantastic. What would we do without computers?" Unlike some other senior officers, Zelensky was completely at ease with modern technology and he used it extensively. But he could never quite get over the contrast with the early days of his career.

"Here's what I'm thinking," he said to Foster. "I'll call Calgary police and ask them to put out an APB on the truck. That way we get eyes all over the city, and we'll hear about it as soon as someone spots the truck. Then you and I can take a drive over to Kalinin's place and check it out. It's possible that Andropov went there when he left the hotel, although how he got out of the place beats me. And also they might have taken Sullivan there. But we don't want to go storming in because it's also possible that neither Andropov nor Sullivan is there, and we don't want to tip Kalinin off. So I'll ask the Calgary police to put a stakeout on the house, and then we'll have to play it by ear until something happens. What do you think?" Zelensky usually asked his colleagues for their opinion, even if he'd already made up his mind about what to do.

"Sounds like a plan."

Zelensky didn't say so, but he was getting increasingly worried that he'd put Sullivan in danger. If whoever picked him up this morning was part of Kalinin's gang of thugs that was a very real possibility. He didn't like it but there was nothing he could do about it now. Deal with it, he told himself. He took out his phone and called the Calgary police. He gave them the details of Sullivan's truck and asked them to issue an APB but not to stop the truck – just notify him if it was spotted. It was crucial they find it, fast. And then he said he wanted to pay a visit to Kalinin's house.

"Have you got an address?"

"Have I got an address? I know it by heart." The officer rattled it off so quickly that Zelensky had to ask him to slow down and read it to him again.

This time he got it, and he told the officer he was going over there now. He also asked if they could put a surveillance team on the house, as soon as possible. They should let him, Zelensky, know everything that happens, including detailed descriptions of anyone coming or going. He wanted to know if anyone so much as looked out a window.

"With pleasure," the officer said. "You get *anything* that puts that guy away and you've got friends in Calgary for life."

Even in the obviously well-to-do suburb, Kalinin's large stone house with its carefully manicured hedge looked ostentatious. Two stone pillars flanked the end of the driveway, the lights perched atop them still burning even though the day was bright. Shades or curtains covered every window. "Either Kalinin likes the dark or he's gone to Florida for the winter," Zelensky said as they drove by. "And we know he hasn't gone to Florida." There was no sign of Sullivan's truck.

"That's a big garage," Michael said. "Maybe they put it in there, out of sight. In this neighborhood an old pickup would stick out like a sore thumb."

"Yeah, maybe …" Zelensky pulled the car around a corner and parked where they had an oblique view of the house. For twenty minutes they sat, watching, but nothing stirred. Then Zelensky's phone rang, twice in quick succession. The first call was from Dominic – no sign of Andropov, he said. Zelensky told him to hang in there and then answered the second call, from Calgary police. A surveillance team was being put together for Kalinin's place, two guys in an unmarked car. They should be there within an hour.

They arrived half an hour later, driving slowly past the house and pulling around the corner into the same street where Foster and Zelensky were waiting. Zelensky gave them a thumbs up and turned to Foster. "They don't need us out here. Let's go back to town and bring Dominic up to speed. And wait for something to happen."

But they didn't have to wait long. They had barely sat down in the hotel coffee shop with Dominic when Zelensky's phone rang again. It was the Calgary police. Sullivan's truck wasn't in Kalinin's garage. They'd found it in a suburban park.

"A jogger called it in a while ago," the officer told Zelensky, "We thought it was just another abandoned truck so it wasn't high priority, but then I was looking at the APB and I thought the license number seemed familiar. It's the one you're look-ing for. It's in an out-of-the-way park about fifteen kilometers out of town. The jogger said it looked like the truck had rolled down a hill from the parking area and ended up in the creek below. Not much damage, though, he said. He was on a running path along the stream when he found it. Two of our cars are on their way over there right now."

"Was there anyone in it?"

"No, that's the first thing I asked. Both doors were open but he didn't see any sign of the driver."

"Okay, can you ask your officers not to touch the truck? We'll go out there right away. Give me the name of the park. We've got GPS." They gulped down their coffee and headed back to the car.

"Feast or famine," Dominic said. "Personally, I prefer feast."

Two police cars, lights flashing, were sitting in the parking lot when they pulled in. Several curious onlookers stood nearby, talking among themselves. Zelensky identified himself to the police officers and asked what they knew.

"Nothing yet," one of the officers said. "We only got here a few minutes ago. They told us to wait for you and make sure nobody touched the truck. We asked those people over there if they'd seen anything" – he pointed to the onlookers – "but they haven't been here long either, and they hadn't even noticed the truck. You wouldn't, from up here. The jogger who called it in is long gone. He told the dispatcher he was getting chilled and he couldn't wait around or he'd catch pneumonia. They've got his name and phone number though."

"Good, we may need to talk to him later. Where's the truck?"

"It's right down in the creek. We checked it out. The hill is pretty steep, but there are some stairs you can go down."

The officer turned and pointed to his left. "See where those bushes are flattened over there? That's where it went over. It doesn't look like an accident to me. Looks like the driver just decided he was going to go over the cliff. Or somebody pushed it over."

Zelensky thanked him and said they would go and take a look.

"We'll be here," the officer said. "Take your time. We're supposed to stick around until you're through, and then we'll get a tow truck and pull the pickup out."

Michael and Dominic were over by the flattened bushes, kneeling down and peering at the ground. "Whoever was driving gunned the motor then let it go," Michael said.

"Yeah," Dominic said, "I can see where the wheels spun on the gravel. But then he must have taken his foot off the gas and let it roll because the tread marks are clear over here in the mud. He was just coasting toward the hill. It's pretty steep; if anyone was in the truck he'd really be shaken up when it hit the bottom, to say the least. He'd probably still be there. If you ask me, whoever was driving probably jumped out before the truck went over."

Zelensky came up and looked over the edge. The truck was upright but it was lying at an awkward angle. It had fishtailed part way down the hill and had ended up perched precariously, its right front wheel in the water, the left one not even touching the ground. "Let's go down and take a look," he said.

The keys were still in the ignition, but otherwise the cab and the back of the truck were empty. "Have you got the gloves, Michael?" Zelensky asked.

Foster reached into his pocket and brought out a bundle of latex gloves and Zelensky pulled on a pair. He didn't like wearing them but he didn't want to mess up any prints they might get from the truck. He reached in and pulled out the keys, looked at them and dropped them into the plastic bag Dominic was holding. "No blood on the seat or the steering wheel, no cracks in the windshield. I think you're right, Dominic. There wasn't anybody in this thing when it came down the hill."

He went around to the other side of the truck, the water almost up to his knees, and gingerly pushed the door open a little wider. The hinges screeched and Zelensky winced at the sound. He opened the glove compartment and reached in with his left hand; it was almost empty, but he pulled out three small items: a mini flashlight, a chocolate bar, and a blank piece of paper. He turned the paper over. Scrawled across the back in large untidy letters were the words, 'I'm sorry.' Underneath, the letter 'T.'

"Oh, Christ," Zelensky said, and stepped out of the water. "Look at this." He held up the note.

Michael squinted at the paper, shielding his eyes. "A suicide note? You think he killed himself?"

"It's possible. Either that or someone wants us to think he killed himself." Zelensky dropped the things he'd taken from the glove compartment into another plastic bag. "Come on, we'd better go tell our friends up top what we found. Best to keep them in the loop so nobody gets uppity about whose investigation this really is. So far I can't complain. They've been amazingly cooperative." They started up the stairs. "I think we'd better organize a search. I have a bad feeling we're going to find Sullivan somewhere nearby."

It was one of the Calgary policemen who found the body. He was a new recruit and he was young, and when he came up to Zelensky his face was as pale as snow. "Over that way," he said. "About five minutes' walk. In a clump of trees. He shot himself; there's a lot of blood."

They called in the others and the young policeman led them to a dense grove of pine trees and pushed through the branches to a small clearing. It was peaceful; the sun slanted through the pines and the ground was covered by a thick carpet of needles and Zelensky had the absurd thought that it would be a good place to pitch a tent. In the middle of the clearing lay a crumpled body; beside it, not far from the outstretched right hand, was a pistol. For a moment no one spoke and then Zelensky said, "Stay back until I get some pictures." He took out his phone and circled the body slowly, taking pictures from all angles. There was no question; it was Sullivan. It looked as though he had put the pistol in his mouth and pulled the trigger. Zelensky could see a large, ragged exit wound on the back of his head and his stomach tightened. He wondered if he should have done things differently. If he had, Sullivan might still be alive. He shook his head, dismissing the thought. Second guessing wouldn't help now.

He put away his phone and said, "You'd better call this in. Get them to send out the homicide unit. I know it looks like he did this to himself, but I have my reasons." He didn't elaborate. Only Foster and Fournier knew the background, and he didn't feel the need to explain it to the Calgary police team.

"Michael," he said, "I need the gloves again." The others watched as he walked up to the body, careful not to disturb the ground around it, and knelt down. Sullivan's padded jacket was open and underneath he wore a tan hunting vest, studded with pockets. The one his wife had told Zelensky about. Methodically, Zelensky checked the jacket and then all the vest pockets, patting each one gently. Most of them were empty, but in one he found a small box of matches, in another a cell phone, in a third a pair of pliers. And then, from a zippered pocket near the top of the vest, he pulled out a pen. He looked at it and then glanced up at Michael and Dominic. It was the recording pen. If Sullivan turned this on, he thought, he's one of my heroes.

CHAPTER 35

They left two policemen with the body and headed back into town. An ambulance and the homicide unit were on their way and there was no reason for the RCMP team to stick around. Zelensky was sure Andropov had murdered Sullivan, but he needed proof, and if Sullivan had turned on the recorder, he might have it.

"Forget the speed limit," Zelensky said, "we need to find out if there's something on this thing, the sooner the better." While Foster drove he called his Commanding Officer at RCMP headquarters in Vancouver. During the previous week, while he had been waiting for reaction to Sullivan's sudden 're-tirement' from his job at the Diatek mine, Zelensky had laid the groundwork for a series of coordinated raids that, if his hunches proved correct, would sweep up the principals in the diamond smuggling ring. He filled in his boss on the events in Calgary and asked him to put the teams on standby.

"If it's going to happen," he said, "it will be soon. I don't want to move until we're sure we have Andropov, and we still don't know where he is. But we'll find him, it's just a matter of time. We're watching the airport because he's got a return ticket to Moscow; it's an open ticket but I'm guessing that now Sullivan is dead he'll leave tonight. One of the CBSA people at the airport is coordinating things for us. We just have to make sure that nobody does anything that will tip Andropov off in advance."

As soon as they got to the hotel Zelensky took out the pen he'd recovered from Sullivan's vest and plugged it into an adaptor, which in turn plugged into his laptop. He waited for the pen drive to come up, then breathed a sigh of relief. There was a file there, a large one. Probably at least a couple of hours of audio.

"I just hope it didn't get turned on accidentally sometime last week," Zelensky said. "But I think we may be about to find out what really happened at that park. Sullivan must have put this thing in his vest when he went out Sunday morning. If he turned it on we should have a record of everything." Zelensky paused. "You know, I wasn't sure about Sullivan when I first talked to him, but I may have misjudged him. If there's useful stuff in this file he deserves a medal."

He downloaded the file and turned up the volume but for a time all they heard was random noises: rustling, scratching, humming, banging. "The microphone is very sensitive," Zelensky said. "But he had a jacket on over the vest and it was in a zipped pocket. I hope we get something." Then a woman's voice, faintly, somewhere in the background. "His wife," Zelensky said. "I think we're okay. It's picking up voices." Again they heard a voice, a man's this time, too faint to decipher. Then, much louder, a single word: "Okay." A moment later there was a screech and the sound of a door slamming.

"That was Sullivan," Zelensky said, "I recognize his voice. And that screech was from the pickup. The hinges made a noise just like that when I opened the door at the park this morning."

The recording played on and again they heard nothing but background sounds for several minutes. Zelensky didn't want to miss anything but he was impatient and he ramped up the speed and the three of them listened intently to nothing but random noise for several more minutes. Then there was a burst of squeaky voices that sounded like Mickey Mouse on steroids. "Whoa," Zelensky said, and clicked the pause button. He went back and started the playback at normal speed. They heard a voice giving directions and Sullivan asking what they were doing at a park and then the truck doors opening and slamming shut again. Zelensky could picture the pickup pulling into the parking area where they had been just an hour before, Sullivan and whoever was with him getting out.

Suddenly there was another, different, voice on the tape. A foreign language.

"What the hell? What is that?" Dominic asked.

"They're speaking Russian," Zelensky said, and clicked pause again. "I'm going to put on the headphones so I can hear this better. The sound is bad enough when they're speaking English. I'll have to really concentrate to get the Russian."

When Zelensky took off the headphones twenty minutes later his face was drawn. He looked over at Dominic and Michael and shook his head.

"That bad?" Dominic asked.

"Worse than you can imagine. I'll get the lab to work on it and see if they can enhance the voices, but I got the gist of it. There are two people speaking Russian and one of them is Andropov. I'd recognize his voice anywhere; I listened to him for hours on those NSA intercepts. The other one is probably Kalinin. Of course they spoke English to Sullivan. They made him write the note we found in the glove compartment and then they joked around with him about committing suicide. No matter how brave he was, the poor guy must have been terrified. It sounded like he tried to get away once and they hit him a few times, just enough to hurt but not do any serious damage. But the whole time – it must have been while they were taking him over to that clearing – he was talking. Babbling almost, but when I listened to it carefully I think it was an act. I think he wanted them to believe he was really scared, but actually he was doing it for our benefit because he knew the recorder was turned on. He told them he wouldn't retire, he'd go back to the mine and smuggle the diamonds for them, anything, if they'd just let him go. That got *them* talking about the smuggling operation. It's all there. Unbelievable."

"Jesus," Foster said. "I'd like to have met this guy."

"Yeah. He even said a few things about his wife. I'll have to get copies of that part made and give them to her. I had the impression they weren't very fond of one another, but it doesn't sounds like that on the recording.

"Then when they got to the clearing one of them held him and the other one forced the gun into his mouth. I think it was Andropov who pulled the trigger, he's up close to the microphone and you can hear him breathing. He says a few things

368

to Sullivan in English, like it was an ordinary day, like nothing was happening, and then you hear the shot. After that it gets fainter, but I think they just stood around there talking for a few minutes after they killed him. Bastards. It sure as hell wasn't suicide."

As background for the investigation, Foster and Fournier had heard bits and pieces about Andropov, but they hadn't been prepared for what Zelensky told them was on the recording. Now, like their boss, they wanted the Russian badly. It was visceral. They knew their best chance was to take him at the airport when he was leaving to return to Moscow. Assuming he was traveling back with British Airways, the same way he had come, there was only one flight a day he could take. Calgary to Heathrow, leaving at eight in the evening.

Zelensky called Craig Hill and told him they were coming out to the airport to monitor passengers for the BA flight. "If he shows up," Zelensky said, "we'll arrest him at the gate. I don't think he'd risk carrying a gun through security, but you never know, so you should be prepared. We'll try to keep it low key."

Hill met them and told him he had the passenger list live on his computer. "I see every update," he said. "So far Magnusson's not on it. It's still early, though, and he's got an open ticket, so he can just show up and get his boarding pass at any time. There are still quite a few empty seats in business class."

They went to Hill's office and watched CCTV feed from the check-in area and the gates. The minutes ticked by and there was no sign of Andropov.

"When do they start boarding?" Zelensky asked.

Hill looked at his watch. "In about twenty minutes. Around seven-thirty."

"Let's go to the gate then. We don't want to miss him."

Hill led the three of them through security and they picked up coffee and stood across from the gate, talking among themselves, Foster leaning against the wall. They looked for all the world like a group of bored, middle-aged passengers waiting for their flight. But when the announcement came that boarding was about to begin there was a subtle change in their posture and they scrutinized every passenger that came forward. First class and business went first, but Andropov wasn't among them. Foster and Fournier moved closer to the gate and checked passengers boarding through the economy lane, just to be sure, while Zelensky and Hill monitored the few remaining passengers who came through the priority lane. But by twelve minutes to eight they hadn't seen Andropov and the gate area was almost empty. Zelensky went up to the desk and asked if they were expecting any more passengers. The gate agent looked at him and said she couldn't give out that information and Zelensky sighed and pulled out his badge.

"Oh sorry," she said, "I didn't realize ... yes, we're waiting for one more, he's a business class passenger. He's in security right now; he's only got carry-on so as soon as we get him seated they'll push back. There's a good tailwind," she said, "they're expecting an early arrival in London." She smiled.

Zelensky thanked her and nodded to the others. No way you're arriving early in London, Mr. Andropov, he said to himself. They spread out and moved closer to the gate, ready to stop Andropov when he arrived. But then the last passenger hurried down the hall pulling a small suitcase behind him. He was short, fat, and red-faced, and he was out of breath and panting. "Sorry," he said to the gate agent, "I got held up." She took his ticket and glanced up at Zelensky. He shook his head almost imperceptibly and turned away in disgust. Dammit, he thought, where the hell is he?

They waited until the cabin door was shut and the airplane pushed out from the gate, and then they watched it turn and roll slowly toward the runway, running lights flashing.

"Shit," Zelensky said. "I was sure he'd be on that flight. Let's go."

On the way back to the city they began to consider the possibilities. The obvious one was that Andropov would be on the BA flight tomorrow. Meaning they'd have another day of twiddling their thumbs. "Or", Foster said, "he could have decided not to use his return ticket just like he didn't use that hotel room. He's a cagey bastard. He might fly with a different airline, maybe even from a different airport. Using a different passport. Maybe he's already gone."

Zelensky realized he'd been too focused on the BA flight. He should have tried to put himself in Andropov's shoes, think like his adversary. "I hope you're wrong, Michael. I hope his imagination isn't as good as yours. It would be ironic if we were watching Calgary and he flew back from Vancouver."

They were pulling into the hotel parking garage when Zelensky's phone rang. It was Calgary police.

"Zelensky."

He was quiet for a long time and then he said, "Jesus Christ … okay, we'll head over there. There are three of us. Where are your men?" Again the car was quiet. Then Zelensky said, "Hold on for a second, I'll put this on speaker so one of my guys can take down the phone number." The voice on the phone read out a number, and Foster wrote it down. "Okay," Zelensky said, "we've got it. Tell them to sit tight and we'll be out there as soon as we can." He paused and then said, "Can you put your SWAT team on standby? We might need them."

"If it's to go into Kalinin's place the guys will be lining up," said the voice from the phone.

"Thank you," Zelensky said and hung up. He exhaled noisily. "That was Calgary police, as you probably guessed. I get the impression they really don't like Kalinin." He chuckled. "It's a good thing we asked for surveillance; Kalinin just arrived at home in his Mercedes, the same one he used to pick up Andropov at the airport the other day. He had a passenger with him and they drove straight into the garage so the watchers didn't see much before the door came down. But they're certain the driver was Kalinin. They don't know about the passenger, they didn't get a very good look at him but it wasn't anybody they recognized. All they could say was that he was a big guy – tall. There's a good chance it's Andropov. Let's get over there."

CHAPTER 36

The watchers from Calgary police were parked under the branches of a large pine tree, half a block from Kalinin's house. Dominic turned off his headlights and coasted in behind them. Zelensky noticed that curtains and blinds still covered the windows of the house, just as they had when he drove by earlier, but at night the place didn't look quite so deserted. Here and there light leaked around the edge of a curtain, and behind the hedge that ran along the front of the house a row of spotlights threw light and shadows up the stone wall. It actually looked quite beautiful.

Zelensky got out of the car and went up to the watchers' vehicle. When he tapped on the window they opened the door and he climbed into the back seat. He asked them what they'd seen.

"We've watched Kalinin before," one of the men said. "That was definitely him in the car. The Mercedes is his favorite; I don't think he lets anyone else drive it. I don't know about the big guy; it's not someone we recognized. But unless they're magicians, they're both still inside. They probably know we're here, though."

"You think so?"

"Yeah, for sure. We play cat and mouse with Kalinin all the time. Mostly we try not to be too obvious, but a strange car parked down the street? He keeps his eyes open, so he's gotta know. Once in a while we park right in front of his house, just to let him know we haven't forgotten about him, but they told us not to do that tonight. We've even had him down at the station a couple of times, but he's got money and a few friends in high places and he calls his slick lawyer and he's out of there in no time. We've never been able to catch him red handed." The cop sounded frustrated.

"This time," Zelensky said, "it's going to be different." He paused, then continued. "I talked to your colleagues downtown earlier and they put the SWAT team on standby. Can you call and tell them it's a go? I'll pull around the corner at the cross street so I won't be visible from the house. Tell them to meet me there."

Twenty minutes later a black SUV pulled up beside them and four men in bulky black clothing tumbled out. They could have been aliens from another planet, helmets pulled low on their foreheads, masks over their mouths and complex looking weapons in their hands. Zelensky knew they'd been told that he would be in charge but he also knew they wouldn't like taking orders from some Vancouver RCMP officer they didn't know. He kept his comments brief.

"We'll have to play this by ear. I'll go up to the door with my two partners, we're all armed. You guys stay out of sight but spread around, just make sure you can see us at the door. You know the drill. One of you should stay near the garage in case they try to get out that way; shoot the tires, not the people, because we need to interrogate them. Okay?"

Several heads nodded. "How many inside?" one of the men asked.

"Two men we know about; one's a tall guy, a Russian, and he's dangerous and probably armed. The other is Alex Kalinin. From what I hear most Calgary police know who he is."

"Oh, we know Kalinin," one of them said.

"There might be others but I just don't know. I also have no idea how they're going to react, so you should be ready for anything when I get to the door. If there's no trouble when we go in, move up as close as you can, but don't let them see you. Two of Calgary's finest are down the street – they've been watching the house all evening – and they'll come up closer too, although I'm hoping we won't need them. But they'll give you the signal to come into the house when I need you – I've already set it up with them. Anybody have questions?"

Silence.

"Okay, I'll wait here for ten minutes while you get in position." Within seconds the four men had disappeared into the dark, as quiet as ghosts.

Zelensky got back into the car with Michael and Dominic. "Crunch time," he said, and they checked their weapons and talked about how they would approach the house. Exactly ten minutes later he said "Okay, let's go," and Dominic pulled the car around the corner and stopped directly in front of Kalinin's house. Zelensky felt a familiar detached calm come over him.

It always happened in dangerous situations; maybe it was the adrenalin, but the fear suddenly fell away and he was left hyperalert and focused. He went up the walkway, Michael and Dominic on either side and slightly behind him. He couldn't see the SWAT team but he knew they were there. As they approached the door a bright motion-sensor light switched on. Zelensky rang the bell and Michael and Dominic, pistols drawn but down at their sides, stood pressed against the wall on either side of the door.

"Who is it?" A woman's voice, muffled, behind the thick door.

"Police. I need to speak to Mr. Kalinin."

Zelensky could hear scraping noises and then a low murmuring of voices. Then a man's voice, louder: "Hold up your badge so I can see it. Up, to the left." Zelensky glanced up and saw the camera. "And tell your men to put away their guns. This isn't a banana republic. Or the United States."

The man chuckled at his own attempt at humor. Either the guy is a very good actor or this is going to be a total anticlimax, Zelensky thought. He shook his head slightly to Foster and Fournier: keep your weapons ready. He held up his badge toward the camera and when he heard the door being unlocked he tensed, his hand sliding down to grip his own gun. This is it, he thought, not knowing which way it was going to go. But when the door opened it revealed a short, smiling man with a protruding belly, wearing jeans and a sweatshirt that had the outline of a bucking bronco on it with the words 'Calgary, Alberta' in large letters across the front. On his feet he wore scruffy brown leather slippers.

He didn't invite them in. "I have to be careful who I open the door to," he said. "It's not you guys I'm worried about. It's just that there are some people in this town I wouldn't let in at night. Or any other time, for that matter. I need to be careful. To what do I owe the pleasure, officer …"

"Zelensky." Surely it's not going to be this easy, he thought. "And are you Mr. Kalinin?" Zelensky had never seen the man, not even a picture, he realized.

"Yes, that's me."

"Mr. Kalinin, you're under arrest." Zelensky nodded and Foster and Fournier stepped forward, one grabbing each of Kalinin's arms and swinging him around. They cuffed his wrists behind him and they all moved into the house, Zelensky shutting the door behind them.

"There must be some mistake," Kalinin said, still relaxed and acting unconcerned. He'd been through it all before. "I need to call my lawyer. You're supposed to tell me I can do that."

Zelensky gritted his teeth. What he really wanted to do was wipe the smile off Kalinin's face with a punch to the mouth. But instead he said, "No mistake this time Kalinin. You can call your lawyer in a minute. First you need to tell me where Magnusson is. Eric Magnusson."

Kalinin looked genuinely perplexed. "I don't know anyone named Magnusson," he said.

"Okay then, how about Dimitri Andropov? When you picked him up at the airport Saturday night his passport said he was Eric Magnusson. It's illegal to enter the country on a false passport."

"You want to talk to Dimitri? Why didn't you say so? Just a minute." He raised his voice and called out rapidly in Russian: "Eva, go get Dimitri. Tell him it's okay. And call my lawyer." A woman's voice answered from the next room, "Da," and they heard footsteps going up the stairs. Foster and Fournier, still holding Kalinin's arms, looked at Zelensky but he just shrugged. He didn't want Kalinin to know he understood Russian.

Kalinin still looked completely unconcerned, and Zelensky thought, this guy just doesn't get it. He's so used to having his own way that he thinks money and his lawyer will get him out of this. Andropov too. He's got a surprise coming.

Just then Andropov came into the room and stopped, glancing from Kalinin to Zelensky and back again, a wary look on his face. Like a cornered animal, Zelensky thought, looking for a way out. He's still dangerous.

But then Kalinin spoke to him in Russian and the tension went down a notch: "Don't worry Dimitri, these clowns don't know who they're dealing with. I've got friends downtown and Eva's calling the lawyer. We'll have it sorted out before you know it."

Don't bet on it, Zelensky thought, and he tapped his phone. It was his prearranged signal to send in the SWAT team.

Andropov replied to Kalinin in Russian: "What's going on?" In spite of the tension Zelensky was enjoying himself. He knew exactly what was going on; neither Kalinin nor Andropov had any idea. Just as Kalinin started to reply Zelensky heard the door behind him crash open and he saw Andropov's eyes widen and his hands go up, slowly. He glanced behind him and saw two of the SWAT men with their guns at the ready, still looking like aliens.

Andropov, at least, knew what he was facing and he wasn't going to argue. And for the first time since they arrived he saw Kalinin's shoulders sag slightly. He nodded to Michael and Dominic and they let go of Kalinin and grabbed Andropov's arms. After they'd handcuffed him they patted him down and found a Beretta tucked into his belt. Dominic held it up, grinning.

"Dimitri Andropov, you're under arrest," Zelensky said in perfect Russian. "These men will take you downtown." Both Andropov and Kalinin looked at him in disbelief. He stared back at them for a moment without saying anything, then turned to the SWAT team. "Okay guys, they're all yours. We'll see you downtown."

The next twenty four hours were a whirlwind. Zelensky's meticulously choreographed operation – he'd called it 'Project Ice' – went off without a hitch. As soon as he confirmed Andropov's arrest, his Vancouver police colleague Helen Williams personally led a raid on the Kitsilano house where Viktor Churkin and Igor Petrov lived. She arrested the two men on suspicion of internet fraud and took away six computers for detailed analysis. Among other things they would be searched for information relating to the Diatek diamond smuggling scheme, and the mugging and attempted abduction of Rick Doucet.

At about the same time, the RCMP posted two officers at the Diatek offices. Another team would search the premises the next day, but Zelensky had insisted on the overnight guard. He didn't want anyone coming into the building in the dead of night and taking away sensitive data. And in Calgary, Kalinin's house was locked down, no one to come in or out without permission. Calgary police would go through it with a fine toothed comb. They could hardly wait; Zelensky knew they would miss nothing.

And why did Zelensky call his operation Project Ice? someone asked him. "Well," he told them, "I usually put a lot of thought into the names of my operations, but this one just came to me. It's the diamond connection. People use 'ice' as slang for diamonds. I'd heard it in movies or books or somewhere, and when I looked it up I found out that if you put a diamond to your lips it feels as though you're kissing a piece of ice. It's not that they're cold, it's just that they suck out the heat so quickly they *feel* cold. They're very efficient heat conductors, way better than metals like copper. Diamond dealers can tell a fake just by touching it to their lips."

At exactly nine-thirty the morning after Andropov and Kalinin were arrested, a squad of six RCMP officers arrived at Diatek headquarters with a search warrant and spread out over the two floors that the company leased. Their appearance caused total confusion. Rick Doucet, already at his desk, was less surprised than most of his colleagues; he had been expecting something like this. He hadn't heard anything from Zelensky for the past few days and he knew nothing about the events in Calgary. But he knew *something* was about to happen. Later, Doucet discovered that Sarah's document about Diatek's finances had been the basis for the search warrant.

And there was one additional component to Project Ice. Thompson had told Zelensky that the diamond shipments arrived at his Vancouver apartment in ordinary cardboard boxes. The return address on the FedEx form was always the same: a hobby and craft shop in Ottawa. Thompson had no idea why packages of diamonds should be coming from a hobby shop, but he knew the address off by heart. He had checked out the shop on the internet and it appeared to a small, family-owned business specializing in model railway trains. It all seemed very odd, he said to Zelensky.

So at the same time the RCMP team arrived at Diatek headquarters – nine-thirty in the morning in Vancouver, twelve-thirty in Ottawa – two RCMP officers entered Bob's Crafts and Hobbies and confronted the startled owner with a search warrant. He was an elderly man, alone in the store, sitting at a work table peering at a tiny model steam engine through a magnifying glass. Around him were scattered the tools of his trade – small screw drivers, jeweler's tweezers, and dental tools – and dozens of model trains, cars and trucks. He was bewildered when they asked him about a customer in Vancouver named William Thompson.

"Of course we ship things all over the country," he told the officers, "even to the U.S. But I never shipped anything to a William Thompson in Vancouver." He peered at them over the glasses that were propped on his nose. "I might be old, but I know my customers." He showed them his shipping records, a shelf full of black notebooks in which each order was neatly entered by hand, complete with its cost, the sales tax calculation, and the full address of the buyer. "You won't find anyone named William Thompson here," he said. "I guarantee."

The officers browsed through the lists of shipments that had been sent out over the past few years and found no entry for a William Thompson. There were not even many shipments to Vancouver. It was possible the old man was hiding something, but they had a gut feeling he was telling the truth. However, they told him they were going to take away his notebooks and make copies. They'd bring them back the next day, they said. And if he had any thoughts about why someone named William Thompson should be receiving packages with his return address on them, he should let them know.

If the visit to Bob's Crafts and Hobbies was a fishing expedition, the RCMP team at Diatek headquarters knew exactly what they were looking for. The first thing they did was secure every computer in the CEO and CFO offices and disconnect them from the internet. The CEO was on an airplane on his way back from a meeting in Toronto and blissfully unaware of the events taking place in his office, but Jim Mulroney, the CFO, was at work when the RCMP arrived. He was a slightly pudgy man, medium height, and he grew red in the face and fairly shook with indignation when they came into his office. He protested loudly at the intrusion. "Stop," he said, "you can't do this. The information on these computers is proprietary. I'm going to call our legal people."

"Be my guest," one of the officers said as she turned off his computer and started pulling out connecting wires. "You can call anyone you like, but it won't do you much good. We have a search warrant."

Mulroney spluttered and swore under his breath but a flicker of fear swept across his face. He couldn't let them take his computers away. He had to find a way to stop the search. He went out into the hall and called the lawyers.

But the Diatek lawyers had no more luck stopping the raid than Kalinin's lawyer in Calgary had in freeing his client from police custody. The search warrant was watertight, and in Calgary the voice recording on the pen Sullivan had been carrying was all the evidence needed to charge Andropov and Kalinin with murder, with no possibility of bail.

With the two Russians safely in jail Zelensky's work in Calgary was finished, and he and his two partners headed back to Vancouver. They arrived just after eleven in the morning, and because none of them had had much sleep over the past several days, Zelensky told Foster and Fournier they should take the rest of the day off. He didn't follow his own advice, however. He went home from the airport, took a quick shower, changed clothes and had a cup of coffee with Heather, and then went to his office. He still had work to do.

CHAPTER 37

Zelensky's colleagues filled him in on the morning's raid at Diatek headquarters. Several of the computers were already at the lab being examined, they said, and three officers were still on site, sifting through files and questioning people. A couple of lawyers from a prominent local firm had shown up part way through the morning and slowed things down for a while, but there was nothing they could do and eventually they left.

Zelensky asked them what had happened in Ottawa.

That, they told him, was a dead end. Some old guy in his shop, no way he could be involved in diamond smuggling. They had taken his customer records, though, and would make copies and send them out.

"Good," Zelensky said, "I want to see them as soon as we get them." It was still a loose end. Why was the hobby shop the return address on all those packages?

When they were through he called Rick Doucet on his cell phone. "Are you at work? Can you talk?"

"Um, I'm at a coffee shop actually. A bunch of us from work are here. There's some problem at the office." Doucet tried to sound as normal as possible. Just talking to a friend.

"Got it. Can you meet me here at my office, as soon as possible? I'm going over to talk to Thompson and I'd like you to be there."

"Yes, sure, I think I could do that. I doubt I'll be able to go back to the office this afternoon anyway." Doucet sat with his colleagues for a few more minutes, finishing his coffee. As far as he could tell none of them had any idea what was going on.

"Well guys," he said eventually, "I have to run an errand. Then I think I'll go home. Maybe things will be back to normal tomorrow." But he knew they wouldn't be. Nothing would be the same at Diatek again.

At the safe house that afternoon there were just the three of them. Zelensky said he wanted to bring them up to date.

"And also," he said, "I know we've been through everything many times already, but there are probably things I've missed. You two are on the inside, you know Diatek a hell of a lot better than I do. So interrupt if anything occurs to you."

He told them how he had confronted Sullivan about his bank statements. "I was bluffing, of course, but I told him we knew the cash deposits were payments for smuggling diamonds into the mine. He denied it at first, but when I told him he had a choice of cooperating with our investigation and getting immunity or being arrested, he came around pretty quickly. He told me everything.

"I already had the outlines of a plan, but when Sullivan told me he was getting ready to retire and that the money from smuggling the diamonds was going to be his retirement nest egg, everything fell into place. I needed some way to draw out whoever was really behind this – I think we all suspected it was Andropov, but we didn't know for sure. So Sullivan didn't go back to the mine as he was supposed to; he emailed his boss and told him he just couldn't do it anymore, and said he was retiring immediately. Just like that. And he sent a text message saying the same thing to the contact number he had for the people who sent him the diamonds. Then all I could do was sit back and wait. That's why nothing much happened for a couple of weeks."

"You're not kidding nothing happened," Thompson said. "I was climbing the walls. Still am."

"Yeah, but now it's all coming together. As Rick knows."

"My office is in chaos," Doucet said. "A squad of RCMP officers came in this morning and started turning off our computers and opening up filing cabinets and asking questions. After a while they said we were free to go and most of us left. No way we could work." He glanced over at Zelensky. "Your colleagues are pretty thorough. They wouldn't let us take anything out of the building, not one scrap of paper."

"Glad to hear it," Zelensky said, and grinned. "To make a long story short, the plan worked. So far, anyway. The messages that Sullivan sent got someone's attention, fast. Dimitri Andropov arrived in Calgary on Saturday evening using a false passport." Zelensky looked over at Thompson, who had a stunned look on his face.

"I sure as hell hope you arrested him," he said.

"Yes, we did. But not right away. I really didn't think Andropov would show, I thought they'd have local people deal with Sullivan. But then I got information that Andropov was on a British Airways flight to Calgary and I went out there with two of my people and tracked him for a couple of days – I'm leaving out a lot of details here – and he's now in jail. Along with another guy, a Calgary-based Russian who was working hand-in-hand with Andropov. As soon as we arrested those two we set a bunch of other things in motion, including the raid on Diatek headquarters. So we can all breathe a little easier. Thanks in large part to the two of you."

"What happens now?" Doucet asked.

"Well, for starters you can go back to your apartment in a day or two and you won't need a bodyguard trailing you around. We arrested two people here in Vancouver this morning who are prime suspects for the break-in and everything else that happened to you. I don't think you need to worry anymore." Zelensky paused. "And we're hoping to fast track the trials for Andropov and Kalinin. Bill, you'll definitely be called to testify. Still under witness protection, so you won't be identified except to those who need to know. I don't think you or your friend Sarah need to be involved, Rick, at least I hope not. We have the Diatek computers so all the evidence we need should be there. It's better – safer – if no one knows you or she had anything to do with it."

"What about Sullivan?" Thompson asked. "Will he testify too?"

Zelensky shifted in his chair. "I'm not proud of this. It wasn't supposed to happen this way, but Andropov got away from us for a while in Calgary, and he and Kalinin got to Sullivan before we could stop them. They tried to make it look like suicide, but they killed him. They've both been charged with murder."

"Shit," Thompson said. "I didn't particularly like Sullivan, but nobody deserves that." The room was quiet for several minutes, Thompson thinking about how close he had come to Sullivan's fate, Doucet trying to digest the brutality of people like Andropov. Why do they do it? Is it all about money?

Zelensky turned to Thompson. "Now that we've got Andropov, you need to start thinking about the future. He's going to be in prison for a very long time, but his boss won't be happy that his protégé has been locked up. From everything we know about Vasily Gagarin he has a long memory and a long reach. It's up to you, of course, but we can keep you in witness protection after the trial is over, with a new identity and a new life. Preferably far away from here. It means you would never be Bill Thompson again and I'm not saying it would be easy. But we could set you up somewhere abroad, like Australia for instance. We've got good relations with the Australians. And they have a very large mining industry; with your experience and possibly a little help from us I'm sure you could find a good job. It's unlikely even Gagarin could trace you there. We can't force you into it, but if I were you I'd do it."

Thompson put his hands on the table in front of him, palms down. It was as though he was going to make a speech. "It's something I've already thought about," he said "Actually, I've thought about little else for the past few weeks. I really don't think I could do it. Even after six months in Mexico I'd reached the end of my rope; I couldn't have taken much more of being someone else.

Besides, there's my daughter and my wife in Ontario. Sharon never remarried; what I really want to do is go back to Sudbury and start over, or at least give it a try. I'll testify for you, that's not a problem, and I appreciate the offer of protection. But when it's over I want to go back to being me. I know it's a risk, but hey, I could get hit with a cement truck crossing the street too."

Zelensky frowned. He hadn't thought the engineer would be so stubborn. "Not a good idea, Bill. Don't rush into this decision. If you go back to Sudbury as Bill Thompson it wouldn't be hard for Gagarin to find you."

"Okay, if it makes you feel any better I'll think about it some more. But I don't think I'll change my mind." Thompson glanced over at Doucet. "While we're talking about the future though, I have a confession to make. Rick already knows about this, but I wasn't sure I should tell you. It's another thing I've been wrestling with for the past few weeks. But I think the right thing to do is to come clean." He told Zelensky about the diamonds he had siphoned off and put in his safe deposit box. "It's strange, but I don't even feel bad about it. If I'm honest with myself I guess I stole them, but if it's Andropov or some Russian billionaire that I was ripping off I don't really care. But equally I don't want them to come back to haunt me. If I walk free after this, in witness protection or not, I don't want the fact that I took those diamonds to complicate things."

Zelensky coughed and looked around. "You're not going to get any grief from me. If you turn them in they'll probably end up being sold in an auction. The police will get a little money from it, but usually the big profits on things like that go to the buyer. They just turn around and resell the goods at retail prices – or higher. That doesn't seem fair to me. Why don't we just agree we didn't talk about it, okay? Nobody's taking notes today. I don't know anything about diamonds in a safe deposit box."

Thompson looked relieved. "Thanks," he said, quietly.

Zelensky said they should call it a day and they went downstairs for coffee and the fresh donuts that one of the minders had just brought in. With all the fast food they ate, Doucet wondered how these people stayed fit. It was okay for Thompson, who had lost a lot of weight in Mexico, but the rest of them … He shook his head, and helped himself to another donut. As his mother always said, he was a growing boy.

Two days later the shit started to hit the fan. Zelensky had expected some blowback, but the scale of it took him by surprise. The first indication that it was going to be a difficult day came at eight-thirty in the morning, when he took a call from his commanding officer.

"Ed, I got woken up this morning by a call from Ottawa. It was a conference call, the two Members of Parliament from the Arctic, they were calling about Diatek. One's Conservative and the other is NDP, but they sure as hell didn't have any difference of opinion this morning. I don't know where they got their information, but they seemed to know quite a bit about what we've been doing. They chewed my ear off for half an hour and acted indignant and said Diatek is a fine company and we're damaging the reputation of Canadian diamond mining. They said it's going to hurt the Northwest Territories and Nunavut and unravel a lot of the hard work they've done to attract investment to the north. Basically they called me an ass-hole, although not in so many words, and the implication was we should back off. I was furious and ready to hang up, but they are MPs after all, so I listened until they were finished and thanked them politely for their opinions. But we have to go on the offensive about this."

"Shit," Zelensky said. "They have no idea what they're talk-ing about. They should be passing out medals to the RCMP for shutting this thing down."

"Yeah, well, they're politicians. I know you wanted to keep this under wraps until all the loose ends are tied up, but they are going to blow it sky high anyway, so we should get our version out first. You need to organize a press conference. Today, early afternoon so it's on the evening news. I'll be there to back you up. It needs to be simple and very clear; just the basic facts but emphasize that we've closed down a major international smug-gling operation."

Zelensky sighed. "There will be a ton of questions," he said.

"No kidding. We need to keep the answers as vague as pos-sible. No names yet, and nothing about the money laundering through the Caymans ... Ed, you've done a fantastic job on this, and I'm not just saying that. It's probably the biggest and most audacious scam I've ever come across, and thanks to you we have the key players in custody."

It got worse. By the end of the morning Zelensky had had sev-eral more phone calls, two of them from National RCMP head-quarters in Ottawa and one from the mayor's office in Calgary. The Russian ambassador to Canada, it seems, had learned of Dimitri Andropov's arrest and had protested to the Canadian government, and his protest was referred to the RCMP. Someone must have made a mistake, he said. Mr. Andropov was a respected Russian businessman and he should be released immediately and allowed to return to his own country. The ambassador had great respect for the Canadian justice system and he was sure that Mr. Andropov would be exonerated. In the meantime he was prepared to quickly arrange for any reasonable amount of bail …

The call from Calgary was in the same vein except that it concerned Alex Kalinin. The caller – it was an aide, not the mayor himself – also said that the whole thing must be a mistake. Mr. Kalinin was a well-known figure in Calgary, an immigrant success story. He was exactly the kind of person Canada needed, a good example of the positive impact immigrants have on the country.

Bullshit, Zelensky thought. He couldn't believe what he was hearing. The mayor's office certainly had a different perspective than the Calgary police.

"Mr. Kalinin is a generous supporter of local charities, you know," the aide said.

Zelensky wondered if the mayor and his cronies were among them.

When he put down the phone he shook his head in disgust and looked at his watch – if the phone kept ringing like this he wouldn't be ready for the press conference. He gathered up his Project Ice files and went down the hall to a small conference room, put the 'do not disturb' sign up, and closed the door.

Somehow, word had spread quickly and there was a packed audience for the press conference. Zelensky was a veteran of these events but he had rarely seen so many reporters in one place. Several TV crews stood near the back of the room adjusting tripods and cameras. "Good afternoon," he said into the microphone. The din of voices quieted immediately. "This investigation is in its early stages so I can't give you many details. But I'll read a short statement and I'll take a few questions afterwards." He took a piece of paper from his pocket and unfolded it, then began reading. He'd worked hard on his statement, discarding several drafts; he wanted to make sure he got it right. When he finished, there was a short silence while reporters finished making their notes, then hands shot up around the room.

"Do you have suspects in custody?"

"Do you know where the diamonds come from?"

"What will happen to Diatek? Should shareholders be worried?"

"Mr. Zelensky, if I remember correctly you are in the organized crime unit. Is this the work of a criminal gang?"

The questions kept coming and after about ten minutes Zelensky caught the eye of his chief, who was standing beside him. He nodded and Zelensky, with a sigh of relief, brought the press conference to a close. He thought it had gone well, but it all depended on what the reporters wrote. He had only really ducked one question, from a reporter he didn't know, who asked whether the recent arrest of a Russian national in Calgary was connected to the investigation. That was a loaded question, Zelensky thought. Someone must have briefed him.

After the press conference he went back to his office and put his feet up on the desk. He moved his phone over so it was within easy reach and closed his eyes, trying to relax. Over the years he had cultivated relationships with two Vancouver journalists, both of whom he trusted with off-the-record comments. It was always delicate and he knew that many of his colleagues wouldn't touch a journalist with a ten foot pole. But he knew that when it worked it was a win-win situation; the journalists got their stories, he got the RCMP version of events into the media anonymously. He'd spotted the two journalists at the press conference but neither had asked questions. He was sure they would call, soon.

He didn't have long to wait long. He had barely settled back in his chair when the phone rang. He set up meetings with both of them for later in the afternoon, separately, at two different coffee shops. He would have to decide how much to reveal; that was something he needed to discuss with the chief.

That night he got a phone call from his son, who lived in Toronto. He had recently graduated from university and was starting a career as an investment adviser, something Zelensky couldn't see the point of – how could that possibly be interesting work? But he was happy that his son seemed to be thriving in the business world.

"Dad, I just saw you on TV. I had the ten o'clock news on but I wasn't really paying attention and then I heard a familiar voice and turned around and there you were. You were great with the questions."

Zelensky was surprised. Yes there had been a lot of interest at the press conference, but he had thought that was mainly because Diatek was a Vancouver company. He hadn't anticipated it would be a national news story, not yet anyway. In the late 1990s and early 2000s Canada's diamond mining boom had caught the public imagination and had been big news. Journalists and TV crews had invaded Yellowknife, the jumping off point for the mining operations, and the lucky ones got invited to the mine sites and filed their stories. But interest had waned when the prices of rough diamonds declined during the Great Recession, and even though prices had now recovered the industry seemed to have dropped out of view. Zelensky had the feeling that was about to change when the full details of the Diatek story became widely known.

CHAPTER 38

To some extent, Zelensky was right. As the Diatek investigation unfolded it grabbed headlines across the country and internationally, not so much as a story about the diamond industry as one about greed, corruption and the malign influence of organized crime. Within days of Zelensky's first press conference, Diatek's CFO, Jim Mulroney, had been arrested and the company's CEO had been questioned. Diatek headquarters became a crime scene, and when employees turned up for work they were sent home. Buyers abruptly refused to purchase diamonds from the company's stockpiles and the mine temporarily ceased operations. Creditors circled, and rumors circulated about a buyout by DeBeers or another unnamed mining company. Soon virtually all activities at the company ground to a halt.

Like almost everyone else at Diatek, Rick Doucet suddenly found himself unemployed. Not formally – no one had received termination notices – but practically. He doubted that Diatek would survive in its present form, and even if it rose again under new owners he wasn't sure he would want to work there. He had been more prepared than others, but still it was a shock. He hadn't realized the extent to which he lived for his work. He was restless; a few days of forced vacation was okay but he didn't want to spend day after day twiddling his thumbs, waiting for something to happen. He began to look around for new job opportunities.

His confidence was boosted when he started to get feelers from other mining companies. The first came from his old employers, DeBeers, a week and a half after the Diatek story broke. No pressure, they said, but they were open to negotiations if he didn't see a future with Diatek. He had to stifle a laugh. A future with Diatek? Who were they kidding? Call any time, they told him. If he was serious, they'd fly him out to South Africa. He was flattered – *South Africa*, they'd said, not the headquarters of DeBeers Canada in Toronto. But he tried not to let it sway him. He still wanted an academic position if he could find one, or perhaps a job with an NGO. He wasn't sure he saw a future for himself at another mining company, even a high profile one like DeBeers.

One evening he called Sarah and told her about the offer from DeBeers. "Don't rush into anything," she said. "You're not broke, you can survive for a few months. Give yourself some time to think. Actually I wish I hadn't been quite so quick to take this position in Seattle." It was the first time he'd heard her say anything negative about her job. "It's not that I dislike it, the people are nice and the organization is great, but at the moment I feel like I'm treading water. Not learning anything new, just doing what I'm told and not having much of a say in strategy or even day to day operations." She laughed. "I actually had a lot more fun working through all the Diatek financial stuff. I guess if I'd taken a little more time to think things through, working out where I'd like to be in four or five years, I might not have taken this job. The moral is, take your time."

Unlike Doucet, Zelensky was up to his eyeballs in work. The Diatek investigation kept him busy from the moment he woke up in the morning until he went to bed at night. And even then it sometimes kept him awake because there was a piece of the puzzle missing, a big one. It had bothered him from beginning. How did they get the diamonds into Canada? Sure diamonds were small and easy to transport, but this involved large quantities brought in regularly, not some one-off operation. The only clue he had was the return address on the packages Thompson had received, the Ottawa hobby shop.

But the Ottawa team had questioned the owner again, and they were convinced he had nothing to do with the smuggling scheme. Nevertheless, when copies of the account notebooks from Bob's Crafts and Hobbies arrived in his office Zelensky set aside time to read through them carefully. He started with the shipping records; many of Bob's customers were collectors who didn't live locally. Zelensky had already been told there were no shipments to Bill Thompson listed in the account books, but he checked every entry for the past few years just to be sure, and he made a note of all customers with Vancouver addresses. There weren't many and the probability that any of them were connected with the scheme he was investigating was small, but he decided he would check them out anyway. Then he turned to the lists of in-store customers, the locals who had walked in and made purchases in the shop. No addresses here, just names and a description of the items they purchased, along with the prices. In a few cases, for more expensive items, the customers had used credit cards; for those he'd be able to get addresses if he needed them. He didn't think this section would be very useful, but here too he scanned through every entry. You never know, he told himself, if I don't check I might miss something.

There were a few Russian-sounding names among the Ottawa customers, but that wasn't unusual; there was no shortage of Russian surnames in Canada. But one of the Russian names kept recurring. A regular customer, who spent a lot of money at the shop. I wonder, Zelensky thought. Surely someone wouldn't be that stupid. But if he doesn't want to use his own address, and he knows this place well … he looked at his watch then reached for his phone. The hobby shop should still be open.

The owner answered and Zelensky identified himself and said he had a few questions about one of his customers. A man named Boris Pugin.

"Boris? Sure, he comes in a lot. I always tease him because his name sounds like Putin." He laughed. "He's got a pretty strong accent. Sometimes I can hardly understand what he's saying. He's a good customer, though."

"What kinds of things does he buy?" Zelensky asked.

Bob – Zelensky had determined that the owner's name really was Bob – didn't hesitate. "Trains. Model steam trains. He loves them. He's an older guy, not quite my age yet but he's close. He talks a lot when he comes in; he's told me stories about taking the Trans-Siberian when it still ran on steam. He's bought several old steam models from me, real antiques. I keep my eye out for them and whenever I find one I let him know."

"Any idea what he does in Ottawa?"

"Yes, he told me once that he works at the embassy. The Russian embassy. We've got people from all over the world at the embassies here. A few of them are customers, like Boris."

Of course, Zelensky thought. It's obvious. I should have known.

"Thank you, Bob. This has been very helpful." Zelensky paused. "If I ever take up model trains I'll be sure to give you a call." He hung up and sat at his desk, a smile on his face.

The revelations kept coming. Mulroney, on the advice of his lawyers, had declined to answer questions, and admitted nothing. The RCMP brought in outside financial experts to review the files from his computer, and they discovered that Mulroney had been presiding over large scale money laundering and misrepresentation of Diatek finances from the beginning, even before Thompson started taking diamonds to the mine. It was enough to charge him, but he raised the necessary cash for bail and until he was tried and sentenced he was more-or-less a free man. More-or-less because he was considered a flight risk; his passport was confiscated and he had to report regularly to the police. Zelensky was convinced that the CFO was complicit in the smuggling operation but that was one thing for which he had no hard evidence. He was also sure the CEO must have known about the money laundering, but the evidence was circumstantial. He decided to confront him directly.

He met the CEO at his home, and he found a pale, drawn man with large dark circles under his eyes, sipping peppermint tea at his kitchen table. He offered to make some for Zelensky, but the policeman declined. Zelensky sat down and looked across the table; with large ears and sagging cheeks and chin the CEO looked like a caricature of a very sad bulldog. Considering what Diatek was going through, Zelensky wasn't surprised that he looked so haggard.

In contrast to Mulroney, who had been aggressive and vocal during initial questioning and then fiercely silent once the lawyers showed up, the CEO seemed to shudder and withdraw further into himself with each question Zelensky asked. Most he refused to answer, saying simply that he had no comment. He denied any knowledge of wrongdoing at Diatek, by Mulroney or anyone else, including himself. Zelensky didn't believe him.

That evening, as he and Heather were finishing a very late dinner, Zelensky's cell phone rang. He picked it up and listened for what seemed a long time, then said thanks and hung up. He turned to Heather – from whom he had no secrets, work or otherwise – and said, "I'll be damned. I questioned the Diatek CEO this morning, and tonight he tried to kill himself by swallowing half a bottle of his wife's sleeping pills. There has to be a connection, don't you think? He feels the net closing in around him, maybe? His wife came home early from some function and found him slumped on the sofa with the pill bottle beside him. They got him to the hospital in time and pumped him out and it looks like he'll be okay. He'll be groggy for a day or two but they think he'll make it. When I talked to him this morning he denied everything, but as soon as he has a clear head I'm going to pay him another visit."

Two days later Zelensky was at the CEO's hospital bedside. They had been pumping him full of liquids to flush out his system, but he still looked slightly confused. Zelensky wondered if it was an act. He told the CEO their conversation would be recorded, and he set the recorder on the bedside table and started asking questions, most of them variations on the questions he'd asked two days earlier. At first the man didn't say anything; his eyes darted around the room, looking anywhere but at Zelensky. Then he held up a very shaky hand. "Stop," he said, and swung his head around so that he was facing the policeman. "The other day, after you came to see me at home, I sort of decided that life wasn't worth living anymore. But when I woke up in here" – he waved his hand feebly at his surroundings – "I realized how precious life is. And so, Mr. Zelensky, this time I'm going to answer your questions. I don't need our lawyers. In fact I don't *want* our lawyers, they would just complicate things."

For the next hour – until the nurses came and told him it was enough, their patient had to rest – Zelensky mostly listened. At first the CEO spoke hesitantly, as though he wasn't really sure he should be doing this, but gradually he gained confidence and his tale came pouring out. Zelensky had seen it before in people who, in spite of misdeeds, still had a conscience. Once they'd made a decision to talk they were hard to stop. It had been the same with Sullivan. He couldn't imagine

Mulroney confessing like this, though; he was a much tougher nut to crack. But it wouldn't matter. He was getting everything he needed from the CEO.

Most of what the man said corroborated information from the Diatek computers, but some went far beyond what they already knew. The CEO had been briefed by Andropov about the plan to launder the illicit diamonds, and some of the skimmed-off profits had gone directly into his Swiss bank account. He had also played an active role with Mulroney in falsifying the company's finances. Zelensky shook his head slowly as the CEOs story unfolded. There was no question the man would be going to jail; he might get some leniency for cooperating, but he had committed crimes and admitted his guilt. Zelensky had it all, right there on the recording, in the CEO's own voice. He almost felt sorry for him. How do intelligent people let themselves get caught up in these situations? he wondered.

The CEO's confession broke the log jam; the company lawyers couldn't defend their client against himself. The combined evidence was so overwhelming that in the trials that followed Zelensky didn't need to mention the data collected by Sarah Patterson. He was pleased. It had been crucial for identifying the fraud in the first place, but it was better that her role not be known.

On the strength of the evidence both Jim Mulroney and the Diatek CEO were convicted and sent to jail. The CEO was given a reduced sentence because of his cooperation and his obvious remorse. Mulroney refused to admit any guilt.

And in Ottawa a low level clerk at the Russian embassy named Boris Pugin was brought in for questioning. To the surprise of his interrogators, he confessed everything before they asked him a single question – and then he asked for political asylum. He loved Canada, he said, he had been forced into it by the mafia. If he went back to Russia he'd be killed. If he went back to the embassy he'd be killed. The packages had arrived in diplomatic pouches, he said, and they'd made him box them up and take them to FedEx to send out west. He had no idea what was in them. He'd used Bob's Crafts and Hobbies because the people at FedEx said he had to have a return address, and he couldn't use his own or the embassy's. He knew the owner at Bob's well, he was a nice man. The police were still scratching their heads, trying to figure out what to do with him. But they sent all the information he provided to Zelensky.

On the afternoon Mulroney and the Diatek CEO were sentenced, Rick Doucet got a call from Zelensky. He had not spoken to the policeman for several months. "Meet me for a beer," Zelensky said. He named a place and time. To Rick it sounded like an order.

Zelensky got two beers and sat down across from Doucet at a corner table. "Cheers," he said, and they clinked glasses. It was still early and the pub was quiet.

"I know I'm not always great about complimenting people, Rick, but I wanted to say a big thanks to you – and your friend Sarah," Zelensky said. "By the way, I haven't met her yet. I'm waiting."

"Yeah, yeah, I know, it's just that … I promise, if she comes up here for a visit … *when* she comes up, I'll call you."

"Anyway, I don't think a lot of this would have happened without you two. I'm serious."

Doucet was a little embarrassed by this tribute from the policeman. "Well, I'm glad it worked out the way it did. Although it has cost me my job, I guess."

"I wouldn't be so sure," Zelensky said. "Apparently there are a couple of mining companies interested in buying Diatek at a discount – from what I hear the mine is pretty valuable – and they would probably want to keep the best Diatek employees, which I imagine includes you. Although I don't know whether anyone will be able to sort through the finances. One of the analysts we brought in told me that the holding company with the Caymans registration has suddenly disappeared. I don't quite understand it, but he said it happens all the time. Suddenly WWME or whatever it was called disappears, and another company with a similar name and the same directors shows up, same address. He said it's like whack a mole, you get one and another one pops up. There's no legal way they can get to the old company, because it doesn't exist anymore."

Doucet laughed at this. "I like that, the image I mean. Whack a mole. But you know, I don't think I would go back to Diatek now, even under different ownership. Too much bad karma after what's happened. I've had plenty of time to reflect since the company closed down, and I've done a lot of reading. I've come to the conclusion that there are better uses for my talents than finding diamonds, or other minerals for that matter. Funny thing is, it was Sarah who got me thinking about this. I know it's a cliché but she's really changed my life. I thought I was set, I thought I knew what I wanted to do, but actually it was mainly because I was in a bubble at Diatek. I mean I liked it, there were lots of challenges, but when you're in the midst of it, working all the time, you forget that there are other things out there. Now I think differently."

Doucet shook his head and grinned and then he told Zelensky how climate change was altering the water cycle on the earth, and how water was going to be one of the crucial resources in the future, especially in Africa and India but even in places like California and Australia. He told him how disappearing glaciers in the Andes and the Himalayas were affecting the water supplies of millions of people and how disputes over water could lead to wars. It's becoming a national security issue, he said. And then he told Zelensky he'd been looking at academic jobs, and also at international agencies and non-profits that were focusing on these kinds of problems. They all need geological expertise, he said.

"Wow. You sound like you've got religion, Rick. But good for you. I'm starting to feel left out here; first Bill Thompson tells me he's going to change his life and go back to Ontario when this is all over – I'll come back to that in a minute – and now you're telling me you're going to reinvent yourself too. Even your Diatek CEO seems to have had an epiphany in the hospital; he says he's going to start over in jail and devote himself to teaching other prisoners about business so they can have a real life when they get out. Good luck to him. Me, I'm still doing the same thing I started right out of university." He shook his head ruefully. "But to come back to Bill Thompson – are you two in touch?"

"We email once in a while, but I haven't spoken to him for a while."

"Can you do me a favor? Could you see if you can talk him into staying in witness protection? It doesn't have to be forever, but at least until the furor over Diatek dies down. It's for his own good; if Gagarin and his crew go after anyone, it will be Thompson. I don't know for sure if they already know he didn't die in that attack in Mexico, but Andropov will figure it out from everything that's coming out in the trial. And if Bill goes back to Ontario like he says he wants to do, he'll be a sitting duck. We won't be able to protect him."

A few months later both Andropov and Kalinin were convicted on multiple counts of smuggling, coercion, fraud, and murder in one of the fastest trials in Alberta history. Both men were sentenced to a minimum of twenty-five years without the possibility of parole and sent to a maximum security prison in Edmonton. There was persistent political pressure to have Andropov returned to Russia to serve his sentence, and there was also pressure to strike some kind of deal for Kalinin, but fortunately the justice system prevailed.

Zelensky had been commuting between Vancouver and Calgary during the trials to help the prosecution and to serve as a witness; when news of the sentencing finally came it brought him tremendous relief. A few days later, at home, late at night, he did something he had done several times over the past half year: he composed a hand-written letter. It was addressed to Sergey Melikov in Moscow, Russia. A decade earlier, in 2003, Sergey had been sent to Canada as part of an exchange program involving police in the two countries. The idea was that they could learn about each other's procedures and foster collaboration, but the RCMP had been reluctant partners; they had been concerned about the high levels of corruption in Russian police forces. However, they had little choice – the idea for the exchange had come from politicians, not from within the RCMP.

Sergey was one of the Russian participants, and because of his fluency in Russian Zelensky had been assigned to accompany him as he traveled around the country. They became close friends, and Zelensky learned that far from being corrupt, Sergey was a straight arrow who had more than once been roughed up and publically humiliated in Moscow for relentlessly tracking down and revealing government officials involved in high level corruption. Each time he had returned to his investigations more determined than ever.

Zelensky had not seen his friend for several years, but they corresponded periodically, usually by email. However, on very sensitive matters they communicated the old fashioned way: they sent letters in the regular mail. It was slow, but surprisingly secure. The spooks had amazing technology; they could intercept email and phone messages, but who bothered with ordinary letters anymore?

In his letters Melikov had been scathing about Andropov and Gagarin. He had also provided vital information that helped Zelensky during the investigation of Diatek. Now Zelensky wanted to tell his friend that Andropov would be spending a substantial part of the rest of his life behind bars. He knew Melikov would be pleased.

CHAPTER 39

Seattle, early autumn 2013. Rick Doucet couldn't remember a time when he had been happier. He had sold his apartment in Vancouver, put his furniture in storage, loaded everything else into his car, and driven to Seattle. Now he was living with Sarah Patterson, teaching a class in mineralogy at the University of Washington as a part-time lecturer and working as a volunteer with two different research groups, one focusing on climate science, the other on hydrology. His entry into the world of water was how he thought of it; he wasn't making much money but it was fun and he was learning every day. And he had time – more time than he had had in years to go for long runs, to sit and read for half a day, to go on hikes with Sarah on the weekends.

Once in a while he heard from Bill Thompson, who had moved back to Ontario despite Zelensky's advice and Rick's entreaties. He was doing well, he said; he saw his daughter regularly and was slowly reestablishing a relationship with his ex-wife. He didn't have a job yet, but he was in no hurry – I have my insurance policy, remember? he said. You don't always get a second chance, so I'm embracing it.

But then, one hazy morning in early October, Doucet got a call from Ed Zelensky. He had not been in touch with the policeman since leaving Vancouver.

"Rick, hi, I'm afraid I have bad news." That was Zelensky, no preliminaries. "Bill Thompson is dead."

There is never an easy way to tell someone a friend has died, or to hear the news. Doucet was stunned. Finally he managed to reply. "How? What happened? I can't believe it, I heard from him about a week ago and he sounded very happy."

"Mm. You're right, I think he was really savoring his new life. I've been communicating with him regularly, just to check in and see how he's doing, and it was certainly my impression that he was happy. I don't have many details because I just heard the news, but apparently they're treating it as an accident. Hit and run; he was out walking on a quiet road. His wife said he went out every day about the same time unless the weather was really bad. I wish I'd known; I would have told him to be more careful, to mix it up, just to be safe. There weren't any witnesses. I can't say for sure, but between you and me I think there's a good chance it's payback, not an accident. So keep your head down, Rick. Or rather, keep your eyes open. You and Sarah both. Only a very few people know about your involvement in the Diatek investigation, so I doubt there's any problem. But we don't want any more unexplained accidents."

That night Doucet couldn't sleep. He told Sarah the news when she got home from work and they sat for a long time talking about Thompson and Diatek. Finally he told her she should go to bed; she needed to be fresh in the morning and he wanted to sit and do some thinking. He allowed himself a large shot of whisky, but he stopped at one. Getting drunk wouldn't solve anything. Mostly he thought about Thompson, replaying in his head the time he'd spent with him.

Early in the morning, as the eastern sky was beginning to lighten, he fell asleep on the living room sofa. At some point he was aware of Sarah moving around the kitchen, and then she was kissing him on the cheek and saying goodbye, she'd see him tonight. He mumbled something in return and she laughed and the next thing he knew he opened his eyes to full daylight. It was almost noon.

The first thing Doucet did when he was fully awake was call Thompson's lawyer in Vancouver. He'd thought about this last night. As far as he knew, he, Rick Doucet, was still executor for Thompson's will. Changing that was probably one of the last things on Thompson's mind as he started to rebuild his life in Ontario, but Doucet didn't think it was right. Thompson had said he was reconnecting with his ex-wife. If anyone should be executor, it was her.

The lawyer did not know about Thompson's death. He had only learned that Thompson was still alive after the engineer left the witness protection program a few months earlier.

"I've never been involved in anything like this before," he said. "First he's dead, then alive, now he's dead again. Are you sure?"

Doucet told him he was sure and explained that he thought Thompson's ex-wife was the right person to be executor. The lawyer said Doucet could simply withdraw, but it would be better if he formally appointed the ex-wife in his place. He didn't need to seek her permission first; however, it would probably be best if he contacted her. He gave Doucet her phone number.

When Doucet reached her and told her how sorry he was to hear about Bill, she broke down. He waited until she could talk again. "I'm sorry," she said, sniffling, "I know it's silly. We haven't been together for years and for a long time I thought he was dead and then he showed up alive and came back and he was so happy and we were talking again ... oh, I'm sorry to go on so. Bill told me about you, Mr. Doucet."

"Please call me Rick." Doucet told her about the will and said he really thought she should be the executor, not him. After some hesitation she agreed, and he said he'd work it out with the lawyer.

"Bill really admired you, Rick – it seems strange to call you that when I don't even know you. He talked about you a lot. And just this morning I found a package addressed to you over at his apartment." She started to cry again. "I'm sorry ... this is hard. I had to go over to get some clothes ... for the funeral home. He must have been getting ready to send it to you." There was another catch in her voice and Doucet could hear her sniffling again. Thompson had told him once that he still loved his wife; it appeared that the feeling was mutual.

"I'll put it in the mail to you soon, Mr. Doucet ... I mean, Rick. I'm glad you called. I think I should go now, but I hope we can talk more later, when I'm in better shape."

A week later the package arrived. It was a mid-sized padded envelope, and very light. Doucet wondered what it could be, and when he opened it he found a card and a small wrapped box. Thompson had written a long note on the card thanking Doucet for everything he'd done and saying that this was something to remember him by, that it would remind him of everything they'd been through together. 'And maybe,' Thompson wrote 'like that jewelry from your grandmother you told me about once, this is as much for that girlfriend of yours as it is for you.'

No, thought Doucet, he couldn't have. He opened the package. Inside was the yellow diamond, still in the same little plastic box he remembered from when Thompson first showed it to him. He turned it in the light, watching it sparkle as the tears welled up in his eyes and coursed down his cheeks, tears for the past and for friendship lost, tears that blurred and multiplied the diamond's sparkle like a kaleidoscope.

Vancouver, February 2014. Ed Zelensky had the flu. He was rarely sick, and he blamed this one on the air travel – he had finally found time for the Hawaiian vacation he'd promised Helen ages ago, and as soon as they returned the flu had hit him like a cement truck. He'd been in bed with it for two days already; his muscles ached, his eyes hurt, and all he wanted to do was sleep. Heather brought him chicken soup and told him he looked like death warmed over, which he didn't think was very funny. A couple of people from work had emailed to say they hoped he'd be back soon, but wasn't it strange that the one time he got sick was during the winter Olympics?

Today he actually felt well enough to get out of bed – and there was a hockey game on TV, Russia playing the U.S.

He got settled on the sofa and asked Heather if she wouldn't mind bringing him some chamomile tea – he wasn't ready for coffee yet – and turned on the TV. The game hadn't yet begun; the fans were still getting to their seats, the players were warming up on the ice, and the TV announcers were making inane comments to fill in time. He turned down the volume so he wouldn't have to listen. The camera panned around the arena and zoomed in on a group of well-dressed spectators. There was Putin, the Russian President ... and someone sitting nearby who looked vaguely familiar. "Jesus Christ," Zelensky said out loud, and sat up straight, his flu forgotten. "It's Vasily Gagarin." He had stared at that face in the RCMP files so many times that he'd recognize it anywhere. He turned up the volume in time to hear the commentator talking about Putin and "the prominent Russian businessman Vasily Gagarin whose companies have played a major role building several of the Olympic venues."

"Yeah, and I'll bet they skimmed off a lot of money in the process," Zelensky said back to the TV.

The camera focused on a stunningly beautiful young woman sitting between Gagarin and Putin. "That," said the commentator, "is Alexandra Gagarin, a true Russian beauty and her father's favorite. It's rumored he gives her anything she wants and she's already fabulously wealthy. She lives in London now but comes home often, and she's the belle of the Sochi Olympics."

Zelensky could feel his blood pressure rising. He had not thought about Diatek or Andropov or Gagarin for a while now; he had moved on to other things. But seeing the sleekly groomed, self-satisfied looking Russian on TV brought it all back. The name Gagarin had been absent from the Andropov and Kalinin trials, but Zelensky and a few others knew it was there, in the background. Surely, he thought now, there must be a way to get at him. For starters we could make another effort to convince Mulroney and Andropov to talk. Time in prison may have softened them up a bit. We could look again at the electronic records of all those financial transactions in the Caymans and Switzerland – and Russia. There's a new willingness to tackle corruption in Russia, even if it involves the high and mighty – maybe even *especially* if it involves them.

He thought for a moment and then turned off the television. The game could wait. He went to his desk and got out his pen and writing paper. 'Dear Sergey,' he wrote, ...

Made in the USA
San Bernardino, CA
26 April 2016